Angels In Stone

BY

TANJA KOBASIC

Published by Stone Series Publishing

Bibliographical Reference:
Cartographer: Donald Pratt
English Translation of Manuscript 512
Background information: Colonel Percy Harrison Fawcett, Jack Fawcett and Raleigh Rimmell's ninth and final expedition into Amazon jungle to search for a Lost City - renamed Z by Colonel Percy Harrison Fawcett.
The Templars and the Ark of the Covenant-Graham Phillips: Researcher
Detailed documentary-referencing to The Stones of Fire –
Old Testament
Exodus 28:15-30
Ilha de Queimada Grande – Snake Island Brazil
WGS84 24° 29' 0" S, 46° 41' 0" W
-24.483333, -46.683333
978-0-9881554-1-1 (e-book)
978-0-9881554-0-4

For more information visit: www.StoneSeriesPublishing.com

What is more evil —
a soul that knows it's evil, or a soul
that doesn't?

Perception is everything...

Prologue

"It's cold down there," Rebecca whispered, leaning over to her big sister. "Mommy's gonna be cold," she insisted, seated in a chair, facing their mother's casket. Claire looked down to her left and realized that Rebecca's shawl had slipped, and the cold winds of Minnesota had turned her ears red. Claire reached over and readjusted the scarf, tucking the ends into her coat.

"She's gonna be cold, Claire," Rebecca said again. "Do something, please?" With her hand still placed on her sister's chin, Claire leaned in, kissed her cold cheek, and then rubbed it with her thumb. It was the way their mother had done it. A comforting sequence that Claire hadn't even realized she was doing, until it was done. Rebecca stared up at her with those blameless green eyes, a red braid poking out of the collar of the black coat Grandma Preston had bought just a few days earlier. *"Black is a color worn in sadness,"* Grandma had said.

Claire had somehow tuned out the stream of prayers led by Father Riley and searched for the right words to pacify Rebecca. "Mommy's dead, Becca," she blurted, unable to control her emotions. "Mommy can't feel a thing…not anymore," Claire persisted in a voice too loud, hoping that her father, sitting just a few chairs over, had heard her. Rebecca blinked a few times as if in disbelief; her lower lip jutted out and quivered. *She looks like a tiny doll*, Claire thought, *all dressed up in patent leather shoes, tears running down her ruby cheeks.* Claire regretted being so cruel and pulled her onto her lap, allowing her to weep into her neck. She felt Rebecca's warm tears against her skin, along with the scent of lilac, their mother's perfume which Rebecca had sprayed into her hair before falling asleep in Claire's bed the previous night.

While consoling her sister, Claire peered a few feet over to her right to where their father sat slumped over in his chair. He was staring down into the hole where their mother's mahogany casket would soon be lowered. He had that same faraway expression in his tired eyes. Grandma Preston sat on the other side of their father, holding his hand and wiping her tears with a crumpled tissue. Behind them, the entire town had shown up to support the Prestons, and when it began snowing, it occurred to Claire that everyone responsible for her mother's death had shown up.

Snow, father, and God.

When Father Riley indicated with a small nod to the pall-bearers, they proceeded to the casket and began lowering it into the ground. Claire felt the cold squall coming in from the north. It was almost poetic: her tears and the snow blinded the vision of the white roses being dropped onto her mother's coffin by the ones whose lives she'd touched. Grandma Preston stood over them and passed a rose to both girls. "It's time, wee ones," she whispered. Claire didn't move. Instead, she pulled Rebecca closer.

"It's time," their grandma said again, setting an understanding hand on Claire's shoulder. Claire took the rose but made no move. Grandma Preston scooped Rebecca into her arms and brought her over to the hole. "Drop the rose, wee one," she whispered. Rebecca dropped it without looking down and whimpered again. Their grandmother carried her away and sat back down, coddling her with soothing words.

Claire stood up and walked over to the hole still clutching the white rose between her fingers, unable to drop it. It was so final. Father Riley led his congregation with the dreaded prayer, but Claire stood numb, her gaze still drawn into the darkness below. The rose began to shake in her hands as the wind ripped a few petals off, scattering them away.

"For everything, there is a season and a time for every matter under heaven. A time to be born and a time to die; a time to plant," Father Riley began, "and a time to pluck up what is planted; a time to break down and a time to build up; a time to weep and a time to laugh; a time to mourn and a time to dance."

Rebecca was wailing now. She broke free of her grandmother and stood over the hole, screaming and tugging at Claire's arm. "She's cold, don't leave her down there. Please, Claire, make them stop!" She wrapped her tiny arms around Claire's waist, weeping. Their grandmother, along with a few other parishioners, reached for her and took her away. Rebecca cried into her grandmother's bosom as she rocked her in the chair.

Claire understood exactly why it made no sense to this sensitive five year old. She turned to her father, who wept into his hands and did nothing to bring his youngest child comfort. *So useless*, Claire thought. And despite the frigid cold, the icy winds that were increasing, Claire felt herself sweating beneath her coat. She turned to her father, causing Father Riley to stop mid prayer. The coffin made a thudding sound as it hit the ground.

"Of course she thinks her mother's cold!" Claire screamed. "It's because she doesn't understand; she never got to see her dead." Apart from the wind, and the call of a hawk in the looming distance, there was silence. All eyes were on Claire.

"But how could she, Father? It was a closed casket because our mother's face was destroyed. Tell her! Tell your baby girl how her mother's face was unrecognizable! Tell her...be a man and let her know what you've done!" The entire parish did nothing. "She doesn't understand, but I do," Claire said, looking directly at her father. But he couldn't bear to face her and kept his head down. No one said a word as the tension mounted. Claire struggled against the urge to sob; her gaze fell on the countless headstones, names of the departed etched into the stonework. What would her mother's stone read? Beloved wife and mother? Gone too soon?

Claire felt a prickling sensation burning her scalp and addressed her father again, the tone in her voice cutting.

"Do you see what you've done to her? She couldn't even have a decent burial. You and your God," she mocked, addressing everyone present, before dropping her rose into the hole. She watched it land on top of the others, the last and final rose, dropped by her mother's first born.

Claire couldn't bring herself to move. Father Riley gave her a meaningful look and continued from the beginning of the prayer. Their town Priest was a smart man, who, she knew, felt that Claire had a right to mourn in her own way. She knew that in a few weeks he would turn up at their door with kind words of advice, which Claire would disregard. He had married her parents and baptized both her and Rebecca. He knew everything.

"For everything, there is a season and a time for every matter under heaven: a time to be born and a time to die; a time to plant," Claire felt the prick of tears begin behind her lids but fought against it, "and a time to pluck up what is planted; a time to break down and a time to build up; a time to weep and a time to laugh; a time to mourn and a time to dance."

It was unexplainable how alone Claire felt in that very moment. It was as if she, herself, were being covered by the cold dirt and unforgiving snow that was now coming down so hard in the form of a thin, crystal veil, separating her from everyone.

"For everything there is a season and a time for every matter under heaven." A swirling wind ripped right through her, lifting the hem of her warm coat and reaching her sweat covered back.

But she felt nothing—absolutely nothing.

Nothingness

Janice Felder waited silently behind the flicker of a lit candle; her hand rested over her swollen belly. Remembering her child, she drew in a shaky breath, hoping to shield him from the stress that burdened her. She bent her neck forward, while memories of her son played in her mind: his first words, first steps, first day of school. The milestones of his short life quickly fast forwarded, then stopped on the dreadful day she'd found him, dead and cold, lying face down on his bed.

The crackling wax of the candle caught her attention. Janice looked across the table to see if the voodoo priestess had any news. Nothing. Instead, the burning white candle, which separated her from the priestess, stretched itself tall and then began bouncing as if the flame were alive and toying with her. Janice tore her gaze away and focused on the woman across from her.

Esperança's vacant, ebony eyes revealed her ethereal state. Janice comprehended the importance of this moment. She had waited a very long time for this old woman to emerge from the world between the living and the dead, and deliver her decree. She checked her wristwatch: forty-seven minutes, to be exact. But he was worth it.

Sighing, Janice's eyes darted to her aged hands, and she remembered a time when those same hands were once young and unflawed, caressing her son's tiny brow as he suckled her young breast. Could these long-deserted breasts be enough to nourish her precious boy? Would she even be able to produce milk? She bowed her head as a lock of hair unfurled from behind her ear and rested on her cheek. Sounds of a couple arguing carried through the thin walls while in the streets below loud rap music roared from the inside of passing cars. A painful reminder of how out of place she was.

To keep herself calm, Janice kept a steady gaze on the candle. Esperança had explained that souls were drawn to fire. Fire was life, Esperança had said, and this candle was lit for James. After many long minutes of watching it, the tempo of the waving flame seduced her and made her sleepy. She shut her eyes and thought of her boy—alone and lost—in an eternal sphere of Nothingness and became anxious once more. Janice went back to praying, hoping that the fallen angels would find her son and guide him home, guide him to his flame.

Melted wax overflowed around the top and dribbled along the stem, hardening at the candle base. *Why is she taking so long?* She checked on Esperança again and noticed something outside the window directly behind her. A large white bird peered in. Pigeons were common in the Bronx, but this thing outside was no pigeon. This bird was bigger, its beak curved. It moved its head from side to side, bobbing impatiently, seemingly waiting for the priestess to return from her trance. She wished it would fly away and felt ashamed. The thing outside of the window stared directly at her as if it knew what she had done to bring her dead son back.

A grunt from across the table took precedence over the bird. Pushing the stray hair behind her ear, Janice bit fretfully on her lower lip and waited.

"Call his name," Esperança mumbled through her stupor. "Call his name now. He needs to hear your voice."

The priestess's words sent a tremor down Janice's spine. "I don't know what to say. What...what do I say?"

"Call his name, quick...before he slips back."

Janice moved into the table, looking directly into the flame. "Jimmy, baby. It's mom, don't be afraid. You're close, you're home. It's your mother..."

Janice felt a painful kick as the old woman came to, blinking several times and gulping mouthfuls of air. Instantly, Janice felt her equilibrium shift, and the entire room began to close in; it was swallowing her whole. Struggling to breathe, her ears popping, Janice watched the priestess sitting across from her. She seemed unaffected; her hands were perfectly folded on top of the table. A sense of heaviness was descending on the room, removing any oxygen. Sputtering, the candle on the table, shrank, quivered, and died. Black smoke and a mood of finality encircled the two women.

Then, abruptly, the heaviness eased.

Clearing her throat in the gloom, the priestess pulled a thin, white candle from under her chair. She licked the stem with her tongue and spit pieces of wax into the darkness and replaced the spent candle with a new one. She struck a wooden match, and a new flame was born. Through her wheezing, she studied the lit wick as it rose four inches. The priestess turned to her left, watching as the flame threw shadows against her wall.

Following the priestess's gaze, Janice stared at the wall, trying to understand its meaning. She turned to the priestess. "What is it?" she asked urgently, turning to the wall. "Did they find him?"

Esperança struck another match, letting the matchstick between her fingers burn to ashes. A whiff of sulfur dioxide settled around them, and the old woman wheezed and coughed even more.

Janice swallowed hard, suppressing her anguish and waited for an answer.

Coughing up a gob of phlegm, the priestess finally recovered. Her hair, which had been tied up, had loosened. She flicked a gray strand away from her face and asked, "Look at the wall, how many shadows you see?"

Janice counted three, and then the third disappeared. In a simultaneous instant, she felt her son kicking inside of her, painful kicks that caused her to flinch. Once recovered, with her hands rubbing her belly, she whispered. "It's him isn't it? I know it's him. My son…he's back."

"It wasn't easy," the priestess continued, "his soul was still caught in the sphere. Nothingness. I told you before it wouldn't be easy." Esperança almost envied her.

"But he's here with me," Janice said, looking down at her belly, her eyes filling with tears. It was true, Janice thought. There was no denying that she felt her son was safe again. It was a feeling to which only a mother could relate. Janice felt another string of welcomed kicks.

"Yes." The priestess looked at the woman's stomach. "He shares your nutrients. Like I said, his soul's been found. The angels pulled him back. He's resting inside the fetus."

Janice began sobbing with relief. "Thank you," she managed, looking up through a blur of tears. "If there's anything you and your people ever need—" She stopped speaking, realizing that Esperança was elsewhere.

The angel came to Esperança again, to deliver a message from the King. The voodoo priestess zeroed in on the communication, her conscious state again fixed among the living and the dead. She whispered, "Wait. I could be wrong...."

Not about my son, Janice thought, and panic began to strip away the first real joy she'd felt in years. "What is it? Please, Esperança, tell me my son's all right!" The priestess had that faraway expression in her eyes, her eyebrows pinched together. The old woman saw something, Janice knew, and Janice didn't know whether the tears she shed should be for loss or for recovery. It took everything in her not to leap across the table and shake the old woman back among the living.

Broken wing, Esperança thought, while seeing her perfectly. Red hair, anger...the angels wanted her, Satan wanted her. "He's fine," Esperança finally said, giving Janice her full attention. "This has nothing to do with him."

Janice exhaled and took in a deep breath of relief. The priestess explained, "But there's a woman, a woman you'll cross paths with soon."

"A woman? Who is she to me?"

"She's nothing to you, but she shares your struggle," explained the priestess.

Janice tried to understand the old woman's explanation, but her mind went blank. This was no time to be playing guessing games.

The priestess closed her eyes, squinting as the vision played behind her lids. "This woman is infertile, can't have children.

You'll know her when you meet her. She's fiery, beautiful… very beautiful." She opened her eyes and glared at her. "Rage, the color of rage. Send her to me. Tell her we'll give her the child she needs."

The color of rage? Janice thought, then focused only on her unborn child. "You're sure my son's soul is—"

"—His soul's fine."

Before she could think, Janice's joyous emotions overwhelmed her. She leaned back to face the dirty ceiling and the damning words flew out of her mouth. "Thank Go—"

On the other side of the table, a hand hammered down, causing the flame of the candle to bounce.

Janice clapped a hand over her mouth. "I didn't mean it! I'm so sorry."

The angry eyes of the voodoo priestess reprimanded her through the flame. "Remember, God has nothing to do with this!"

2

The Forsaken

The alarm clock glared at Claire: 4:43 a.m. Even if she were to try to fall back to sleep, her anxiety, now in overdrive, would prevent her. Doctor Sidle, her gynecologist, had explained that her hormone overload was causing the insomnia, but Claire had had sleep issues long before her fertility treatments had started. On her left, Jonathon faced her, his breathing pattern signifying deep sleep. The green light from the clock illuminated his face revealing the masculine contours of his jaw. The cute pout he wore while sleeping made her husband look even younger than he was.

She slid out of the bed. Not wanting to awaken him, she moved with caution, but on rising she pulled the warm comforter with her.

"No," Jonathon said in his sleepy voice. "Come back to bed." His arm went out to reach for her, but she pushed it back.

"Go back to sleep. I'm going for a run."

He mumbled something, pulled the covers over his shoulders, and turned over onto his other side. Claire slipped out of their bedroom, eased the door shut, padded down the hallway and into her private bathroom. Locking the door behind her, she switched on the bright light. Squinting, she rummaged around in the bathroom cabinet, sorting through the syringes, alcohol swabs, and containers she used to mix the different fertility drugs. She took out the pregnancy test, tore into the box, and moved toward the toilet with it. Balancing awkwardly, Claire urinated, holding the pregnancy stick between her legs, allowing it to absorb some of the stream. She felt a tinge of hope. Fourteen months of painful injections, gaining five pounds, and last month giving up caffeine completely, would surely make a difference. This was it; it had to be. She placed the test flat on the counter reminding herself to remain calm. *Five minutes, no more, no less.*

Worrying her lower lip with her teeth, Claire pulled her pink satin nightgown off and caught the reflection of her nakedness in the mirror. A dark bruise on her stomach looked ghastly in comparison to her pale skin. As much as Claire hated needles, never mind giving one to herself, she'd been faithful. Once a day she had suffered the needles, once a day for twenty-one days each month. Once a day for the last fourteen months—and it was taking an enormous toll on her.

She took her sports bra and jogging fleece from where they hung on the door and forced the garments on. She reached for her toothbrush, squeezed some toothpaste onto it, turned it on, and began brushing.

Four minutes.

Staring at her own reflection in the mirror, and still working the toothbrush over her teeth, she inspected her skin up close. The recent Botox injection had done its job perfectly; there was no way she looked forty-three.

Three minutes.

Her mind roamed as she rinsed her mouth. She thought of her young husband who slept with ease in their bed. Because Claire was a master at hiding her emotions, he had no idea of the hell she'd been through over the last year and some months. He wasn't the one taking drugs, suffering migraines, and losing even more sleep. Thinking back to how peaceful he looked all curled up in the warm sheets, a part of her felt like smothering him with a pillow.

Two minutes.

Reaching for her hairbrush, Claire pulled the elastic from her head, allowing her red tresses to fall around her face. She noticed something. *Shit, a gray hair.* Claire plucked out the nasty evidence and washed it down the drain. Jonathon could never know that the silky red mane that he loved to run his hands through was no longer natural. In fact, she had gone almost completely gray. Fortunately, Claire's talented stylist hid her little secret behind a curtain of Fox Red Number 23. She pulled the brush through her hair and fastened a neat ponytail.

One minute.

She looked down at the test. It was a simple thing, not much more than a stick. But to Claire, the pregnancy test held hope and fear in equal measure. It was the same game she'd been playing for over a year. The test teased her, drove her to frenzy. Doctor Sidle had given her just a five percent chance of success. There was also serious scar tissue left by an abortion she'd undergone years before she'd met Jonathon, so the likelihood of Claire carrying a child to term was slim to none. *So Doctor Sidle said.* But Claire wasn't someone who gave up easily; somehow she always managed to get her way.

Zero minutes.

She snatched the test from her cluttered counter of designer fragrances and lotions, knocking over a tall bottle of Givenchy perfume, and forced herself to look.

Negative.

The same bad news. She leaned her back against the wall, slid to a sitting position, crossed her arms, and stayed that way for several minutes. She had no choice but to sit. Every time Claire took the test, she experienced this same reaction. She could only wait for it to pass. The cold wall and chilled tile floor sent shivers through her. Claire's body began to tremble, and her heart began to race. *Breathe. You're in control, don't let it happen, don't let it happen.* But of course, it always did. Claire's throat felt like it was swelling shut as if she were being strangled by invisible hands. "You're in control," she whispered out loud, hoping her pep talk would make the anguish go away. Then her nose began tingling, the warning that she was close to tears. She would never permit herself to cry. Hell no. *Fuck him for wanting kids.* Claire pulled herself up off the floor and remembered who she was. The woman she had trained herself to be. The urge to cry was replaced, once again, with the anger that had become her constant companion. She wouldn't permit herself to cry.

She grabbed the pregnancy test and empty box before exiting the bathroom. She made her way downstairs and moved through the dark house, entering the cold garage. Her breath puffed white before her as she marched toward the back wall. She opened a green bin used specifically for dumping the cat litter. Claire made her usual deposit of the used test materials, along with the vials and syringes, and then slammed the lid shut. Jonathon would never look in there, of that she was sure.

Preparing herself for a cold morning, all Claire wanted to do now was run.

Miles into her jog, on a stretch of woodland adjoining her New Jersey estate, Claire felt somewhat better. She hoped the extreme cold could force her not to think of anything else. This morning was no different, apart from the newly fallen snow which covered the frozen ground like a surface of gleaming porcelain. Steadily breathing, twisting, turning, heart pounding, she piloted her way along the familiar path she'd beaten into the frosted forest. The world was hers alone, and the captivating sight of iced branches took her back to her childhood, to a time when fairy godmothers existed, and, if she believed hard enough, one touch of a magical wand would freeze the world's imperfections and all her dreams would come true. She trusted in the power of the mind, so perhaps this was the universe's way of giving her what she wanted. But when the snow began falling through the trees, her love-hate relationship with it crystallized, as the firm grip of melancholy wrapped around her throat like the fingers of a murderer. The bloody weakness was back, and even the ice-cold air wasn't enough to freeze it out.

She stopped running and found a tree to rest her back against for a few moments. She immediately regretted interrupting her perfect pace. Her mind flooded with memories she could only block out by keeping herself busy. It made no sense to revisit the past, and she hated doing this to herself; but something about the snow—which she pegged "the beautiful killer"—made it impossible for her to think of anything else.

Beautiful though the snow looked, if one got stuck in it too long, it was game over.

"Fucking snow," she muttered, her breath rose in a visible curl against the moonlight.

There was that sensation again, light-headed and weak. She continued to lean against the tree for support while the plump snowflakes moistened her lashes and blurred her vision. Caught inside of the illusory setting, she soon saw the dreaded vision; a mahogany-lacquered coffin lowered into the ground. Roses, white ones, their petals scattered over the lid that enclosed her mother. It had snowed that day, drifts of fernlike flakes that melted into her tears. Claire blinked several times before taking another long look at her surroundings.

The scene around her had opened the floodgates to the emotions she'd managed to suppress for so long. Snow evoked Claire's most painful memory, just as a certain smell or a song would. Winter used to be Claire's favorite time of year; it was also her mother's. As a little girl, Claire and her mother would stand outside, in the midst of a snowstorm, with their mouths open. *Mommy would say that the flakes were gifts from the heavens, frozen into beautiful little sparkly packages, given to us by God.* Claire had no way to know that snow would one day help to kill her mother. And the three things that her mother had cherished— God, snow, and her father—would all be to blame. It was ironical that all three had shown up at her funeral.

Thirty years ago, on a cold November night, during a massive snowstorm, Claire's mother, Connie, had plunged their family Buick into a ravine and died.

Closing her eyes, Claire rehashed the sequence of events, hoping after this that she'd never be haunted by it again. She saw herself at thirteen; Rebecca was barely five. They stood together lighting a candle by the window, praying, *God, please bring mommy home.* On the third day the local police had found her car, their mother dead inside. Daddy said that the snow flurries and icy road conditions were the contributors to her death, but Claire knew better. It was also her mother's drinking that took her mother away from her and her baby sister—the drinking that was a direct result of her father's cheating. Claire felt the strength returning to her legs. Anger began to course through her veins as her hatred of God and her father reminded her of who she was—Claire…in control and indestructible. Preparing herself for another mile, she stopped mid-stretch and felt its eyes on her again.

For the fifth morning in a row, she was not alone. Looking around the pathway through the dense forest, Claire stopped before a crab-apple tree. Her gaze followed from the base of the trunk and gradually moved toward the top. Two inch thorns covered the bare branches, creating an eerie pattern against the charcoal sky. There, in the midst of the pointed barbs, was the bird again: an enormous white bird in the shape of a black raven. Claire knew her birds, having grown up in rural Minnesota where ravens were very common. They were known for their powerful bills and shaggy throat feathers. Their eyes were always watching as if they knew something that humans didn't. These birds were communicators with distinct and robotic vocals. So far this white raven was a mute. The bird gave her the creeps, and it didn't matter where Claire jogged, the white raven simply followed her, flying from tree to tree.

Claire took a handful of snow in her glove, and formed a snowball. She moved back a couple of paces and whipped it toward the bird. "Hey asshole, you like that?" The ball moved through a thin branch and broke apart. Claire made another one, and aimed it at the bird. To her amazement, the bird began moving its head from side to side.

"You're a fugly bird. I hope a coyote makes breakfast out of you!"

The raven swooped off of the branch, almost grazing the top of Claire's wool hat. She watched it as it soared over a thicket of evergreens. This bird was ballsy.

Shaking her head to free her mind from the eerie bird, she faced the wintry scene to ground herself in the present. Claire took a deep breath, thrilling to the sensation of ice-cold air entering her lungs, and resumed running. She was always running. With each pounding step she hammered down on her childhood scars and reminded herself of an old Japanese proverb, *a tree that has grown in the wind has stronger roots.* And what didn't kill her surely made her stronger. Racing over the ice-caked path, she ran her course with newfound motivation.

She pushed harder. The snow continued falling and melting

against her hot cheeks. She couldn't help but feel that God was taunting her, sending down the same type of stellar dendrite flakes, which had cloaked her mother's car. Looking up, she spotted the white raven flying low; its massive wingspan propelled it into another tree.

Although tired, she decided that there was enough time to complete one last track. There were more cobwebs that needed cleaning inside her head, and the muddle of memories frazzled her.

First, there was the negative pregnancy test, then the thoughts of her dead mother, and now there was Jonathon, the young and beautiful husband she was trying desperately to hold on to. They had married despite the thirteen-year gap between them. His youth made her feel old and she had to work even harder to preserve the perfect body and her youthful appearance. As much as she loved him, a part of Claire despised him for exposing her.

He knew a piece of her that no other man had ever known.

It was a well known fact that men always wanted what they didn't have, and their interests only increased by their need to know what lay hidden inside the pretty box. Somehow he had managed to lift the shroud which protected her mystique, but more importantly, her heart.

He had matured and wanted more, and Claire realized that, for her, "more" was like squeezing blood from a stone.

Through the thick brush, she pushed herself harder, the iced branches snapping under her feet. Coming to a clearing at the back of her house, Claire spotted the white raven and followed its flight as it soared over the top of her majestic home. The rising sun made its snow covered roof sparkle.

The extra mile had exhausted her.

She slowed her run to a walk as she approached the cobblestone walkway which led to her door. The negative pregnancy test resurfaced in her mind. She knew that if she didn't give Jonathon a child he would leave her. And, although he never said as much, the unspoken threat hovered over their marriage.

Claire had bought him from the outset, appeased him in every materialistic way imaginable, and yet he'd become unsatisfied. Jonathon wanted a child. He wanted to rub his hands over

Claire's swollen belly and feel the movements under the layers of her skin. She was able to control and manipulate every aspect of her life, but this was the one part of her life over which she had no power. It was her own body—yet it betrayed her.

The Color of Rage

Waiting in Doctor Monroe's office, Claire shifted with unease in her chair. Her file hung on the door. It contained the results of the exam she'd taken four days prior when she'd been picked, probed, and completely exposed. Rebecca had recommended the doctor, and she swore she was a guru when it came to fertility. The doctor had been a guest on a few syndicated talk shows throughout the country and was well respected. Claire had done her research, and she was somewhat impressed with her. And Doctor Monroe was thorough enough, even going so far as to have Jonathon's sperm count retested. She was scrupulous.

Glancing about at the doctor's personal effects, she focused on the framed photos of her children showcased on the immaculate desk. *How fucking rude*, Claire judged, while pulling out a tube of hand cream from her purse. What a boastful show for desperate women, shoving their faces in how fortunate she is to have children.

If *fortunate* was even the right word.

In frustration, she rubbed the lotion into her skin. *Homely bitch. No wonder your husband left you.* Rebecca had filled Claire in on the doctor's personal struggle, her husband leaving her for a young blonde. It gave her a wicked satisfaction.

One photo revealed her son, no older than four, who closely

resembled his mother. He had her same thin lips and large ears. Like Doctor Monroe herself, he was awkward and unattractive. For a while Claire couldn't take her eyes off his picture. The poor boy would have a hard time later in life. Children could be so cruel to one another.

Recalling the day she and Jonathon had first met this woman, Claire smiled faintly. After the doctor had seated them, she'd closed the door behind her, and the hint of envy in her watery eyes was as unmistakable as the extra-long stare at the pair. No doubt about it: their children would be beautiful, filled with beautiful genes.

The doctor had been easy for Claire to read. She'd fumbled and knocked over the penholder while explaining to Jonathon the type of tests involved. She'd even blushed.

Claire was sure that Doctor Monroe didn't expect her to look as she did, especially with Rebecca as her introduction to the family. Unlike Claire, Rebecca was simple, very plain. She had the same red hair and green eyes as her sister, but she was put together differently. While Claire oozed sexuality, Rebecca appeared wholesome. She hid her shape behind long skirts and loose blouses, and her eyes were partially masked by oversized glasses. She looked like she should be stacking books in a library.

Women never ostracized Rebecca because she was shy and easily walked over. It made sense that she'd made many female friends. Claire, on the other hand, had absolutely none apart from her sister. She'd encountered many women over the years and knew she was unfairly hated on the basis of her intense beauty. But that wasn't what bothered Claire. It was when Doctor Monroe had asked Claire her age—that was printed in plain view in her records. Then the doctor announced, "Fertility declines with age." That comment alone made Claire loath the woman.

When Doctor Monroe entered, she cut into Claire's memories. "Mrs. Preston-Lockwood, and how are you today?" Her straight black hair was brushed behind her big, unsightly ears. She walked in and plucked a file from the pouch on the door before closing it behind her.

Claire was especially eager to intimidate the doctor with her splendor and was glad she'd taken the time to be particularly dazzling that morning by wearing her favorite black skinny jeans, black Christian Louboutin knee length boots, and red, fitted, cashmere sweater. Claire pulled out her compact and gave herself a quick perk, recoating her pout with red lipstick. Smacking her lips together, she sighed out loud before placing the compact back into her purse. A full smile escaped Claire's lips. "I'm well, thank you," she said in her crisp, business-like manner.

The doctor glanced at the empty chair beside her. She was a little disappointed that her striking husband couldn't make it; she'd looked forward to this moment.

"My husband couldn't make it today." Claire made a point of letting her know she was one step ahead of her.

Doctor Monroe forced a smile and pushed her glasses further up the bridge of her nose. "So, we do have your results."

Claire felt herself getting hot. She said nothing, and the temporary silence hit hard.

"Your husband's sperm count tested well," Doctor Monroe announced.

Claire's file remained closed. Clearly the doctor had memorized the results, had taken a personal interest. "And me?" Although her anxiety was growing, she kept it in check.

Doctor Monroe looked Claire over before answering. Claire was truly stunning, she thought. *But she had to have work done; no woman at forty-three could look so young.* While glancing at Claire's chest, she remembered how disappointed she was during Claire's clinical procedures. She was certain that they were implants; no, they were not. A perky C, and apart from being a real bitch, Claire's breasts were the only real thing about her. "There is significant scarring in your uterus consistent with…a previous abortion. And apart from that, there's the issue of your age." Doctor Monroe paused, referring to the notes attached, without actually reading them. "I see from the information Dr. Sidle sent that you've been diagnosed with diminished ovarian reserve, premature ovarian failure. I'm sorry, but…I have to agree with Dr. Sidle. I would say it's physically impossible for you to bear children." She flipped through Claire's file, this time pulling out a page. "You've also been on a strong dose of

DHEA for quite some time. No success there."

"The word is 'dehydroepiandrosterone.'" It enraged Claire that Doctor Monroe was so casual about her situation, reciting Doctor Sidle's diagnoses word for word: diminished ovarian reserve, premature ovarian failure. It was as if it pleased her enormously to remind Claire of her failure. Yet, when it came time to pronounce the fertility drug in its full name, Doctor Monroe was too lazy, using the abbreviation DHEA.

The doctor did a double blink, a real quick bitch, she thought. "Regardless, I would still have to concur with Doctor Sidle. The probability of you producing your own eggs then actually being able to carry a child to term…well, it's physically impossible." She then proceeded to open a pamphlet. The title: *Surrogacy an Option?* The doctor opened her mouth to speak but was thrown off by the fury in Claire's eyes.

"Impossible? Are you out of your mind? Nothing's impossible!" Claire all but shrieked.

The doctor's head jerked back as if she'd been slapped. "Mrs. Preston-Lockwood, please. I understand you're upset, but listen to me carefully. There are options. Egg donors and many women in your position arrange for a surrogate mother to carry a child to term."

"No, that's not an alternative," Claire countered. "I won't have another woman carrying my husband's child. Not happening." Claire felt a prickling sensation moving over her scalp. She knew that her ears had turned red. The Irish-Preston temper, on Claire's father's side, as her mother used to say.

"Well, adoption is another alternative," Doctor Monroe suggested. *This is getting ugly.*

"No," Claire affirmed, looking her dead in the eyes.

The doctor removed her glasses and wiped the perspiration from her nose. "Mrs. Preston-Lockwood, the fact remains…" She paused and chose her words carefully. "The fact remains that it is clinically impossible for you to ever carry a child."

With each word spoken, Claire felt her strength draining from her body, the numbness filling her extremities. She concealed her trembling hands into her lap.

"I'm very sorry, and as I pointed out before," Doctor Monroe continued, "your age isn't the only risk." As uncomfortable as she was, she needed to embrace her position and take control. She began to speak with closed eyes, tuning out all distractions in order to articulate her advice.

The doctor's words weren't penetrating, and Claire felt that she relished her professional position, her influence, along with the sound of her own voice.

"I'm sure your husband will agree that my suggestions are viable alternatives. I'm sure this is not what you wanted to hear, and I truly am very sorry," the doctor added—*Bullshit*.

As Claire watched the gynecologist express her regret, it seemed that the doctor's mouth moved out of sequence with her words, like a strange, incoherent, foreign film. What the doctor didn't know, as she folded her hands softly on her desk expecting full acquiescence, was how she'd finally whittled Claire down, chiseled away the last bit of her patience.

"You're pretty pleased with yourself aren't you? I don't think you're sorry at all. I think you take pleasure in all this!" Claire stood up, grabbed her file from the doctor's desk, and moved fast through the door and into the reception area.

Doctor Monroe stood up and followed her. "Mrs. Preston-Lockwood... I'll need that file."

"Wrong. These are my results and I'm taking them with me." Claire regained her composure. "You see, I know exactly what your problem is." Claire pointed an accusing finger at her. "The photos on your desk scream to the world that you have children. Bravo for you! But I know something more about your life. Oh yeah, that's right. At least my husband didn't leave me for another woman, a much younger woman with blonde hair, at that. Definitely an improvement over you. So your issues with me are apparent. I'm beautiful, rich, and my husband loves me. And you just adore being the bearer of bad news, don't you?"

Doctor Monroe stood speechless on the spot. *Please don't give her the satisfaction of crying*, she thought. This woman was dangerous.

Claire paused for a moment and lowered her voice to a whisper. "You never know, maybe the blond might give your ex-husband beautiful children. I'm done here!"

Charging through the doctor's office, Claire headed for the

door leading to the hallway. A startled pregnant woman, also leaving, held it open. In her haste, Claire dropped her file, and its loose pages scattered along the floor. Furious, she half knelt, trying to reassemble the papers.

"I'd help you, but I can't bend over," a pregnant woman wearing a great pair of Roger Vivier flats offered. Claire could spot the black patent leather and rounded caps anywhere. Claire stood up, and came face to face with the pleasant-looking woman who held the door for her.

"I'm Janice Felder," she introduced herself, tucking a gray and blond hair behind her ear.

Still flustered, Claire shook the offered hand and noticed the Harry Winston diamond that Janice wore on her left ring finger. It was similar in design to Claire's; naturally she had replaced the original ring with which Jonathon had proposed to her. Odd, but she liked the new woman. "Claire Preston-Lockwood."

"Well, that was worth the ticket." Janice fished out a candy from her coat pocket and popped it into her mouth. "You were a little hard on her though." *Claire's a knockout*, Janice thought, with her tall and slender body, along with the faultless features of a delicate geisha. Janice's gaze focused on Claire's generous mouth, coated in a deep red. *Rage, the color of rage.* There was no doubt in her mind that this was the woman Esperança had referred to.

By this time Claire had carefully placed the pages back into the folder. Janice gave her a sympathetic smile.

"The color of rage," Janice said, looking deeply into Claire's wide set and bewitching green eyes. "Shall we?" Janice motioned toward the elevator.

Claire nodded as they walked in silence. She wondered if Janice was referring to her blood-red ears, which were now starting to itch.

Janice rubbed her belly. "This elevator can take forever."

As they stood waiting for the elevator, Claire was intrigued by the older woman carrying a child. She couldn't stop herself and asked, "How far along are you?"

Janice's smile spread into her tired gray eyes. The question pleased her. "Just a little over eight months now."

Her voice was soothing, seeming to come from a contented

heart. Calmer, Claire wanted to ask her more questions but was relieved to see that Janice almost read her mind.

Janice pointed to the results of her ultrasound, which she held in her hands. "I'm fifty-one, and my son is very healthy."

"That's very good."

Janice studied her briefly. "Don't give up, Claire." She gestured to Claire's file. "May I?"

"Sure." Claire surprised herself by letting this perfect stranger read her personal information. There was something soothing about the intrusive woman who had befriended her.

It was hopeless, Janice thought, while leafing through the pages. She'd seen it all before. "Not good, right?" She handed the file back to Claire. "I've been exactly where you are." She spoke quietly. "Monroe really is a good doctor, but it sounds to me like you'll be seeking another opinion, right?"

Claire nodded.

Janice produced a card from her purse, and handed it to Claire. Claire took the card and, searching for answers, stared into the face of this person named Janice.

"Call me. We should talk. I, of all people, understand perfectly what you're going through."

Janice's tone was simple, though somewhat sincere. Her abrupt offer somehow made complete sense to Claire, who had never felt such a natural connection to another woman before. She felt neither threatened nor on guard.

The elevator doors opened and they entered. Janice hummed quietly to herself as they cruised the short distance from the fourth floor. The whole time she stared at the ultrasound of her son. Claire glanced at the grainy gray and black picture which brought so much joy to her new friend. His legs appeared crossed, and he was sucking his thumb.

There was something inexplicable about Janice, as if she had important information to share with her.

"Don't lose my card," she urged Claire after the elevator stopped, as they went their separate ways in the lobby.

Like a child, Claire obediently listened to her; and she looked at the card closely for the first time.

It read very simply: JANICE FELDER, followed by her telephone number.

4

Fishy

riving into Manhattan, Claire's cell phone rang; it was Jonathon. She put him on speaker, "What's up?"

"Hey, babe, you busy?" He sounded energetic.

Claire said, "I'm on my way to the office. Why?" Jonathon often checked in around five o'clock in the evening to tell her that he wouldn't be home for dinner.

"Well, I just wanted to let you know I have some paperwork to catch up on. I might be a little later than I thought."

"Fine, I have a closing to work on anyway." Claire knew exactly what he'd say next; she could recite the words by heart.

"All right then, I'll pick up some sushi from SonVi." Son-Vi—again. She and Jonathon had eaten sushi twice that week and, interestingly enough, on the exact same days as the week before, and so on.

"Love y—"

Claire terminated the call. His constant "I love you" bored her at the best of times. Lately, however, the sincerity in his voice seemed tainted. The way he said it these days sounded more like standard procedure. Something other than Sushi smelled fishy to her.

The office was her home away from home. She stored many of her personal belongings there, over two decades worth of memories, including a private box of memorabilia in the locked, bottom drawer of the file cabinet. Whenever she found herself missing her mother's loving advice, Claire would sift through it, staring at old photos, wondering what her mother had been thinking at the time.

Tonight seemed like a good time to get out the box. She walked over to her file cabinet and unlocked it.

"Hey you, what are you doing here all by yourself?"

"Huh?" Claire turned around, surprised. Harvey Wyatt stood in the doorway. He looked pale and wobbled where he stood. His zipper was undone, and his dress shirt was crumpled and partially tucked in. Normally, he kept his hair cut low, but now he looked more like Bozo the Clown rather than the owner of a multi-billion-dollar real estate firm. Clearly Harvey had been sleeping on the sofa in his private office again.

"I'm fine," Claire finally answered, "just catching up." She took the box out, placed it beneath her desk and sank into her cushy leather chair.

"We go back what, twenty…twenty-three years?" Harvey blinked, as if the luminescent lights hurt his eyes.

Claire ignored his question, hoping he'd go away.

Harvey didn't get the hint. "You were a regular firecracker. One of my best guys."

The booze on Harvey was obvious as he ambled over to Claire's desk and held himself up. Claire knew that he'd been bunking in his office. The rumors around the office were that Harvey had taken to another woman—a woman he'd been seeing on the sly. Apparently, she gave exactly what he wanted. Soon afterwards, however, she'd threatened to tell Libby, Harvey's wife of forty-two years, about their affair. If the rumors were right, Harvey had been giving her ten grand a month to keep her mouth shut.

Harvey glanced down at her file and picked it up. "How do you do it?" He was staring at Claire's recent closing, his heavy-lidded and bloodshot eyes scanned the document.

Claire snatched the paperwork from his sweaty grasp and placed it into a folder. "I've learned a thing or two from you, but the rest is simply learning how to swim with sharks."

Harvey snickered. "Tell me the truth…do you still wear men's cologne when you close these big deals?"

"Sure I do," Claire played along. "And under this skirt, I have a big set of hairy balls."

Harvey let out an unruly laugh and shook his head. "Tongue in cheek, Preston, tongue in cheek. If you need me, I'll be in the man cave."

Preston-Lockwood, Claire wanted to shout after him, as he waddled away. She reclined back and pondered about him some more.

Preston was Claire's maiden name, but for some reason, even after five years, Harvey couldn't warm up to Claire's new title. *Preston* rolled off of Harvey's tongue with such pride. Preston was a name held in high regard in the real estate world. Harvey would say, *Claire Preston, proficient and polished, working with high-profile clients and ultra-luxury properties.* Regardless, Claire's new name, Preston-Lockwood, didn't have a negative impact at all. She still held her spot as one of Manhattan's top agents, branded as a rival who walked tall in designer shoes, dressed like a lady and cussed like the rest of them, if you pissed her off enough.

Nevertheless, despite Claire's efforts, the business performance of Wyatt Real Estate during the past two years had been negative. The competition had more than caught up and was now in the lead. Harvey was making bad decisions. He'd become irrational and unstable, losing his top agents and hiring amateurs. These newbies had no business selling property in Manhattan, and might as well have gotten their real estate licenses from the bottom of a Cracker Jack box. Harvey was too drunk to see his mistakes and was chiefly responsible for the lack of sales.

Claire gave her head a pathetic nod, reached down for her box and placed it before her. It was an exquisite piece, a lacquered box with solid bronze hinges, which Grandfather Hayes had crafted with his own hands. Preparing herself, Claire fingered the intricate floral markings carved into the wood and placed a cautious hand on the lid. "Do I really need to do this?" Claire whispered. And then she opened it.

The scent, a familiar mix of old prints and pine, escaped from its confinement and played with Claire's vulnerability. The box itself had been a keepsake Rebecca had given her years ago. Her sister had it delivered to her workplace, and for some reason, Claire hadn't wanted to take it home with her, nor did she have the heart to toss it. She'd skimmed quickly through pictures of her and Rebecca, cards she'd received, letters from her old boyfriends, but she stopped at one photo which had left a lasting impression on her.

It was a picture, taken on her thirteen birthday, of her mother a few weeks before the fatal accident. She was leaning over the table, putting vanilla icing on Claire's cake. Studying her mother's face, Claire noted the sadness that covered Connie's unresponsive green eyes. Her weak posture spoke volumes, as if to say she'd already given up on happiness—and on life. It was difficult to look at her mother's earlier photos, when she was vivacious, with her gorgeous red mane and radiant smile. Connie had a beautiful smile especially when she wore red lipstick, Claire reflected back, and it wasn't just any woman that could pull off such a bold color.

"And all because of a man," Claire whispered, staring down at the frayed picture of her mother. She'd almost forgotten what her father looked like, having long ago destroyed the photos of him, along with any other shred of evidence that he'd ever existed. She never forgave him his affairs, betrayals that had pushed Claire's mother to alcohol instead of sending her out the door.

Growing up in Sartell, Minnesota, Claire had always been haughty of her "gifted" status. She had graduated easily with honors; some of her instructors hailed her as brilliant, a genius, and they guaranteed her a future filled with success. But her most valuable lesson was the one she had learned while studying her father's conduct. This was where Claire came to understand the complexity of men, or rather the simplicity. Men craved the challenge, not the prize beneath the shroud.

Watching him from the sidelines, as a young girl, she had observed him as he prepared for his evening dates with other women, by splashing himself with the cheap cologne Claire and her baby sister, Rebecca, had bought him for Father's Day. He always winked at his daughters on his way out the door, planted an obligatory dry kiss on their mother's cheek, and drove off without a second thought.

Her parents had been high school sweethearts. Claire's father was a good-looking man with thick brown hair and hazel eyes. From what Claire knew, they were madly in love. They married and decided to stay in their hometown of Sartell. It was a peaceful place to raise children, with its old-fashioned values. This was a place where people understood the importance of family, and where friends and neighbors wished each other peace and love.

But the tranquility hadn't lasted long. Her father grew tired of the humdrum routine and found new interests that led to gossip in the town. Adultery.

To her mother, the word itself was the ultimate betrayal. She couldn't—wouldn't, believe it. Eventually she relied on vodka as a way to deal with the shame and pain that ate away at her faithful heart. Claire remembered clearly how it began with one glass of vodka and orange juice to calm her through the dark hours while Grant was out of the house.

After the first year of ignoring his affairs, Connie had graduated from one glass to a whole bottle, minus the orange juice. Claire bore silent witness, hiding in the corners of the family room, watching her mother withering away into a shell of what she once had been. She'd lost her grace, stumbling around drunk, searching for her imagined strength in a bottle of vodka.

It fascinated Claire all the more when, not long after her mother had died, her father suddenly changed again. Grant became doting, spending time at home with his girls. He even tried to bake with them, though Rebecca was barely five at the time. Claire's little sister had been easy to pacify, but not Claire. She despised her father and openly wished it was he who had died.

What stung Claire the most was the way her father wallowed in agony over Connie's death. At the funeral, he had sobbed like a child and, no doubt, begged for forgiveness. Rebecca did not know, as Claire did, about their father's many affairs. Soon he became obsessed, creating a shrine of pictures in the bedroom they once had shared: their first dance, their wedding, the places they'd been. Letters written by her to him lined the walls. He spoke to his daughters about how no other woman would ever be the angel she was. How much he loved her. Oh, how he loved her. He was such a hypocrite! Grant died eleven years later of a massive heart attack. It gave Claire a great deal of satisfaction to conjecture that the attack had possibly been the culmination of years of guilt.

Claire picked out a photo of her mother, holding a glass in her hand. Before the affairs, her mother barely even touched a glass of wine; Claire's thoughts drifted over to Harvey. He, too, seldom drank prior to the mess he'd gotten himself into. She wondered if there was something she could do to help him. Normally she couldn't have cared less if people wanted to waste themselves, but when it came to Harvey, a part of her felt obligated.

Claire opened the door to his office and immediately wished she hadn't. A rotting stench hit her hard, and snoring through his drunken sleep, there was Harvey, curled up in a ball on the floor. Vomit covered the half-eaten pizza in its open box. Inside the aquarium, on the surface of the water, floated three of his prized clown-fish; their once shiny scales of yellow, white, orange, and black looked sickly. Not only was Harvey himself a mess, everything connected to him was falling apart.

Claire felt instantly enraged with the pitiful man. *And you used to be my mentor,* Claire wanted to shout at him. Any concern she had felt for him as a person evaporated, replaced by thoughts of how his loss of reputation could be a direct hit on her. Was her own career hanging by a thread? Despite her confident persona, the prospect of working elsewhere filled Claire with dread. She was as rooted as a redwood tree. This was her golden egg. Wyatt Real Estate had made her very wealthy.

Seeing him passed out on his floor was like witnessing a crime scene. "Wake-up, Harvey." Claire poked him three times with the toe of her shoe.

"Just let me be..." He slurred and then rolled onto his other side.

"Fat bastard." She went to his desk and wrote a quick message on a large, pink post-it note:

Stop drowning yourself
into a drunk and grow
a pair!
Preston-Lockwood

She stuck it to his forehead and hoped that when he awoke it would still be there for him to read. But as she prepared to leave, she stopped.

Fuck me.

Claire turned back, walked over to his sofa, and yanked his blanket off. Standing over Harvey, she felt a startling thrum reverberate behind her chest bone. It was a pitiful moment. She covered him and slid out of the office, closing the door behind her.

The post-it note was still stuck to his forehead.

5

Crazy is as Crazy Does

Claire sipped discreetly from her jasmine tea while waiting for Janice to arrive. It had surprised her when Janice suggested they meet at Son Vi, located along the lively Manhattan strip—kind of a coincidence. On the phone, Janice had told her to find a table near the back. She emphasized that everything must be confidential, and Claire must come alone.

Claire sensed her new friend held a possible solution to her seemingly impossible situation.

A young Asian woman, looking more like an awkward child, placed a plate of lemons before her. "You ready to order?" She had a strong accent. Claire put up her hand and wiggled her fingers to suggest five more minutes.

Janice poked her head around the circular partition. "May I join you?"

The sight of Janice's sunny smile, as well as her being on time, pleased Claire. Janice settled in the chair across from her. Her Channel suit fit snugly over her obvious bulge, and her hair hung in loose blond and gray curls, topped with a matching cream angora beret. She looked like she might have just finished strolling in the park without a care in the world. To the waitress, she said, "I'll have green tea, your decaffeinated kind. And would you bring us each a menu?" Taking off her brown leather gloves, Janice asked, "So, how have you been?"

Claire had to pause before answering. "As good as expected."

Several seconds passed. Janice stared at her, expressionless. The waitress returned with a pot of tea and two menus.

Janice hummed a familiar tune as she squeezed a lemon into her tea, ensuring the leaves settled at the bottom of the cup before taking a small sip. "I love this stuff—so good. I have a box of the finest green tea from Japan. It's from the first pick you know, the same kind set aside for the emperor." Delicate auburn brows rose. "Perhaps you'd like a bag?"

Claire blinked at the offer. "No thanks, I get mine from Chinatown."

Janice opened the menu. "It's really not the same, but as you wish." She continued humming while mulling over her order. "I think I'll try the grilled chicken served over a bed of bok choy. Normally I'd get the curried crab, but my boy really never liked curry." Then she closed the menu and put it aside. "What about you, Claire? Have you decided on anything?"

Claire was stunned. What the hell did eating curry have to do with her kid? Something was odd about Janice. Claire was now even more intrigued.

"I'll have the same." Claire didn't care what she ate. Her motive for lunch with Janice had nothing to do with food, or the emperor's damn tea for that matter.

While waiting for their orders, Janice made small talk. "So," she asked, "do you have any brothers and sisters?"

"I have a younger sister, Rebecca."

"And what does Rebecca do?" Janice asked.

"Rebecca's a stay-at-home mom, and her husband's a contractor. Vince rebuilds homes and does renovations."

"Do they live close by?"

"Fairfield. They live in Fairfield," Claire said without elaborating.

"Ah, any children?"

"A set of twins, boys. Their youngest is a girl…they named her Olivia, after Vince's dead grandmother. She was Sicilian or something." Claire held back what she really wanted to say. Jonathon loved Olivia and it was her fault that Jonathon became insistent on becoming a father. Claire suspected it had something to do with the fact that he had been around when Olivia was born. He loved holding her and almost cried when she took her first steps. It made Claire sick.

"Do you like children?"

Claire wondered if she read the revulsion on her face regarding her sister's children. "Sure I do," Claire replied. *Only when they're sleeping.* Unlike Jonathon, Claire had never wanted any children. She outright despised them. They were like little explosive devices, loud and dirty noisemakers.

"And your husband, what does he do?" Janice took a quick sip of tea.

More questions. "Jonathon works as a stockbroker, Kerrigan and Lockwood."

"And yourself?" Janice seemed even more enthralled.

"I'm a senior agent with Wyatt Real Estate."

"A self-sufficient career woman," Janice said, with an undeniable measure of respect in her voice.

"Yes, I've done quite well." Claire liked hearing that combination of words, and judging by Janice's expensive tastes, she, too, liked money; perhaps she was a career woman as well. Claire had earned her success through years of determination and drive. She had come from nothing. She'd literally stepped off the train from Minnesota with everything she owned in a suitcase and small duffel bag. After two years of selling real estate, she'd purchased her New Jersey property outright. It was a perfect semi-rural location near Montville, an easy thirty-five minute commute to Manhattan.

"And you live in New Jersey?"

"Montville," Claire specified.

"Really?" Janice thought for a moment. "My husband and I also live in Montville…that is, when we're not away on vacation. Wow, it gives rise to the phrase, six degrees of separation," she said taking a longer sip. "So tell me, what are your plans for Christmas?"

"My husband and I go skiing in Colorado every year."

Janice set her cup down. "You don't celebrate Christmas?"

Claire's response was clipped. "No, I don't. Actually, I don't believe in God." She was beginning to lose her cool, and Janice had pressed the wrong button. But for some reason, Janice seemed fine with her response and simply smiled. And thankfully, the string of questions stopped.

Janice ate with an enormous appetite as Claire nibbled on what she could. There was the usual dinner conversation, but none of the topics really caused Claire to pay attention. She was disappointed. This was not what she'd hoped for. Janice was simply a nut.

Groping through her purse, Claire pulled out her hand lotion. Out of sheer boredom, she asked, "Do you have any other children?" Claire rubbed the cream into her hands. She had grown annoyed hearing about Janice's family company, and how her great-great-grandfather had arrived from Germany in the late seventeen hundreds and traded furs with the Indians, or how in the later seventeen hundreds, they started their first fur shop in New York City. Her question, however, provoked the strangest look on Janice's face.

"Yes. I mean, no." Janice placed a trembling hand over her mouth. Her gray eyes darkened, like rain washed stone. "I had a son." Janice's eyes filled with unspent tears.

Claire realized she'd touched on something. "Had?"

Janice stared off into space before opening her purse. She pulled out a small photo of a handsome youth and slid it toward Claire. "This is James, Jimmy. Jim Junior…" Janice pulled a tissue out of her purse and daintily blotted her eyes.

Studying the photo, Claire was far from her comfort zone and tried not to sound remorseless. "He looks like you. What happened to him?"

"James was nineteen there, and he died three months later." Janice took back the photo and slid it carefully into her purse. "Drug overdose…I found him in his room. He was cold. His lips were blue." She trailed off, lost in her memories. "Jim and I had no clue he was using."

Although she wanted to say something, nothing came out of Claire's mouth.

"But we can't talk about that anymore," Janice reminded herself, forgetting that Claire was sitting across from her. "And now everything is as it should be, and Jimmy has come back into our lives again. I do give thanks for that."

"Huh?" The statement caught Claire off guard. "He's come

back into your lives?"

Janice placed a loving hand on her belly. "He's right here."

Claire finally clued in to the insanity Janice was saying. "You're naming him Jimmy?"

Janice swallowed, her stare stone cold. "He is Jimmy."

This takes the bloody biscuit, Claire thought. The woman was a loony. She bit off a retort as Janice forged ahead.

"What if I were to tell you it wasn't our good doctor who helped perform this little miracle?"

"I don't know what you're getting at."

Janice combed the room with her eyes, and dropped her voice to a mere whisper. "Listen, what would you be willing to do to carry a child of your own?"

"Practically anything," Claire went along with Janice's madness. "Why?"

"My son died almost two years ago. He was my world, our world." Janice spoke in a soothing tone, glancing down at her unborn child as if she were addressing her dead son. "I know we spoiled you, gave you too much." She looked at Claire as if she remembered to include her as well. "But we loved him. You know?"

Claire nodded, but for a second time, felt she could say nothing. Still, she felt fascinated, getting to observe a nut-case close up.

"We tried for more than a year, even went to Europe seeking cures—a fortune spent on fertility. They all said the same thing: I was infertile. And even if we had a surrogate, it would never be the same. It wouldn't be Jimmy."

"What did you do?" Claire whispered.

The silence lasted several, long, 'Mississippi' seconds.

"Do you know anything about voodoo?" She studied Claire's face for a response.

"Voodoo? As in shoving needles into those tiny dolls resembling real people?" Claire was annoyed, and worse, her anger was rising. "What is this bullshit?"

Janice took hold of her arm when Claire reached for her coat. "If you go, you'll always wonder if what I'm saying is true. I went to the trouble of getting her number for you. At least call and see for yourself. Take this, call her...you'll see for yourself." She practically shoved a card into Claire's hand. "I thought the same thing as you when I first heard about her."

"Do you actually expect me to bite?"

"I expect you, if you have the courage, to think outside of everything you know. There's a world out there, Claire, a world where Satan is listening." Janice steamrolled on. "Look at me; thirty-six doctors and specialists from all over the world, acupuncturists, you name it; one by one, they told me to give up, that I'd never be a mother again, to let my son's death go. And I swear, on my unborn son's life, whatever the magic, voodoo, or whatever it is she did, I have my son back. Not just a replacement, but my boy—his soul. She gave him back to us. So when I asked what you would do to have your husband's baby, I didn't ask for the sake of something to say."

Claire's mouth became dry. She was spooked but also curious. Glancing down at the card, she said, "And you think this voodoo lady can help me?"

"Did you not hear anything I just told you?" Janice said. "Satan has been watching you."

"What, he knows if I've been naughty or nice?" Claire pulled her napkin from off of her lap and threw it onto the table.

"Whether you know it or not, you've reached Satan, and he wants to help you. Just as God can see all, so can he. And there are people who can channel him," she explained, tapping her finger on the card. "She's a voodoo priestess. And yes, I do know she can help you. I also have it on very good authority you will give birth to your first child. It'll be a girl, by the way."

"What makes you say that?" This got Claire's interest; it was no secret that Jonathon wanted a girl.

"The woman who helped me is going to help you. She saw you in my path—saw you coming. She told me to tell you this." Janice's eyes seemed cloudy, as if in a trance. "She sees things... in the walls. Shadows."

Claire let out an unrestrained laugh, one that turned several heads. "You're nuts, lady!" She got up to leave. But before exiting, she added, "And you're paying for my lunch!"

6

Vial Woman

One mile into her morning jog, plump snowflakes began falling and blinding her vision. She stopped running and used her glove to dry her lashes. But before she resumed her run, Claire noted that there were drops of blood off the beaten trail. She followed the crimson droplets with her eyes and saw what looked like a dog in the near distance. Claire sunk her boots into the knee-deep snow until she was able to see the animal up close. A horrified breath escaped her. A dead, gray coyote lay stiff, on its back, its belly ripped open, and perched on the animal's ribcage was the white raven. Its entire beak and plumage was stained with the animal's blood, while it pecked large pieces off of the animal and turned its neck up to swallow the meat. Once it managed the bite down, it met Claire's stare and began bobbing its head and spreading its wings.

Janice's words from a few weeks ago came back to haunt her. So far, every morning, the white raven had stalked her, flying low and moving from tree to tree.

Claire had whipped rocks or frozen pieces of ice at the bird, followed by her usual barrage: *I hope a coyote makes breakfast out of you.* Was the raven more than just a bird? Was it satanic? Was Satan really watching her?

Claire studied the bird as it sunk its beak into the bloody flesh and yanked on another piece of tissue.

The whole idea of Satan was a mystery. But unexpected warmth circulated through Claire's body while contemplating him. God had failed her, and because of that, she had lost her faith. That energy had morphed into hatred over the years. Maybe Satan did notice her as Janice had said. Maybe, without even realizing it, Claire had placed *that* energy into Satan.

He applauded selfish and reckless behavior. Claire was all of those things. Staring down at the goriness, Claire wondered if evil could be personified through the eyes of the sinister raven. But what exactly was evil? The world was imperfect, and Claire was merely doing what she needed to do in order to survive in its imperfectness. Perhaps that was what Satan was: another divinity which opened a window when God had closed his door.

The raven pulled its head up and spread its wings. It seemed as if the damned thing was reading her mind. Claire pulled the hood from her jacket over her head and left the scene running.

The house was quiet; Lady mewed at the top of the winding stairs. Claire's white Persian cat was hungry. Claire made a quick stop in the kitchen and opened a fresh can of gourmet pet food. Lady rushed to Claire's feet and ate elegantly from the plate.

This is going to be one long day. Sweaty and tired, she opened the refrigerator door, took out a jug, and drank from her personal recipe of dark berries and pomegranates. It reminded her of the blood-soaked raven. She wiped the red stain from her lips and reached toward the back of the fridge, picking out two different vials of fertility serums. As she began making her way upstairs, the telephone rang.

In her rush to reach the phone, Claire dropped the vials, but they didn't break. Instead, they went sliding across the granite floor. "Shit!" she swore, as she checked the call display. It was her sister, and after the morning she'd just had, the last thing she wanted to do was to play nice and pretend to be happy. Unlike Claire, Rebecca was always cheerful.

"This better be important," Claire said, picking up on the

third ring. Lady went chasing after the vials, swatting at them with her paws. The thick glass made scratching sounds against her floor. What a joke her life had become. The cat was now playing with her only hope.

Clearing his throat, Vince said, "Hey, Claire. Hope…I mean…I didn't wake you, did I?"

Her sister's annoying husband always mixed his words around her. She made him nervous, and it gave her a perverse sense of pleasure.

"Oh, what's up?" Claire said, watching Lady as she chased the vials. One slid beneath the fridge, the other Claire stopped with her foot. She bent over and picked up the second vial, placing it on the kitchen counter.

"You're supposed to…" Vince cleared his throat again and started over. "Jonathon said he'd give you our tickets, and that you'd drop them off around noon. I would pick them up myself, but I have to take the kids to Nutley. My parents will be keeping them for a few days." He cleared his throat again.

Claire bit her lip. The occasion was Rebecca and her husband's tenth wedding anniversary, which happened to fall on New Year's Eve. The night was planned around the New Year's Gala at the Metropolitan Opera. It was the affair of the year, although Claire had no desire to go.

"He did, did he?" Claire was unaware of any plans.

"I'd get Beck to do it, but the guys have my truck," Vince explained.

"And what time did you guys have in mind?"

"I—"

Claire cut him off. "I have a private showing today, plus it's New Year's. The traffic is going to be brutal." Then she remembered the weather. "And… it's a fu…freaking blizzard outside."

"I just thought Jonathon told you."

"*Told me?*"

"I mean, asked." Vince quickly corrected himself, but it was too late for that.

The anger in Claire began to increase. The more she thought about it, the angrier she got. Jonathon was taking too many liberties with her lately and now this, having to drop tickets off at the last minute.

"I work. I don't just sit around all day watching soaps and playing mommy," Claire barked. Whoops, too late. She'd said it. It was difficult to keep her irritability in check, specifically given the situation of her morning. Her sister's trust in Vince drove her mad.

Vince cleared his throat again. "That's okay, Claire, I'll drive into Montville, don't worry."

"You're not getting it, Vince, I have a very big client who's looking into buying a multi-million dollar home. I can't predict what time I'll be done. I'm not selling hot-dogs and fries here."

"So…okay, why not just leave them in your mailbox?" Vince suggested.

"And who'll open the gate? No one's here and I'm sure as hell not leaving costly tickets in my mailbox," Claire snapped, feeling a bit embarrassed by her lack of control. She hated when people saw that side of her. Claire's cat began pulling herself through her legs, purring incessantly. The sound of her pet calmed her some.

Sounds of children spilled through the phone receiver. "Cheerios," Vince said, cupping the mouthpiece, but his voice carried through anyway. "Make your sister some toast."

He came back to the phone and said, "Sorry, Claire, I figured it was New Year's Eve. I didn't know you had to work."

Money never sleeps, Claire wanted to say, but she held back. Following a taut moment of silence, coupled with Vince's heavy breathing, Claire felt the need to redeem herself. "Don't worry about it…I'll drop the tickets off after my meeting."

"You sure?" There was lightness in his voice.

"I'm sure," Claire said, wanting to get off the phone. By the sounds of it, the Greco family was stirring, and the last thing she wanted was to have her niece grab the phone and start babbling. Or worse yet, her sister coming to the phone and expecting Claire to offer her congratulations on being married ten years. "I have to go, tell Beck I'll be there by three."

"Thanks lots. I…I mean, thank you," he stumbled in perfect Vince fashion.

Putting the cordless back onto the cradle, Claire picked up the vial from the counter and moved toward the fridge. She crouched on the cold floor and felt around beneath the freezer door, fishing out the other vial. Still positioned with her head close to the ground, Claire found herself face to face with her cat. "Lucky you, Lady. You're old and spayed, but at least someone still loves you." She reached over and scratched behind her cat's ears.

On her way toward the double-stair foyer, Claire paused at the beautiful, travertine mosaic landing which led to her torment upstairs. Cupping the vials in her hand, her nose began to tingle. Another humiliating round of injections.

Where did she go wrong? How did she not see this coming?

She ran her free hand along the cool, wrought-iron railing. Her eyes slowly drank in the splendor of the Italian stone stairs and stopped at the brilliance of the Austrian crystal chandelier. The rays of light that shone through the delicate crystals dazzled her. Claire thought longingly about Vince.

Of course, that was it: the mistake—where she went wrong.

Claire thought back to the day she had hired Vince. It was a choice between him and another guy who stank of sweat and tiger balm. *If only he hadn't stunk*, she thought. Then Rebecca would have probably stayed a spinster and Jonathon wouldn't have met Vince, or their kids, and she wouldn't have to be stabbing herself with another round of drugs.

She made her way upstairs, recalling the day that she had introduced her sister to him eleven years earlier. Despite his virile good looks and quiet disposition, Vince was no more than a blue-collar worker, dependable and honest. So she had no other use for him, made no moves, and he never tried any of his own.

It still secretly bothered Claire that she had been responsible for the day Rebecca and Vince first met. Rebecca was spending the weekend, and Vince had dropped by to pick up his check. He was tongue-tied trying to introduce himself, nervously stumbling over his words, as he usually did.

But who in the hell would have thought that renovating her home would lead to this? She hadn't even known Jonathon then.

Stealing into her bathroom, she locked the door behind her and placed the vials on the counter. Looking in the mirror, Claire saw that the woman staring back at her was sad. But somewhere, close to the surface, there was this other woman, an angrier woman who kept things in check.

Taking out the syringes and rubbing alcohol pads from the medicine cabinet, Claire began preparing her ritual. There was a war going on inside of her as she opened the vials, a struggle that pulled her in two directions.

Claire thought about Jonathon and having to spend New Year's with Rebecca and Vince, pretending to be cheerful for their so-called happiness. Tonight they would celebrate, toast their ten years of marriage and their three children.

She pulled off her shirt and flinched when she saw her bruised stomach. Claire didn't know what was harder, pretending to care, or pretending not to.

7

Crystalline

hot shower loosened her muscles; she knew they would ache later. With her hair wound in rollers, wearing just a black silk robe, Claire added the final application of mascara. She stared into the mirror, but the satisfaction with her appearance wasn't enough to lift the miserable mood she was in. Opening her robe, Claire glimpsed her naked body in the mirror. The bruise on her stomach was no longer visible due to an amazing product that actors used called "pancake make-up." She'd been using it for a while and was grateful for it; Jonathon didn't see the hideous telltale marks on her. Every few weeks she would switch things up by injecting her legs or arms. Sometimes, the injection areas would become irritated and form small scabs. Other times, she was lucky—like this morning—Claire thought, admiring her work.

She closed her robe and squirted a generous amount of lotion into the palm of her hand. Inhaling the sweet scent of cocoa butter first, she began rubbing the cool cream in a circular pattern onto her thighs. Distracted, she wondered if Janice's insistence about the voodoo was true. But what if it wasn't? And time waited for no one, not even Claire.

There had to be a way, even if she were to hire a surrogate. Claire herself would have to form a bump and keep the woman in hiding until it was time to birth it. But what if Jonathon wanted to touch it, feel the movements? Shaking her head, she decided that she'd cross that bridge when she got there. For now, she needed to put together a plan of action. First, she needed to find a good doctor, a gynecologist who was willing to do exactly what Claire wanted. In-vitro fertilization was an obvious solution, but how would she get Jonathon's sperm? Or better yet, how was she going to get an egg donor with the same red hair and green eyes as hers? What about Rebecca? What could be a better plan than that? But, knowing her sister, it wouldn't be easy. Manipulating people wasn't in Beck's nature, and she couldn't tell a lie if it would save her life. Looking in the mirror, and staring into her own eyes, Claire determined that there had to be a way. There had to be a way to keep Jonathon from finding out that she was unable to produce an egg. He would see her as a hopeless failure, an old, infertile failure. *What the hell is wrong with me?* Claire thought. *Have I lost my fucking mind?* That had to be the hormones talking, making her contemplate such absurd thoughts.

Turning her attention away from the mirror, Claire caught the smell of coffee that drifted beneath the closed door. Jonathon would be up soon with the dreaded, decaffeinated brew in tow. Even the enjoyment of a cup of coffee had deserted her.

Claire gave herself a slow once-over in the mirror and exited her bathroom.

Powerless to put her reflections aside, she listlessly made her way down the long hallway toward their bedroom. Her long silk robe tangled itself around her calves like ankle chains. She truly was a slave to her predicament: trapped and without a remedy. There were women who killed mothers and stole their babies. While most people would gasp with disgust, Claire understood perfectly what motivated them.

Walking directly toward her bedroom window, Claire watched the morning sun spill over Montville. It was breathtaking, and the view calmed her as she prepared to face Jonathon. She traced her slender finger along the misty windowpane and stared as the snowflakes flew at her, stopped, and melted against the warm glass. Jonathon was as beautiful an individual as the tiny flakes that disappeared before her. If she failed him by not giving him the child he so wanted, he too would disappear.

"Snow is a precipitation of crystalline formed within the earth's atmosphere from the freezing of water vapor in the air and consisting of multitudes of snowflakes that fall from the sky," Claire whispered, reciting the information she'd collected thirty years prior following her mother's death, "and no two snowflakes are alike." But how would researchers know that? They would have to capture each and every fallen flake, and that would be impossible.

Jonathon would soon be coming upstairs with coffee. She needed to resist the primal feminine urge to be vulnerable and uncontrolled. She must not lose her common sense to emotions of helplessness.

"Morning, Mrs. Lockwood." Jonathon set Claire's coffee mug on her bedside table.

She didn't turn around to face him. Instead, she said, without the same warmth, "I want you to tell Bruno that we have a dead coyote in the back. Tell him, before he does the driveway, to find its carcass. I want that thing removed."

"Okay."

"And tell him there's a bird he needs to watch out for. A white raven. I know that it killed it."

Jonathon chuckled. "Birds can't kill coyotes."

"This one did."

"I seriously doubt that. Besides, ravens are black. What you saw was probably a turkey vulture," Jonathon said. "And the coyote was more likely dead before it got to it."

"Whatever." It was, without a doubt, a raven.

By her cold reply, Jonathon knew she was in one of those moods. While she stayed at the window, Jonathon studied her beautiful figure from behind. With her long legs and perfect posture, she had an incredible grace, and made just staring out the window a work of art. Her black, silky robe molded beautifully over the outline of her curves, accentuating the perfect rise of her buttocks. A part of him wanted to join her and take her in his arms, and the other part of him wanted to bounce out of there.

Jonathon flopped down on the bed causing a few tiny feathers to escape from the comforter's fabric. "You have an open-house today, right?"

Claire turned around to face him, avoiding his eyes. "Not an open-house, a private showing. I'm sure they'll bite...it's a gift for their daughter." She grabbed her coffee and took a sip. "Wedding present."

"Damn, what's wrong with Tupperware?" Jonathon said, hoping to get a rise from her. "I made you an egg-white omelet, it's in the microwave," he offered, as she entered her walk-in closet. "With spinach and goat cheese," he added.

Jonathon figured she was mulling over which power suit would best close the deal. He had come to understand Claire's moods and patterns. This was one of those days when he need-ed to keep his distance, but at the same time, remain within her reach.

Lady gracefully leaped onto his lap, purring for his atten-tion, and Jonathon groaned, "Lady? Come on, girl, look what you did." The cat's white Persian hairs covered his two-thou-sand-dollar Versace suit. He gently set Lady down onto the hardwood floor.

Claire emerged from the closet wearing silk stockings and a pale-pink bra and panties.

She was something. Even with her hair wrapped in big plas-tic curlers, any man would have thrown her onto the bed and taken her right there. Jonathon watched as Claire opened her bedside table drawer to retrieve the lint brush. He straightened to allow Claire to glide the brush over his suit. *God she's beautiful*, he thought to himself. The morning sun, which poured through the bay window, caught the emerald-green pigment in her irises. They were hypnotic and one of her best features. He relaxed at her touch. He wanted her.

Claire sensed his desire. She felt his eyes touch every curve of her body. She wanted him too, but found it difficult to keep from reflecting on how much he'd changed in just a few short years. She continued to glide the lint brush over the fine fabric of his sleeve. She remembered when she had first met him. His choice of music had been Eminem, and his wardrobe consisted of blue jeans and sneakers. It often amazed her how naïve he was about his effect on women. He didn't see the eyes that were gawking at him, their mouths open in long, salivating gulps. But Claire took notice of the stares and reveled in it. Jonathon stood an athletic, six-foot-two, with a tuft of chestnut curls and thick-lashed eyes, which made his blue eyes burst. She loved when Jonathon anchored them on her, that prelude to sex. Her gaze darted to the small scar, below his right eyebrow, which only added to his appeal. A bad-boy with a permanent cock to his brow.

"Lift up your arm," Claire said. He studied her, while gently biting on his lower lip. Another turn-on, with his strong jaw-line and almost perfect teeth. His two front teeth were slightly overlapped, and his permanent smirk made him appear naughty, though boyishly handsome. But Jonathon was all man. She smiled inwardly, while working with the lint brush, as memories drifted into her consciousness: his first time on a plane (he had taken the window seat, bursting with enthusiasm), his first custom Armani suit. That was just the beginning, a first of many things that had needed doing in order to ensure that her young lover complemented her own expensive taste and style. Eventually, he gave up the window seat. After all, that was what a gentleman would do: give the lady her choice. And Claire always chose the window.

Claire gently put the lint brush down. "All done." She paused to tighten the clasp on his diamond encrusted, white gold cuf-flinks. The reminiscing made her feel things she hadn't felt in a long while. She missed him, remembering what things were like before the whole infertility problem.

Sensing her affection toward him, Jonathon drew her closer. He'd been yearning for his wife, forgetting the reasons why he fell in love with her. She'd always been aloof and not easily im-pressed. Claire was the kind of woman who people took notice of: beautiful, extremely intelligent, and scrupulous. Her interest in him made him feel special and incredibly alive.

His lips parted as he brushed them over her cold shoulders and then traced them along her neck. He stopped at her mouth and whispered again, "Good morning, Mrs. Lockwood."

She teased him and licked his earlobe. "Mrs. Preston-Lock-wood. And I heard you the first time."

Jonathon sat back on the bed and looked up at Claire while she stood over him. "You never said good morning back," he reminded her, looking up through his lashes.

Claire slithered onto the bed and spoke into the curve of his neck. "Well, Mr. Preston-Lockwood, let's make it a good morning indeed." Claire carefully unwound each curler, moving slowly, knowing the important poise of foreplay. Her red tresses landed on the surface of her pale shoulders. Jonathon wound a curl in his fingers, stared cravingly into Claire's eyes, and dropped it. The curl uncoiled and fell across her collarbone.

Adoring the attention he paid her, she watched him remove his suit jacket and pants, his penis stiff in his boxers. It pulsed through the thin cotton as Claire undressed before him.

She moved toward her husband and reached for his tie. Her heart stopped, heavy in her chest, and then accelerated. The tie was new; she'd never seen it before. She studied it carefully, inspecting the thin silk threads.

"What?" Jonathon was confused.

Quiet at first, Claire's mind went to work. She knew he lacked coordination skills when it came to color. This was a dead give-away. "New tie..." She wasn't asking him. She watched his face as he squirmed under her examination. He was on the stand now.

The tension in the room returned. Claire said nothing as she continued to examine the evidence. The tie was spectacular. The threads were exact and harmonized Jonathon's azure eyes. Someone had to have cared enough, looking deeply into them, to see that there were tiny flecks of gold and copper running through them.

Jonathon rose and reached for his pants. "It's a gift from a client."

She knew he was lying, but allowed him to sink himself further.

He slanted her a look, while zipping up his pants. "Another satisfied customer."

She shook her head but kept her comments to herself. If she'd learned anything from spending as much time as she had with the many men in her life, it was that saying nothing was like having them walk through a minefield.

"You hate my tie that much?" Jonathon struck a pose. Nothing got past Claire.

Claire did her best to compose herself. Another lesson she'd

learned from her mother, who, unlike Claire, would have started questioning him, showing her vulnerability. The cold air
raised goose bumps all over her pale skin. She lay on the bed
and wrapped her naked body under the soft covers, looking at
him, expressionless.

He worked quickly and slipped back into his suit jacket. "I
like it." He straightened the tie in the dresser mirror.

Claire huffed out a laugh. "It looks like azurite exploded on
it."

Jonathon turned around. "What?"

"Azurite, it's a mineral. That tie looks cheap…and way too
busy," she lied with ease.

Jonathon took a long look at his reflection and smiled
through the mirror at her. "Well, I'm a busy guy." Moving from
the dresser, he leaned to kiss her.

She turned her head so that he caught her hair instead.

"Oh, before I forget. I have Rebecca's anniversary gift." He
opened his jacket and pulled out an envelope. "See if you can
get there an hour early. We're wrapping things up by two today."

Taking the envelope from him, Claire remarked, "My meeting should be over by three. I'll arrange for a ride into the city."

Claire peeked inside. "Box twenty-nine."

Jonathon grinned. "Die Fledermaus, the second act."

"Yes…and the best seats in the house," Claire added, thinking about Vince and Rebecca's good fortune. All eyes would be
on them, the bigwigs seated in box number twenty-nine.

"Patrick's a member…and you know how he is, anything
less won't do." Jonathon fussed with his hair in the mirror. He
seemed preoccupied, as if he was primping for something—or
someone.

It was true what he'd said about Patrick though. Anyone
who knew anything about the stock market had heard of him.
He was a businessman, a renegade, and was known for going
off the reservation. He almost always got what he wanted. Case
in point: the Parterre Box for the New Year Gala.

"I guess Patrick and his wife are sitting with us?" Claire
probed. Jonathon turned around with a genuine smile.

"Where else? As Patrick says, if the section is good enough
for the Clintons, it's good enough for him."

Claire loathed the way he valued Patrick. Jonathon loved being able to use the man's name so freely, loved to be partnered with one of Manhattan's biggest achievers. It gave him a sense of worth. For Jonathon, raised by a single mother who had given him up for adoption when he was nine, Patrick was more than a partner. Patrick had become the father he'd never known.

But what truly disturbed Claire more, as always, was the effect Jonathon himself had on everyone he met.

People were naturally attracted to him. Without any effort on his part, they genuinely liked him. Claire had worked long and hard to master what Jonathon owned naturally. An invisible sunshine seemed to follow him as he floated his way through life. From a lowly deliveryman with no future, Claire had made him over in her image—a class-conscious, financial success. In short, she had created a beautiful monster, and now he was overshadowing her. She was a rose in the shadow of a big, beautiful oak tree, unable to absorb the rays of the sun.

Claire continued to study the tickets. "I don't know why you bother spoiling my sister that way, it's not like she and Vince know any better."

Jonathon had regained some of his composure and answered innocently enough, "What do you mean?"

"Please," she went on, "they're drinking champagne on a Kool-Aid budget."

Beer budget, he thought. Claire's cruel play on words made him want to defend them, but decided against it. He took offense to her harsh judgment of her sister's family, considering he had been in a worse predicament when she'd first met him.

Claire studied Jonathon again, as if she were looking at a perfect stranger. Less than six short years ago, his idea of a night out was eating out of a foam container and sipping drinks through a straw. Her influence had taught her young husband that hard work and discipline were the only way. And now he was showing her. How quickly he'd moved up the corporate ladder, although, unlike her, he had done it without stepping on anyone. Unbeknownst to him, she had done that for him.

He scrambled around before finding his keys. "See you tonight." He slipped out the bedroom door.

With the comforter wrapped around her naked body, Claire

went back to the window. Lady purred at her feet. "It's going to be a long day, Lady. You'll have the whole house to yourself." Claire watched as Jonathon backed out of the driveway in his Mercedes.

Falling into another meditative state, Claire found her vision blurring as she watched the countless snowflakes that flew toward her and hit the glass. *What is it about the crystalline?* What was it about snow that slowed her down and caused her to analyze her life, piece by piece?

This was a new year—but what new beginning? She knew how important having her husband's child was to their marriage, but it wasn't something she even wanted. Maybe it was the guarantee she wished for. The guarantee that no one would ever hurt her the way her mother had been hurt; the guarantee that if she gave Jonathon a child, he would never leave her.

Of course, that was it. It became clear to her as she watched the same beautiful frozen water patterns that had killed her mother. A guarantee for a perfect life. Thinking about the lousy morning she'd had, she wondered if Satan was trying to reach out to her. Maybe, just maybe, Satan really was there. Perhaps he really did open a window when God had slammed his door on her. If Satan was truly listening, she knew exactly what she would ask for. Claire caught herself smiling. *Full control.*

Movement on the outside caught Claire's attention. The white raven swooped in, just a few feet away from her bedroom window, and perched on top of her crystalline-covered roof. The thing seemed very comfortable as it began preening its blood stained feathers. In that thrilling moment, it became crystal clear that Claire needed to rethink what Janice had said. Maybe some dreams weren't just that after all.

8

What a Tangled Web We Weave

Five towering stone arches divided the glass façade. From the outside, the setting sun reflected off the surrounding glass structures, casting a red glow upon the edifice. The magnificent spiral staircase inside invited the crowd in to celebrate the New Year. Claire stepped into the scene, entering through the revolving glass doors that led into the lobby. A blur of fine wine, furs, and jewelry filled the bustling entrance of the Metropolitan Opera. The smell of leather and perfumed fragrances swirled about, and the shine of black polished shoes and elegant tuxedos gave an ambiance of rich, Hollywood glamour. Women, both young and old, were dressed appropriately: hair was beautifully coiffed and faces were exquisitely painted, like delicate Japanese lanterns.

Claire walked alone, familiar with the opera house and uninterested in the building's grandeur. Her hair, pulled into a tight knot, highlighted her long, delicate neck, which was decorated in a diamond-studded collar. She wore a white lynx fur which covered her bare shoulders, and her sleek black dress moved with the rhythm of her body. Claire strode with a mission, her head held high, stealing the attention away from the crystal chandeliers, which dropped from the ceiling like exploding suns. She savored this moment, noting the eyes that followed her, wondering who she was, and who the lucky person accompanying this exquisite creature might be. She passed the works of Marc Chagall, not so much as glancing at them, and moved toward the concrete and marble staircase with its maroon carpet and hammered bronzed railings. There, through the crowd, she spotted her husband. Jonathon stood near the red velor-covered wall, admiring the works of Aristide Maillol.

He turned to her and seemed to stand even taller, inflated with pride at seeing his ravishing wife. "Look at you," he whispered into her ear.

She smiled politely, not returning the compliment, although Jonathon was undeniably handsome, even in the midst of such brilliance. Here was a man who could look good in anything and wearing a tuxedo brought out the territorial woman in Claire. She would ensure to keep him close tonight. "Where's my sister?" Claire roamed the room impatiently with her eyes.

"They're running a little late, had some issues with his car earlier, but Vince figured it out."

Claire rolled her eyes. "It figures. They're always late."

"Don't be so hard on them," he said, taking her hand. Unlike himself, Vince didn't have luxuries. Jonathon and Patrick belonged to an elite club, where they had spent the afternoon being massaged and primped for their evening out. Poor Vince had been running around all day making arrangements just to give his wife the night of her dreams. Then their car broke down and they ended up having to take Vince's company truck. Jonathon had offered to rent them a limo, but Vince wouldn't hear of it and felt that the gift of seeing *Die Fledermaus* was even too much. Jonathon had had to convince him that the tickets were complimentary, because of his connections with the firm. Even if he had paid for them, he would never have let his friend know. Vince naturally worked hard. He was generous to a fault, known to help friends and family when they fell on hard times. A few years back, Vince had gone into partnership with a guy who ended up almost ruining them both. Since then, Vince and Rebecca had been battling a large debt and their savings were nearly depleted.

Jonathon left a message on Vince's cell phone. "I let them

know where to find us." He nibbled the back of Claire's hand and managed to get a smile from her. "We should go, Patrick and Bernice are waiting."

Claire and Jonathon walked arm and arm into The Founders Lounge and made their way through the lively crowd. Surrounded by elegance, Claire spotted a few wealthy, high profile people who traveled in her social circle. Some people held champagne flutes, while others clutched thousand-dollar handbags. The room reeked of money, new and old. Like a lingering trail of first and second hand smoke. Tonight, there were more *first hands* in The Founders Lounge—prosperous and self-made.

Those that Claire recognized, she smiled politely to, keeping her head held high while Jonathon made several stops, shaking hands and making small talk. Jonathon held on to her waist and pulled her close to him while they made their way toward the bar. Claire spotted Patrick, dressed in a black tux, paired with a white, silk vest. On his arm was his wife, Bernice, who, for a woman in her fifties, was no less beautiful. She wore a lovely champagne-colored gown and her blond hair was swept into a loose up-do. She smiled brilliantly as Claire and Jonathon joined them.

"We were starting to worry someone had taken you away," Bernice said, offering Claire her hand.

"It's good to see you again, Bernice," Claire said, giving her hand a squeeze and addressing Patrick with a curt nod.

"Evening, Mrs. Lockwood," Patrick said, turning his full attention to Jonathon. "Come here partner, there's someone I want you to meet."

"Ladies." Jonathon excused himself and left Claire and Bernice alone. They stood in silence, both watching their husbands as they shared a toast with a group of men—most likely investment bankers or prominent men with money on their minds. Regardless, they looked especially blissful, laughing and buoyantly slapping each other on the back. It was obvious by Patrick's posture and loud behavior that he had had a head start in celebrating. He held the full glass of champagne, began laughing at what he thought was a great joke, and spilled some on his tuxedo jacket.

Bernice gave a soft chuckle. "He'll be three sheets to the wind." She turned to Claire, her laugh gone, and said with sincerity, "I have to say, if it wasn't for your husband, I don't think we could have made it through this last year and a half."

Claire studied the appreciation on Bernice's face; her dark eyes were soft and glassy. "He did what he had to do, I'm sure he felt an obligation."

Bernice shook her head. "Obligation is forced. What your husband did for us, especially during Patrick's radiation…" She gave her head a quick shake and held up her glass. "I'm a cheap drunk…this stuff brings out the softy in me."

Claire thought about what Patrick had gone through. He had been diagnosed with stage three prostate cancer, and throughout the entire ordeal, Jonathon had gone above and beyond to aid his boss. From spending all his time at the firm and landing huge accounts to ensuring that Bernice was taken care of in every way possible, Jonathon had become the son they never had, a constant source of strength for them. It enraged Claire, having Patrick and Bernice rely on him the way that they did, especially those middle-of-the-night phone calls or the times when Jonathon insisted on staying with Patrick during his radiation treatments. Judging from the obvious display of happiness, Patrick was here to celebrate.

Bernice looked over at her husband again. "This is the first time he's been able to enjoy himself. I think I'll give him a pass."

Jonathon came over with a glass of Perrier, decorated with a lime. "For you, Claire bear."

"Thank you." Claire took a small sip.

"Jonathon turned to Bernice. "Don't worry, I'll take the bottle away from him soon."

Bernice laughed, taking his hand. "I was just telling Claire that we'll give him a pass tonight…just as long as we can get him into the car."

Bernice and Jonathon shared a private moment, as they both looked over at Patrick. He raised his glass up and bellowed across the room. "To my wife and my business partner…here's to Kerrigan and Lockwood."

Jonathon raised his own glass and said, "The blue chip in

your wallet."

"They'll have to give us our own shade of blue," Patrick shouted back, stirring up a roar of laughter from the men who all shared the same, 'my dick's bigger than your dick' attitude. He slugged back more champagne, then wobbled slowly toward them, a glass in one hand, the bottle in the other.

"Where's that brother-in-law of yours? I wanted to talk to him about some work we want done." Patrick placed the bottle and glass onto the bar and took his wife's hand. "My lovely here wants to build a greenhouse in the back, says we need to go organic."

Bernice smiled, "So that we can keep you here a little longer." She turned to Claire. "I heard your brother-in-law has done some impressive work. He built a greenhouse for the Jeffreys…their house in Water Mill."

Claire nodded. "That's what he does," she said under her breath, looking around for Vince and Rebecca.

Jonathon took his phone out and made a call. Claire watched Jonathon but felt Patrick's eyes on her. She turned her head and found herself staring into his heavy eyes. He had a dumb expression, his mouth slightly parted. Incredibly uncomfortable, Claire leaned closer to Jonathon. He snapped the phone closed.

"Looks like they can't figure their way around. I'm going to get them."

"Why don't I join you?" Bernice suggested. "That way I'll have a chance to talk to Vince about my greenhouse."

Jonathon gave Bernice his elbow. "Shall we then?"

"We shall." Bernice turned to Claire before leaving. "Watch my husband for me while we're gone, and make sure he doesn't break into his Tom and Jerry act."

Claire forced a laugh and leaned against the bar. Sipping her drink, she felt Patrick's eyes on her. Without turning to face him, she said, "You're doing it again."

Patrick teetered where he stood. "Doing what?"

Claire watched him from the corner of her eye. "You're staring."

He leaned closer to her and said, "Maybe you shouldn't have painted that dress on."

Turning to face him, Claire wondered, judging by the drunken state he was in, if it was wise to test him. "I didn't wear it for you, of that I'm sure."

Patrick edged even closer, speaking into the curve of her neck, "Sweetheart, doesn't matter what you wear, because I know every curve and every turn that leads right into your honey-pot—"

"That's enough," Claire said, raising her hand to him. "I suggest you stop drinking before you say something we'll both regret."

"Regret?" He sized her up with an irritable gaze. "I regret the day Claire Preston walked into my life. I should have thrown your ginger ass out, the moment I saw your true colors. Cold blue."

"Will you *please*..." Claire checked to see if anyone had heard. "Your wife and my husband will be back at any moment." Judging from the look on Patrick's face, Claire's warning seemed to penetrate. He placed his drink down and exhaled slowly.

Claire shot him a withering look. "Now you know why I left you. Two bulls in pen could never work."

An extended silence followed, Patrick's shoulders settled on his tall frame. "Sorry, it's...being here...with you...you remember, about twelve years ago, I took you here to see...what was it...*The Great Gatsby*?"

"That was a long time ago, before Jonathon, before I was married." She studied him more carefully. His full head of salt and pepper hair, his handsome square face, and his alluring brown eyes reminded her of how easy it had once been to be around him.

"Yeah, but I was married," Patrick said in a voice too loud. He was restless again. "You said you'd never marry, no commitment. Whatever happened to free rein?" Patrick felt lost again, finding it hard to look away. Even now, after almost fifteen years of knowing Claire, he still desired her. But remembering Jonathon, he said, "You're gonna swallow him and spit out his bones."

"Excuse me?"

"Excuse me?" he mocked her. "Claire Preston-Lockwood, what a sham. A God damn joke."

"It's been years, Patrick, surely you can get over yourself."

"It's not me I'm worried about, it's Jonathon…he's a good kid."

Claire stiffened at his reference to her husband as a kid. "Well, Patrick, this has been a very *fruitful* conversation," she said, regarding the open champagne bottle and wishing he'd shut the hell up.

"He's like a son to me and Bernice. Not even our own daughters cared as much. He took care of her while I was sick," Patrick continued. "A man knows who his friends are when—"

"—Yes, I know all about it," Claire said, cutting him short, "and I'm glad it all worked out for you."

Patrick raised his brows and laughed out loud. "Yes, it did work out, didn't it? And here you have to spend New Year's with your ex-lover and your husband." Patrick shook his head, amusing himself, "Oh, what a tangled web we weave…you know, years ago, your blackmailing me really did me a favor, because our Jonathon's one of the sharpest men I've ever trained. And the business loves him. I got guys right now that would sell or trade their left nut if he said the word."

Yes, Claire did blackmail Patrick. In fact, it wasn't the first time Claire did what she had to do to get what she wanted. Was Satan really watching her? If he was, did that make her evil? Claire began to rewind all the 'evil' things she'd done over the last two decades. Patrick was merely a teensy notch on her belt.

"Do you know why they would?" Patrick went on.

"No, I don't? Why don't you fill me in?"

Patrick snickered. "Because Jonathon's word is gold. He's got great instincts, good intentions. At least something good came out of us."

Claire bit her tongue while studying Patrick through her glare. Patrick had never demonstrated such a protective interest in Jonathon before. Claire knew it was the drink that made Patrick emotional, but she also worried that he'd lose control and spill the beans about their affair, which had ended over a decade ago.

Patrick leaned into her and pulled her chin up toward him with his finger. "You better not break his heart."

"And what if he breaks mine?" Claire said, wishing for some

reassurance.

Patrick pulled his hand away and shook his head. "Sweetheart…that would be impossible, because you can't break what's not there." Looking up, Patrick spotted Jonathon and the others walking toward them. "Well, look who finally decided to join us."

Claire looked up and put on her plastic smile.

9

Boomerang

till reeling from Patrick's insults, Claire managed to appear relaxed as her family and Bernice made their way toward them. Rebecca and Vince's rosy faces and labored breathing hinted that they'd most likely walked a few blocks to avoid paying for valet parking. Claire made her usual inspection, starting with Vince. Thankfully, he was dressed suitably, but to her disgust, Vince was sporting Jonathon's Brioni tuxedo. Claire knew that Jonathon hadn't yet worn this newest addition to his wardrobe. Vince looked incredibly dapper. His thick, black hair was combed back, and his dark eyes sparkled. Like Jonathon, he was well built and just as tall. But the tuxedo jacket fit him a tad tight and strained at his biceps as he shook hands with a few men who'd joined their circle. At a glance, Vince could have passed for a gentleman, but on closer inspection, calloused hands gave him away. A tiny piece of tissue was stuck to his clean-shaven face.

"You forgot something," Claire pointed it out, enjoying the moment.

Vince smiled at his sister-in-law. He felt embarrassed and peeled off the morsel of tissue. "Shaving cut."

Claire sighed wearily to herself, watching as Rebecca allowed Patrick to kiss the back of her hand. It was the first time her ex-lover had met her sister, and Claire knew that Patrick delighted in the fact that Claire was uncomfortable.

Rebecca giggled. She looked thrilled as she read the program for the show. This was a rare treat. She'd never been to an opera. Claire looked her sister over from head to toe, and once again, felt embarrassed. Her sister wore shiny red shoes to match a reddish dress that hung sloppily off her shoulders, creating a droop above her breasts. And her hair was even worse. An attempted up-do looked more like a bird's nest with strands of gray hair sticking out. All this angered Claire; she'd have to take her to Emilio and have him fix the mess. Rebecca's carelessness might make Jonathon wonder why Claire herself hadn't yet begun going gray. Yes, she would convince her to go, but it wouldn't be easy. She'd have to be discreet about the cost. Rebecca was ultra conservative and would never allow Claire to pay three hundred dollars for a simple cut and dye job.

Rebecca adjusted her dress, lifting the fabric around her bosom. She gave Claire a smile. "You like my dress?" Claire's eyes were focused on the beautiful set of pearls that shone around Rebecca's neck. It had belonged to their mother, Connie, the special piece that she had worn on particular occasions, and on Sundays when she had gone to church. The strand had been handed down from her maternal Great-Grandma Hayes who, having been brought up in England, had been taught that social interactions were governed by strict rules of etiquette. Connie had often shared these traditions with her daughters, but Rebecca was far too young to remember. Claire, on the other hand, had a photographic memory.

Claire nodded. "It suits you."

Vince interrupted, as he usually did. "She's got the 'Pretty Woman' look, don't you think?"

"Yeah," Rebecca added, "except I couldn't find the white gloves."

"Why didn't you just knit or sew them?" Claire asked under her breath.

Jonathon glanced disapprovingly at Claire and made his "please don't start" face. He turned to Rebecca, "You look truly beautiful tonight, Rebecca."

"Yes, she certainly does," Patrick announced, over the noise.

"Let's toast to the foxiest redhead in the room." He looked over to Claire and swallowed another mouthful of champagne.

Rebecca blushed happily and buried her face in her husband's shoulder.

Claire turned away, unable to comprehend how both Jonathon and Patrick were able to sound so convincing.

"Look," Patrick said, pulling Vince toward him, "I want you to build my wife the biggest greenhouse ever. I don't give a hoot what it costs…just build whatever she wants."

Claire observed as Bernice gave her husband a tolerant smile. "I have already talked to them about it."

Patrick gave Vince a hearty slap on the back. "I've got something else for you."

Patrick was just getting started, Claire knew. He had this gallantry about him, this need to help out certain people. Claire used to refer to it as *P-lights*—Patrick lifting people's plights. Tonight, Claire concluded, Patrick's light shone down on Vince. Claire wondered just how much Jonathon had told Patrick, regarding Vince and Rebecca's quandary.

Patrick pulled over a business acquaintance of his who was deeply engrossed in a conversation with a group of men gathered a few feet away. "You see this guy?" Patrick pulled the tall man into their group. "This is Walter, the founder of Ross and Butler, one of the biggest oil companies in the world."

"This takes the bloody biscuit," Claire muttered to herself.

Walter shook Vince's hand, nodded politely at the ladies, and smiled at Claire, cocking a dark, well-groomed brow. "Nice to see you again." He had a perceptive wink in his russet brown eyes. Walter was privy to the fact, that Claire was once Patrick's love interest, and Patrick, years before, had insisted that Walter retain Claire as his realtor when he'd purchased his home in Hudson Valley. Satisfied with Claire's competence and sharp mind, he later used Claire's services on a few other deals, and he'd always remained professional. He had made the Forbes list more than once, and anyone who was anyone knew who Walter Ross was.

"Nice to see you as well," Claire said, wondering when Vince was going to start jumbling his words around.

Patrick jabbered on. "Now Walter here has a job for you,

needs some work done on his property in Nassau County before he sells it."

Vince's eyes lit up. Claire watched as Rebecca gave her husband a slight nudge. To Claire, it read, *See, things are looking up.* "Yeah…I'll give you my number," Vince said.

Just send in the clowns, Claire thought. She could only imagine the conversation between the two: a money mogul talking to a paper bag.

"No need," Walter explained, pulling out a business card from the inside of his tuxedo jacket. "I'll give you mine." This was something Walter infrequently did. He looked over to Jonathon, then back to Vince. "I trust any brother-in-law of Jonathon Lockwood's." And judging by the look on Walter's face, Claire knew he meant it.

Vince gave Rebecca the card. She opened her knock-off Gucci clutch and placed it in the inside compartment.

Vince pulled his wife even closer. "Let's have some wine."

Of course, Claire thought. *It is free, after all.*

A "New York moment" can mean many things to many people. For those who were stylishly dressed and fortunate enough to welcome the New Year at the Metropolitan Opera, this was a classic New York moment.

The lights, adorned with gilded accents, dimmed as the hum from the enthralled crowd waned to an expectant hush. The exploding suns began to rise, swallowed by liquid gold, allowing the majestic red room to fade to darkness.

In box twenty-nine, Claire and Jonathon sat in the third row, Vince and Rebecca in the first, and Patrick and Bernice in the middle. The conductor took the podium, extracting a first anticipated note from the orchestra as Claire settled into her seat. As the ornate curtain began to rise, she began to reflect on the night that had barely started. The opera had begun, urging the attention of its audience, but it would take a lot more than the second act of *Die Fledermaus* to get Claire's.

From behind, she had a perfect view of the people who had taken center stage in her life. Beside her, she saw the neon light coming from Jonathon's cell phone. Seven thirty, without looking at her watch, she was certain of it. Jonathon had been getting phone calls every night at the same time. Seven thirty or nine o'clock—no matter where he was, with the exception of tonight, he'd leave the room and take the call. Sometimes he even went into the bathroom. And he whispered in the same tone he had once reserved for Claire alone. She'd tried, without success, to make out what he was saying. Whoever the woman was on the phone, she was able to bring out in him what Claire could not: she made Jonathon laugh. Apart from her wicked sarcasm, Claire had no sense of humor, and Jonathon's many attempts at humor left her annoyed.

She studied his face, pictured him in compromising positions with his mistress, and wondered if he used his mouth on her.

Is he careful? Does he use protection?

Claire almost panicked at a single notion: *what if he got her pregnant?* She recalled the time she'd discovered she was carrying her lover's child. He was married, but when she informed him of her plans to have an abortion, for some reason he had practically begged her to keep the baby. *Would Jonathon beg for another woman's child?* Claire's heart began to race, and her adrenalin caused her face to flush.

Jonathon turned to her and said, "You okay?"

She nodded and made sure to look straight ahead. Claire was always the other woman, never the wife. She'd have to move with utmost caution. She knew exactly how to think like the other woman by continuing her observations and keeping mental notes of any suspicious activities. Claire was good at that. Her mind worked in multi-layers. So far she had two key pieces of evidence: one, a new tie; and two, Jonathon received calls every night at the same time.

She looked over at Vince and Rebecca whose eyes were on the stage. Claire had a perfect view of Rebecca, who gave her a backward glance and smiled, before returning her gaze to her husband. Rebecca was completely immersed in the play. Her eyes danced from the stage to Vince, as though to draw him into her happiness. Claire watched as Vince lovingly caressed her sister's bare shoulder and then kissed her cheek. Observing the couple, Claire filled with rage, wondering when Vince would destroy her sister and kill the only family—apart from Jonathon—she had left.

Her eyes moved to the center row and rested on Patrick and Bernice. It was obvious by the way his head kept nodding that he was incredibly drunk and most likely falling asleep. He placed his head on Bernice's shoulder. She was patient enough, lightly patting his cheek, as if to say she understood and that it was all right to go ahead and snooze.

Jonathon reached over and kissed Claire on the cheek. She remained focused, her thoughts solely on Patrick. Her mind wandered to the day she had made the biggest mistake of her life. It played before her, in her mind's eye. And if Roderick Benedix were alive today, he'd have written a comedy about what Claire did to get Patrick to hire Jonathon. He would have titled it *Boomerang*. Because here it was, the effects of what she'd done. The boomerang had returned and was seated in box twenty-nine with her. Claire couldn't help but wonder if Satan took a front-seat view of all her performances. If he had, he would have given her a standing ovation.

The curtain in Claire's mind rose, and she saw herself, six years earlier. She and Jonathon had been dating for several months when, out of the blue, he mentioned that he had a license in stock trading and felt that it was time to use it. He felt that Claire deserved a real man, with real capital, and he refused to live off the woman he loved. In any case, this caught Claire's attention. She knew he worked as a delivery man but had no clue that her young lover readily understood numbers and was strongly analytical. Jonathon had a natural burning desire to succeed. His tenacity and fervor reminded her of one man in particular: Patrick Kerrigan, a self-made billionaire who had founded and owned one of the largest stock brokerage firms in Manhattan. His confidential clients ranged from A-list actors to the some of the world's most elite entrepreneurs. If anyone could mentor Jonathon, it was Patrick.

Years earlier, Claire and Patrick had been lovers. He was married, of course, but at one point, he became controlling and somewhat possessive. The relationship wasn't fun anymore, which was when Claire put the brakes on. This shattered Patrick's heart and wounded his ego.

One night, Claire had scheduled an appointment with Patrick, who was surprised and delighted to cancel his evening plans. Immediately, he began fantasizing about what might take place in his comfortable office, where many times before Claire had taken him to the highest levels of ecstasy, and then brought him to his knees.

He opened a bottle of his finest cognac. "Drink?" He was merely being polite; he knew Claire never drank. Patrick gathered it was her way of keeping herself and her surroundings under control.

Liquor had killed Claire's mother, and drinking the enemy would have been like conceding to a truce. She was steadfast in her abhorrence of alcohol; it fueled her anger.

He drank slowly, allowing the cognac to wet his lips. "Are you sure you won't share just one glass with me?"

"You know I don't drink," Claire responded, as she smoothed her skirt. This was an uncomfortable, albeit expected, situation. She'd seen that look in his eyes many times.

Loosening his tie, he returned to his desk, where she sat in front of him. "You look great," Patrick stated. He appraised her over the rim of his glass as he sipped from it. That familiar hungry glint in his eye conveyed everything to her.

For a moment, she was tempted. Patrick always gave off an appealing scent of masculinity. She shifted in her seat. "I am not here for that," she snapped.

Patrick's face changed, and he tried to replace his sexual thirst with his business face. He cleared his throat. "Well then, what brings you here and at this hour?"

Claire understood Patrick's temperament. He was not one to play with, so she got straight to the point. "I'm here for a favor, a professional one."

This piqued his curiosity. In all the time he'd known her, Claire had never expressed an interest in stock trading. She never gambled with her finances, no matter the guarantee. "What kind of favor?"

Claire explained, measuring each word with caution. "I need you to hire someone, show him the ropes."

Pushing his drink aside, he processed her request in bitter silence, his brown eyes drilled into hers. "You want me to show some guy the ropes?" .

Claire nodded, a slight smirk played on her lips.

His eyes narrowed on her expression. "Does he come recommended at least?"

Claire knew she was reaching, but she was up for the challenge. "No, he has no experience, but he's licensed."

Patrick waited for her to continue. He hoped she was joking. Still, he knew she never joked. Claire was serious.

Understanding Patrick's nature, it was obvious, judging by his constricted pupils and the flush in his cheeks, that she'd enraged him. In order to quell his anger, she decided that a gentler approach was necessary and spoke convincingly sweet. "He kind of reminds me of you actually. Very clever and very determined. But he'll need training; I was hoping you could teach him. You are the best."

"I don't train fucking cherries," he finally said and walked toward the windowed wall. The view was stunning: the horizon, fronted by some of the tallest buildings in Manhattan. Claire remembered what it was like to deal with the man who had everything and hated to lose. He was notorious for getting what he wanted, but then again, so was she.

Walking behind him and resting her chin on his shoulder, Claire said in her soft voice, "I wouldn't ask you if it wasn't important to me."

Patrick turned around to face her. He looked hurt. "You've fallen in love."

Claire laughed at his accusation. "You should know me better than that. I don't fall in love, I stand in it."

He almost believed her, but having known her for just under a decade, and having loved her for years, he'd never seen the side she was showing him now. Claire was ruthless and although it was what had attracted him to her in the first place, her callousness was what had ultimately ended them. He studied her, noting the flicker behind her gorgeous eyes. They looked dangerously alive.

"He must be an amazing man," Patrick stated. "Tell me more about him."

This bothered Claire. Patrick was wasting her time with inconsequential details. She hated to see him so insecure. "He's young, easy on the eyes. And yes, I do…have a soft spot for him."

"Why in hell should I do a favor for him?"

Claire paced around and observed him like she would a piece of art in a museum. "Because…I'll return the favor," she said. She stopped and stood before him, tilting her head playfully to one side. A lock of hair fell against her cheek. It took his breath away, remembering the mischievous way she used to look at him after hours of lovemaking.

Being so close to her made Patrick realize how much he'd missed her. Her splendor was intoxicating and played with his mind. He wanted nothing more than to rip her clothes off and ravish her.

Claire felt the shift. "Not that, you dirty old man. I mean my silence." She gazed into his eyes, preparing for a duel. "I'll never let Bernice know how much I loved her boudoir or how much I loved her husband's face between my thighs."

He laughed out loud and his face turned bright red. "You really are a vicious bitch!"

"Yes, a vicious bitch who helped you to buy that condo on Broadway. Then again, there was that lovely little place in Bridgehampton. You remember the vacation house you bought for your wife, the house that she just had to have? If I recall, I had to jump through a lot of hairy hoops for you and your wife to get that property."

Claire edged closer toward Patrick, leaning suggestively into him. His eyes softened again. He wondered if it was Claire or the drink, but his judgment was quickly drifting off kilter.

Just like the dog you are, Claire thought as she gently massaged the back of his neck. All he had to do now was rollover for her and submit. She stood face to face with him, her lips just inches away from his own.

"It's just one little hoop, Patrick," she whispered. "I've done it for you…and for her, too."

Patrick pulled away from her, and gave his head a slight shake. Some of his best men couldn't have sparred with her. He eased back into his chair and finished the rest of his drink. Following a moment of silence, he said, "What is this, tit for tat?"

"Quid pro quo," Claire replied. She picked up his linen business card from the desk. "Listen, six months, okay? If it doesn't work, then it doesn't work."

"And if it does?"

Claire glanced over at his premium imported bottle of cognac. "If it works out, you'll send me a bottle of your finest. That's what you do when a deal works out, right?"

"You don't drink."

"No, but Jonathon sure does. And unlike Bernice, who loves her martini with a splash of vanilla and a drizzle of chocolate, he loves a good, stiff drink." *I just like him stiff*, Claire almost blurted out loud.

Claire had Patrick exactly where she wanted; she was aware of his life's most minuscule details. She could easily ruin him, and if need be, she wouldn't hesitate.

"So what do I get out of all this?"

She pointed to a picture of Bernice and their daughters. "You get to spend your golden years with your lovely wife."

Patrick remained silent, staring down at his glass. By this, Claire knew she'd won.

Claire remembered the look on Jonathon's face when she'd produced Patrick's card; his eyes had shone in disbelief as she passed him the card during a private dinner. His response was exactly what she had anticipated: Jonathon worshiped her even more.

"The Patrick Kerrigan? You can't be serious." He was elated.

It was irrelevant whether or not Jonathon would succeed in his mission. Claire had succeeded in hers. If he were to question her supremacy, or what she was capable of, she had just demonstrated to him that she was not to be underestimated.

She hadn't anticipated the following months after Patrick's approval of Jonathon's six-month trial period. A seven and a half thousand-dollar bottle of Martell Creation cognac arrived at Claire's door with a note that simply read: THANKS.

Last year, because of Jonathon's loyalty to Patrick and his commitment to the firm, Patrick had taken Jonathon on as a partner. That's when the changes began to happen. Looking to her left, Claire saw a very different man. He was made, and she had created him. There was no way another woman would reap the rewards of her labor. If she couldn't get pregnant and keep her marriage, she'd destroy him, and like Patrick had said, spit out his bones.

10

Human Depravity

Explosive lights, from outside, flickered through the window, throwing colorful shadows against Esperança's walls. Fireworks cracked in the bustling streets, while a culmination of pleasure and blithe overflowed through the gutters and walkways of Castle Hill. Tomorrow there would be vomit and urine flowing along the roadside streams, promises of change and resolutions swept away with the melting snow and human depravity. The world over would speak of peace, a coming of nations, a time for change.

Change....but everything stays the same, Esperança thought, with her spine pressed up against the wall, the cold, hard floor cutting into her tailbone.

She picked up her courage, still wrapped in a paper bag. She put the bottle to her mouth and took a long drink. The rum burned as it went down her throat and traveled into the deep recesses of her empty stomach. Just like the polluted sewers outside. The empty promises carried away by poison.

She placed the bottle down and set it to the side, while she reached for her box of matches. She pulled one out, dragged the red tip along the rough strip, and a flame was born. "Forty-five," she said, pinching the stick between two fingers. She kept a close watch on the moving flame as it tore through the wood. She turned the charcoaled end around, studying it as it burned through and through. Retrieving the bottle, she placed the hot cinder onto her tongue, received the hissing sound, and washed it down with a swig of rum.

She gazed out the window again and looked for the moon. It was almost time; the moon would soon surface, find its way, moving a full hand-width to the east. She would bring the New Year in with an old friend. *You made a promise*, the moon would say to her. *You promised me to her, and then she was gone.*

Esperança picked up the matchbox again and pulled out another stick. She struck the tip against the side as she whispered, "Forty-six."

The strong flame weakened between her fingers, burning through the wood. She turned the stick around, completing the ritual until it was all black. She placed the cinder into her mouth and let out a small whimper. She could taste blood from the tender blister formed on her tongue and washed number *forty-six* down with a final swig of rum.

Esperança placed the bottle down, setting it a few feet away. She drew her knees up and tucked them inside of her nightgown to keep warm. With her right ear pressed against her knees, she kept her gaze steady on the moon outside. It was always on time. But movement outside blocked Esperança's view: a white raven, its eyes boring right through her, was at the window.

"Move." Esperança straightened up, pulled her legs out of her gown, and waited. But the raven relaxed, its plumage fluffed, while it began preening itself. It wasn't going anywhere.

Esperança rose with a wobble, her legs asleep. She leaned against the wall waiting for the sensation to pass. *Bird must be cold, even hungry*, she thought. When she opened the window, cold air rushed into the small room, passing through the thin, over-washed fabric of her gown. She held out her wrist, allowing the raven to hop onto it, and pulled it closer to her. She scratched the bird around its neck, lightly tickling it with her nails.

"You must hungry," she said, running her free hand along the bird's back. Its eyes were closed, seemingly enjoying her touch. "So hungry and cold," Esperança said, moving toward her table. There were a few scraps of pizza crust leftover in a paper plate. She held up the crust and cupped it in the palm of her hand, while the bird pecked at the bread before losing interest. "Ah," she said, pinching a morsel of ground beef between her fingers, "you like meat." The bird swallowed the scrap and looked up, wanting more.

"It's never enough is it?" she said, wrapping her free hand around the bird's neck. She walked back over to the open window and began to squeeze, holding the flapping bird steady in her grip. The bird thrashed in her grasp, its wings flapping. She held on to the creature; falling feathers moved in the icy coils that entered through the window. She kept her gaze on the moon as the intense squawking dropped to garbled protest, then silence, the raven's body lifeless in Esperança's calm hands.

She dropped the bird into the urine and vomit covered streets below. "Some promises are easier than others."

She closed the window and moved back to her sitting position by the wall. But as expected, another white raven flew in and perched itself outside, obstructing Esperança's view yet again.

"Depravity." She reached for her courage and swallowed a mouthful.

Beautiful Strings

The last time Rebecca had spent time inside a tent, Claire thought, was when Rebecca and her family had been camping. But this was Damrosch Park. Claire noted the way Rebecca and Vince were continuously turning their heads in awe, whispering to each other, and discreetly pointing. It was obvious they were lost in their own piece of heaven. Claire had been watching them for a while.

Jonathon had left them in order to assist Bernice and their driver. Patrick was done for the night and was in no shape to have dinner with them. Following the play, he had completely fallen asleep in his seat, and it took some heavy maneuvering to get him out of it. Claire was glad, and, as the clock approached midnight, she couldn't help but feel that something in the air was changing; something huge was coming her way. Claire turned to the empty seat beside her. Was Satan keeping Jonathon's chair warm for him? Was Satan, disguised as a human, watching her from across the room? Claire tuned her head slowly in search of anyone suspicious.

Nevertheless, the room was a portrait of elegant romance. The entire area was draped with white lilies. Balloons that looked like ivory pearls were suspended from the ceiling, and cream and golden silk backdrops blended into the floor, the slight seam linking them as delicate as a line inside a shell. The space was dreamy. Every chair and table was carefully wrapped in a soft cream silk, while the shine of polished silver and Swarovski crystal chandeliers reflected beautifully against the cream palette.

"It looks like we're inside an oyster," Rebecca said, as if she was reading Claire's mind. Dinner music began to fill the room, while the sounds of toasting glasses hit their own signature notes. A waiter came to their table and filled their glasses with champagne. Watching Rebecca's face lit with happiness as she held up her glass brought out the softer woman in Claire. She almost pitied her sister, wishing that, like herself, Rebecca could control the urge to surrender to joy. Happiness was a smoke and mirrors trick that could destroy you if you believed what you saw. Seeing that side of her baby sister, Claire thought of their mother. They both had that same flaw: they lacked control of their emotions.

Jonathon slid into the seat beside Claire and startled her. "What did I miss?"

"What did *we* miss?" Claire was dying to know if Patrick had vomited on the maroon carpet or, better yet, on himself.

"Nothing." Jonathon held up his glass while the waiter poured him a drink. "We got him into the car, and the driver's going to make sure that he gets to bed."

"Good," Vince said. "Then all's well." He held up his glass, suggesting a toast. Claire raised her glass of Perrier and clinked it with the other three. Looking at Vince wearing Jonathon's tuxedo, Claire almost forgot how much he annoyed her. He seemed relaxed and even confident as he pulled his wife closer. For a New York minute, Claire found her brother-in-law to be appealing. Vince sincerely looked like a man in love.

Jonathon pulled Claire closer to him, and planted an un-rushed kiss onto her cheek. "And you…you're a dime and a half tonight." They stared into each other's eyes. "I love you."

Realizing she was looking into the eyes of the man who had lied about his tie that morning made it difficult for Claire to believe him. *Treat him mean and keep him keen,* said the angry voice inside. Claire simply nodded.

The evening dinner started with a watercress and endive salad and ended with white truffle pearls served on oyster shells, coupled with champagne sorbet. Sipping real coffee, surrounded by her family, Claire found herself falling for the moment. Several times during dinner, Claire had studied Rebecca, discreetly, while she ate. It induced a memory of a time when Rebecca was a gangly teenager and came to visit Claire in New Jersey. Rebecca was uncultured and had no life experience apart from country living in their hometown of Sartell, Minnesota. Raised by their father, and having no mother to teach her how to be a lady, Rebecca was very much a tomboy. Claire, by then in her mid twenties, had had years of practiced refinement. Rebecca adored her big sister and loved the week they had spent together. Claire had taken her baby sister shopping in the Big Apple and treated her at a five-star restaurant she frequented, located along the Manhattan strip. Because Rebecca had no idea what dining etiquette was, Claire spent a lovely autumn afternoon teaching Rebecca where to place her napkin and what forks to use first. And now, this evening, seeing Rebecca across the table brought a tingle to Claire's nose. Claire had taught her sister well, and she observed her with a rare pride as Rebecca used her knife to cut delicately into her prime rib—a small habit of their mother.

Left on their own, Claire and Rebecca had the chance to do some catching up. "This was really something," Rebecca said, looking around. "It almost makes me dread going to The Flame and Grill now."

Claire smiled with sincerity, "I'm glad you enjoyed yourself." Claire watched her sister with vast interest as she surveyed the room with her pretty green eyes. Apart from the gray hairs and lack of style, Rebecca was an attractive woman. They both shared the same wide-set green eyes and snub nose, sprinkled in freckles. But where Claire had a heart-shaped face, high cheekbones and straight teeth, Rebecca had their father's flat oval one, along with a slight overbite and plush lower lip. But there was something enticing about it, Claire always thought. Imperfections were sometimes a good thing, because people naturally stopped searching for what wasn't perfect. Claire's mind wandered over to Jonathon, that scar below his brow and that perma-smirk of his. She searched the room for her husband and spotted him a few chairs over. He must have been thinking about her too. Their gazes collided and he gave her that smile, followed with a puckered kiss. Jonathon was New Year's drunk, his face sheathed in a glow and his hair was starting to curl under. Claire shook her head with a laugh, but her laugh dissolved at the thought of another woman, loving those same flaws.

"Gosh, if Dad could see us now," Rebecca said, stirring her coffee. "He would have loved this." She caught herself, remembering that Claire was sensitive about their father. Sadly for Rebecca, she had very little memory of their mother, and because Rebecca was raised by their father, she was extremely close to him. "I'm sorry."

"Forget it." There it was, the good old anger waking from its nap. Changing the subject abruptly, she asked, "So what did you get for sticking it out for ten years?" Claire's question was calculated, she knew Vince couldn't afford anything much more extravagant than a box of chocolates. To her displeasure, Rebecca's answer was not what she expected.

"He built me my dream home."

Face twisted in confusion, Claire looked at Rebecca for an explanation.

Rebecca laughed it off and pulled out a folded piece of paper. "I don't mean an actual house. He wrote me a promise."

Claire took the paper and scanned it. In addition to expressing his undying love for her, Vince made a vow to build her the dream home she so deserved. "What is this dream home?"

Her sister giggled and pulled out a tiny, hand-carved, wooden replica. "Tara.' You know, from Gone with the Wind." She balanced it in the palm of her hand.

Laughing at what she thought was a great joke, Claire said, "That? Wow, did you get the deed to it?" Rebecca's smile disappeared. She carefully wrapped the house up in a tissue again and placed it into her purse. Her lower lip quivered as if she might cry.

Rebecca's sensitivity always drained Claire's patience. No wonder she'd never made her mark anywhere. "Oh come on, Rebecca. I'm kidding. It's sweet, really."

Studying Claire's face closely, Rebecca wanted to believe her. She practically pouted, "It is sweet, and Vince is an amazing husband and father. Not everything is about money all the time, you know. He's never let me down yet. Anyway, I'd live in a tent with my family if I had to."

Just like Mom, Claire mused, *such a loyal fool*. Meanwhile, Claire looked around at nothing in particular.

The silence between them lasted half a minute. Rebecca disliked conflict. In her usual cheerful tone she asked, "How's the baby making coming along, and Doctor Monroe?"

"Don't ask," Claire snapped. Again, her mind wandered back to Satan and the whole voodoo business. Interestingly, right there at that moment, Claire decided she would go and pay a visit to that voodoo woman, whose card she couldn't bring herself to throw away.

Rebecca joined hands with her sister. "You have me if you need me, just say the word."

"Aww, loving sisters," Vince teased, as he returned to his seat.

Claire pried her hands away from Rebecca while Jonathon took his seat beside her. A small crowd formed around their table, and a waiter balanced a tray, placing it before Rebecca. On the silver tray, set in the middle, was a small, round cake, encased in ivory fondant. Along the top, framing the outside of it, were tiny golden roses, delicate and paper thin, surrounded by beautiful silver leaves.

"What's all this?" Rebecca asked, looking around. The waiter handed her and Vince two small gold forks.

"A little something we arranged for you. That's twenty-three carat edible gold on there," Jonathon said, enjoying the moment.

Rebecca tapped the fork to the roses. "I can actually eat these?"

"Of course, you can," Claire said. "It's in its pure state. It's harmless."

"You had something to do with this?" Rebecca was on the verge of tears.

Claire shook her head. "Jonathon's idea."

"I don't know what to say…" Rebecca began.

"It's okay," Vince said, rubbing her shoulders.

"Patrick and Bernice send their apologies for having to bail tonight. They also sent this message for you." Jonathon opened his phone and read out loud. "May your years turn silver, but your love for each other remain gold for all eternity." Then Jonathon added, "I'm sure those words came from Bernice. Patrick's counting sheep right now. And if it was Patrick, he'd say something like, 'Too late, don't stop now.'"

"Or," a senior colleague of Jonathon and Patrick's piped up, "the higher the investment, the higher the reward."

The small crowd laughed and clapped for Vince and Rebecca, while they shared a kiss. Tears spilled over Rebecca's cheeks.

"Dang, you're not supposed to cry, you're supposed to eat," Jonathon said with a soft laugh and passed Rebecca a napkin.

Rebecca nodded, unable to speak. Vince plated a small piece for Rebecca and offered a sample to the others at the table before cutting a piece for himself.

"You take that home for the kids." Jonathon settled back into his seat and took Claire's hand in his. "What about us, will we have all eternity?"

Claire snatched her hand back. "That's up to you." The angry woman was back and screaming inside Claire's head. Watching her sister's happiness only reminded her of what was inevitable. Rebecca would be crushed one day, and because she was weak and not armed, the heartache would kill her.

Jonathon pulled out a brown envelope. "And that's not all." He pushed it toward Vince and then shot Claire a fleeting smile without making eye contact.

"What's this?" asked Vince.

"Inside is an all-expense-paid weekend at the Whispering Winds." Jonathon knew the private bed and breakfast on the outskirts of New Jersey would be perfect for them. A weekend getaway was exactly what they needed.

Rebecca looked touched while reading the pamphlet. "Balloon rides? Wine tasting? Oh my God, guys, thank you!"

Vince was speechless; his friendship with Jonathon had developed into a brotherhood.

"And you don't have to worry about the kids," Jonathon added. "We'll be more than glad to have them."

Rebecca threw her arms around her sister in appreciation. "Thanks so much."

"No problemo," Claire imitated this warm response while sending Jonathon an angry look. She had no clue about this gift and hated being taken by surprise. She stood up and excused herself. "I need to go to the ladies' room."

Rebecca stood up, still gushing over the loving gesture. "I need to go, too. Thanks again, brother-in-law. We'll never forget this night!"

Jonathon smiled as he watched her almost skip away to catch up with Claire's march. *She's so easy to please.*

"You made her very happy tonight." Vince spoke as he swirled the glass of wine in his hand.

Jonathon's eyes softened and he answered with deep conviction, "She deserves it. She's a great girl."

"Yeah." Vince stared pensively around, taking in the glamorous scene. "Just bothers me I can't give her more." The saxophone player had begun to play, so Jonathon leaned in to better hear Vince. Strangely, the musical melody matched the somber mood that showed on Vince's face. He was an emotional man.

"Vince buddy, listen, I have a few leads coming up, and I promise we'll get you set up," Jonathon assured him.

Vince sighed, "I hope so. I'm worried. Maybe it's just the liquor talking."

The car ride home was tense. Jonathon was prepared for it. He knew what he was in for. Claire kept her hands on the wheel and her eyes focused on the road ahead, while biting on her lower lip.

Jonathon blurted, "I know you're mad."

"Your point?"

"I didn't say anything because I knew you would've been opposed to it."

Claire tightened her grip on the steering wheel. "And if you knew that, then why the hell did you do it?"

Jonathon fiddled with the dashboard, trying to turn up the heat. "It's cold tonight." At the same time, he was busy thinking of a good answer, one that would calm her.

"Well?" She was losing her patience, and Jonathon, still feeling the effects of alcohol, was unable to hold back.

"Because I happen to love them. They're the only family I have apart from you." Then, more subdued, he said, "I wanted to give them that."

Claire kept quiet. She wondered if Jonathon's new lover was a kind, gentle woman. With an unfamiliar urge to convince him that she also had the ability to show kindness, she replied, "I'm fine with it. I just wish you had…prepared me."

"I know what you're thinking, but don't worry, I'll watch the kids." Jonathon knew she hadn't recovered from the last time they had her sister's children stay over for a few nights. The boys played football in the parlor and put some noticeable dents in the mahogany table, an antique dating back to the Civil War.

"It's your party." Claire's mind wafted over to the voodoo woman.

Half relieved, Jonathon exhaled. He'd expected her to react explosively and insist that he renege on his offer to take care of Rebecca's kids. Something was off; he could sense it.

For the remainder of the ride home, Jonathon was forlorn. He had a beautiful woman sitting next to him, and yet he found himself still searching, yearning. The snow fell heavily, causing the sloping road ahead to look like a ski run going much too far down. He pushed 'play' on the CD button and reclined the seat.

Claire rolled her eyes. "Not this crap again."

Jonathon ignored her. Nothing would distract him from his moment, his song. Piano keys played in beautiful rhythm with the windshield wipers. Jonathon drifted into his thoughts. The bass sounded, filling gaps in the dark road ahead. And the violin was his favorite part. The strings lifted his spirits; he loved where they were taking him. He couldn't stop thinking about her, and in his head, he slowly said her name.

Nicolette.

12

The Voodoo Priestess

The phone call with Esperança was, surprisingly, not so creepy. The woman's slight Brazilian accent did not hinder her instructions in any way. She'd ordered Claire to bring with her a picture of Jonathon. This made sense. Then the woman instructed her not to apply any kind of deodorant or perfume. Though this sounded bizarre, Claire went ahead with it.

She decided to dress down and keep her jewelry at home. Her seven-karat Harry Winston would have made for a great pawn. After checking herself in the mirror, she decided her appearance was appropriate for a woman about to venture into the Bronx. New York's boroughs had many great histories, but Castle Hill 'in the Bronx' was not somewhere Claire could usually be found. Glancing again at her blue jeans and powder blue sweater, she threw her reflection a scornful look. Going to this silly voodoo woman to fix her infertility problems. Did she honestly think that some sinister woman was going to perform a miracle? Still, it was something she needed to resolve, and she couldn't think of any acceptable alternative at this point.

Claire grabbed the keys to her Hummer. It was the one vehicle she owned that would surely prove intimidating should she find herself in a dangerous situation—which was a solid possibility considering her destination.

Getting to the Bronx wasn't a problem. January's usual cold temperatures prevailed, but only two inches of leftover snow lay on the ground. Once she arrived in Castle Hill, she slowed down and swallowed hard to take it all in. A Latin food market occupied the main floor of the building, and Esperança's apartment was located above it. Of course Claire knew this beforehand, but actually being there was twice as bad as she'd guessed it might be. The dirty and dilapidated old neighborhood was an assault on her senses.

Pulling up alongside the entrance to the store, Claire watched customers carefully wading in and out, while local riff-raft loitered outside an adjoining door leading to the upstairs. Claire couldn't imagine how Janice had found the nerve to come here. She hadn't appeared especially street-smart. What could possibly have possessed her? But the answer was all too obvious. Like Claire, Janice had been desperate.

For a long time Claire remained in the Hummer, heater cranked against the cold, as she gazed at the entrance of Esperança's apartment, weighing the pros and cons. It looked no more foreboding than any of the other entrances.

She opened her visor mirror and stared intently at her reflection. Her perfect nose spotted with tiny freckles required no powder. The emerald green circling her pupils looked almost indigo as the sun's rays glanced off it. Glimpsing her perfect white teeth and smooth, glossed lips, Claire smiled to herself.

Beautiful as ever. She snapped the visor closed. Still, she remained uncomfortable, out of her element. Checking her beautiful face hadn't returned to her the confidence she'd hoped for, and she lacked the courage to leave the protection of her Hummer.

A strong combination of sewage and sulfur escaped through the manholes, followed by a pungent steam which crept through the closed truck and settled around her. *What the fuck am I doing here?* She nervously looked through her black leather purse for her hand lotion. Shadows behind the tinted windows caused her to look up.

Then Claire saw her. A beautiful, stylish woman exited the building. Her blond hair hung in deep silky curls to the middle of her back. And she had expensive tastes. The Prada bag that her gloves clenched coordinated perfectly with her cream-colored cashmere coat, the same coat Claire had recently had her eye on in Saks Fifth Avenue. She'd have no qualms shelling out a few thousand dollars for it, if only it came in black.

The woman didn't fit in. She was a white water-lily floating down a filthy sewer. "What the hell is she doing here?" Claire muttered to herself, as she watched the woman walk boldly over to a young Latino man. His dark green bomber jacket was unfastened, partially revealing a white wife-beater underneath and a mesh of black tattoos covering his neck. Tiny fog clouds in front of their faces revealed an exchange of a few words between them. She passed him a few bills, and they both smiled. Surely the woman wouldn't be buying drugs in a place like this. She could easily get her fix in a more affluent, respectable part of the city. It made no sense.

In her rear-view mirror, Claire watched the woman walk to a black Porsche where another strong young Latino stood, his back leaning against the driver's door. He flashed a smile, gleaming gold with dental work, and moved out of her way. Just before the woman shut the door of the Porsche, her face was perfectly captured in Claire's mirror.

"Cynthia Jennicks." There wasn't a better-known criminal lawyer. One of her famous clients was Juan Ramirez, a Columbian mobster and drug lord recently in the news. He'd been on trial lately in connection with the murder of a state witness. But thanks largely to Cynthia, he'd walked away a free man, found "innocent." The media called her "The Sleeper," a nickname she'd earned through her effect on jurors. She practically hypnotized them with her words, her flair.

Claire envied her.

Fuck it! If Cynthia Jennicks can handle herself in this neighborhood then so can I. Hell, she had sparred with some of the meanest sharks in the real estate world. Surely she could deal with a few poor punks in the Bronx.

Claire turned the engine off and unclasped the seatbelt. Drawing in a courageous breath, she opened the door of the Hummer, and then locked it. She stepped out and in her long black boots, walked meticulously around the garbage, strewn all over the trampled, brown snow. As a pack of wolves, the young men converged on Claire. They said nothing at first, walking in sequence with her, like wasps protecting their territory. Their gold smiles taunted her and hands reached for her hair. Words spilled out from one of them. "*Copo de nieve.*"

Claire slapped at his extended arm, "Get your dirty hands away from me," she snapped, more annoyed than afraid.

The smaller of the group plucked out a lock of Claire's hair "What's your name, *Rojo*?"

She elbowed him hard and held up a defensive fist. "When I tell you to get away from me, do it!" She pushed her way through the men.

A rapper-looking wannabe rounded her. "My boy's takin' to you. Be nice and say hello."

Claire took out her cell phone. "Don't try me…I will call the police."

"Easy, Red," said the smallest of them with a wink, then offered Claire his cell phone. "Take mine and dial the po-po with it." The laughter was contagious, hilarity spreading like a bad cold. A heavily blanketed, frail, old man sitting on a fold-up chair in the narrow doorway also got in on the fun.

"Chino!" a gruff voice boomed into the crowd. "Leave my money alone, and keep your wanksta friends off of her truck." The familiar tone came from a window above the market, but no face appeared.

"Esperança…" Claire whispered the name. Whoever or whatever she was, none of the men dared ignore her.

"No worries, Red," Chino cowered. "You heard the Jefa," he ordered his crew with a snap. "Step away from the lady's whip."

Claire prepared herself, then walked unflinchingly through the local crowd to the door. She entered and was met by a long, narrow, and crooked flight of stairs leading to a door that somehow spelled an ascent into doom. She heard music, a combination of rap and salsa. A siren wailed in the streets, and a baby cried on the other side of the wall behind the stairs. Claire's senses whirled as she caught the smell of fried onions, tomatoes, and the sharp odor of marijuana. Another scent insinuated itself, but what it was she couldn't tell. The uncertainty only added to her uneasiness.

Claire's eyes focused on the steep steps leading to the landing where Esperança stood. She was so tiny, probably less than five feet, with a small frame and short limbs.

"Come on, come on. Too slow," Esperança urged, with her wrinkled hands resting on her miniature hips. Not at all what Claire pictured a voodoo priestess to look like, wearing a yellow DON'T WORRY BE HAPPY T-shirt, loose fitting jeans rolled to her mid-calves, and white bobby socks.

Claire wondered if she should simply forget all about this stupid idea.

"Don't be such a coward," Esperança teased. The smiling happy face on her shirt was such a contrast to the miserable woman who greeted Claire with a scowl. Close up, the old woman appeared in her seventies at least. Her gray hair was pulled into an unkempt bun. Claire thought that the voodoo woman had a face that resembled a desiccated, golden delicious apple with two wormholes for eyes.

Claire caught a whiff of body odor laced with baby powder. She looked down at Esperança condescendingly, and muttered, "Coward, you say?" She walked swiftly past the old lady and into a dim, red-lit room. Strange, unidentifiable aromas welcomed her.

Esperança cleared her throat and slammed the door shut before she said something in a foreign tongue and spit against the door.

Disgusted, Claire turned and fell into a padded kitchen chair, where she drank in her creepy surroundings.

A picture of Juan Ramirez sat in plain view, along with a list of names. Esperança stood over Claire and asked, "You know him?"

"Not personally," Claire admitted, placing her purse on her lap. Eyes adjusting to the alien setting, she tried keeping her stern self intact.

The amber red glow of dancing flames cast shadows on the dark walls. Dozens of photos covered every inch of the floor at the back of the room. Hard, melted wax clung to the frames of photographs: brides and grooms, parents and their children. The brown table held odd knick-knacks and something else, too. Claire strained her eyes to see. It appeared to be a thick lock of dark, human hair, but she wasn't certain.

"You're in the boss's seat." Esperança pointed to a stripped wooden chair. "There," she directed her.

Claire stepped carefully around Esperança, as if she might catch some horrible disease from the woman if she didn't keep her distance and reluctantly settled into her appointed seat. Her eyes immediately stopped at the center of the woman's flattened hills of flesh where her breasts should have been. The woman was completely flat.

Esperança smirked and Claire drew her attention to the old woman's face again and took another long look at her. Voodoo priestess or not, she was an ancient, vile woman. At one point in her life she may have been beautiful, with her exotic features and high cheekbones. But what Claire was seeing now were a pair of angry eyes. Reflective black circles wrapped around twin bottomless pits: pits that had seen the depths of hell and had returned—only to drag others back with them.

A quiet moment passed between the two women. A lit candle placed on the table separated them, and the light shone onto their faces. A merciless energy exuded from both sides: each woman battling the other, neither blinking an eye.

"Broken wing," Esperança whispered almost to herself, breaking Claire's stare and deliberations.

Claire's brows pinched together, waiting for the woman to enlighten her.

"A bird without flight. So broken, so exposed. What a shame." Esperança shook her head, expressing genuine pity.

"You have something you want to say?" The voodoo woman had her full attention. Claire crossed her legs and leaned back.

"The little red bird fell from its nest and broke its wing." Esperança clicked her tongue in shameful tut-tut, while studying the beautiful redhead. On the outside, she was perfect. Her gaze was perfectly level and those green eyes were like two emeralds set in cold, expressionless stone. This woman, Claire, was unlike any other she had ever met—in this life, or any previous ones. She was beautifully broken, and a perfect warrior to add to Satan's battle.

Claire was internalizing. *Broken, broken wing, exposed?* What the hell did she mean by that? Broken meant weak. She was anything but that. Esperança was quiet, staring off into the dark wearing a distant expression.

"Hello, is anyone home?" Claire was losing her cool. "It's been a real slice lady, but would you mind telling me what the point of all this is."

"The point," she said, turning her attention back to Claire, "was that you broke your wing on the day that you buried your mother...but you had something to do with it, didn't you? And instead of dealing with it, you blame everyone else. What is it, this thing that's been eating away at you, this thing that broke your wing?"

Claire was silent.

"Someone once told me that you're only as sick as the secrets you keep. So how about it, got any secrets? Something to do with your mother?"

Claire repeated the woman's question in her mind, but then her anger caught up with her again. "Look, I didn't come here for this, and I won't tolerate you using my dead mother to fuck with my head!"

Nodding emphatically, Esperança said, "Fuck? Oh, ho, you swear..." She pointed an accusing finger at Claire.

Claire wasn't sure how to respond. The woman's tone was playful, yet there was a vicious glint in her eyes. Claire was almost afraid of what she would say next, especially where her mother was concerned. Did Janice do a background check on Claire? Were the voodoo priestess and Janice in cahoots together?

"You've been a bad girl," Esperança said, with a lazy smile. "Got a lotta fuckage on you."

"Fuckage?"

"What I'm getting at, is that you fucked over a lot of people. Fuckage...like baggage. The depravity that you drag around with you like a ball and chain."

But Claire sat silently, biting her lower lip.

"Oh, come on," Esperança urged, "don't be like that." She taunted Claire with a wicked satisfaction. "I'm playing. I can't help myself." A winning smile escaped the old woman.

She has great teeth, Claire thought. *The better to eat you with...*

Esperança let out a mad laugh. "You're a little undernourished, not enough meat. But looking into your soul is like getting three cherries on a slot machine." Staring into the burning flame of the candle, without so much as blinking an eye, Claire continued to bite her lip.

Under hooded eyes, Esperança leaned into the table until she locked into Claire's glare. "Ding, ding, ding…"

Claire's heart raced and her eyes dilated, yet she spoke in a cold, steady tone. "Don't fuck with me, old woman."

With enormous pleasure, Esperança clapped her hands together, producing one swift slap. "Feels good, doesn't it?" She watched the pupils of Claire's eyes shrink back to normal size, allowing the emerald color in them to return. As Esperança noted the flush in the woman's cheeks, she was reminded of a porcelain doll whose beautiful face she had once smashed into thousands of pieces.

Claire stood up, and prepared to leave. This was bullshit, and Janice would pay for dragging her into this shit-hole. She reached inside her purse, feeling around for her car keys, when Esperança began speaking. What she said made Claire freeze.

"You met your husband in a lounge, a block away from your office. He was paying for a drink, a few bills and loose change. He dropped a quarter, and you picked it up, put it into his hand." Esperança paused, with a smug expression, allowing Claire to gather her wits.

"From the first glimpse, you saw how young he was, twenty-four as it turned out. But the attraction was instant, there was no rhyme or reason…it just was. You hid him away for the first few months, humped like rabbits, and in between that, you taught him the rules. He learned manners: how to stand, shake a hand. You started taking him out to public functions. You loved the way he looked on you. Like one of your designer purses." Esperança glanced at the purse which Claire held in her hands.

Completely mesmerized, Claire eased back into the chair. But the voodoo priestess wasn't done just yet.

"He would need new clothes, so you took him to De Lica's… no," she said, closing her eyes, as if she saw the answer behind her eyelids. "Deluca's," she finally said, fluttering her eyelids open. "An expensive boutique in Manhattan that specialized in the finest menswear." Esperança smiled at what she saw in her mind's eye. "Oh, how uncomfortable your young buck was the first time you took him shopping for new clothes. So awkward. He'd never been fitted or measured, didn't even know his own neck size. How fascinated you were, watching Mario Deluca explain to your young lover…"

Esperança stopped speaking, then changed the pitch in her voice into a masculine one, and tweaked her accent, emulating Mario's Italian enunciation spot-on. "The importance of a masterfully crafted suit or dress shirt depends on the fabric. It too has to be luxurious and of the highest quality."

Claire let out a gasp, her lips parted in complete awe. Esperança gave her a playful wink, and dropped her impression.

"Your baby-faced boyfriend was completely grateful for the experience and the tutelage. And he made a promise to you, after you trashed all his jeans and sneakers, that once he had made it and was a financial success, he would reimburse you for every dime you spent on him. And, true to his word, he did." Esperança took a long pause, her eyes downcast.

"But I will say this…he has very nice eyes. Kind blue eyes."

Claire moistened her lips and straightened up. "And how did you know all that?"

Esperança's gaze lifted to meet Claire's penetrating eyes and heart-shaped face. "How, you ask. I know you did a lot for him: blackmailed your ex-lover, who gave him his job; made him shine like a new silver dollar. But now he wants kids, and you can't have them. And that makes you feel old," Esperança said. "And yet, here you sit…with that ball and chain. *Fuckage.*"

"You're pretty pleased with yourself."

Esperança's cocky expression didn't waver. "What can I say?" She all but shined her nails against her T-shirt.

"Impressive," Claire admitted. "And yet you failed to see how my husband's enormous dick motivated me."

The lewd remark drew another deep-throated laugh from Esperança. Once recovered, she wagged a teasing finger at Claire.

"Oh, I like you. But you are one crazy biatch. A brazen biatch, that's what you are."

Claire's lips curved into a half-smirk. She found Esperança

to be quite the comedian.

"You know, I'm sure you're already aware, that you have two people inside of you." Esperança held out her right hand. "One is a sad and lonely girl who just wants to be loved, wants to be saved." Esperança held out her left hand. "And one is an angry, sour bitch. An angry woman, who sends the girl away and builds a wall of expensive clothes, cars, homes, vacation properties, a boat she used twice in three years: things…nice things that mean nothing; a wall of vanity that buries the sad and lonely girl alive."

"I'm a sucker for poetry," Claire said. "Love metaphors. But I believe it's called dissociative identity disorder." She tried to remain completely composed and uninterested, although on the inside, she was full of turmoil and amazed at Esperança's insight. She always knew that she was dealing with a split personality. She had even gone so far as to research her symptoms, wondering if the constant back and forth meant she was truly mad.

"Who gives two rat's titties what the terminology is," Esperança said. "The question is what happened to you as a child? What was it that split you in half?"

Claire remained quiet.

"So, which one will win?" The priestess looked first left, then right. Dropping her hands into her lap, she said, "You can't go on like this forever, Claire. It's one or the other, the left or the right. The middle is maddening. You'll go crazy." She was taking in the redhead's beauty again. It far exceeded what she had foreseen over a month ago. Of course Satan liked her; he did have a passion for pretty things. "You need to choose or you'll end up with nothing at all, stuck between worlds."

Waiting for a response from Claire, the old woman began sucking at bits of leftover food stuck between her teeth.

"I need to choose God or Satan, is that what you're telling me?" Claire probed.

"Your actions have chosen for you."

"Well then…"Claire said settling into her chair, "why not use your powers, and thank Satan for me. Actually, I'll tell you what to say: 'Dear Satan, thanks for my affluence, my connections, and setting a kick-ass example.' Because I could care less what God thinks of me. So if Satan has something he wants to say," Claire said, feeling an array of emotions surfacing, "tell him I'm here, ready and waiting." She waited for a response. But the voodoo priestess was quiet, staring off at the wall.

Claire found herself thinking back to a time when life was simple, before her father's scandalous affairs. They were a family, picnics and baseball games following Sunday church services. Daddy was Claire and Rebecca's hero. The two girls used to stand on either side of their father, each taking a hand, as they climbed their way up the stairs and into the church.

Claire had forced that memory out, and she wasn't prepared for the culmination of emotions that continued to surface. She struck again. "Once upon a time my actions said otherwise. I used to believe in God, I had faith. So if you have something you want to say to me, I'm right here!" she said, directing her statement to Satan, but still Esperança had yet to respond. And in that still moment, a palpable presence entered the room, and it wasn't something the human eye could see.

Esperança's face awakened; she turned to Claire, the black in her eyes reflected like polished, black pearls catching the bright flame. "Do you know how long you've been holding Satan's hand?"

It wasn't the question that caused the hitch in Claire's breath but rather the confirmation. Satan was paying attention. She tried to hold on to her advantage by replying nonchalantly, "No, I don't. Why don't you tell me?"

Esperança's eyes relaxed and the heaviness subsided. "Since the day you found out your mother died. The moment you realized God didn't listen to your prayers."

Claire felt those familiar, invisible hands, slowly choking the life out of her.

"You lit the same candle every night for three days," Esperança sneered, "and God did nothing. Isn't that right, Claire? It was all God's fault, daddy's fault, and even the snow's fault. And instead of listening to your prayers, God made it snow, the biggest blizzard in years!" She screamed at the redhead, apparently happy at having dug up her most deeply buried secret. The secret she'd left frozen beneath thirty years of fallen snow. "Isn't that right, Claire, because a little blue bird told me everything!"

Claire was paralyzed by the emotions that gripped her, flustering her into shock. This was a subject she had never dared to discuss—her darkest pain that lay buried and unturned since the day she had laid a single, white rose on her mother's coffin.

In the dead of winter, after a bout of drinking, Connie had driven the family's Buick front-first into a deep ravine, where it had split in two. No one knew it had happened. For three days she had been officially declared missing, before a local woman reported something resembling a car hidden under a layer of fresh November snow.

Much later, Claire found the medical reports that would haunt her for years. Mom hadn't died on impact as Dad led Rebecca and her to believe. She'd survived for seventy-two hours, slowly bleeding to death. The image of her mother suffering alone, in so much pain, left a hole in Claire's heart. She was never the same after.

Her mother never realized how absolutely beautiful she was in the eyes of Claire and Rebecca. Before Grant's affairs, Connie's love for her husband was clear in everything she did, and friends and neighbors admired her zest for domestic life. She was the one other women went to for advice, or at least for a smile, a hug, and a friendly ear. After Grant's unfaithfulness, however, Connie became a cardboard cutout of her former self, like a ghost in search of its deserted body.

The couple agreed to stay together "for the sake of the children," but keeping up appearances didn't hide the scars for long.

It was impossible to imagine Connie, bereft of family and friends, in her final hours. And yet she died alone, except for the empty bottle of vodka and the groceries which had spilled from the bags. The same bottle that contributed to her death also kept her company as she took her last breath.

Claire was thirteen when she buried her mother. She remembered sobbing, placing a hand on her mother's closed casket, and telling her that she loved her.

Claire recoiled, replaced her pain with anger, and soon felt a hot prickle moving over her scalp. She had to fight to stop herself from slapping the old woman for toying with her. She got up and smacked her hands hard against the tabletop, causing the candle to tip over. Hot, red wax rolled toward Esperança and hardened at the edge of the table, but she didn't flinch.

"You fucking bitch!" Claire screamed pure hatred. "God didn't give a fuck about my mom or me! He left her to die; did you see that too? Did you? A billboard the size of this fucking building hung over the ravine where she was dying, and God couldn't see her? He didn't care to see her. He left her there bleeding to death!" Her voice cracked at the end of her tirade.

She caught her breath for a few seconds and waited for a reaction that did not come. Then she looked fiercely into Esperança's eyes. "So to hell with God and to hell with you, too." A long moment passed and paranoia set in. Claire's eyes darted around the room.

Esperança rose from her chair and applauded. "Bravo, very good. Now tell me, how does that feel?"

Calmer, Claire muttered with an unexpected relief, "Feels pretty good." She sank back into the chair, crossed her arms, and blew a wayward hair away from her face.

"You know, anger is a cover-up for hurt." Esperança sat back down.

"Where did you get that line from?"

"A client of mine." Esperança reached under her chair, placed a white candle into the holder and struck a match. "She's a psychiatrist. A good one," she elaborated further, lighting the wick.

Claire Smirked. "Why on earth would a psychiatrist come to you, of all people? And I suppose you've helped out Cynthia Jennicks with her career?"

Esperança obviously found the banter entertaining. "The psychiatrist came here for personal reasons. Her husband was cheating on her. I got rid of his lover for her, and she helped me with one of my problems. We traded services."

"It's called bartering," Claire informed her. "Wait, if you're a voodoo priestess, why wouldn't you just cast one of your black magic spells to get rid of any problem you might have?"

"You got a lot to learn." Esperança stood up and walked over to a small shelf. After gently jostling around, she pulled out a bottle of Bacardi 151 rum, opened it and tilted the bottle to her lips, upending it.

Claire watched as the strange old woman took a big gulp.

"So, you're an alcoholic?" *What is it with everyone and alcohol? My mother, Harvey and now her.*

Using the back of her hand to wipe her burning lips, Esperança nodded. "I was good for a few years, but then the psychiatrist moved to Pennsylvania, and…" She paused, looking for an explanation, but found none. "You know how it goes." She took another swig and studied Claire through her veil of liquor.

Claire shook her head slowly. *How does this woman command such power?* The local thugs fear her, people like Cynthia Jennicks and a psychiatrist do business with her. But what would turn an old woman into an alcoholic?

Esperança returned to the table and eased back into her chair. "Why do people drink? Why do people do anything they do? Different tokes for different folks and a lid for every pot. But in the end, we all bleed, shit and die. So, why are you here, charming me with your wonderful personality?"

"You means strokes. And you know why I'm here."

"Give me the picture," Esperança ordered. "And the tie."

"How did you kn—" Diving inside her purse, Claire handed Esperança a photograph of her wedding day, along with the rolled up tie.

Esperança held the tie in the palm of her hand, a few inches from the burning flame. She turned her head toward the left and studied the shadows against the wall. "Hmm," she said, the silky tie slipping between her fingers and grazing the top of the flame. "A little gift…from a client. Another satisfied customer."

Claire grabbed the tie from Esperança's hand to inspect the damage from the flame, and knocked the candle over in the attempt.

"A client he's in love with," Esperança added, not quite finished with her findings.

"What client? Who is she!"

"Pain in my ass." Esperança shook her head and took another gulp of her rum. She picked up the tipped-over candle and relit the wick. "Now, I'll tell you what I see. You keep quiet."

Claire nodded and Esperança reached over, taking the tie back and resumed her position. She stared at the wall and said, "She hired him, a money thing. It worked out for her, and she came back to give him a present."

Esperança looked down at their photo. "Now the picture." Esperança's eyes were closed and she moved her fingers back and forth at a snail's pace, about half an inch above the photograph on the table. Her voice dropped to a coarse whisper. "So, your husband, he's a good man. Very different from you. He has empatia."

Opening her mouth to ask her what the word meant, she was halted by Esperança who held up a finger in front of her mouth. "Ah-ah-ah, remember what I said."

Claire let out a weary sigh.

"Empathy," the old woman said the word slowly, correcting herself. "He feeds hungry people."

"Feeds hungry people? What do you mean?" Claire also wondered what it had to do with getting her pregnant.

But the old woman ignored her question and rattled on. "He still loves you, but it's not the same anymore. A man wants to be a man. And he can't love you the way he loves the other one."

Claire leaned forward. "Who is she?"

"Look, you shut up now. I'll let you ask me any questions when I'm done," Esperança barked.

Claire pressed her lips together, watching her with a skeptical glare. On the outside, Esperança was everything a creepy voodoo priestess was expected to be. Although, there was a certain astuteness and in Claire's own experience, intelligence was often coupled with danger. She continued to observe her.

"He does love another…but she doesn't know this yet…and he doesn't know that she's in love with him, either," Esperança clarified.

Claire felt a trickle of sweat creeping down her spine.

Esperança blabbered on, "She's young, maybe twenty, twenty-one…comes from a wealthy family, but she's not spoiled. She helps people…cold, hungry people." Esperança focused even more. "Your husband, he helps her."

She studied as Esperança became immersed in a mime. Her hands moved as if she were playing an invisible violin. She stopped and said with complete awareness, "She plays music… incredibly talented."

"How nice," Claire said sarcastically, "she feeds people and plays music while my husband dances around like a monkey."

She jolted back into the reality of her everyday existence. "Does she serenade these famished people with her violin while they eat?" Claire shook her head in laughter. "I can't believe I fell for this nonsense!"

Esperança's face became deadly serious. "Nonsense? You uppity bitch. I just gave you a heads up. Deal with it."

"Deal with it? So, what should I do? Get rid of her? You want me to pay you, is that it?"

Esperança shook her head. "Stupid, stupid woman. A woman's intuition is a gift. Listen to it, don't fear it."

Claire was prepared to leave.

Esperança began to speak more softly, and Claire's resolve melted. "If you don't get rid of this other woman, he'll make his choice. And it won't be you."

The tension held for a brief moment, then the madness was dissolved by a beautiful voice coming from behind a beaded curtain. "Grandma? I'm leaving soon."

"Yes, yes." Esperança fanned her off.

The voice sprinkled sweetness over the evil room like magic angel dust. "Make sure you eat something...I made you some soup."

Esperança noted Claire's pinched brows and explained. "It's my granddaughter, Paciência. Patience, in English."

"Patience?"

"I named her Patience because when she was a baby she never cried when her diaper needed changing. She was very enduring, even when she was hungry. Of course, I liked the name Patience a lot better than Enduring." She gave a lax, one-shouldered shrug. "Patience flows better, sounds prettier, suits her."

Speaking of her granddaughter seemed to calm Esperança. She drank once more from the rum bottle.

Claire considered the priestess's words. The old woman had an uncanny gift, knowing her deepest secrets. Was this the answer she had been waiting for, the key to saving her marriage? Few people ever surprised her or terrified her into compliance. She hesitated, then said, "What do you suggest?"

But Esperança was gone, staring at the wall again. That damn wall. Claire's smooth expression fell, once she realized that the voodoo woman had a troubled look in her wormhole eyes. *Now what?* She waited one, long, agonizing minute.

"What?" Claire demanded, her gaze moving from the wall, then back to the priestess. "What is it?"

"What do you see in the shadows?" Esperança finally said, in a low and detached tone.

Claire studied the wall. "How in the fuck should I know? There's shadows... everywhere. Just say it!"

Esperança pointed to Claire's shadow and explained, "You see that long shape?"

Claire strained her eyes to look, focused on her outline.

"There's something in your colon, something you need to take care of right away. Something that could become a serious problem."

"Don't tell me that," Claire said, hugging herself. "It's cancer isn't it? My grandmother and aunt died of it."

"It's in your ass," Esperança furthered. "This thing. This big...long..." she returned her attention back to Claire and lifted her eyebrows. Claire leaned in pleading with her eyes, while digging her teeth into her lower lip to still the quiver.

"Stick," Esperança said. "A big, long, stick in your ass."

"You old crone," Claire said through gritted teeth. Esperança was laughing now, her entire body was draped over the table, until her hoarse laughter turned into a thick coughing fit. It got so bad, that her hair had come undone. She looked like a washed-up Sea Witch, Claire thought. How she wished for a can of disinfectant, she would have doused the old bitch in it.

Esperança managed to contain herself, once she realized, that Claire wasn't amused. She coughed up phlegm and spit into a tissue. "We do it in steps," she explained, straightening up and inspecting what she'd spat up. She crumpled the tissue in one hand and was all business again. "First the girl, then we take care of the baby. That works for you, no?"

Claire came around to the bottom line. "So, just how much money are we talking?"

"Ten-thousand for the girl. When we're finished, he'll never want to see her again."

"Ten-thousand? Are you mad? I should pay you to get rid of some girl?" Claire rose from her seat and grabbed the tie, stuffing it into her purse. "You may have suckered Janice, but not me. What do you do with all the money you make from your rich clients? Look how you live. There's something weird about this, and I'm not buying it. You won't get one red cent from me for this hocus-pocus crap."

Esperança watched, making no attempt to stop Claire. She bolted down the stairs, preparing herself to deal with the thugs from earlier. Once outside, her rage intensified, sending her into battle with anyone who tried to cross her. The men pulled away from her path as she charged for her Hummer. She pulled out Jonathon's tie from the inside of her purse, and dropped it down the sewer.

In the apartment above the market, the window opened, and Esperança's head popped out. "I take only cash," she said, convinced that Claire's tantrum was both amusing and temporary. She laughed. "And when you do come back, make sure you bring me another bottle of rum. Bacardi 151."

Opening the truck door, Claire shouted back, "Fuck you, lady!"

Esperança roared in a new burst of laughter, which made her look like a mental patient hanging from the unbarred window of a psycho ward. "And fuck you, right back!"

13

Limbo

In the span of two weeks, Claire unwillingly visited three more gynecologists. They all concurred with Claire's original gynecologist, as well as Doctor Monroe. She was infertile, and worse, she'd never be able to carry Jonathon's child, or any child.

She hadn't slept well for days, nor managed to hold much food down. Her struggle to hold herself together induced emotions she couldn't remember having experienced before, emotions that trapped her somewhere between anger and fear. The effort to contain herself made her whole body numb. Even jogging was impossible, for fear that the white raven was out there ready to taunt her. If Satan was listening, and the voodoo woman was the answer, then the truth was that Jonathon was in love with another woman. And that was something that Claire wasn't willing to believe.

That morning she'd approached Jonathon, who was putting on his suit jacket. "Guess what?" she asked with a pretend look of joy.

Jonathon was preoccupied. "Hmm? Oh, sorry, what was that?"

Standing behind him in her fur housecoat, she had wrapped her arms around his broad shoulders. "The gynecologist we saw a few weeks back, Dr. Monroe? I wanted to tell you tonight, but

I can't wait. All the test results came in and she said there's no reason I can't have a child."

Jonathon had turned and smiled faintly. "Good to know. We should talk about that later."

Taking her arms off him, she stood, searching his face. Of course she'd just lied to him, but for fuck sake, it hadn't been the first time. True, this was one of her big, bald-faced lies, not a little white one like the others. Still, there was no way he could see through her. No one could. "This is what you wanted, right? I can give you a child."

Nodding, he said, "Absolutely." Then he added, "Listen, Claire, I might be a bit late tonight."

"Okay." Claire was bewildered, as she watched him walk out. Clearly he was distracted, detached. The numbness tightened its hold on her. She was losing him, and worse, she was losing control.

The house had become too quiet for her liking. Claire sat alone in her den, researching foreign doctors who specialized in possible remedies for infertility. Her eyes were red rimmed, burning with exhaustion. The tick-tocks and chimes of the grandfather clock echoed through the marble halls. Deeply engrossed in her research, she hadn't realized how much time had passed until she looked out at the descending darkness.

She felt alone and yearned for companionship. Rubbing her fingertips together, she discovered that her hands were dry from the many pages of paper she'd handled. She pulled open her desk drawer and fumbled around inside for the tube of hand lotion. Fishing it out, she snapped open the lid and squeezed out the remaining cream. A loud sucking sound from the emptying tube alerted the cat, who had fallen asleep by her feet.

Lady surprised Claire by jumping softly onto her desk, scattering several printed pages, and purring, as if she'd sensed her owner's desperation.

"I know, girl," she whispered to her pet. "You miss him, too."

She picked up the cordless and dialed Jonathon's cell. The call went directly to voicemail—he'd shut off his phone. Then she tried his office line. It rang and stopped at the answering service. Her mind ran amok with suspicious questions. Who is he with? Where are they? And the worst thought of all: what are they doing?

She called both lines persistently, each to no avail. Whatever he was involved with, Jonathon clearly didn't want to be disturbed. Normally this wouldn't worry Claire, but in all the years they'd been together, he had always been available for her.

It was Wednesday. He had meetings all day, or so he'd claimed. She paced the room saying aloud, "Think, think, think." Then it occurred to her. Adrenaline rushed through her weakened body and fed her energy like a double shot of espresso.

Claire tore through the house and into her four-car garage. Jonathon had taken the Mercedes Roadster to work. Perfect.

Several minutes later, after making the call, Claire traced the location. He was in his Manhattan office.

Upstairs in the bedroom, she threw on her pink fleece tracksuit and pulled her hair up into a loose knot. Next, she bolted back to the garage.

Pulling out into the driveway and approaching her gate, Claire spotted something along the top. High beaming the object, Claire saw that it was the white raven, perched up, and looking right at her. Claire put the truck in park and exited from the running vehicle, walking toward the bird. The raven spread its wings apart, as if it was ready to fly, but instead, it began bobbing its head.

"What do you want?" Claire screamed at it. The raven continued to bob its head, toying with her, and pulling the rage from deep inside of her. The raven was laughing at her: *Jonathon's cheating, and you're too old to have a baby, nah, nah, nah, nah, nah…*

"Fuck you…You hear me," Claire screamed. "Fuck you, and the whore that birthed you." She wasn't directing her rage at the bird anymore: it was at Jonathon. She got back into her truck and opened the gate. The raven flew off and followed in front of the running vehicle, as if it was guiding her. Then, it disappeared.

Speeding like a mad woman, Claire slammed the driving wheel hard with both hands. "He's making a fool out of me!" she screamed. "I'll fucking kill him!"

A solid yellow color flashed in front of her eyes and she was forced to swerve her truck, just missing a parochial school bus. Children waved at her through the window, some laughed, and others showed the peace sign. Giving them the middle finger, Claire felt some degree of satisfaction. "Stupid Bible freaks, starting them so young!"

Pushing down even harder on the truck's accelerator, the speedometer passed 140 miles per hour. She couldn't escape the feeling that she was not so much running toward Jonathon as running away from herself.

Something scalded deep within the pits of her soul. Confusing waves of pain swept through her aging, barren body. Claire's husband, cheating on her. *How could I have been so stupid? What an idiot I am.* The pain succeeded in insinuating itself into her carefully crafted, censored heart but then it diminished, replaced by anger. Her anger worked like effective chemotherapy, killing all the cancerous pain. She knew her personal rule, the one she dared not break. No pain allowed! Pain equals sadness; sadness equals weakness. And Claire willed herself to never, ever, give in to the very thing that killed her mother. She damned Jonathon.

Pulling into the forty-three floor building, Claire was determined to catch him in the act, and then plot her revenge.

She entered at the front where high-tech security monitored every movement. Naturally, she knew the Indian head guard, Rajiv, who worked the evening shift. He spoke in the best English he could muster. "Good evening, Miss Claire," he said, with his gap-toothed smile. "Long time I don't see you."

"How are you, Rajiv?" She smiled, stopped, and leaned with her elbows on the counter-top of his security desk.

He whispered back, "I'm better, now that I see you." His gaze was drawn to the open zipper of her fleece tracksuit, no doubt enjoying the view beneath her thin, white tank top.

She giggled. "Can you let me pass? I need to drop off these documents to my husband."

Rajiv's smile had a hint of lewdness in it. "No problem, I'll buzz you in."

Claire moved quickly before her magic wore off. He hadn't even noticed that she had no documents in hand. Rajiv was breaking the rules, now unknowingly aiding in the crime which she was about to commit.

In the elevator, intoxication filled her during the long flight up. She'd destroyed the pain, and her newly charged anger was something she savored. It worked like a drug and surged through her veins, and just like an addict, she felt intensely alive. Her anger had been a driving force for most of her life—it understood her, made her who she was. And, at the moment, she was a woman scorned.

The elevator doors closed behind Claire. For a moment she stood still and alert. From wall to wall, the broad-loomed floor was asleep. Claire prowled the length of the hallway and entered the private sector where only the top dogs were fortunate enough to do business; she had the good fortune of being one of them. Once upon a time, every inch of this four-thousand-square-foot space belonged to her and Patrick. He'd given her free rein to run completely naked if she wished. Back then, it had given her a smug satisfaction, knowing the desks they used awaited their owners the following morning with secrets of their own.

The dimness made her other senses more attuned. Finally, she stepped swiftly to his office door. Her right hand trembled as she gripped the doorknob. Her blood ran cold.

Soft murmurs came from behind the door. The woman's voice was raspy. Jonathon's laugh annoyed her to the core. Behind the mahogany doors, she would find her husband inserting what belonged to her into another woman and doing so in the very platinum office which Claire had arranged for him.

Her throat closed in on her and, for a second, suffocated the purpose that brought her there in the first place. She wanted to run, afraid to face what might destroy her. Then she heard the woman's voice say, "A little finesse wouldn't hurt."

Claire all but kicked the door in, but nothing could have surprised her eyes more.

"Hey, Claire bear, what brings you to this neck of the woods?" Jonathon asked as he struggled with an espresso machine. Claire searched for the right words.

Patrick and his wife Bernice were also there. Big boxes surrounded them.

"What do you think?" Jonathon asked, with arms open and

signaling the jumble.

Claire moved through the boxes and joined her husband at the machine he worked on with a screwdriver.

"I have two machines set aside: one for us, and one for Vince and Rebecca. They're the real deal. Direct from Italy," he grunted, "if we can ever get them to work."

Patrick laughed, "This is a fine mess."

Shaking her head as an amused mother might, Bernice said, "These guys think that reading instructions doesn't apply to them."

Claire faked a smile.

"Well, it's kind of hard to read instructions in Italian," Jonathon defended.

Claire looked around. "What is all this?"

Bernice motioned for Claire to take a seat beside her, and she did so reluctantly.

Patrick stared at the dynamic redhead whom he had known so well. Claire didn't stare back, still angry over his low blows from the night of the gala.

As if she had a personal stake in it, Bernice explained to Claire, "It's a gift from a client. He's invested in a growing company in Europe. He predicts that in a few years, every corporate office will have an espresso machine. Apparently it's a real time saver."

Patrick chimed in, "Well it beats going down the street and waiting in line for one." .

Claire smiled politely. She suddenly felt the sleepless nights catching up with her. Sleep had cast its net, and her body was relaxed enough to surrender to it. The adrenalin settled, leaving her grateful for the hundreds of innocent boxes surrounding her.

So Esperança was wrong, there was no woman taking what belonged to her. Her man had been faithful. Like a newly found gray hair, the awareness of how much she needed him showed itself to her. This sensation sobered Claire immediately. Not since her mother had she needed anyone. Her eyes met Jonathon's, and warmth surged through her body. As he fiddled with the screwdriver and the machine, he looked so goofy and charming. In her own way, she loved him.

Claire rose from her seat and walked over to him. "Pass me

the instructions."

Her admiring audience watched her as she read the foreign words. She operated on the machine with the skill of a surgeon. In no time, she had it pumping like a healthy, beating heart. Claire poured the dark liquid into the tiny porcelain cup. It smelled earthy, as though the beans had just been roasted over a blazing fire.

"Voila!" She passed the cup to Bernice.

Bernice sipped the espresso as the men waited in anticipation of her opinion.

Claire shook her head in a kind of joy. Minutes ago, she'd been prepared to conquer and destroy, and now here she was making coffee for her ex-lover's wife as her husband looked on. She contemplated how life could be so hard-nosed on the one hand and yet so gentle on the other. A person being squashed under the tires of a bus had no idea how comfortable the ride might be for unaware passengers inside the vehicle. Despite the happy ending of her recent brush with fear. Claire knew the importance of never again letting down her guard.

Half an hour later, it was no coincidence when Claire and Jonathon walked to their favorite coffeehouse, arm in arm. Several months had flown by since they'd last enjoyed the Manhattan streets, accompanied by a silver moon. A contented Jonathon thought, *People write songs about stuff like this.* He loved her, especially tonight. She'd surprised him at the office; made an effort to socialize with his extended family. How natural and comfortable she looked. Even without make-up, wearing nothing but her old fleece jogger, she was perfect. There were no eggshells to walk over tonight. If only she could be like this more often, maybe he wouldn't have been so tempted.

A homeless man caught Jonathon's attention. His face was lined with the scars of street life, his body layered in all the clothing he owned. Although missing teeth, he smiled at having bumped into an old friend.

Jonathon smiled in return. "Hey, Jack, how goes the reading?" Jonathon bent his knees to make eye contact with him.

Making no effort to conceal her disgust, Claire stood as far away from the homeless man as she could. "I finished the bagful." The man gestured to the small gym bag he carried and then said, "Who's this pretty lady?"

"This is my better half. Claire, this is my friend, Jack."

Jack saluted her like a sailor floating off to war. Jonathon signaled for Claire to formally introduce herself, but she didn't budge. He sighed, thinking he should have known better. She had no empathy for the homeless and frequently dismissed them as "lazy parasites" who were either drunks or drug addicts.

He had lost himself in the almost perfect evening and forgot who Claire really was. She was nothing like Nicolette. To Claire, a man like Jack was nobody.

Jonathon opened his wallet and passed a twenty to him. "I'll get you more stuff to read next week." He wanted to remind him to get something to eat with the twenty he gave him, not spend it on another bottle, but decided it was none of his business.

Jack took the money and pushed it into his sock. "Thanks for that, I appreciate it." The man pulled off his grimy glove and extended his hand to Jonathon.

Claire turned her head. She couldn't bring herself to watch her husband shake hands with the filthy man. She also couldn't wrap her head around how polite, friendly, and comfortable Jonathon seemed with him, as though he'd run into a prestigious client or an old school chum. She began walking again, showing them both that her time wasn't worth wasting any further.

Catching up to her at the entrance of the coffee house, Jonathon raced to open the door for her. Once they were inside, Claire said firmly, "Before you do anything else, wash your hands. I'll be in that booth in the corner."

The evening wore on. Coffee and desserts were delivered and consumed. Jonathon's romantic notions of the evening drooped into mechanical motions performed by them both. Jonathon couldn't dismiss Claire's insulting behavior in front of Jack. *Can I spend the rest of my life with this woman, who has no compassion?* She had given him a life in the lap of luxury, and he was grateful for it, but her heart was frozen. Jonathon needed to believe that a child would soften her heart, change her for the better, and renew the waning energy in their marriage.

Children always transformed him for the better, the way

they worked their tiny hands into his; and it made him realize his life wasn't complete without the ring of their innocent laughter.   Jonathon loved it when Vince and Rebecca's kids came to visit.

"I was thinking," Jonathon spoke as he drew his fork into his favorite Harvest Cake. "If we have a baby by next year, why don't we take some time off? Go to the Dominican for a couple of months. Take a break."

Claire's expression of rage escaped her before she had a chance to assume her poker face.

"Did I say something wrong?"

She hated this. Claire's lie from that morning came back to her. Eventually, Jonathon would know the truth. "Why must we have a child?" Her bold question surprised even her.

"Because I want a family…a real family."

Claire didn't look up from her frozen blueberry yogurt. "I see. I'm not enough."

Jonathon charged ahead. "Look, I was brought up in the foster care system, in case you'd forgotten."

Rolling her eyes to the ceiling, Claire spouted, "Here we go again."

A cute, blond waitress set a small cup on the table in front of Jonathon. "A dollop of whipped cream, the way you like it." She had a Texan drawl, and she didn't acknowledge Claire in the least.

Jonathon gave the waitress a thin smile. "Thanks, Jenny."

"If you need anything else, just flag me." Again, she addressed Jonathon alone.

Claire slid the girl a glance. "She's crushing on you." She pegged Jenny as the kind of girl you'd find in a country bar, wearing a pair of cut-off jean shorts, while straddling a mechanical bull.

"Jealous?"

"I cut jealousy off at the knees, but you know that already."

"Yes, I do know that." Jonathon wanted to break through her hard exterior, and practically prayed for her to be less in control all the time. More vulnerable and loving.

Claire jumped back into the nitty-gritty. "So, you were saying before Dingbat interrupted, you want a real family."

"Right." He stared at the whipped cream and plopped a spoonful onto his cake.

Claire felt uncomfortable, not knowing exactly what to do with him.

Jonathon looked over at a little boy who peeked around from another table at them. His mother grabbed his hand, and playfully scooped him into her arms.

Great, thought Claire, *as if he really needed to see that right now.*

"I never told you how my mother said good-bye to me." Jonathon held his breath, stopping the tears from forming.

Noting his nervous body language, Claire decided this situation called for a different strategy. Sometimes Jonathon seemed to need her to act in a sensitive manner, so she put on a show for him. As she'd done before, on occasion, she faked her concern. "Go on."

"My mom was seventeen when she had me, we were alone. I don't remember ever having a father or grandparents. She did have a lot of men over, though." Jonathon paused and swallowed hard. "When I was nine, me and some kids from the block were playing baseball, and I ended up getting hit with the ball. Right here," Jonathon pointed to his eyebrow. "It was really bad, became infected. She was so mad at me that she beat me. A few days later, she could see the cut was getting green and smelly, so we took a bus into the city, Detroit's main hospital…" A long silence prevailed. He sniffled "…and she left me there. Made arrangements to have me put in foster care."

But Claire, blank faced, didn't say anything. And all this time, Claire never even bothered to inquire about his scar. Claire would never look at it the same way again.

"She didn't say good-bye, and I never saw her again." He looked at her, waiting for a sign of comfort. "I tried finding her, but after a few years of dead-ends, I just gave up. I don't think she wanted to be found."

Claire absorbed the new details of her husband's woeful upbringing with silent bitterness. She'd never mentioned her wretched past to him nor would she ever consider doing so. The very idea of whining like a child, and being sad about things that happened during childhood and could not be changed, was appalling to her. Where was his gratitude? Had it not been for her, Jonathon would not be among the movers and shakers of the financial world. *I rescue him from his doleful life and this is how he repays me?*

Nevertheless, Claire was clear on why he wanted so desperately to have children. And she feared he would not stay in their marriage without a child. It meant everything to him. She decided to go with her original plan of hiring a surrogate and holding the woman in hiding until she gave birth. She was prepared. Jonathon would never know she wasn't able to give birth herself. If Claire had to tie a goddamn pillow on her stomach to somehow keep up a nine-month charade, then so be it. She had made her man, and now she had to make his child.

Jonathon spent a long time staring at her.

"Try not to worry," Claire said in her usual, convincing tone. "We'll have a child. But I can't promise you the Dominican. Maybe the Bahamas?"

Jonathon chuckled. He reminded her of a child who still needed his blanket. "Let's go make babies," she suggested, in a silky voice. They both laughed, and all the tension broke between them like a tsunami warning suddenly called off.

At home, Claire took a bath in her deep soaking tub. She lathered every muscle of her long legs in cocoa butter soap. Her breasts floated on a sea of bubbles, and her red nipples hardened each time she exposed them to the air.

Jonathon stood naked at the open doorway. "Got a package for a Mrs. Lockwood."

Claire studied his athletic body, standing in the shadows of the bedroom. A roaring fire crackled behind him, casting a red glow over his skin that stretched tightly over his firm muscles and ripped stomach.

He walked in slyly and stood above her, licking his lips masterfully, while staring down with heavy-lidded eyes. Claire's eyes journeyed over to the boyish tousle of brown hair, to the shadow of his beard and then settled on his erection. She rubbed herself under the soapy blanket.

Jonathon worked the right muscles, and got his penis to move up and down, then side to side. "Hi, got room for me?" He used his deepest voice and drew a genuine laugh from his wife.

"There might be room for you, Big Ben." Claire traced her finger from his scrotum to the tip of his penis. He shivered at her touch. "But I don't know about Jonathon."

Jonathon sank into the tub with an audible sigh. He submerged himself completely under the bubbles and then resurfaced, his hair dripping wet. He positioned his head between her breasts.

Claire wrapped her legs around him, and ran her tongue along the side of his neck. He made a groaning sound and sank farther into the deep tub. He turned to face her. His cheeks were flushed, his lashes wet and dark, intensifying the blue in his yearning eyes. He stared at her with that cocked brow and licked at the soap that tickled his lower lip. She let out a breathy moan and squeezed him up against her body.

He started at her neck, stopped at her mouth, licked her bottom lip, and then sucked on it as though it were the special place between her legs. Claire moaned in anticipation of what would come next.

He lifted her buttocks, and placed her before him, her legs spread. Caressing her inner thighs with his tongue, he stopped at her opening. He rubbed his nose in the warmth and smelled the sweetness that oozed from within her. Claire grabbed his hair and pushed his face into her. He used her lips as if they were her mouth. She shivered from the tips of her toes and released her juices into his mouth. Jonathon rose from the tub and lifted her into his strong arms.

He carried her to the fire, gently placing her into the soft throw he'd put there earlier. He loved her at that moment. Lovemaking was the only time she allowed him to take full control and have his way with her.

He whispered into her hair, "I love you."

Claire closed her eyes. "Me too." She brushed her lips up the curve of his throat.

Something changed for Jonathon. The intensity evaporated along with his hunger. His erection was replaced by a deep moral conflict moving back into his conscience, making him feel guilt-ridden.

"What's wrong?" She nestled at the pulse beating at the base of his neck and felt him swallowing several times.

Jonathon pulled the covers over their naked bodies. "I guess I'm tired."

Claire kissed his chin and then rested her head on the pillow. "Then, sleep." Jonathon curled at her side, gazing at her delicate profile. He saw her lashes flutter closed and waited for her breathing to change. After a few minutes had passed, he covered her exposed shoulders and left her by the warm embers of the fireplace.

He went into his pants pocket and pulled out his phone. Nicolette had called at nine o'clock as usual, but left no message. He wished she had, so he could hear her voice.

He looked at the woman he'd married—she looked peaceful as she slept. Claire was his wife, he loved her, and she'd made him the man he was.

Nicolette was his friend. He loved her, but he also desired her. And his guilt was no less, simply because Nicolette was unaware.

He was in limbo, trapped between two things. Caught between two very different women.

14

Old Square Britches

airfield, New Jersey, a picturesque township located in northwest Essex County. Rebecca and Vince had made it their home and owned a small, detached, two-story house of red brick there. Standing on its threshold, Claire rang her sister's door bell. Olivia opened the door wearing a pink, frilly princess tutu and tiara, her face and hands covered in chocolate. Seeing it was her aunt at the door, Olivia smiled timidly.

"Aren't you going to let me in?" Claire asked.

Rebecca approached, wearing a filthy white apron, and moved Olivia out of the way.

"Hey, what brings you by?"

Claire stepped into the hallway as the smell of baking welcomed her. She stood by the door, still holding her purse and car keys in her hands.

"Takeoff your shoes and come in the kitchen, we're making cupcakes," Rebecca announced.

"Chocolate and vanilla," Olivia said, holding up her chocolate-covered hands.

Claire faked a laugh, while balancing against the wall, and pulled her boots off.

"Go wash your hands, Livy. And put your cartoons on. Mommy and Auntie Claire are going to talk for a bit."

Claire followed Rebecca through the hallway, took a seat at the Greco's kitchen table, and began rummaging through her purse. Smiling shyly again, Olivia moved toward Claire and pulled her doll off the chair. Claire sat still, watching her niece from the corner of her eye.

"She's dirty too," Olivia explained, pointing to the chocolate on her doll's face.

Rebecca laughed, as she untied the dirty apron. "I gotta throw this in the laundry pile," she said, leaving the kitchen. Claire smiled politely and pulled out her hand sanitizer, pumping a few squirts into her palm. Her niece watched her curiously and, thankfully, didn't annoy her with any questions. Doll in hand, Olivia left the room, leaving Claire alone.

Claire looked around; the entire kitchen was a mess. Measuring cups, baking trays, and flour lined the kitchen counter. In the sink, a pile of mixing bowls and other bulky kitchen items were stacked on top of one another, unwashed and sticky.

Rebecca re-entered the room. "Let me just get these things out and I'm all yours."

"Sure." Claire studied her sister with interest. She couldn't fathom living in such chaos and was astounded to see how contented her sister looked. Rebecca's hair was a sweaty disaster, as if she hadn't washed it in days, and her oversized, gray track pants and blue T-shirt made her look even frumpier than she already was.

Bending over, Rebecca pulled out a tray of cupcakes from the oven. Hot air escaped from the door, creating a misty film over the kitchen window. Rebecca cracked it open and took in a deep breath. "I'm so hot," she said, looking over at Claire. "The twins have their play tomorrow night…I said I'd make my famous Peace Cakes."

"If peace was possible by eating chocolate and vanilla cakes," Claire said, reaching over for one which was already iced and plated, "then I'm sure Betty Crocker would have joined the Peace Summit." Claire took a small bite of the cake and held it on her tongue. "Coconut oil?"

"Just a tad. Sweet butter, too. But the icing's Mom's." Rebecca watched Claire take another bite, and noted the warmth in her sister's eyes. "You want coffee?"

"No," Claire said, looking over at the espresso machine Jonathon had given them. "What I'd like is a cappuccino to go with this." She held up the cupcake. "Just don't tell my husband."

Rebecca nodded. "I do mean cappuccino, and Vince picked up some amazing coffee from the deli." She got up and moved toward the espresso machine, placing the countless eggshells and empty boxes in the trash bin to make room. "This machine's unreal." Rebecca reached into the cupboard for a red tin. A plastic cup fell out and dropped to the floor. Claire got up and set it on the counter.

From her perspective in the kitchen, Claire was able to see into almost every room on the main level. Looking around, she remembered why she avoided visiting her sister. The place was an utter disaster: toys and sports equipment in every room, dolls and coloring books scattered on what used to be a dining room table. Looking up at the vaulted ceilings, she admired Vince's handiwork and then dropped her gaze to the floor. It was breathtaking; the intricate design, using various colors of wood inlay, spread across the entire main level. It was amazing what Vince was able to do, crafting a lovely herringbone pattern that spread from room to room. But regardless, the messy collection of children and toys ruined what could have been a pretty, if modest, home.

Sounds of powerful steam escaped the espresso machine in the Greco kitchen. Turning her head to the right, Claire watched her sister working away on the cappuccino preparations. To her left, just behind the wall that separated the kitchen from the family room, was Olivia, completely immersed in her cartoons. Claire's niece sat comfortably on a throw cushion, her tutu fluffed over the edges with her doll seated next to her. She giggled, lost in her own little world where Wiley Coyote set bombs for the Roadrunner. Claire wondered what having a child in her own perfectly kept home would feel like, but more importantly, wondered what Rebecca would answer to what she had came over to ask.

Claire observed Olivia's dark eyes and her deep brunette curls and was reminded of Vince's Sicilian heritage. It was quite natural that Olivia and her brothers looked nothing like Rebecca. Claire pondered the possibility she had come to discuss: it was likely that Jonathon and Rebecca's child would have lighter skin, given that Jonathon had a peachy complexion and brown curls. Thinking about the child's eye color, Claire felt indifferent. It didn't matter, because both Claire and Rebecca shared the same green irises as their departed mother, although Claire's own eyes were a far more striking than her sister's.

"Your cappuccino, madam," offered Rebecca. Claire turned around to see her sister placing the frothy cups onto the table. Taking a seat at the table with her sister, Rebecca reached across to the stack of cupcakes.

Claire took a quick sip, the foam tickling her upper lip. "It's the real deal," she said, to flatter Rebecca, although it really was very good.

"Oh, we love this thing. Me and Vince are bouncing all over the walls at night." Rebecca peeled the paper wrapping from the cupcake and ate the cake part first, saving the icing for last.

"You still do that?" Claire said, amused, raising the cup to her mouth. She took another slow and careful sip.

"Guilty as charged." Rebecca watched Claire reach for the cupcake she'd selected earlier. She picked at a small amount with her fingers and sampled the icing again. Rebecca could see the obvious look of worry which escaped her sister's eyes. Claire never came to visit, not even for the children's birthdays. She'd send Jonathon with a gift, usually a gift card. It was Jonathon who made the extra effort and went out of his way to wrap some personally selected toy or crazy thing he'd ordered online. Jonathon was especially attentive to Olivia, scoring a coup when he'd tracked down the Princess of Pink doll for her fourth birthday. She loved that thing and dragged it everywhere with her.

Claire was strangely calm, Rebecca noticed. She wondered if it had anything to do with the special icing that reminded them of their mother, because she seemed sad while she continued to sip her drink and pick the dessert apart.

Rebecca took a long sip. "You ever think of her?" she asked, blinking over the cup's rim.

"Our mother?"

Rebecca set the cup down. "Yeah…do you ever think of her?"

Everyday, Claire wanted to say. "Sometimes, when it snows or…" Her throat tightened around the words.

"Or what?"

Claire avoided talking about their mother. She had tried to suppress the painful memories by getting rid of reminders of Connie, even going so far as to give Rebecca all of their mother's recipes and most of her personal effects. Rebecca was barely five when their mother had died and had no memory of her. The only thing she knew was what their father had told her. Claire, on the other hand, knew a part of their mother that she kept from Rebecca.

Claire straightened her thin shoulders. "I do think of her… when I'm around you." She held back the part about where the similarity ended. Unlike Connie, Rebecca was a slob. Before the drinking, Claire and Rebecca's mother had been strikingly beautiful and had run a clean and perfect household. You wouldn't have caught their mother wearing track pants and T-shirts. But just like Rebecca, she was also a fool for her man.

Rebecca, oblivious to Claire's inner dialogue and only aware of Claire's great love for her mother, was deeply touched. "I remind you of our mother?"

"Yes, you do." Because she was there for a favor, she held back. What she wanted to say was that Rebecca would end up just like their mother. And because Rebecca was so close to their father, she had to keep her wicked thoughts on him to herself as well. Still, not everything about Rebecca exasperated her.

"Really?" Rebecca leaned forward. "How? In what way?"

"Your hands," Claire replied. "You have our mother's small hands…her mannerisms. The way you bend your wrist and the way you raise your pinky when you're doing something, like holding cutlery. I always think of her when I watch you."

Rebecca straightened up and looked her hands over. "My hands." Rebecca's eyes lit up like sun-dappled moss. "I have our mother's hands." Unshed tears held on the brim of her lashes.

"Make them stop Claire," Claire remembered Rebecca's words. *"Mommy's gonna be cold,"* Rebecca said, on that winter day. Rebecca had that same expression, those blameless green eyes staring up at her, begging Claire not to leave their mother in the dark hole. And here she was begging again, that same little girl,

turning to her sister for comfort.

Claire caught the tail-end of her breath, blinking hard at the memory. As the swell of guilt rose, so did the anger. "Do we really have to do this?"

Rebecca wiped her tears with the back of her hand and offered a small nod. Claire reached for a tissue in her purse and passed it to her, then turned away. Immediately forgetting her own need to hear more about their mother, Rebecca dabbed at her cheeks and focused on her big sister. Claire seemed lost and somewhat depressed. It was a Monday afternoon, the beginning of a crazy week and here was Claire, sitting at her kitchen table eating a sugary and fatty cupcake. Finally, Rebecca asked, "Are you okay?"

Following a taut moment of silence, Claire spoke. "No, I'm not all right."

The admission worried Rebecca. Claire was always strong, always in control. *Was she sick? Was Jonathon leaving her?*

"I'm infertile. Five doctors, including Dr. Sidle and that... Dr. Monroe you sent me to, say it's impossible for me to conceive. And even if I was fertile, there is zero chance I could carry to term. I have some scar tissue on my uterus."

"Oh, Claire, I'm so, so sorry...what does Jonathon say?"

"He doesn't know." Claire gave a warning glare. "And I would appreciate it if you didn't tell your husband."

"Of course not, whatever you say."

Studying her sister's expression, Claire decided not to waste another minute playing nice and eating sugary crap. She needed to get to the point if she wanted to leave in time to beat the traffic. "I need your help."

"Sure, anything you need." Rebecca pushed the coffee and cupcake out of her way and stretched her hands toward her sister, waiting for the moment Claire would accept them, for support. It made Rebecca hopeful to witness vulnerability in her normally cold sister. She yearned for the day that Claire would become warm and receptive, so that they could share a genuinely loving relationship. After meeting Jonathon, Rebecca had been optimistic: elated to see her sister with such a kind and compassionate man. But even he couldn't melt the coldness in Claire.

"I've been doing some research, looking into hiring a surrogate. But there's also this thing about egg donors," Claire explained in her business tone. "I'm not comfortable having some stranger's egg. I want my blood—our mother's red hair and our mother's green eyes—to remain in our family."

Rebecca's empathetic eyes began to glaze over.

"And I'm asking you to donate your eggs to me…so that I can give Jonathon a child."

Rebecca spoke, without a second thought. "You want me… to give you my egg?"

"Yes."

"Oh my God…Claire. Yes, in a heartbeat, whatever you need." Rebecca nodded and wiped her tears with the same crumpled tissue. "I'd have to talk to Vince though, see how he'd feel. But he loves Jonathon. He'd do anything for him and—"

"No," Claire said, cutting her off, "Vince can't know. No one can." Claire stopped speaking, seeing that Olivia was standing in the doorway of the kitchen.

"You need something, Livy?" Rebecca asked. Olivia walked to the counter and selected a cupcake with chocolate frosting. She caught her mother's stare. "You've already had way too much today."

"It's for Princess Pink." Olivia padded out of the kitchen, cupcake in tow.

Rebecca went back to the statement. "What do you mean Vince can't know? Of course we have to tell him. I'd be pregnant, with your guys' baby."

"Listen to me," Claire said, back to her normal self. "I've been doing some research, and I found a few gynecologists I might be able to work with."

Rebecca nodded reluctantly.

"You know, get Jonathon's sperm, and tell him we're doing in-vitro so that it'll speed things up. In the meantime, I'd hire a surrogate and keep her in hiding: somewhere close, so that I can keep an eye on her. And as the pregnancy progresses, I would wear a prosthetic bump. I've seen a few online; they're very real looking, made by movie make-up people, or whatever they are. Anyways, I'd figure all that out later, but for now, I need your help."

Hearing the words out loud hit both Claire and Rebecca hard. It sounded insane, completely off the charts insane. But it was too late, the words were out, spilled over the table, surrounded by Rebecca's Peace Cakes.

Rebecca blanched. "No, I won't do it. I won't play these games with people's lives, especially the life of an innocent child."

Fury began to build in Claire. "You're kidding?" But why did it surprise her? Maybe it angered Claire to have stooped that low, begging her sister for the one thing she actually did well—fertility.

Rebecca folded her arms over her chest and felt heat rise to her cheeks. "When Jonathon married you, he did it because he loved you. I can't imagine him leaving you over not being fertile. That's not like him. He would understand… My God, even if you guys adopted, he'd be happy. He's a good man, Claire, he doesn't deserve this."

Claire could feel the hot prickle moving over her scalp.

"You made a promise when you married him," Rebecca stated in a voice too loud. "And he made his to you. Kids or no kids."

"A promise is a comfort to a fool," Claire snapped. "You make it sound as if I don't deserve him, or even children for that matter."

"I'm saying that if you do this to him, then yes, you don't deserve him. And there is no way, that I'd help you play him like that. It's wrong, morally…" The telephone rang. "I have to get this," Rebecca said, reading the call display on the cordless, "it's the twins' school calling for the baked goods."

Claire fanned her off, as Rebecca moved toward the other side of the kitchen to answer the telephone.

Meanwhile, Claire decided it was time to go. Walking past the living room, Claire saw her niece, sitting on the loveseat, engrossed in her cartoons, as she picked at her cupcake. It was strange how quickly the rage she was feeling passed. Olivia was so calm and innocent. Claire was curious. What would it be like to talk to Olivia one-on-one? What was it that Jonathon loved so much about her?

"Scoot over," Claire said.

Surprised by her aunt's interest in her, Olivia moved her doll away so that Claire could sit beside her. Looney Tunes, an old favorite of Claire and Rebecca's, played on the big screen. Foghorn Leghorn rambled on, *Whoa, Nelly!*

Olivia turned to Claire with a laugh. "Whoa, Nelly!" Olivia giggled, causing a few crumbs to fall from her face. Her two front teeth were missing, making her even more adorable.

Claire soon became lost in the world of cartoons, watching the loud, Texan rooster courting the old hen with her blue bonnet and thick glasses. Olivia turned to Claire. "The other chickens call her Old Square Britches."

Turning her attention back to the cartoon, Claire enjoyed the happy nostalgia. For a moment, it felt like home—the feeling of innocence. Looney Tunes, and the smell of baking.

A laugh escaped Claire's lips; she caught Olivia's interest. "Wherever did you get these, they're classics."

"My mommy," Olivia said. "Her favored."

"Favorite," Claire corrected her, without turning away from the screen. "My favorite, too."

From the kitchen, Rebecca watched her sister, sharing a moment with Livy. It quickly erased the anger Rebecca was feeling. Maybe Claire really did want to be a mother. Maybe there was a way that Rebecca could help. If only Claire weren't sneaking around behind Jonathon's back. She continued to watch her sister and Livy, unseen.

Claire turned her attention to Olivia, her innocence, how precious she was. Olivia tore the paper off her cupcake and began eating the cake part first, just as Rebecca had always done. Olivia caught her staring and turned bashful.

"Your mother used to do that," Claire said, leaning down to the level of Olivia's bowed head.

"Do what?" Olivia asked, scrunching her nose as she looked up.

"When she was a little girl, your mother used to save the icing for last."

Olivia's tiny brows pinched together. "You knew my mommy when she was a little girl?" The child was completely amazed.

"Of course," Claire said.

The lightness Claire was feeling surfaced through her tone.

"She was my little sister."

Rebecca continued to eavesdrop from behind the wall.

Olivia pressed the pause button on the converter. Her tiny finger left behind a sticky icing print. She gave Claire her full attention. Olivia's ebony eyes were wide with awe.

"You were little too?"

Claire let out an unrestrained laugh and amusement colored her cheeks. "Well, I sure wasn't born this way." Claire was surprised to find herself so taken by her niece. She thought of her mother and how much she would have adored this child, her granddaughter.

"Your grandmother would have loved you," Claire uttered. She hadn't meant to compliment her niece, but, for some odd reason, the truth would not be stopped.

Olivia put her cupcake on the armrest and turned to Claire. "My Nonna always says she loves me and my brothers."

Claire shook her head and lightly brushed the crumbs from Olivia's face. *So soft.* "I meant my mother, your mommy's mommy… It's a pity you never knew her," Claire's voice was subdued to tones of placidness. "She would have adored you." Looking at the crumbs on her niece's face and lap, Claire dug into her purse and pulled out a package of tissue. "I suppose this will have to do," she said, opening the tissue into a square.

Olivia watched her with keen interest. "You see this?" Claire asked.

Olivia nodded eagerly, her curls bouncing.

"Your grandmother, Connie, taught your mommy and me a little trick. The next time you eat anything, especially a messy cake," said Claire, placing the napkin on her niece's lap, "you'll remember to be a little lady and not make a mess."

Claire inclined her head to get Olivia's response, and was touched by the child's smile.

"She was pretty like you and my Mommy," Olivia said. "Mommy shows us grandma's pictures all the time."

Behind the wall, Rebecca had her hand to her mouth waiting to hear more. This was the first time Claire had ever said so much about their mother.

Claire nodded, folding her hands in her lap. It was difficult for her to talk about her mother, but she found Olivia's sweet nature engaging and easy. "Yes, I guess we do look like her. But your mommy is actually a lot like your grandmother was. Your grandmother did a lot of fun stuff with us too. We played games, baked and we even played dress up..."

Claire fiddled with her wedding band as she fell deeper into her memories. "Your grandmother used to let us put on her clothes and high heels and wear her red lipstick." Claire smiled at the recollection.

"She had the most beautiful clothes." Claire turned to her niece who was captivated by the story of her grandmother. "She was a wonderful seamstress," Claire added, but noted that the word 'seamstress' confused Olivia. "She made her own dress-es," she clarified.

Olivia nodded, her mouth in the shape of a cute *o*.

"Oh, but I loved her style...I always said that when I grew up, I'd dress as nicely as your grandmother did. Her dresses were especially nice."

"Sparkly dresses," Olivia suggested.

"Sure, sparkly." Claire concealed her smirk. "But your grandmother was a fabulous lady, a real Grace Kelly."

"Who's that?"

"Never mind that." Claire moistened her lips. "Your grand-mother really loved us. She really did. We would sit around the dining room table. Drink tea from the special teacups she bought us, and we'd get all dressed up with white gloves and hats. Your mommy, she was too young to understand...and she'd say, 'Is it hat day today?'" Claire's voice fell to a broken whisper. "It's too bad that your mommy can't remember anything. She was just a little girl, not much older than you."

"What else?"

Claire paused, then softly cleared her throat. "Oh, well...we would talk about very important things while we sipped tea. I was a little older, so I would talk about school and projects. And your mommy would discuss what cereal she wanted or things she had going on." Claire stilled at the memory, and placed her index finger to her lip. She turned to Olivia.

"There's something else I remember, it's about your grand-mother. She had these wonderful pearls. They were really spe-cial and she only wore them on special occasions. Anyway, your mommy always wanted to wear them, but so would I. We'd fight over them...cry and scream at each other. We both loved those pearls," Claire paused and chuckled at the memory. "We eventually made a pact."

"What's a pact?" The kid missed nothing.

"Well, it's kind of like an arrangement. One week your mother would wear them, and the other week I'd get the chance to."

"Take turns," Olivia offered.

"That's right, take turns," Claire agreed.

Behind the wall, Rebecca burst into tears, realizing that when Claire had surrendered the pearls to her, it was done out of love. She had absolutely no memory about the pearls or the tea parties and more importantly, about how much Rebecca was like their departed mother.

Claire's smile dipped to a frown. "Your mommy was about your age when God took our mommy away…"

She looked at her niece and realized she'd said too much. "Anyway, it was a long time ago. Just be glad you still have yours," Claire added and looked straight ahead, with her hands still folded in her lap.

This was too much for Rebecca. She ran upstairs. "You wanna watch cartoons?" Olivia asked excitedly.

"Sure," Claire said, not wanting to leave. A small part of her was tempted to hold the child; apart from holding Rebecca as a baby, she'd never held one before.

Another cartoon began titled, Of Rice and Hen. Olivia turned to inform Claire, "The other chickens make fun of her, because she has no baby chickens."

"Oh." Claire remembered it well. The cartoon played before them, the old hen, wearing her blue bonnet and glasses. Old Square Britches, the old eggless chicken.

"Oh, Prissy," said Olivia, following the words in perfect timing, "you don't know how lucky you are never to have had children. They're such a trial." Olivia turned to Claire. "They make fun of Old Miss Prissy. She's too old to make eggs."

Claire felt a warm flush creeping over her face. Olivia turned to Claire and smiled, her little feet kicking with excitement. Meanwhile, the cartoon of the pathetic chicken continued to play. All Claire could think of was Jonathon leaving her for another woman: leaving her because she was infertile old woman, incapable of giving him the one thing he craved. Claire's panic began to mount; she felt her throat closing in. Picking up her purse, she rose from the couch.

"Where you goin'?"

"Just watch your freaking cartoons," Claire said. "Old Square Bitches," she added loud and clear before running out of the room.

Moments later, Rebecca ran down the stairs, holding a blue velvet box that contained their mother's pearls. Entering into the family room, she found Livy happily watching cartoons by herself.

"Where'd Auntie Claire go?"

Olivia giggled with one hand covering her mouth and the other pointed to the TV. "Old Square Bitches made her mad."

Rebecca stood rooted, knowing exactly how hard that cartoon had slapped Claire in the face. Her big sister was losing her mind.

15

Forty-Six

A wave of light moved from the banks of the second river and spread into the dark recesses of the valley. In a silent rush, the entire land was glowing under the light of the full moon and the thousands of moonflowers that illuminated it in a bioluminescent glow.

Sitting between her legs, by the river's edge, overlooking the hills, was her golden child. She was so silent and ever so still. Esperança bent her neck forward and smelled the sunshine in her hair, then saw that there were tears in her peacock-blue eyes.

"Grandma, Grandma…please wake-up."

Someone was nudging Esperança, forcing her awake. With her eyes closed, Esperança's dream of glowing flowers and her babe, slipped into the reality of her existence. Her dream dissolved into the nightmare of the present. Lua in her arms, was gone again.

"Grandma, wake up," Patience begged.

Esperança's head was on the table, the scent of depravity served as a painful reminder. The smell of blood and wax, etched into the wood's grain, assaulted her on every level. Esperança shivered, cold and itchy from the urine that saturated her pants.

"Grandma, you can't stay like this, you'll get a rash again," Patience said.

"I saw her this time," Esperança mumbled. "I could smell her, like the ocean and sun."

"I know, Grandma. I know," Patience whispered, lifting Esperança underneath her arms and pulling her away from the table. The chair, pulled from under her, went crashing onto the floor.

Esperança's eyes remained closed. "She'd be forty-six today...have babies of her own."

"I know, Grandma."

"Her birthday is coming soon. Did I tell you, how she always wanted a party with shiny bows and pretty paper?" Esperança asked.

"You did, Grandma. Let's get you into a bath," Patience suggested, dragging Esperança through the beaded curtain.

"I know you," Esperança said, through her drunkenness, forcing an eye open. Everything was a blur.

"Of course you know me," Patience said with a soft grunt while pulling her into the washroom, "I'm your granddaughter."

16

The Big, Red Button

Claire sipped mineral water from a tall, crystal glass decorated with a lime wedge. The green citrus reminded her of Esperança, the freakish sour bitch. Lately it hadn't taken much for her mind to waft back to the woman and her horrid little space in the Bronx.

She picked up the butter knife from the table and caught a glimpse of her reflection in its shiny silver. Returning the knife to the table, she sighed, while taking a longer look around.

It was the world traveler in Claire that appreciated the French restaurant's rustic decor. The gray slate floors and the exposed brick walls reminded her of the bistros in Paris. But it was the refined woman in Claire that adored the pianist's delicate rendition of Beethoven's, Moonlight Sonata. If nothing else, maybe she could enjoy the ambiance and have a magnificent meal.

Looking her watch, Claire cursed inaudibly. The man was sixteen minutes late. Being forced to wait made her insides simmer. Seeking distraction, she turned her attention to the crystal glassware. Admiring it, she held the glass up to the light and frowned.

A pretty-boy waiter with curly brown hair and feminine features noticed her displeasure as he passed. "Is everything all right, madam?"

Claire clicked her tongue, and pointed to the glass. "I've

changed my mind. The lipstick stain has ruined my appetite."

Dread filled the waiter's face, as though he'd been caught with his pants down. "I do apologize." He winced, examining the glass for what she had claimed to see. "But I don't seem to—"

She rolled her eyes and muttered to the nearby patrons, "And they call this a five star." Then she turned back to the waiter, "I want to talk to your superior."

"Oh, I didn't mean to question your—I'm very sorry, madam. I'll call the manager for you immediately." He quickly moved on.

Left on her own again, Claire began reviewing her opinion about Esperança, while gently scraping her top lip with her bottom teeth. It was true that the despicable woman had talent; she'd been able to read a bit about her history and even some of her thoughts. But she recalled watching a documentary a few months before which explained this strange phenomenon easily enough: certain people, simply more attuned to their senses than others, are able to tap into what idiot followers referred to as the 'supernatural.'

The question lingering uppermost in her mind was whether or not she could believe the old bat regarding Jonathon. His behavior had changed of late, and his performance in the bedroom was lackluster. Something was unquestionably wrong. She could feel it. And despite not catching him with a woman at his office, the fact remained that she was infertile. If Esperança was correct about Jonathon, then the next vital step was to proceed with Esperança's plan. First, get rid of the girl; second, take care of her infertility issue. But before parting with a dime, she needed proof.

The asshole was now eighteen minutes late. She glanced at the entrance. Before hiring him a month ago, Claire's own investigation, back by her lawyer's, showed that he was one of the best in the business. So it shocked her that he looked as drab as he did when they first met. Azad Portoian was at least thirty pounds overweight, no Magnum, PI. The squat private investigator's beady brown eyes brought back memories of her childhood hamster—Harry, not of Tom Selleck fantasies.

In fact, at their initial meeting, Claire had accidentally called the investigator *Harry,* and he reminded her that his name was Azad which, he explained, meant 'free' in Armenian. Because he specialized in domestic surveillance, she sought his services—instructing him to follow Jonathon's activities from the moment he left their house at daybreak to the moment he drove back into their garage after sunset. He showed his surprise when she insisted that he complete a month's worth of work without reporting to her in between. She wanted him to be thorough, including names, addresses, and any other pertinent information. She had to be absolutely sure before she could put Esperança out of her mind forever.

Finally, after twenty-one minutes of tardiness, the fat oaf lumbered in. Claire knew that he was purposely late, it was his way of getting Claire to invest her time. Subliminal manipulation. Azad walked with a cool, though unconvincing, swagger. He also sported a month-old goatee. Claire saw right through his act—including why he had urged her to meet him here at this secluded, fine restaurant. The location of the impressive *Châteaux* next door was no coincidence.

Did he honestly think she would be so vulnerable as to fall into his waiting arms? She almost laughed out loud as he approached the table, but then she felt her anger rising. His supreme confidence might be confirmation that he'd found something scandalous in his investigation of Jonathon, and immediately she resented Azad. Was this how he got all his women, if indeed he got any?

"Good evening," Azad grunted, as he sank into the chair opposite her. "Sorry I'm late. I had a meeting with some big wheels on an espionage case. I'd tell you more, but it's strictly confidential, you understand?" Azad loosened his too-tight belt, and flashed her a quick glimpse of the handgun, which was strapped to his pudgy side.

"Oh yes," Claire replied, pretending to be naïve and lost in admiration, "I wouldn't want to put you in a compromising position." For her own amusement, Claire envisioned the portly PI playing Twister in the nude.

Before Azad had the chance to reply, a well-dressed middle-aged man planted himself beside the table. "Good evening, my name is Claude Moushette, and I am the manager. May I be of assistance, madam?"

"I certainly hope so," Claire said firmly. "Your establishment comes highly recommended and you have a reputation to live up to, don't you?" She held up the faintly lipstick-stained glass to the light.

The manager strained his eyes, then reached into his top pocket to fetch his reading glasses. After a few seconds of further eye straining, he uttered, "Ah!" and blushed. "I do apologize for this," he whispered, looking about nervously. "How may I remedy the situation for you?"

"I'm sure you'll think of something." Claire glanced at her watch. "Come back in eight minutes and let me know what you've come up with. Agreed?"

The blushing manager nodded and made a quick exit.

Claire felt Azad's sharp gaze on her. She turned to him, and caught the sneer that lifted one corner of his mouth.

"I never had the chance to order a glass of wine," Azad stated. "And I don't like having a woman talk for me."

Of course, she thought. *The picture of a male chauvinistic pig.* She slid her glass of ice-water toward him. "You're hot enough. Wine will only make you hotter." This made him smile. Her eyes caught a strip of white cardboard dangling from the side of his new tweed jacket. "You forgot to take off the sale tag."

Azad struggled, twisting his ample body around before finding the telltale evidence of a deep discount price tag. In typical manly fashion, he ripped it off and held on to it.

Staring at the bulky, coffee-colored envelope sticking out of his inner pocket, Claire said, "So, you have what I need?"

"Yes." He passed Claire the envelope and watched as Claire slid the contents into her attaché case. "Now, I think we should go through the surveillance footage together," Azad said, raking a hand through his thatch of black Armenian hair. "That way I can fill you in on the more pressing details." He smirked and licked his lips. "And I don't think this is an appropriate place to do that."

Claire watched Azad as trickles of sweat collected on his brow, forming into a big, fat drop. It was like watching a sausage, stuffed in its tight casing, starting to sizzle in a hot pan. His pathetic scheme to seduce her certainly angered her, but she decided to play it through in order to punish him.

Claire smiled and summoned her most sensual voice.

"Where would you suggest?"

"Well, we could go through it in my truck, but maybe I should rent a room," Azad replied, while he used his thumbnail to peel off the yellow price tag sticker, rolling it into a small ball. "It's just…I need to explain some things to you as the video rolls. I'm sure you understand." His rodent eyes dropped to Claire's breasts.

Clearing her throat, Azad got the hint and lifted his eyes to meet hers. "I bet that a lot of women can't help themselves around you." There was a gentle and seductive lift to her voice.

Azad licked the corner of his mouth, "I get by." His eyes greased over and slid back to Claire's bosom.

Claire reached for the butter knife, tilted it, so that the silver caught the light above their table, then beamed it directly into Azad's eyes. He blinked through his stupor. Claire set the knife down and tilted her head to one side. Azad's thirsty gaze gulped every inch of her.

"You like looking at me. Don't you, Azad?" She raised her brows and parted her lips suggestively.

Azad huffed back a laugh. "I could take it or leave it. But I doubt any man would throw you out of bed for eating crackers." He mindlessly ran his index finger along the outside of his water glass, running lines into the condensation. He had black wiry hairs on each of his knuckles, Claire saw; an indication that Azad was a hairy man, and most likely had hairy shoulders.

But he was good, she realized. At some point in Azad's miserable life, he must have come to the conclusion that confidence was key. "And what would we do in that room?" Claire crafted her question deliberately.

"That depends."

She let out a breathy laugh. "Meaning?"

"On whether or not you have what it takes. Just because a strawberry looks ripe doesn't make it sweet."

Yes, Claire thought, *time to punish Azad.* "I have to say, you have this whole sasquatch thing working for you."

Azad raised his phantom unibrow, waiting for Claire to elaborate.

"It's a hairy beast. Big Foot," Claire said.

"Yeah, I know what it is. And I don't like being compared to an animal." Deep frustrated lines grooved his forehead as he waited for her to explain herself.

"Ouch, so touchy." Claire smoothed out the creases in her cream cashmere sweater. Her moves were slow and deliberate. All the while she felt Azad's angry stare roving over her flesh. She peered up at him through her veil of coated lashes, wanting to give him impression that she was possibly submissive.

"I have a confession to make. I have a weakness for hairy men. As I'm sure you already know, my husband's too good-looking, too tall and hairless. What a woman really wants is a short and hairy ape. An ape that will ravage her. Hairy shoulders only add to the animalistic attraction."

With a questioning grimace, Azad had yet to respond. Maybe he regretted waxing his back, Claire mused. "Tell me, are you a hairy beast...or am I just wishful thinking?"

There was a lethargic beat. "No, but it'll grow back."

Claire leaned into the table. He followed her lead and turned a cautious ear to her. "Whatever you do, don't press the big, red button." She eased back into her chair, crossed her legs and left him chewing-over the comment.

"I'm not following you."

Claire dropped the charade. "You tell a person not to press a button and that'll just *make* them want to do it. Reverse psychology. Then there's the double reverse psychology, which would be to ploy someone into thinking you're using reverse psychology. But let's not forget the triple reverse psychology, which would be to trap him or her into thinking you're using double reverse psychology so that he or she will do the opposite. I have to hand it to you Azad," Claire said, while reaching for the menu and opening it. She merely glanced at the selections, while speaking in a passive tone. "You've accepted that you'll never be tall, lean and desirable. So you've managed to use your profession to rope emotionally unstable woman into bed, and to top that off," she said while turning the page, "you've managed to maintain this supreme confidence."

"Listen here—" Azad began, but was interrupted by their waiter. He stood proud before their table, holding a bottle of wine wrapped in an ivory napkin.

"Complimentary," the waiter said. "Our house wine. It's a lovely... " His words trailed off when Claire held her index finger up. She spoke, sparing him another glance, while mulling over the list. She turned the page slowly.

"I asked for eight minutes, not five. Come back in three, and my friend will tell you what he's having. And we'll have to pass on the wine, thank you. I don't drink."

The waiter bowed out gracefully, leaving behind a sexually frustrated man, sporting a month-old goatee and sweating in his tweed coat. Claire could almost feel the raging heat radiating from him.

"As I was saying, what most unattractive people have yet to understand is that confidence is like a muscle: the more you exercise it, the stronger it gets. Quite the affective tool actually. It all comes down to…I believe it—you believe it." Claire fell silent, her eyes narrowing on a particular item, which was listed as one of the main course options.

While capturing her bottom lip between her teeth, Claire peered over the menu, her eyes locking with Azad's. His face was sheathed in a film of sweat. A devilish smile touched her lips. *That's right Fatso, stew in your own chauvinistic juices.*

"You can coat a pork-chop in the tastiest breadcrumbs, serve it in a rich, creamy brandy sauce, and dress it with a sprig of rosemary. But it'll always be just a pig." She closed the menu, set it down, and found herself looking into his face again.

A scowl flashed across those brows of his, anger darkening his brown eyes. He could not conceal his embarrassment, and this satisfied her enormously.

Claire clicked her tongue. "Come now, don't give me that, 'who sat on my Twinkie' look. This is business. I hired you to do a job, and you crossed the line."

Azad spoke through gritted teeth. "I just assumed you weren't getting any."

His words felt like skin caught in a zipper, but Claire kept her gaze level and her face vacant. She'd practiced that look in the mirror; a mask to hide the vulnerability that was feeling for cracks beneath the ice. Azad worked his tongue over his teeth and snorted at the same time. Claire knew that he savored the moment.

What exactly did Azad Portoian have on Jonathon? Who was Jonathon fucking?

Claire charged at him, causing him to flinch. "What shot of stupid do you think I drank?"

Azad pointed his fat finger at her. "It's women like you—"

"—Yes, women like me. I wrote the book on manipulation, Mr. Portoian. And whatever it is you've found on my husband will make no difference to me. Because, as you so eloquently put it," Claire said, glancing at her breasts, as Azad's fingers curled into a tight fist, "no man would throw me out of bed for eating crackers."

Claire stood up and collected her things. Azad stiffened as she leaned over him, allowing her lips to graze his ear. "Whatever you do don't press the big, red button."

She stepped back and pinned the investigator down with her unswerving glare. Azad's gaze swept her face, passing all too briefly over her legs before returning to her eyes.

"Bitch."

Claire let out a victorious laugh. "Yes, and I wrote and re-wrote the book on that too." She lifted her chin and pulled her shoulders back. "And on that lovely note..."

17

The Warm Hands

In the dark office, she felt around for the light switch. The brightness of the bulbs caused the surreal moment to shock her back into reality, and for a instant, she wondered what she was doing. Do I really want to spy on Jonathon? It was like being back in high school when she had first read Hamlet's famous soliloquy: To be, or not to be: that is the question. She stood for a moment, pondering.

Concluding that she had every right to protect what was hers, Claire walked with new energy and purpose to her own office. She sniffed and caught the aroma of pizza. Harvey must be eating his life away again, but too bad for him. Her first priority was to get into her office and download the last month of Jonathon's life onto her computer.

Thirty shiny disks stacked inside a plastic tower appeared ordinary on her organized desk. However, the rest of her life might well depend on what information Azad had been able to uncover about her husband. A month's worth of surveillance footage stared at her, daring her to take the next step.

Holding on to the sliver of hope that her worries were nothing but paranoia, she couldn't ignore the signs. Whether it be the "women's intuition" Esperança had referred to or Jonathon's recent suspicious behavior, she prepared herself for the worst. "What the hell."

Claire inserted the first disk. The grainy video captured Jonathon exiting their home at 7:23 a.m. Azad had trailed him to his office in Manhattan at 8:27 a.m. The film paused and continued at 5:23 p.m., at which time he was followed back into Jersey, where he stopped briefly to pick up a few groceries. At 7:03 p.m., Jonathon pulled into their driveway and disappeared behind the gates.

"Hmm," Claire spoke to the screen, "day one gone and nothing out of the ordinary."

Claire slid her hand into the envelope and pulled out Azad's chronological notes. Surveillance began on a Friday, so that would have been on the first disk. Azad's notes showed that the three following days were just as uneventful as the initial one. But then something caught her attention.

Tuesday was different. Azad's notes reported that at 5:30 p.m., Jonathon left the office and drove to the west side of Manhattan. He parked at a local garage, around 6:21 p.m. and was seen next at 6:30 p.m., going into a local soup kitchen called 'The Warm Hands.' Claire put the pages down and pushed in the disk showing Tuesday's activities. She forwarded the surveillance footage to the 6:30 time.

Her adrenalin spiked as she took in the video. Azad must have been close behind Jonathon at this point, since she could clearly see the familiar back of her husband's coat. Jonathon moved to the back room and emerged again wearing a white apron. Azad's focus on him wavered, and the sounds were muffled. The focus became clear again, and now she saw him. Standing beside him was a dark-haired woman. She was tiny, maybe five foot two or three. Her presence there with her husband stung her.

There they were, working together behind a counter where chicken, mashed potatoes, and other foods abounded in large stainless steel warmers. Jonathon was smiling, happily serving meals and chatting with the bedraggled people who waited their turn in line. He acted as though he'd known them for years. Claire watched the woman with whom he stood. She wished Azad had zoomed in on her more—she couldn't quite size up little Miss Pretty.

For a long and boring ninety minutes, the footage dragged

on this way. She zipped through most of it, waiting for something to actually happen. Nerve-racking though it was, she had to admit that being a covert spectator of her husband's most private activities was exciting, almost like playing God. She observed everything she wanted to about him, and he was none the wiser. Along with the dread of what she might find, came an undeniable thrill.

Finally, Jonathon disappeared behind the door again, and reappeared minus the apron. Azad followed closely behind. At 8:05 p.m., Jonathon made a quick stop at their favorite sushi place and exited with a take-out order. Then he returned to his car and drove out of the parking lot. Azad followed him home.

Claire shook her head. "What the hell is he doing in a soup kitchen?" She recalled Esperança's words. Feeding hungry people was exactly what he'd been doing. But why? She scanned through Azad's notes, stopping at Thursday—once again, Jonathon was observed going into The Warm Hands. Claire sifted through the disks until she found the one that matched the notes. She inserted it.

At 6:45 p.m., Jonathon entered the run-down, crowded soup kitchen. Everything seemed identical to the previous day. Claire yawned, so far finding the film footage a complete waste of her time. It annoyed her watching her husband stoop to conversing with common street bums. The woman he stood beside—she wished Azad had bloody well focused in on her better—who was she? Esperança's haunting words came back to her. Could she be the one? The one he loved secretly? She watched their body language, but nothing gave anything away, not even a nudge.

Claire dived into the notes once more. She highlighted the days Jonathon went into The Warm Hands. It turned out to be every Tuesday and Thursday. This began making sense to her, the sushi, the feeling that he was keeping something from her.

Scanning through the other disks, it angered her to see that there was really nothing different. She'd gone through almost every one, fast-forwarding for a hint of change. She regretted spending almost thirteen thousand dollars with not a shred of evidence to show for it.

Her disappointment soon turned to relief, and she relaxed.

She was sure to sleep soundly tonight.

The final disk was another Thursday. Jonathon came into The Warm Hands at his standard time. He went into the back and came out wearing the usual apron. Claire nearly pitied him for a moment. She couldn't wrap her head around why Jonathon, whom she'd personally trained to operate in a higher social sphere, would want to waste his time in such a dingy place.

Then she saw the woman much more clearly. She entered and joined Jonathon by the serving counter. This time Azad had captured a perfect shot of her face. First, the camera panned in on her smile. Her perfect natural teeth and her dimples made her look fourteen. After pressing 'pause,' Claire studied every angle, every detail of the young woman. Her high cheekbones and perfect olive skin complemented her almond shaped eyes. She envied her gorgeous, dark locks piled high on the top of her head. She was a natural—no dye and no Botox. It was her: the woman Esperança had warned her of—the woman with whom Jonathon was in love. Claire's hands trembled.

Her phone sounded, causing her to jump in her chair. She put Jonathon on speaker. "What?"

He sounded joyously out of breath. "Claire bear, guess who I have sitting in the truck?"

Claire gave her head a shake. She had no patience for playing guessing games. "Who?"

"Hi, Auntie Claire!" Olivia sang in the background.

Jonathon took back the phone. "I've got the kids, remember? We just had pizza and now we're gonna rent some movies and games for the weekend. Any requests?"

Inside her mind Claire yelled, *Fuck!* Claire thought for a moment and then said, "Yeah, whatever you want, but none of those God-awful chick flicks tonight."

Jonathon inhaled to say something else, but Claire terminated the call.

She replayed the footage, in slow motion this time. The young woman whispered something in Jonathon's ear. He bit on his bottom lip and grabbed her hand as lovers do in a moment of fun. She took something from his pocket, and he struggled with her to retrieve it. His arms wrapped around her tiny frame, and he tickled her until she dropped the unknown item.

Whatever it was made no difference to Claire. She understood their body language, and it was obvious that they sought any excuse to play with each other. Jonathon was happy, even ecstatic, doing that thing with his mouth, that thing that turned Claire on—biting on his lip for Nicolette. And she didn't need Esperança to confirm for her that he was in love with this young woman. It made her sick.

The young woman exited for a few seconds, reappearing with a black case too tiny to house a guitar. While the woman took out a violin, the faces on the hungry homeless people eating their dinner began to shine. The sound was distorted and Claire was no expert, but she knew the difference between a beginner and a professional artist. And this woman was truly an artist. Her graceful posture danced with the instrument, swayed with the strings. The hungry people enjoyed the free entertainment along with the free food. When she was finished, they clapped and cheered. Even some who appeared too weak to do so, stood up.

Claire raced through the pages and stopped at the detailed information regarding the young woman's identity: 'Nicolette Joleigh Vasseur, twenty, student at Julliard, born in Montparnasse, Paris, France. At the age of six, she moved to California with parents John and Angela. Prominent people, own a string of hotels and casinos throughout North America, Germany, England, and France. Nicolette has her own condo in Manhattan and has invested in a soup kitchen, registered in her name, titled 'The Warm Hands.'

Claire skipped over the pages of information regarding the many awards Nicolette had won over the years, both abroad and throughout the United States. She was also actively involved in several charities, including organizing summer camps for underprivileged children who had musical talent. Apart from being young, beautiful, and talented, Nicolette was a do-gooder.

Another piece of information attached to Azad's notes irked Claire to the core: a newswire article reported that Jonathon Lockwood had invested two hundred thousand dollars of his own money into The Warm Hands. He was "actively involved in making a difference."

What is he doing? she wondered. This was much worse than

some tawdry affair. He was making a difference in the community and hadn't said anything to her about it. Instead, he chose to humiliate her by spending time with a twenty-year-old, feeding the scum of society. She wished it had been a dirty affair. But this was different. This was real. Claire was in the fight of her life, because Jonathon was clearly in love with a woman twenty-three years Claire's junior. And the other woman was beautiful, inside and out.

On the spot, Claire decided that she would indeed withdraw ten thousand dollars in cash, and pick up a bottle of Bacardi 151. But, rather than buy just one bottle, she'd buy a whole damn case. Meanwhile, she prepared to leave her office and face the bullshit waiting back home.

Tea for Three

ince and Rebecca's children had the TV room looking like a slumber party. Every comforter in the house
was sprawled over the cherry-stained floors. An open
24-ounce bottle of orange pop, plain chips and onion dip, and
a box of partially eaten pizza teetered on the corner of Claire's
imported coffee table. Blasting from the plasma TV screen was
the new video game Jonathon had bought for the twins. Vinny
Junior and Marco loved Uncle Jonathon, but they made a
point to stay away from Aunt Claire. She wasn't cool.

Olivia watched her brothers dueling with one another in a
screen game of violent knife throwing and gun slinging. Wearing her fuzzy pink slippers and matching pink pajamas, she
looked like a tiny princess. Her long, dark tresses collected at
the top of her head like a tiara of curls. "I wanna try now," she
complained to Jonathon. "They've been hogging it all night."

Jonathon laughed and pinched her nose. "That's not funny,"
she said.

"Hey guys," Jonathon said good-naturedly, "why don't you
let your sister have a go?"

The twins heard him, but there was no way they were about
to let Olivia interrupt their game. "She has her tea set. Why
don't you make Uncle J a tea?" Vinny suggested, speaking over
his shoulder while his eyes never left the screen.

"That's a great idea," Jonathon said, trying to encourage Olivia. "Why don't you go get your set, and I'll boil some water."

Olivia jumped at the suggestion. "Okay." She almost fluttered out of the room.

Jonathon stretched his long legs before getting up. "Great suggestion, guys, thanks."

"No problem, Uncle J," Marco replied. "Have one on us."

Jonathon laughed as he got up. His pajama pants gathered around his legs. He smoothed them out and noticed some cheese stuck on the fabric. He peeled it off and walked into the kitchen. He loved the feel of the house, the sounds of the children laughing, the video game echoing through the usually quiet house. He didn't even mind that the cheese stuck to his clothes. It was a great night. He only wished Claire were there to enjoy this with him. He turned on the water and washed the dried-out cheese down the drain.

Reaching for the kettle, he checked the time. It was late, past ten. *Where is she?* he wondered. He filled up the kettle with water and plugged it in. Jonathon looked through the tea cupboard above the stove. There wasn't much choice, either green tea or chamomile. He kicked himself for having forgotten to pick up hot chocolate and marshmallows. Kids loved those kinds of things. He considered calling Claire and asking her to pick some up on her way home, but decided against it.

The pizza and pop he'd ordered was enough. "Chamomile it is," he said aloud.

Olivia sauntered into the kitchen, balancing a tiny porcelain tea set on a tray.

She looked adorable, Jonathon noted, and he helped her place the tray on the table. He chuckled and thought what a lucky guy Vince was to have children. "The water's almost ready," he explained to her.

Olivia had an infectious giggle that made Jonathon smile. She passed him the teapot. "You can't fill it over the line," she cautioned him, "and there has to be a big person to do it."

He carried the pot over to the counter. "This line, right?" He pointed to the embossed grid.

Skipping over to the counter to check for herself, Olivia said, "Yup, that line."

Jonathon poured the water and popped in the herbal tea. "How about some cookies?"

Olivia nodded.

Opening the grocery bag, he pulled out Olivia's favorite graham cookies. "I'll get a plate, and you take a seat. Okay?" Jonathon guided her as he carried the items to the table. He loved every moment with her. He hid his laughter, though not the smirk on his face, as he watched Olivia take a napkin from the table and place it carefully onto her lap.

"A little lady shouldn't make a mess."

He sat opposite her and followed her cue. "Well, neither should an uncle."

Like a dark shadow, Claire appeared in the kitchen. Jonathon surmised by the sour look on her face that she wasn't amused.

A smile minus two front teeth, brightened Olivia's eyes when she saw Claire. "Want some tea, Auntie Claire?"

Claire put down her purse and walked over to the sink. She used the antibacterial soap and scrubbed her hands vigorously.

Jonathon and Olivia exchanged looks as if to say, 'we're in for it.' Claire conducted her usual one-minute scrub and patted her hands dry on a paper towel.

"Sure, I'm game," Claire answered, as though false enthusiasm was being wrung from her.

Standing up, Jonathon pulled out a chair for her, and Claire sat. Then he returned to his seat, his mind filled with wonder over what might be inside hers.

Placing a napkin on her lap, Claire did her best to remain collected, but what she really wanted to do, was flip the entire table over.

"Ladies first." Olivia filled Claire's tiny cup.

Claire watched her every move. If she weren't so angry over Nicolette, she would have enjoyed the moment with her niece. Judging by her tea set, their little 'talk' the other day had made an impression on her.

"Now Uncle Jonathon," she sang, as she filled his.

"What about you?" Jonathon teased.

Olivia giggled, "I forgot me."

"Allow me." Jonathon took the teapot and filled her cup.

Claire watched Jonathon dote on her niece. Her mind

worked in layers again, filling her head with the images of him and Nicolette. It struck Claire that as a child, Nicolette could have been Olivia. They had a remarkably similar appearance. Her adrenalin rose to the crown of her head. Her scalp burned. Her anger peaked. *She's twenty! What the fuck is he doing?* Watching Jonathon and Olivia drove her to the edge. Claire wanted to seize the teapot and smash it against the side of his head.

"You wanna cookie, Auntie Claire?" Olivia moved the plate toward Claire and accidentally knocked over her aunt's teacup.

Tea spilled onto Claire's lap, and her anger cracked. "You stupid shit! Why can't you be more careful?"

"What's wrong with you?" Jonathon shouted over the table.

In lieu of a reply, Claire jumped out of her chair, snatched her purse, and walked quickly out of the kitchen.

Jonathon walked over to Olivia and put his arm around her. Tears sputtered down her rosy cheeks. "It's okay, sweetie, it's not your fault."

She cried into his neck. "I ruined the party."

"You didn't ruin anything. I'm still here. You've got me, right?"

Olivia sniffled.

Jonathon took the napkin from her lap and held it over her nose. "Here, blow." After a moment he asked, "Better?"

"Auntie Claire said shit," she reminded him.

"But we don't use that word, right?" he asked, sweetness in his voice.

Olivia nodded her head.

"Let's finish our party, okay?"

Olivia smiled feebly, and he gently kissed her forehead.

Claire sat in her den watching the same section of the surveillance footage on her computer. She played it over and over again, like one would a riveting movie scene. She couldn't decipher the words spoken between Jonathon and Nicolette, but she recognized that the two had developed a comfortable relationship. His body language said *free and easy* compared to how he was when he was with Claire. His shoulders weren't tense, and his posture resembled that of a college student hanging out with a sorority girl as opposed to a man who handled millions of dollars for important clients. She studied Nicolette's face again. In addition to her obvious beauty, she detected another important piece of the puzzle. Nicolette had a serious, mature look for her age. Of course, she'd had a prosperous upbringing, probably groomed from the womb to achieve greatness.

Jonathon entered the den. He walked up to her desk and faced her. "We need to talk."

"Later—" Claire spared him a glance. "—I'm busy right now." Her eyes focused on Nicolette.

Jonathon sat down across from her. "I'll wait."

"Fine." She queued up the footage to the beginning. It gave her a demented sense of power to do that.

He waited almost a full ten minutes before saying, "Is whatever you're doing all that important right now?"

Claire met his eyes. "I'll say it is."

"May I see?" Jonathon leaned over to catch a quick glimpse of the computer screen.

Claire enjoyed the game of cat and mouse. She shut off the screen just in time.

"What were you looking at?"

"I'm looking into a few charities online." Claire's tone was smooth. "So, do you have any suggestions?"

Jonathon avoided eye contact with her. "How would I know?"

Claire made a mental note of his response. He avoided eye contact when he was guilty of something. She'd never had such a problem. Before getting married, she wouldn't think twice about going to bed with a man, and an hour or two later having tea with his wife. She looked at her husband and thought, *What a weakling he is*. Finally, she said to him, "So talk."

"It's what you did to Olivia. That was terrible, Claire." Jonathon shook his head like her father used to when he was disappointed in her. "I can't believe you said that to her."

His mimicking an authority figure threw Claire into another boiling rage. She wanted to scream at him, tell him what she knew, and that Olivia had simply been in the line of fire. "I think you need to address your own issues first. I'm the one who has reason to be disappointed. Not you."

Claire's disks fell from her bag and slid like dominoes. She caught the thirty disks, and pushed them back in.

Looking down, confusion took hold of his face, though he didn't raise an eyebrow about the disks.

"Do you think that it's normal for a grown man to like young girls so much?"

Jonathon lifted his eyes to meet hers and hoped that what she had just uttered was an appalling joke. He blinked once, twice. "How can you..." His voice cracked then. He swallowed and forged on, "What exactly are you saying?"

"I'm saying I have to wonder why you're so interested in Olivia. Maybe you have a thing for young girls." Embarrassment colored his face, intensifying the blue in his eyes. She'd never seen him this way and it made her nervous.

"How can you even think that? Wh-what..." Jonathon said on a stuttered breath. "I would never..." His attempt to speak was stopped by an intense pain, and it took everything in him not tear up. He pressed his lips together and turned away from her.

Claire watched Jonathon struggle and offered no way out. She couldn't say what she really wanted to say, the truth of the matter. Instead, she worked her magic and created a far worse situation for him. Besides, Claire felt it was pointless in breathing life into the situation with Nicolette and confronting him on it when she planned to bury her.

She picked up her bag of disks and almost sashayed to the door.

Jonathon remained seated, frozen, as Claire slammed the door behind her.

19

Till Death do Us Part

Claire maneuvered her Mercedes 600 SL aggressively into Castle Hill, the Bronx. There would be no repeat of last time. A case of Bacardi 151 rum rested on the passenger floor, while on the seat was an envelope containing a picture of Nicolette and ten thousand dollars in crisp bills. Entering Esperança's neighborhood, Claire slowed down and quickly caught her complexion in the rear-view mirror. Her eyes looked tired, and deep circles showed through her makeup. Jonathon wasn't speaking to her; it had been two days since their blow up.

She was worried. Never before had they argued to the extreme of sleeping in separate rooms. Even when he'd had reasons to be angry with her in the past, it had never taken her long to make him cave in.

Claire parked her car, got out and walked to the passenger side. She tucked the envelope into her shirt then began struggling with the box of rum.

The man Esperança had called Chino stepped behind her. "Hey, Red, want some help with that?"

"Sure," Claire answered with authority. She was part of the club now, and these guys were nothing more than Esperança's little lackeys.

She followed behind him up the long steps. "That's good there." Claire pointed to a spot on the floor next to the door. As he set the box down, she handed him a bottle from it. "Watch the car for me?"

Chino opened the bottle and took a big sip. "Good lookin' out Red." Wholly satisfied with his payment, he vanished down the stairs, taking them two at a time.

The place was still crappy of course, but it was not nearly so creepy. In a way it had turned itself into a place of refuge for Claire. She was a few minutes early, and she noted through the slightly ajar door that Esperança had company. I wonder what's going on in there? A man spoke softly, and the tone of his voice was soothing. Claire slid silently beyond the door and stood unseen, just inside, so she could eavesdrop more closely. It fascinated her to watch the old woman at work.

Esperança was wearing a neon-yellow T-shirt displaying a happy face again, but this time the words read: SIT ON A HAPPY FACE. Claire's dirty mind went there, and she visualized Esperança squatting over the man sitting across from her. Claire bit gently on her lower lip to prevent herself from bursting into laughter, but when Esperança broke into hilarity of her own, it made Claire freeze. Esperança's sinister laugh stirred movement in the wiry cage placed a few feet from the entrance. Claire figured that they were chickens used as props for voodoo. Esperança was still amused, but the man was silent.

What's so damn funny? Claire thought, edging in a little closer, and glimpsing the laughter on Esperança's face. Could the man sitting across from the voodoo priestess have put her in this great disposition? Unlike Esperança, the man wore a glower: and he seemed irritated. But he had great tastes. He wore a stylish gray suit with crisp white collars. A Rolex watch hung loosely on his wrist, and she noted that his hands were manicured. Though not as beautiful as Jonathon, he came close. In the middle of the table, under a slender black candle, was a picture. A gold ring had been placed around the wax of the candle which represented a finger. The flame flickered high, and then dropped to a small sparkle. It was as though the flame were alive and attentive to them. Claire strained to hear.

Holding a small glass jar of yellow oil in her hand, the voodoo priestess said, "You rub this on her tires, even around the bumper."

"What if she washes the car?" the man asked.

"She's not going to wash the car, don't be stupid!" Into the small dancing flame her eyes narrowed, seeking mystical information.

The man fidgeted in his seat. "What do you see?"

As Esperança stared at the glowing quiver, it rose three inches. Her tone was calm. "Just how sure are you about him?"

"Very sure." The man became eager. "Why? What is it?"

She put her hand up, stopping him from speaking, for she saw something. Looking toward her left, she studied the shadows on her wall. "Are you certain he's finished with his wife?"

The question surprised Claire, who kept herself invisible, but it pushed the man into a state of near panic. "Why? Does he still fuck her?"

Esperança turned to face him, smiling menacingly. "Sometimes, but you should have taken care of that first, before deciding to kill your wife."

"I shouldn't have to manipulate his feelings for me," the man said. "I already told you how he feels about me."

Nervously, the man scratched his arms. He looked crazed. Engrossed in the drama, Claire didn't budge. She wondered how none of this bothered her or why she didn't rush right out of there. Dealing with this type of lunatic fringe was monstrously appalling, but the scene also drew her in.

"What about that shit I did in Brazil, that's only going to take care of my wife right?" His tune seemed to shift. It appeared to Claire that he was toying with the idea that his lover really did need some manipulating after all.

"That's right," Esperança said.

The man kept fidgeting, unable to sit still. "And you're sure this will work?"

She blew out the candle and replaced it with a white one. She was quiet while lighting the new candle and pulling his wedding ring off the black one. "The mission has already started. Once you're ready to complete the task, tell the angels what you want them to do for you. Write the words on the candle and light it. Do it in your basement—don't blow it out."

The man accepted the candle and held it with caution, as if it were a loaded gun, then gently placed it on the floor. "Too bad we couldn't get our wives together in the car." He'd spoken these words off the top of his head.

She raised her brows and let out a soft chuckle. "Good idea. Do they ever drive together?"

He paused, and then he nodded. "They shop on Saturdays."

"And what about the kids?" Esperança reminded him. Claire was gob smacked; she treated the matter as if coordinating a surprise birthday party.

The man shivered. "Christ, I forgot about that." He picked dried wax from the table and thought for a moment before speaking again. "Fuck it, they'll be better off dead anyway. More time for me and Cameron, less distraction."

"Yes," Esperança said, staring the man down. "Just kill them all, right?"

Claire understood clearly what was going on. The man had hired Esperança to kill his wife and the wife of his male lover; the women were friends. But even more insane was the idea of killing both their families. *How bizarre.* Yes, bizarre and completely amazing: to be able to kill someone without having to pull a trigger, without having to hire a hit man. The idea of having such control sent a warm thrill circulating through her body. She suddenly felt thirsty.

"Six birds with one stone," Esperança spoke into the tall, even flame.

The man nodded, still scratching away at his arms. Esperança reached over, grabbed a firm hold of the man's right arm, and slammed his hand flat on the table, palm up.

"Hey, what the hell…" the man said, then, for some reason, fell instantly silent.

Claire edged even closer and stood just behind a shipping barrel, where she had a full view of what was going on. Esperança and the man stared silently across the table at one another; the flame stretched tall enough so that Claire could clearly see that the man was spellbound. His eyes were heavy and his mouth hung open. The silence in the room prolonged into minutes, and drool began to dribble from his lip. Esperança grabbed a small knife and sliced it into the muscle of the man's hand, causing blood to ooze from the incision. But the man didn't draw back. He continued to stare across the table, unable to offer more than a few words in a broken whisper.

"I'm a bad husband, aren't I?"

"You're a bad father, too," Esperança said. "A change of plans, I want you to rub your palms together, nice and slow."

Claire watched the man obey Esperança, rubbing his own blood into his palms. He held up his bloody hands, a faraway expression in his eyes.

"I got blood on my hands," he whispered.

Esperança grinned with those perfect teeth. "Yes, you do... your own blood." She slid his wedding ring to him. "Put your ring back on, you depraved source of disease."

The man nodded. "Till death do us part?"

"That's right, till death. You're a very disgusting man whose children and wife will never know just how disgusting you really are. Now get out of my sight; go outside and stand at the side of the road and make like road kill," Esperança ordered.

He nodded, stood up, and walked swiftly to the door, leaving without closing it.

Esperança exhaled and stretched her hands around her neck. "Did you enjoy the show?" she asked dimly. "You're a dirty girl," she said in her cocky tone, giving Claire a sidelong glance. "Do you really think fuck-head would be happy with me squatting over his face?"

Edging in from the shadows, Claire said with a shrug, "You obviously found it entertaining."

"Entertaining? Sure," Esperança admitted. "But I say that you'll like this better." She pushed her chair out with the back of her legs, stood up, and sauntered over to the window. Claire joined her and stood just a few feet away, wondering what she was looking at.

In the street below, Claire spotted the man, who stood motionless between two cars. Esperança breathed her hot breath against the window, causing it to film up. "Some souls aren't savable," Esperança said, tracing her finger on the window. And when she moved it, the man moved too, taking two small steps. Again, Esperança pulled her finger an inch or so against the glass, and again the man took another two small steps. "Watch this," Esperança whispered.

She pulled her finger forward, moving the man into the busy

street like a puppet, and pulled her finger back, allowing the man to dodge a car. "Witnesses will say that he was crazy, a nut job, who looked suicidal," Esperança added, and then let out a hoarse laugh, with her finger still pressed against the glass.

"In about fifteen seconds, a tow truck will be going south, and you, my friend, will walk right into it." Esperança traced her finger hastily and dragged it forward. Just below, the man pushed himself recklessly into the oncoming truck. Claire couldn't move. She stared down at the commotion below, as awestruck as she was afraid.

The tow truck clipped the man's arm, spinning him into the northbound traffic, where another SUV smacked directly into him. The SUV skidded out and pulled up along the sidewalk, dragging the man's body beneath it. A small group of people gathered, including Chino, who stood with his gang of hoodlums. He looked directly up into the window, and then disappeared into an alley, taking his gang with him. Several more spectators from around the area soon gathered to watch as the crumpled and twitching body of the good-looking man bled to death in a pile of debris and shattered glass.

"I couldn't give two rat's titties, if someone's a fudge-packer or a carpet-muncher," Esperança said, still in her calm and detached tone. "But what kinda man, would want to kill his wife and kids?"

Following a few minutes of staring at the uproar outside, she turned to Claire and said, "Bring me my present. I need a drink after that shit."

20

A Man's Heart

laire placed a bottle of rum on the table and sat across from Esperança, who replaced the white candle with a thin red one. She wiped up some of the man's blood from the table with an old rag. "Your ring," she commanded.

Claire removed her ring and passed it over to Esperança, who slid it down the candle and lit the wick. The flame moved in quick rhythmic bounces before steadying.

Esperança cleared her throat. "You and your husband have been fighting."

"Yes," Claire said, her mind in a fog.

"Pass me the picture of her."

Claire removed the money from the envelope and was shocked by the old woman's wrath.

"Not that. Her picture! Don't pay until I say." Handing her the photograph of Nicolette, Claire waited opposite the old woman and did her best to remain quiet. She couldn't help but think of the man who lay dead in the street. Sounds of a siren wailed outside, and bright red lights flickered through the window. They were scraping up the remains of the man who wore the tasteful gray suit and once crisp, white collars. What made Esperança decide not to kill the wives and children? She seemed so protective over them and almost took it personally. It would have surprised her less had Esperança hacked off the man's nutsack and used it as a purse. She caught the cutting glare of the old woman.

"Will you please shut up?"

"Sorry," Claire said, lowering her head toward Nicolette's picture. The waiting was driving her mad.

Esperança kept her focus on the image. The quality was poor but it didn't matter. She dipped the corner of the photo into the flame. Fire tore through Nicolette's face until it became ashes.

"He's made his decision," said Esperança, after a few seconds had passed. "He's chosen her. And he plans to tell her."

The sound of Claire's own heartbeat filled her ears. "No, did—"

"They haven't fucked," Esperança interrupted, "just kissed." This small detail itself was too much for Claire, and she closed her eyes.

"You have a big mouth," Esperança spoke, while shaking her head in disgust. "He would never hurt a child."

Claire opened her eyes wide and took in a deep, sad breath. "I know," she said on the exhale.

"But he doesn't know you know that. Anyway, we've got work to do. And tonight she's gone. History," Esperança reassured her. "Are you ready?"

Claire had noticed a cage sitting along the back wall while she had been hiding. She pointed at it. "Will this involve those… chickens?"

Esperança waddled away from the table and returned with a cage. She placed it on the table.

Claire looked between the skinny wires at the birds. "Pigeons?"

Esperança held a knife over the flame. "Pigeons, doves, they're both one and the same. But you do know why they use doves at weddings?"

"It's symbolic," Claire offered, "of love."

She shook her head. "More than love. When these birds find one another, they mate for life. The male feeds her when she's nesting. That's something, isn't it?"

Claire nodded.

The voodoo priestess pointed to the table. "You see that small slip of paper?"

"Yes."

"Grab the pen and write exactly this: 'I beg you, King Lucifer, make Jonathon,' and write your full last name, 'love only Claire blah, blah, blah.'"

With pen in hand, Claire paused, the slip of paper still blank. "King Lucifer?" she asked, making sure.

"Yes, King Lucifer, who the hell did you expect, Cupid? That or you can change your mind about the whole thing," Esperança explained, in a measured tone.

Without further delay, Claire wrote the words on the paper.

"Now, take that pin and poke it into the tip of your finger," Esperança directed.

"I'm not pricking my finger with that."

"Why...I suppose you have something better?" Esperança snapped. "You want Satan to help you; he'll need your blood, the essence of you."

Opening her purse, Claire pulled out an emergency needle and thread kit. "I'll use this."

"Hurry up! I can't sit here all day," Esperança urged, slapping her hand several times on the edge of the table.

Carefully removing a shiny needle, Claire applied one of her disinfectant wipes before pricking her finger with it.

Esperança rolled her eyes. "Now, let a drop fall on the slip of paper."

Obediently, Claire did so and asked hopefully, "Is that all?"

"Take the clear tape, and stick it onto the back of it," Esperança ordered, overseeing that Claire followed her instructions thoroughly. "You remember what I said about doves?" Esperança questioned her, once she was done.

Claire nodded "They show more loyalty than humans. They can't live without each other."

Esperança reached into the cage, and removed one of the doves. "The male, he cannot live without his heart." Esperança pointed to a small oil jar. "Open," she ordered.

After opening the jar, Claire waited for another command. "Rub some of the oil onto your chest, over your heart."

Claire looked down at her chest wondering if the oil would ruin her silk bra.

"Now!" Esperança said, pounding the table with her fist.

"Okay, okay," said Claire, inhaling the odorless oil. She took a few dabs of it, pulled her hand under her shirt, and massaged it over her breast. Riding the 'Esperança' roller coaster was beginning to make her dizzy. *So moody*, Claire thought.

"Now, his turn," Esperança said, holding the docile bird in her hands. "Rub it against his chest, and while you do, think of your hearts beating as one. Two hearts, one beat…two hearts, one beat. Do it. Now."

Relieved that Esperança at least held the bird for her, Claire gently rubbed the oil onto the chest of the male dove. His feathers felt soft and warm beneath the tips of her fingers. All the while, he remained calm in the old woman's grasp.

"Say what I say: 'This is Jonathon, my husband, the man I want. He must love only me. Two hearts, one beat; two hearts, one beat.' Say it!"

Hesitantly, Claire repeated the words in something akin to a whisper.

"Say it louder, with everything in you. You must believe and feel it! If you don't, how is Satan supposed to!"

As loudly as she could, Claire affirmed, "This is Jonathon, my husband, the man I want. He must love only me. Two hearts, one beat; two hearts, one beat."

Satisfied, Esperança pointed to the strip of paper. "Now, take the words you wrote on the tape and wrap it around his ankle. Make sure it's on tight."

"Are you sure?"

Claire was wearing down the old woman's patience. "You want this to work? Do as I tell you, now!" Esperança ordered.

After three feeble and failed attempts, Claire finally managed to tape the message onto the bird.

Esperança stepped toward the window, the dove in her hand. "Open the window."

In the street below, a crew was sweeping the remaining debris, and the handsome man was gone. Claire did as she was told, and cold air rushed into the hot room.

The dove stirred in the hands of the voodoo priestess. "Find your heart, Jonathon Lockwood," Esperança said. She let go of the dove, and it flew out the window soaring into the February wind.

"That's it?" Claire asked, hopefully.

"Not even close." Pointing at the table again, the priestess commanded Claire to sit. "Remember what I told you about a man's heart?"

"He can't live without it?"

Esperança smiled and removed the female dove from its cage. "This bird is you, and what you have he can't live without. He'll fly and search, look all over, until he finds it. And he's not gonna find it anywhere else but in you."

Absolute fear prevented Claire from speaking. Staring into Esperança's bottomless eyes, she felt as if she was falling into them, being sucked into a void. "I feel dizzy," Claire whispered, watching the scene in slow motion.

"I'm going to cut her heart out, and you're going to swallow it," Esperança explained. "Just a tiny, bleeding heart…no bigger than the tip of your pinky." Ash coated the sharp edge of the knife that Esperança clutched by its handle. She held the dove's head, kissed it, and said, "Sorry about this, little bird," cutting the knife into her chest. Again, blood spattered all over the table.

Blood, Claire thought. So much blood for something so small. The bird didn't make a sound. In fact, all she saw was blood. No bird, no feathers, just Esperança's hand that reached across the table.

"Eat it!" Esperança screamed. Claire didn't make a move. "Quick, while there's still time!"

Claire held the tiny heart in the palm of her hand and then forced it into her mouth. It felt warm and tasted like copper.

"Swallow!" Esperança ordered. "Do it! You've come this far. If you think this is hard, you may as well quit now!"

Claire's cheeks ballooned. As she swallowed, a sickening smell filled her nostrils. She wanted to retch.

"Don't throw it up! It'll ruin everything. Keep it down! Patience? Patience? Where are you? Bring juice…quick."

"Yes, Grandma," said a beautiful voice behind the beaded curtain.

The nightmarish experience was far from over for Claire. She was bent over in the chair, quivering, with her eyes shut.

The beads swayed as Patience passed through them. She

entered slowly and finally passed a glass of orange juice to her grandmother's redheaded client.

Still unable to look up, Claire grabbed the glass, drank from it, and swallowed. She could swear that the dove's heart fluttered all the way down her throat and into her stomach, but she managed to keep it down. She shuddered, on the verge of tears.

Patience lovingly stroked Claire's hair in an attempt to comfort the upset woman.

Trying to regain control of her mind, Claire opened her eyes and turned to thank the girl. Instead, she screamed in horror. The glass in her hand dropped to the floor but did not break.

A sideshow freak, Patience breathed heavily and her large body matched her gigantic head. Bald areas on her scalp raised in bumps, while the rest of the scalp was covered with weak strands of brown hair. She didn't seem affected by Claire's terrified reaction. In fact, she smiled through her cleft palate and yellowed teeth.

"Go," Esperança roared in laughter. "Go, before you scare the pretty lady away."

But Patience looked at Claire in a strange, compassionate manner.

"I said go!" Esperança shooed her away. "She'll be fine."

Patience moved in an awkward shuffle, her left leg swollen to three times the size of her right leg.

Claire's head returned to hide between her legs. "She's gone now," the old woman coaxed her.

Peeking up at the voodoo priestess, Claire asked in a whisper, "What happened to her?"

Esperança's face turned deadly serious. "Nothing happened."

Claire sat dumbfounded. This was too much revulsion for her to endure. The insanity spun rapidly moving circles in her head. She tried to piece together the puzzle of Patience, as if analyzing her appearance might bring a semblance of order. To have to look in the mirror and see that face day in and day out was unthinkable. Claire felt a rush of relief when she compared her own beauty to the monster she'd just seen. *Elephant man… She'd be better off dead.*

"Enough!" Esperança screamed, clearing everything, including the lit red candle, off of the table in one sweep of her arm. "You've said enough!" In the darkness, the only light came from outside of the tiny apartment window, and the candle's wax left a dotted red trail along the floor. Esperança reached over by her feet and felt around for the matchbox. She slapped it onto the table, locking eyes with Claire as she sat down again, and pulled up a new ivory candle.

Glaring across the table at the redheaded bitch, she licked the stem before lighting it with a match. A part of her wanted to blow the flame toward her and set her hair and face on fire. *Those who feel, know.*

The flame caught the rage in Esperança's eyes, but it also captured a noticeable sadness. Claire had forgotten to keep her thoughts on other things, and now Esperança's ability to read minds had shown itself again.

The bitter silence stretched long enough, until Claire couldn't take it anymore. She shook her head and said defensively, "What do you expect from people? It's a natural response. Look at her! I mean, shit, with all the money you make you'd think you'd do something for her."

The old woman smiled with a wickedness that made Claire wish she hadn't said a word. "She's very beautiful on the in-side." Esperança leaned into the table. "Did you ever wonder what you look like on the inside? It makes you feel so good to see how ugly my granddaughter is, doesn't it?"

Knowing she couldn't deny the truth of her thoughts, Claire swallowed hard. "In a way…it makes me feel even more beautiful. I feel good about myself. But I think that's only natural." Claire flinched, awaiting the response of the voodoo priestess.

"Yes, you feel good," Esperança responded, in a condescending tone. "What if I told you that, on the inside, you look much worse than Patience?" Esperança picked a few ashes from Nicolette's picture, placed them in the palm of her hand, and blew them into Claire's face. "Not like Nicolette, who is beautiful inside and out. If you don't watch yourself, I might undo the spell. Then she can have your husband."

Claire used her fingers to gently sweep the photo ashes from her face. "I didn't mean anything by it. I'm sorry. Sometimes I say stupid things."

Reaching for the rum bottle, Esperança's mood lightened. "Sometimes?" She took a long sip, sat down, and nodded. "Even if I did offer to pay for an operation to make her beautiful on the outside, she wouldn't let me. She loves herself the way she is." In a disappointed tone, she sighed, "Says it's the way God created her," and took another sip of rum.

All this greatly confused Claire. Worshiping Satan and God in the same house? It made no sense to her.

The alcohol soon sent Esperança drifting to a different place; her tone was gentler. She spoke more about her granddaughter. "She teaches at a school for the blind, connected to a church in Harlem." Esperança still had that peculiar look in her eyes. She spoke with such admiration and pride.

"The children there adore her…they love her." Staring into her lap, she went on. "They paint pictures for her. She has them everywhere, all over her room." After a few seconds, Esperança shook her head as if she'd indulged in too much mushiness for one day. "They're just sloppy pictures, messy paints. No big deal."

Claire decided it was best not to say anything.

"Anyway," Esperança focused her attention on her client, "tonight you will have him back, and after, we'll work on the baby."

In silence, Claire nodded, her eyes following the burning flame that rose four inches and then dropped to a mere flicker. She looked at Esperança, whose weary glare looked glassy. Esperança's thin lips barely moved as she whispered, "It's time to prepare for Brazil."

"What are you talking about? Who's going to Brazil?" Claire recalled what the dead man said. He had also alluded to a trip he'd made to Brazil.

Esperança's face took on a trance-like expression. She said nothing for a long while, and trouble shot through her physic tone. Finally, she spoke, her brows pinched together. "There are other reasons you can't conceive. I can't do for you here what needs to be done."

Claire leaned into the table. "What is it? What do I need to do?"

Shaking her head and holding a hand up for Claire to stop

talking, the voodoo priestess listened intently to instructions from the other side. She maintained eye contact with her client the whole time. "There's a force stopping the commencement."

"Commencement?"

"The conception," Esperança clarified. "You had an abortion a long time ago…the force needs to be removed from inside of you. It's the only way. I told you, you want Satan's help, you better be prepared."

The room became ice-cold. Claire tugged her coat up around her neck and trembled. She awaited further explanation, but the old woman focused on the connecting worlds.

After several minutes of raspy breathing, Esperança looked up, alert, having severed communication with the other world. "So, tell me about the man who wants to kill himself?"

The question took a moment to penetrate in Claire's mind. "What man who wants to kill himself? And what does that have to do with my conceiving or not?"

"The man you work with, the man who's losing everything."

Claire gasped. "You mean Harvey?"

"If he loses, so do you…right?"

"That's true." Claire was thankful the discussion had shifted to something other than some creepy 'force' that was stuck in her womb.

Esperança rose from her seat and began searching the floor for the red candle, which had Claire's ring placed around it. She sat back down and passed it to Claire.

"Thanks." Claire placed the ring back onto her finger. She watched as Esperança selected another wooden match. She lit it, allowing it to burn through, then turned it over, burning the other side as well. Clearly, this weird habit of lighting matches calmed her.

"Bring me the names of the woman and man. I'll get rid of them," Esperança said crushing the burnt matchstick in between her fingers.

"What woman and man?"

"Your boss will know," Esperança explained. "Get him to write down their names, and bring them to me. I'll need their info to complete the task."

A strange, enticing energy surged through Claire's receptive body. "And what will I owe you for that?"

Drifting off momentarily, the voodoo priestess was apparently listening to someone or something else. She smirked and shook her head. "Nothing."

Nothing? Claire thought, skeptically.

Esperança read Claire's mind. "For the conception, you pay. One hundred thousand in US dollars." She walked from the table to the shelf, and in the dark, she felt around for a pen and piece of paper.

Claire watched as the old woman wrote something and then walked back to her. "You'll wire the money there. You know why it's an off-shore account. You're a smart financial lady, right?"

Claire sat silently reading the account information before setting the slip of paper on fire.

Esperança smirked. "I almost forgot, your photographic memory."

"It's served me well over the years, made me a lot of money. That's why I have to ask."

"Ask away," Esperança challenged.

"Why not ask me for a million? You know how much I have, and I'm desperate enough to pay it." She immediately regretted opening her mouth. What if the voodoo priestess suddenly changed tactics and demanded an amount far beyond a million? She could do so, and Claire would obviously pay. This could be the beginning of her ruin. But Esperança's answer surprised her.

"Simple. I can only charge you what I'm authorized to… what I'm instructed to charge you."

Perplexed, Claire pressed harder. "But why just a hundred thousand. It doesn't make any sense." For a moment, she became her strong-willed self again. "I won't wire you a dime until you give me a proper answer."

Esperança smiled and gave a lax shrug. "Money and power are Satan's tool. But money alone has no value to Satan. It's the actions, the motivation behind the money that empowers him—and his cause."

Not sure how to respond, Claire waited with her arms folded. It still made no sense. To get rid of Nicolette, the fee was ten thousand, for the conception, a shocking one hundred thousand. "What, Satan just throws random numbers around?"

"Think about it. Satan needs souls like me to build his army, to spread his word. He would rather throw in a freebie now and then, than to lose a soldier because of a few dollars," Esperança clarified.

Understanding dawned in Claire. "So this is about Satan building an army and rewarding us with favors to do so."

Esperança narrowed her black eyes on Claire. "That's right, to see to it that the souls on earth, stained by the Grace of God, switch allegiances, and if they don't, to send them back where they came from. Satan's claiming his world and using people like you to do so."

Claire liked where this was going. "What about Juan Ramirez, the mobster you helped to get off for murder?" Claire asked, thinking back to Cynthia, the brilliant lawyer she saw leaving Esperança's apartment awhile back. "Was he working for Satan as well? Is he killing God's loyal, the stained souls?"

"Stained souls get caught up in the line of fire. But for the most part, people like Juan have their own set of principles. They kill each other. Business is business. It's his sin that spreads into the world like cancer."

Claire was intrigued by this intellectual side of Esperança. She uncrossed and re-crossed her legs. "Care to elaborate."

"I met Juan Ramirez, eight years ago through Cynthia. You'd be surprised to know that he has a degree in marine engineering."

"That is surprising."

"Over twenty years ago, he became one of the most feared and respected Columbian drug lords, who started his entire empire when he designed a custom-made drug sub. A narco-submarine they call it. A vessel used to transport cocaine from Columbia to Mexico, which was then smuggled into the United States. After that, he was smuggling guns into the country and many, many other naughty things. Every time Juan comes to me for help, he surrenders one of his sins in exchange. For the state's witness, the exchange was his prostitution ring."

"You mean as a trade. But why not just pay you?"

"He pays Cynthia, but that's the easy part. A sacrifice is only a sacrifice when it hurts. To give up something that you want the most. For a man like Juan, his money and power is everything."

"And the state's witness—"

"—Was an asshole that the world won't miss. Trust me and don't ask."

Claire wasn't budging. "But this makes no sense what you're doing. It makes you a charlatan."

"One day, I may arrange to have Juan Ramirez killed off, but for now, he's been very useful," Esperança said. "And a fake you say, I would rethink my comments if I were you."

"What I mean is that you obviously have a connection with the devil, yet you use it against him. You're kind of a hypocrite."

"Or maybe I'm just using one hand to wash the other, like fighting demons with demons," Esperança counteracted.

"And the two wives you should have killed?" Claire reminded Esperança with a smirk. "What if you pulled that off, what hand would you have been washing to help the other?"

"God had a place for them." Esperança's voice fell to a whisper. "The place where good people go…It just would have occurred a little faster. Like your mother. She was a loyal servant of God. She had a place waiting for her in heaven. But the circumstances, like her drinking and the snow, just sped things along."

Claire had a wounded look in her eyes. Esperança examined her from across the table. "Sorry," Esperança added with sarcasm, "sometimes I say stupid things." She reached onto the floor and handed Claire the black candle that had belonged to the man who had just died. "Take this home…etch the words into the candle's wax. Let the fallen angels know what you want, in order to help your boss," Esperança explained. "And don't hold back, because the world won't miss them."

"Light it in my basement, and don't blow it out," Claire finished the instructions. "But isn't this candle meant for his benefit?"

"The angels owe me a favor…the man paid his dues in Brazil. Let's just say that this is his way of paying it forward." Esperança picked up her bottle, took a slow swig, and set the bottle down hard, causing Claire to flinch. "And by the way, don't you ever question my work. You want to open up Pandora's Box, you better be prepared for what's inside."

Claire took heed in her warning and simply nodded.

"Because the next time you call me a hypocrite, I'll release the little blue tit bird from its box and send it your way," Esperança threatened. "And you know exactly what I'm talking about."

"There's no need to get dirty," Claire almost pleaded. "It was just an observation."

"I observe too, and you know and I know that you got more dirt on you than you want to admit," Esperança said. "But I'll give you this pass, just so that the next time you'll think twice about questioning my tactics."

Claire forced a cool smile. "Duly noted. I'll try and remember that for next time."

"Don't let your mouth write checks your bony ass can't cash," Esperança groaned.

Claire laughed at this, relieved for the lighthearted retort. She stared back down at the candle in her hand. It was empowering, and Claire liked the cool and greasy feel of it. "Is it all right to pay you now?" she asked under her lashes. "Speaking of checks."

"As long as you know that once you hand over the money, it makes it final," Esperança advised.

"Kind of like a commemoration."

"Or a gesture...this is Satan's official service with you. He does his part, and now you do yours," Esperança simplified. "But you do know what this means? And it's not no Cupid, you understand? It's Satan, the devil himself, and the fallen angels that will make this happen."

Claire smiled, almost to herself. For years she had felt lost, but she saw things differently now. She'd experienced the incredible mind-reading powers of Esperança, and she concluded that her soul had been leaning toward Satan for decades. Her several financial accomplishments had not come through any sweet, loving prayers to God. Clearly, it was Satan who had been guiding her, directing her, and rewarding her. And if gaining the ability to conceive Jonathon's child meant sacrificing her soul to Satan, then so be it. She felt she had given God enough chances to earn her devotion.

"I accept then," Claire said, straightening up.

Esperança nodded, just a tiny head bob. Claire picked up the envelope from off the floor and slid it across the table toward her. Esperança took the money and moved it to the side.

Claire knew that on the next business day, a hundred thousand dollars of her money would be wired to the account number Esperança had given her. She no longer concerned herself with where the money was going. Whether it went into the pockets of America's most wanted or another Hitler in the making, she accepted her alliance with the devil himself.

Esperança caught the satisfaction in Claire's decision, and she swallowed yet more rum. Her lips burned with the sting of the alcohol. She reached underneath her chair and felt around before producing three boxes of chocolates, and slid them over to Claire.

Claire looked down, without touching them, and saw that they were chocolate-covered almonds, and the white sticker fixed to the boxes had the name of some charity—a church in Harlem.

"What's this, a parting gift?" Claire knew better, but the cross alongside the charity's heading gave her the creeps, and made her a little angry. She was just starting to embrace her newfound connection with Satan.

Esperança glared at her. She mumbled, "Five dollars a box. The kids at my granddaughter's school are raising money to build an orphanage for the blind babies in Africa."

Her stern expression didn't waver.

"I don't eat chocolate," Claire replied, not knowing what the right answer was. Esperança's eyes hardened even more. "What?" She said in a meek voice. "I said something wrong?"

"I said it's for the blind babies in Africa." Esperança's tone was calm and unwavering.

"Fine then." Claire reached for her purse and pulled out a twenty and slid it over to her. "I'll need my change."

A smile flitted over Esperança's lips. She lifted the lid on her tin box and rummaged around for a wrinkled five dollar bill. Claire took her change, dropped it into her purse, and rose from her seat. On her turn, Esperança cleared her throat.

"You forgot something," Esperança said, still sitting in her chair and addressing the boxes with her gaze.

Claire was baffled.

"Take them and keep them," Esperança said. "That way you can remember that you did something good."

21

A New Alliance

During the drive home to New Jersey, Claire tried to convince herself that she would soon awaken from her extraordinary dream. Had she really eaten a dove's beating heart? How could she have succumbed to the very things she'd scoffed at? And she wondered how many others like her were out there doing what she was doing. Driving her Benz along the freeway, passing everyday people, seemed surreal. The drivers who cast admiring glances at her and the machine she drove never guessed she'd just entered a world of demonic forces and satanic rituals. Her thoughts tripped back to Cynthia Jennicks, the uncannily successful criminal lawyer. It was clear that she too had sold herself to the dark world. Then Claire thought about the handsome man Esperança had killed; now the man's black candle sat inside her purse like a fully loaded .22 caliber handgun.

For the first time, it dawned on her that the world she'd stumbled upon truly existed. The people involved in it appeared normal enough. They included everyday citizens with children, homes, and responsibilities. Some went to church on Sundays, picked their children up from school, and took part in community activities. Claire decided she must never again underestimate what a person was capable of doing.

Seeking a diversion, Claire checked her reflection in the visor mirror. She no longer looked tired. Her cheeks were flushed and her eyes were alert, although no longer her own. They were wiser after seeing a piece of otherworldly mystery. This was her eerie secret, her new toy to play with, and what she once considered a nightmare was fast becoming a dream.

She caught a glimpse of her lips in the mirror. The dove's blood hadn't left any traces in the cracks of her mouth. However, her emerging self remained calm at the thought of what she'd done; she felt sexy and empowered. She closed the visor and allowed herself to envision the rest of her life. It was no longer "if " this worked, for she knew it would. A dramatic shift in her world had taken place in Esperança's little shit hole of an apartment, and it now rushed over her like a tsunami of pure joy. She felt protected, as if a hidden force watched over her every move. And everything she wanted and needed was going to be hers. Jonathon was hers again; it told her so. He loved her, wanted her again.

An unidentifiable voice murmured indecipherable longings into her ear; her loins responded in anticipation. Even as unknown hands touched her, groped her, Claire gripped the steering wheel and accelerated through the delicious sensations. A masculine voice whispered, *Surrender to me*. Hot breath massaged her neck. Invisible hands touched her in the places that belonged only to Jonathon. Wanting her, the presence smelled her and even tasted her. Claire's body shivered while she struggled to keep her car on the road. She was aware of the danger but did not fight for control of her body.

When she was close to the height of ecstasy, it all stopped. The voice laughed and said, *Go home and prepare for your husband*. After wiping the sweat off her upper lip, Claire noticed her pulse throbbing fast through the veins of her neck. She clicked the window switch and the glass lowered, allowing the cold air to cool the parts of her body which yearned for the voice to come back. Whatever "it" was, she definitely did not fear it.

She pushed in the CD of Jonathon's favorite music. No longer annoying her, the melodies produced a strangely calming effect on Claire. They brought her back to earth, back to the traffic inside the Lincoln Tunnel. She pressed eject, the music stopped, and the CD slid out. She placed it in her purse. Later,

Claire concluded. She would play it for him that evening while he made love to her by the fire.

Claire stopped at a local market in Montville. It had been a while since she'd cooked for Jonathon, and now there was reason for celebration. Why shouldn't she treat him to his most desired dish, fillet mignon and shrimp Alfredo. And because she was in an especially good mood, he would also be treated to homemade fettuccine.

The house smelled fresh when she entered. The cleaning lady left behind a note reminding Claire to pick up more kitty litter and furniture polish. Excellent, Claire thought to herself as she placed the groceries on the counter. She had a few hours in which to prepare Jonathon's meal and get ready for him herself. It was Thursday, so dinner was being served at The Warm Hands.

Claire ran up the stairs and entered her room. She hadn't opened her top drawer in awhile. Carefully unfolding her glossy jewels, she found the designer hot pink camisole with matching bra and panties. She took them out and laid them on her bed. She'd never worn the camisole. Claire gingerly touched the silky lace and ribbons intertwining the paper-thin fabric. The panties were French-cut with a similar silk ribbon woven along the waist and tied into a sexy bow in the back. She'd had it custom designed and fitted.

Claire tore off her clothes and randomly reached for Jonathon's New York Yankees T-shirt. It hung loosely on her willowy frame. Claire breathed in his scent. She treasured the mixture of his natural musk and cool cologne nestled in the cotton fabric. Her insides twisted and ached, needing to be set free. And the proverbial butterflies, more closely resembling birds, flapped their wings inside her.

Claire fell onto the king-sized bed and gave herself a minute to take in what had gone on. She calmly contemplated the voice, wondered where it went, and whether or not it would return. It hadn't been her imagination. It knew her.

She parted her legs and glanced over them. They needed shaving, and she was in need of a bath. Jonathon loved her clean skin, often remarking on the good taste of her buttercream body wash. She rose from the bed and smoothed out the sheets.

There were things to be done downstairs before she could clean herself.

Tiger shrimp cleaned and prepped with olive oil and freshly chopped garlic, Claire sprinkled sea salt and black pepper on them before placing the seafood into the refrigerator. Later she would grill them and prepare her Alfredo sauce at the same time. The perfect beef cuts sat in a ceramic dish wrapped in thick strips of bacon. She poured a handful of peppercorns and dried spices into a grinder, and crushed them into grounds. Wonderful smells filled the kitchen as she carefully coated the beef with the bursts of flavor. She made room in the fridge for them also.

Standing on a stool by the fridge, she pulled down the pasta maker and placed it on the counter. As much as she hated what carbohydrates did to her, she absolutely loved fresh pasta. And if she was going to surrender to her cravings, it might as well be worth it.

Next, Claire took out her mixer and the ingredients to mix into it. She sifted the cups of flour, added egg yolks and salt. The mixer whirred loudly while she added water, producing the perfect dough. Claire pinched it with her fingers. "Good," she smiled and set it aside. "Now the dessert," she coached herself. She washed the berries and set them into two large, see-through glasses. Her travels around the world had taught her many things. Preparing a superb dessert dish was something she learned while spending a few months in Paris.

The cream sauce was a blend of egg yolks and sugar, whisked over a low fire. The chef used only fresh vanilla. Claire split the bean and scraped the tiny grains into the yolks. She whisked continuously while opening the small bottle of vodka and poured the contents into the mixture. It bubbled into a foamy sauce. She doused the juicy berries with the cream.

She finally poured herself a coffee, not decaf, the real thing. The coffee felt good as it moved through her body, giving her that extra boost.

Then she felt him. He breathed on the back of her neck, tracing a finger from the nape of her neck slowly along her spine to the small of her back. Shivers sprayed her skin like thousands of tiny spiders. Claire spoke with an alluring smile.

"You're home early." She turned and halted, looking around the cold kitchen for signs of Jonathon. No one and nothing appeared.

Lady suddenly hissed at the foot of the stairs. Claire walked over beside her. The cat's Persian coat stood at attention; she was prepared to either defend herself or run. This was not like Lady, who was usually sweet and docile. She didn't like whatever was there. Claire spoke to "it" as if speaking to a child, "Leave her alone." And Lady bolted upstairs, probably to hide under her bed.

She returned to the kitchen and picked up the dough. She pulled the perfect noodles through the press and put them onto the floured sheet to dry.

He watched her, studied her beautiful figure under the shirt. Obviously, she wasn't wearing anything underneath it. He hungered for her and, because it was unlike anything he'd ever felt before, it confused him. His immediate urge was to kill her and love her all in the same moment. He wondered what it was about her that drove him to such intense longing.

She moved gracefully as she pulled the noodles through. Her long legs made quick pivots, allowing the T-shirt to lift in an unprovoked tease.

He moved closer and wrapped his arms around her waist, placing his fingertips into her wet warmth. Claire froze. *Who is that*, she asked herself, too stunned to turn around.

Jonathon breathed into her neck. "I couldn't stop thinking about you, Claire. I had to come home."

She turned around and their lips met. "I haven't stopped thinking of you either," she responded in the same mischievous manner. Only Jonathon wasn't playing.

He picked her up and sat her facing him on the kitchen counter. "No," Claire stopped him, "I haven't had a bath or anything. Let me get ready."

A splash of insanity resided in his boyish smile. Then he worked his tongue from her temple to her bottom lip.

"No, really, Jonathon. Not yet."

Again he carried her effortlessly and placed her on the kitchen table. "I need to smell you. Taste you. Don't ruin this."

"Just let me prepare," Claire insisted.

"Give it up," Jonathon said.

His voice was calm and low. It roved over her flesh like a feathered caress. Claire's will fell short, and her body gave in to his request. Her pent-up frustration yearned for him. The hot pink get-up which she had placed on the bed would not be worn, and her skin wouldn't be kissed with the sweet fragrances she'd selected. She hadn't needed them after all.

He'd already been seduced by a force which had drawn him home and into her arms. He moved with newfound hunger. He bit her skin with tiny nibbles and intricate licks. He stopped to smell her in private places, and then brushed his cheek against her wrist.

Claire caught his intense stare. He was looking straight through her as if she wasn't really there. Claire grabbed his face and breathed his name, forcing her mouth over his.

He ripped off his pants and thrust himself into her. Claire moaned, allowing her body to push back into him with a flow of release. She became limp as he pushed even farther into her and screamed her name.

His body trembled, and she wrapped her legs around him, keeping him inside a little longer. She felt his pounding heart as he rested heavily over her.

Jonathon had finally made love to her for the first time in a long time.

This was real—very real. The control with which Claire had manipulated others throughout her life had just been magnified a million-fold.

Jonathon slid away from her and held out his hand. "Let's have a shower together." He didn't give her a chance to respond, but she didn't mind in the least.

The fire breathed warmth over their naked skin. While Jonathon ate voraciously, Claire picked at her food, enjoying their picnic by the flames.

"Mmm," he murmured and moved his plate to the side.

"What have I done to deserve all this?"

A guilty smile tugged at Claire's lips. "I owe you an apology for what I said the other day. I didn't mean it." Jonathon looked away, his stare lost in the red and blue flames.

"I know." He picked up the iron poker, pushed around the logs. "I don't know what I'd ever do if I lost you," he continued without looking at her. "I don't think I could live without you, Claire." He faced her, his eyes bore right through her.

Claire stared back. The roaring fire was reflected in his eyes as she felt his full palm gently against her face. The reality was overwhelming, causing her to close her eyes.

"Let's never fight again," he said, moving his hand to the back of her neck. He began massaging her, kneading the months worth of built-up tension. Her lips parted, lulling her entire body into capitulation. Her eyes snapped open, on hearing the ring of his cell phone.

Jonathon pulled away and dug into his pants pocket before retrieving his cell. He glanced at it.

Claire peeked at her watch: seven thirty-six. "Aren't you going to answer?"

Jonathon turned off the phone. "Nope, it's nobody important."

Claire's heart fluttered. *Perfect*, she laughed inside. Then she remembered something. "Oh, I forgot. I made dessert."

After serving the berries and cream, she said, "We need music, too." Claire retrieved the CD from her purse and pushed it into the player.

"Come sit." Jonathon patted the fur rug under and around him.

She joined him and sat between his legs.

He took turns eating his dessert and feeding it to her. He kissed her in between, brushing his lips across her neck. The music filled the room. "Where did you get that?" Jonathon demanded.

Claire turned to face him. "From your car. It's the music you like. Remember?" She watched as he rose from the floor and moved to the stereo.

He hit the eject button hard and removed the CD. Claire was confused. "What's wrong?" .

But he said nothing for several seconds. He returned to her, and opened the glass door of the fireplace. "I'm just tired of these songs," he murmured, tossing the CD into the flames, and then closed it back.

Jonathon locked into Claire's gaze, but his liquid eyes gave nothing away. "Now, where were we?" He pulled her between his legs.

Claire stared, hypnotized by the blazing fire, where the disk caught on fire. It had been Nicolette's music. How had she not realized this before? She decided that it didn't matter anymore.

Claire laid her head on his chest and breathed in his familiar scent. She shut her eyelids and allowed herself to relax and enjoy the moment as the stress drained from her in a shudder. And while she found herself thankful for finding Esperança, the woman's mystery only deepened. Who was this woman, living with a monster? And why would someone so powerful and so connected to Satan give a shit about blind babies in Africa? Normally, Claire would have tossed the box of chocolates out her car window. But something about the urgency in Esperança's eyes made Claire rethink her actions. In a strange way, Claire felt good knowing that her fifteen dollars might make a difference, even if the paltry sum was nothing in comparison to what they needed. But even stranger, she found herself liking this disturbingly strange woman, this woman that posed as something she wasn't.

Enjoying the feeling of her husband's arms around her, it made no difference to Claire who Esperança really was, because the proof was caressing her naked back and making her sleepy. It had been a long day, and her body surrendered, protected by the warmth of her husband as well as her invisible protector who lurked in the dark corners of the room.

22

Letting Go of the Darkness

The Bronxities referred to Westchester Village as West-chester Square. But to Esperança, the neighborhood in the southeast Bronx was the ideal location, being close to home, only a stone's throw to pickup necessities. For Patience, she would make her routine purchases of milk, eggs, and bread so that her granddaughter could have breakfast in the morning. And, depending on what day it was, Esperança would stop in at Cafeccino's Oven, a Latin bakery. Fridays they made sweetbread—Patience's favorite.

Then there were days like this…

The squalls had tapered off in the early morning, leaving a blanket of slush beneath her feet. Sludge, mixed with pigeon poop and seed shells, covered the grounds where Esperança had taken her usual spot, on a weathered wooden bench outside of the No. 6 train station. She rummaged around in her bags and pulled out a bottle still wrapped in a paper bag and cracked the seal open to take her first morning snort. She was cold. She had forgotten to wear a hat and the warm coat Patience had bought her for Christmas. It would have been ideal on a day like today. The coat was lined in feathers, Patience had pointed out, it was water-proof, and the key feature was that it had a hood. Her gift was still inside its bag, never worn, the tag still on.

Esperança pulled the collar of her woolen sweater up and around her neck before taking three mouthfuls from the bottle. What Patience failed to remember was, that once the rum set in, Esperança would grow feathers of her own and feel nothing.

In the wiry cage beside her, the female dove cooed. Esperança pulled the package of pretzels up and put a salty rod into her mouth. She crumbled a few into the palm of her hands, sprinkling them into the cage, before eating the pretzel as if she was chomping on a celery stick.

It was good, quelling the hunger in her belly. Then a vision caught the corner of her eye.

It was the child, the same little boy she'd seen over and over again; the same time: ten thirty. The motel nearby had a check-out time of eleven a.m. He should be in school, she thought.

He stood just a few feet away wearing the same cheap, navy coat with the too short sleeves, no hat, no gloves. He stood by the exit watching for his mother; the crack head junkie, who told him to wait, and that she'd only be an hour. She lied; it was seven months. For seven months she'd been doing this: having the boy wait for her while she got her fix. The boy's mother had touched her one time in passing. Esperança had "accidentally" walked into her and saw right into the woman's soul. She had none; an empty vessel who sold her body for a hit. An empty vessel that'd lost her other children to the system and refused to surrender this one. She had her reasons.

This boy, the woman wanted. He was a bargaining chip, and she would use him soon, just as she had done the others.

Esperança took another long swig and saw an apparition that iced the rum which kept her warm. She saw the boy, a clear vision. The boy had been living on the run and witnessing his mother's behavior. His mother was using him, keeping him on the streets to panhandle and hustle money for her. People were sympathetic to the child, would drop bills into his hands. She would use that money and rent rooms, buy drugs. She would keep him in the washroom while she did unspeakable things with faceless men. The boy had seen much too much. He was on the precipice and was about to fall into the darkness, and his mother would pull him in with her.

The visions continued, playing in her mind, flashes of repulsion, of what was to come.

The mother would sell her own son's virtue for a hit. She'd allow her John to abuse, sodomize, and destroy his worth. But it was not too late for this child. Esperança placed the bottle down and signaled the boy over. She knew he was watching her, curious about the old lady that reminded him of grandma. The kind old lady that had full custody of him.

The boy looked around then proceeded over with a curious expression in his stolen smile. On closer inspection, standing less than four feet tall, in patch of pale winter daylight, Esperança's stomach bottomed out. She couldn't help but think he resembled someone she once knew; the same greenish-blue eyes, a tuft of black curls, and insight that was not meant for a boy his age. His eyes were scathed, had almost no sparkle. And, along with being cold, the boy was hungry.

Esperança offered him the bag of pretzels. He looked hesitant, though willing. "Take, I know your mother never told you not to take food from strangers," she said, pushing the bag to him.

The boy was slow to move, and he pulled out a single pretzel and held onto it. "Sit," Esperança said, sliding the cage over, "and take these." She forced the bag into his hands.

The boy took a seat beside her and looked into the cage while chomping away. "You a magician lady?" he asked, turning to Esperança with a glimmer in his eyes.

"Yes, you can say that." Esperança tittered to herself and reached into the cage and pulled out the female dove. She held the bird with one hand and stroked the bird lightly with the other. A wondrous expression lit the boy's face as he offered the bird a cupped palm, full of crumbs.

"He likes me," he beamed, as the pigeon ate from his hand. "It tickles." He had a cute giggle. It was like watching a runt fighting for its mother's teat. Yes, this child would fight.

"It's a she," Esperança explained. "I like to use her in my shows."

"Magic shows?"

"Sure, and this little bird is very talented, she can even play dead," Esperança explained. "Although real magic comes from another place. Some magic comes from darkness, and good magic comes from goodness. A real magician doesn't need a bird or a magic wand, but some people have no faith. Some people have to see it to believe."

"What's faith?" He allowed the bird to perch on his wrist.

"Like magic," Esperança replied. "Believing in something you can't see. And the good magic I told you about, like kindness, compassion, understanding. You see how she feels safe with you?" Esperança pointed to the bird. Her eyes were closed, soothed by the boy's touch.

"Your kindness is enough for her to close her eyes and know that she's in good hands. That's the best magic of all, spreading goodness."

The child's eyelids flickered. "What's her name?"

"Heart," Esperança replied, and then pointed to the barren tree before them. "And that's her mate up there, his name's Soul." Esperança made a kissing sound, which set the bird into flight, landing on her wrist. She lowered her wrist and introduced him. "You see, when these birds mate, they bond for life. He'll feed her while she's nesting. Pretty amazing don't you think?"

"Yeah." The boy focused his attention to the bird's foot. "It has something on its foot."

The female dove flew off of his wrist and landed a few feet away, perched on the black, wrought-iron fence.

Esperança picked up the male and carefully removed the note which Claire had taped on just the day before. She rolled it into a ball and chucked it. Getting Claire's husband to love her again was as simple as lighting a red candle and writing the request to the fallen angels. But in order to keep Claire's interest, it had to be dramatic. "Just give me a second here," she said, transferring the male onto the boy's wrist before pushing her hand into her pocket and removing a small strip of paper and tape. Esperança picked up the bird again and worked like a pro, having done it countless times before and taped the new message onto its foot before letting him join his partner.

"Whadja tape on his foot?"

"A wish," Esperança replied, "for a lady I know. A lady with no faith. Wishes are also powerful, another word for hope."

She reached over and touched the fabric of the boy's coat between pinched fingers. His mother had found the coat in the garbage.

"How would you like to be my assistant?" Esperança asked.

"Magician's assistant?"

"Yes, a magician's assistant."

The boy's face changed, a lovely smile, the light in his eyes stirring even more. It made her emotional.

"What'll I do?"

"For now, you'll wait here while I go and get you your costume. But you have to promise not to leave. You stay right here, and wait for me to come back."

The boy nodded. Esperança knew he wasn't going anywhere. Her only regret was that her knees were aching. The walk home would be hard. "Twelve minutes," she said, and picked up her bottle while rising to her feet. A shooting pain rippled through her knees, making her jerk back. "Make it sixteen."

When Esperança had returned, the boy had eaten the entire bag of pretzels. This pleased her. She took her seat again and set the bag, containing the coat Patience had given her for Christmas, down by the boy's feet. He looked down, his eyes wide. Esperança reveled in the joy that transformed the boy's face. He was in disbelief while looking into the sparkly, red gift bag.

"Well," Esperança said, catching her breath and rubbing her knees, "put it on."

The boy tore through the bag, in the way children are meant to do, and pulled out the light-blue, feather-lined bomber jacket. He held it up, between two hands, both disappointed and elated. This was not the coat of a magician's assistant. Esperança expected this reaction.

"Put the coat on, boy, and let's get to work," she said.

The boy nodded, stood on his feet, and began pushing his arms into the sleeves. "No, no. Take off your old coat first," she schooled him.

"My bad," the boy said, too excited. He pulled off the old coat and reached for the new one.

Esperança noted that he had several T-shirts on and two pairs of pants. It was everything he owned, while living on the run. He pulled his arms into the plush warmth of his new coat. It was almost a perfect fit. A bit too big, but the child would grow into it.

"Come, come," Esperança said, pulling the boy close. She zipped him up, pulled the hood over his head, and tucked his loose curls away from his face. "You need a haircut, you look like a girl," she said, angered that his mother was keeping his hair long on purpose for the sake of the Johns. Those sick types liked both. She soon saw another vision, of the boy's mother applying makeup on her son. It was difficult trying to keep her anger under control; she felt like smashing something.

The child took his seat beside Esperança again and looked up at her with those familiar eyes. She read the different emotions running through him. The boy wanted to thank her but couldn't bring himself to do it, for fear of crying and looking like a baby. The child had cried enough, and Esperança knew what that felt like.

"So, what's your name?" Esperança, asked, maintaining eye contact with the boy. She was reaching inside his mind, preparing him for the magic he desperately wanted to see, wanted to believe existed. Hope, a word more powerful than any abuse, inequity, and horror the boy was subjected to.

Hope—a light in darkness.

She would give him magic.

"Theo...you?"

"Ghost," she answered evenly. "Theo, I want to give you a lesson about something important. Something magical inside you."

"Me?" Theo felt as if he mattered. It was exactly the feeling she was aiming for.

"Your grandma, she lives on Long Island, right?"

"How ya know?"

"I'm a magician...I know things. I also know that your grandma is supposed to have you, and the law says that your mother isn't allowed to see you unless she's supervised, right?"

Theo nodded. "Yeah, she said we were gonna get me back-to-school clothes. She promised me new kicks. My Nana gave her money."

"That was months ago, Theo. When you were five, now you're six. And you should be in school."

"You really are a magician."

"I told you I was. But you see, when I went to my magic store, I saw something in my magic ball… something that made me sad. Your grandma misses you."

"I miss her too," he said. "And I think of her all the time. She said if I call Nana, something bad'll happen."

"She lied to you, nothing bad will happen. But you know, it was your grandmother who named you after the great president, Theodore Roosevelt. On the day that you were born, your grandma held you in her arms, and she said that at that very moment she knew that you were a survivor, and that you were special…meant to do great things."

"Because I was born addicted."

"That's right, because you were born a fighter, with magic inside your heart. And you overcame the drug addiction."

This made Theo smile; a real smile, one that took her breath away. "Now, you want to see some real magic?"

Theo nodded, the light in his eyes stirring again. Esperança held out two closed fists. "In my left hand, I have for you a ball. It's black, cold, and very sad. It's a ball that holds your future. A life of drugs, jail, early death," she added. Theo was horrified, but that wasn't going to stop her. That was the problem with this world, people afraid to tell the truth to children, yet the horrid truth was occurring anyways. "Your mother is a very sick woman. She does drugs and sleeps with men for these drugs."

"I know," Theo admitted.

"And if you pick the ball in my left hand, then that, young Theo, will be your life."

Tears welled in Theo's eyes. This child was no idiot, Esperança thought. He knew exactly how this would go if he stayed.

"But there's good news. That ball in my right hand, is a magic light. It's a very powerful light from the angels in heaven. You see, if you choose the ball in my right hand, then that will be your protection. You'll go home today, home to grandma. You'll go back to school and start over. And because you're smart, you'll make up for the last year."

Esperança paused. "Mind me now, Theo, if you choose this magic light in my right hand, then I want you to understand something very important. This light comes with responsibilities. You take this light everywhere with you. Keep it in your pocket; keep it on you at all times. Even in your sleep."

Esperança needed to make eye contact with Theo again to connect with him, so that she could have him see what she wanted him to see. "Life is full of bad things, Theo; you'll face them for the rest of your life. You must be strong, smart, know the difference between good and bad, wrong or right. Think, Theo! Actions have reactions. Even the tiniest stone will cause a ripple in the ocean. Do you understand what I'm telling you?"

Theo's lips were parted; his eyes were relaxed. He managed a small nod. Esperança was pulling the poison from inside of the boy's essence: the damaging visions that haunted him and kept him up when he should have been asleep. One day, Theo would become a man, and that man would take a wife, and later, that man would become a father and have kids of his own to raise.

Esperança still held her two closed fists out. "Now choose," she said, straightening up. "If you choose the ball in my left hand, I'll still let you keep the assistant's coat, but if you choose the ball in my right, you'll have to do exactly what I say. That means, always think of the consequences of your actions. One hit off the crack pipe, one tiny stone in an ocean. Because whether you understand this now or later, every stone counts."

She steadied her gaze on him, before asking one, last time. "Are you ready?"

Theo shook his head. "Yeah."

"Then choose," Esperança said.

Theo reached out and tapped Esperança's right hand ever so gently, and then pulled away, as if something so holy was caught inside of her clasp and ready to escape.

"So we're letting go of the darkness."

Theo nodded as his eyes glazed over. He gasped in utter fear when Esperança opened her left palm and released what Theo saw as a swirl of red and orange rising into the cold, gray sky then turning into black ash before disintegrating. To a bystander, there was nothing in her palm, but to Theo, the vision was very real.

With his neck still turned up, Theo said, "But howdja do that?"

She gave him a playful wink. "My secret. Come close child, I want you to take your gift and be mindful about it. When I give you the ball of light, I want you to say, 'My name is Theo, and I am a survivor. I will carry this light with me wherever I go.' Do you understand?"

"Yeah," Theo whispered.

Esperança opened her palm, and inside Theo saw exactly what Esperança wanted him to see: a glowing ball, swirling in the palm of her hand. "Take it, quickly now."

Theo reached over and held out his tiny palm as Esperança transferred the light into his hand. He looked down into his palm; tears formed in his eyes and fell down his winter-bitten cheeks and chapped lips.

"Now say the words," she coached him. "My name is Theo, and I am a survivor. I will carry this light with me wherever I go."

Theo recited the words with unconditional commitment. The light in his eyes bloomed into the most incredible enlightenment. That was how a child should look, Esperança thought.

"For me?" Theo said, choked up, looking up at Esperança then back down into his palm.

His endearment toward her circulated in warmth through her cold body, for she was trembling from the icy rain that began falling. But despite the cold, Theo was worth the sickness she was catching.

"Put it into your pocket, child, and remember what I said," she said through chattering teeth.

Theo stood up and pushed the light into his jeans pocket. Esperança rose from her sitting position and pulled out a hundred-dollar bill from inside her pants pocket, handing it to him.

"You'll ask the people inside the train station to help you, tell them you're going home to Long Island. This'll be enough to get you home and buy you something to eat. Understand?"

Theo nodded, his nose running along with his tears. Esperança wished she had a tissue for him. "Now mind me, Theo, you will make no other stops; straight to the station, and when you get off, you'll use the change to call your grandmother. Don't be afraid to call her...nobody will ever hurt her or you. I promise."

"What about my mother?"

"For some people there is no light, child. Sometimes it's just too late," she said, not wanting to lie to him. He'd been lied to enough. "You stiffen up that upper lip, and hold onto that light...you hear me?"

Theo reached over and wrapped his tiny arms around Esperança's waist. "Thanks, Ghost." She was moved by the boy's touch, there was no more poison in Theo's soul.

"Yes, yes. Off with you now," she said, ensuring that the money was safely tucked into his coat pocket, and then she remembered to rip the tag off. The last thing the boy needed was to be jumped for the coat.

"All right then, you better go." Esperança patted Theo on the head.

Theo pulled away, and he ran against the rain. He stopped just a few feet away, and struck a pose, his little fingers spread into a downward peace sign. "Deuces, Ghost," he called out, looking like a baby rapper. Theo was happy with a kick in his step, as he ran to the train station's entry. He looked back at her for one last time, with those greenish-blue eyes, the tuft of black curls.

Why can't all little boys stay that way forever?

For a moment, Esperança felt as if she wasn't even there. She tuned out the noise pollution, drowned out the screeching reverberation of metal to metal, along with the acrid steam that rose from the manholes. Bottle in hand, Esperança stood trembling, her hair stuck to the sides of her face, and her forehead pricked with the ice rain.

A harsh burst of wind skidded up behind her, lifting the edge of her sweater, and shocked her back to the present. She blinked back the drizzle and finally returned the silly peace sign.

"Dueces, Kamau," she whispered, before fanning him off. His mother was close by and vomit was rising in her throat.

The boy's poison made her queasy.

Theo lingered before disappearing from her sight. On her turn, Esperança slipped on the frozen concrete and landed hard on her right knee. She stayed there for a moment, groaning, lying face down, and spotted her bottle which had slid over to the roadside, still wrapped in the paper bag. She groped over the frozen ground, sliding through pigeon poop and ice covered gravel. She could feel the sour taste of vomit in her mouth as she pushed herself toward the bench and managed to crawl her way up. The world was spinning before her eyes, and the pain in her knees was excruciating. She bent her head forward and vomited. On her rise, she spotted Theo's cheap, navy coat and used it to wipe her mouth. But instead of leaving it behind, she needed it, for the final act. The coat had Theo's mother's essence on it. She would never again come back for her son.

If his mother wasn't already dead inside, she'd have taken care of that, too.

23

Gone

Working behind his desk, Jonathon looked at his watch—an appointment at four, and then, at five, a quick drink at Platinum's with Patrick and some investors from Hong Kong. He thought about Claire. Damn, he missed her already. He tapped his fingers against the desk and considered calling her again. He wondered where the hell she was. She'd told him at breakfast that she had a client interested in listing a property, but eleven had come and gone. It wouldn't have taken her four hours. Jonathon decided he would call but got her voicemail instead.

Rather than simply hang up and try again later, he left a message. "Claire, where are you? Call me." Hesitating, Jonathon wondered why he needed to speak with her so urgently. He went on, "I just need to hear your voice." After leaving his message, he tried her at the office. There was still no answer.

To divert his focus, he got up and walked toward the new espresso machine. Operating the complicated piece of equipment took his thoughts away from Claire momentarily. Jonathon filled the silver dish with coffee grinds and pushed in the dish. He inhaled deeply and tried to unravel his feelings. But in no time a horde of 'what ifs' returned to wreak havoc upon his attempts to get back on task. He wondered what was wrong with him lately, why he had this insane desire to be with her all the time, and why he felt so paranoid of finding her in another man's arms. He pulled the latch, and watched the hot coffee dribble into the cup. After it was filled, his desk phone rang, and he quickly answered it.

"Yes, is it Claire?"

"No, Mr. Lockwood, there's a young lady here to see you… says her name is Nicolette Vasseur."

Jonathon held his breath, then let it out slowly before answering, "Send her in."

Led by Jonathon's assistant, who quickly returned to her desk in the waiting area, Nicolette entered.

With a professional nod, Jonathon gestured for her to have a seat in the chair.

She shifted with uneasiness, and her sneakers rubbed together, making a squeaking sound.

"It's wet out there," he said, scanning between the blinds of his office window. He turned around and walked to the desk where he began sifting through files.

Nicolette bit her lip in frustration. "Will you please sit down?"

Their eyes finally met, and he sat down awkwardly behind his desk.

Not so long ago a stare into his eyes was all it took, and the communication between them was perfect. Many times he had said he loved her without saying anything at all. Now his eyes were vacant. He was… gone.

Nicolette looked away from him and fiddled with a thread which hung from her checkered blouse. She spoke, looking through her thick, dark lashes, "You haven't answered my calls."

Confusion whirled around in his head as his fingers fidgeted on the arms of the chair. Had he loved her? He must have, but he couldn't remember much about it. Instead, he studied her beautiful face, her lovely cheekbones, and hazel eyes. Was she crying?

Her lips parted, she wanted to say something to him, but she lowered her head instead.

Jonathon disliked seeing her this way. He felt responsible and swallowed hard and fast. Following a long silence, he said, "I'm sorry you're hurting."

Nicolette lifted her head, and tears ran rivers down her cheeks.

He passed her a tissue.

"Thank you." She dried her face. "Um, I didn't come here to cause you any problems. I just needed some closure."

His face showed a blank expression. "Closure?"

She sat there, amazed. "I needed to know why you disappeared."

"Disappeared?" He picked up a pen and drew circles on a piece of scratch paper. "I'm still dedicated to the program. You understand how important homeless people are to me."

"Yes," replied Nicolette. She then erupted into sudden, insane laughter for several seconds while he watched cautiously, and with concern. Recovering, she shook her head and whispered, "Actually, Jonathon, I was talking about us."

Now his mind became clear. It was her fault. She'd had no right to interfere in his marriage. Claire deserved his loyalty. "Us? I'm married, and happily. I have a wife. You know that."

"Yes," Nicolette answered, "but you kissed me anyway."

Bewildered, he barely looked at her. Yes, he'd kissed her. But why? "That was a very wrong thing for me to do, and I apologize. Please forgive me."

She stood up and searched his face for traces of the man she'd fallen in love with. His unique blue eyes with tiny shimmers of gold reminded her of the days she'd lost herself in them and had written the song, "Gold Rain." His strong jawline flexed, drawing her attention to his soft, pink lips. She yearned for him even more. "What has she done to you?"

"Done?" Jonathon looked angry.

"Did she threaten you? Hurt you? Tell me, please. Just tell me the truth!"

The accusing tone annoyed him, and he wanted desperately to get rid of her. "I won't be going back to the kitchen. I have to focus on my wife, my family. But that doesn't mean my commitment to street people will stop." Jonathon looked at his watch in hopes of sending her a message that it was time for her to leave. "You became a distraction at a difficult time in my life. I never planned on you."

Knowing it was over, Nicolette nodded in bitter acceptance.

"I think it's best if you never call me again," he concluded. She was about to say something when his office line beeped.

Jonathon held up his finger. "Excuse me." He spoke into the phone, "Yes?" It was Claire. His face changed. "Claire bear, where are you? I've been missing you." He burst into a wide smile.

Clutching her purse and keys, Nicolette ran out the door.

He didn't acknowledge her exit; she merely escaped from his thoughts.

Claire hung up the phone with Jonathon and glanced over the newly arrived fax once more. The offer on the property she'd listed only days before was the cherry on her sundae. Today was great. Sales were up, and her husband couldn't get enough of her. He even asked her to come home early because he had a surprise for her—again. Claire gave her head a shake and tried to focus her attention back to the computer screen.

While leaning back in her chair, Claire reached for her box of chocolate-covered almonds. She ate one at a time, allowing the chocolate to melt onto her tongue, before crunching the nut. A few weeks back, Claire had bought three boxes off of Esperança, and had made her contribution of fifteen dollars toward the construction of a blind school in Africa. In the days that followed, Claire had done her homework, having her lawyers research the project to ensure that the orphanage for the blind in Nigeria was legit. As of that afternoon, Claire's contribution had increased, making the total three hundred thousand and fifteen dollars. She insisted that the charity project's manager, keep her informed on the school's development. More importantly, that Claire's identity remain anonymous. This was her secret and she didn't want to explain it to anyone. She caught herself smiling.

"Good news?" Harvey poked his head into the door-way.

Great, now Harvey caught her smiling too. "Yes, actually." Claire shut off her computer screen and focused her attention on the offer. She pointed to it. "They gobbled it right up. I didn't even need to arrange a virtual tour."

Harvey stepped through, clumsily dragging his feet, and

dropped himself into a chair with his head hung low. "I gotta say, kid, you never stop amazing me. You did me good all these years." He'd been drinking, nothing new there.

She leaned back into her chair and faced him.

He stared at the large oil painting which hung directly behind her. It was a new canvas, a gift from Jonathon. "You ever wonder what happened to them?"

"Who?" Claire asked, looking around. "What happened to whom?"

Harvey struggled to stand, and with his index finger, indicated the painting: a beautiful man and woman, wrapped in each other's arms, resting happily in a hammock. The serene background, painted in rolling hills and trees, featured pockets of sunrays casting a shine over the couple. The painting was titled Bliss.

"It's a painting Harvey, not real."

Teetering from one leg to the other, he said, "Bliss doesn't exist here." His eyes strained to focus on the small gold plate which identified the painter's name. He lost his balance and flopped on the floor.

"Damn it, Harvey, you need to pull yourself together." Claire walked over and offered her hand to help him off the ground.

Instead, he yanked hard, causing her to fall onto him.

"What in hell's name are you trying to do?" Annoyed, Claire slid toward the wall, and rested her back against it. They sat there on the floor, staring at each other.

Harvey broke out laughing, loud hysterical laughter. His round face turned red as he began choking. Hunched over and hacking away, he reminded her of Lady trying to cough up a fur-ball—but nothing came up. Finally recovering, he sat up again and blinked a few times, as if wondering where he was and how he'd gotten here. Then he began sobbing, sobbing feverishly, face down, his tears wetting Claire's slate floor.

She watched him and understood her new responsibility in the matter, remembering Esperança's words about him. Her boss looked like a man on the brink of suicide. "Harvey?"

He was delirious and mumbled into the floor. "Pay attention, Harvey! I'm talking to you."

Looking up from the floor, and using his tie to wipe his face, he sighed. "I messed up. I really messed up bad this time."

"Stop whining and tell me what's going on."

"Macarena and her husband are blackmailing me," he explained, without filling in the holes.

So it was true.

"Who the hell is Macarena? Sounds like a dance or something."

Harvey tried his best to answer, but only managed to slur a few consonants together.

"I can't understand you. Tell me about Macarena."

Harvey swallowed. "She used to clean the office at night. I saw her for a few years, just for sex." He stopped.

Claire remembered seeing her a few times, and was shocked that this was the woman responsible for Harvey's demise. She was a ragged mouse-like woman who was in her early fifties. "Go on."

"Well, I tried to call it off with her, but she turned on me—said she'd tell Libby everything." He shook his head. "I don't get it. I've been paying her ten grand a month to keep her mouth shut. She has some video and pictures of us in bed. In our bed, Libby's and mine."

My specialty, Claire thought. She knew exactly just what kind of power Macarena had. "How very bold of her," Claire said, clenching her fists.

"They're asking for millions now. My kids' future. I don't know what else to do. If I keep giving in to them, they'll just keep coming back for more. First it was thousands, now millions. What next? I'm tired, Claire; I'm so done with this. So, so done."

Listening in bitter silence as Harvey rambled on, she bit gently on her upper lip.

Harvey began sobbing into his tie again and then added, "And Libby has cancer. Ovarian. They started her on chemo. She's so weak. So damn weak."

Claire felt an unfamiliar empathy for Libby. She'd grown fond of her over the years, and although she'd never gone out of her way to get close to the woman, she did tolerate her. Libby often prepared lunches, bringing in great baskets of homemade sandwiches and gourmet salads.

"I can't let her know about this. Not now," Harvey jabbered on. "It'll kill her." Harvey sniffled, "I'm better off dead."

Anger boiled deep within Claire. How incredibly stupid and spineless to give up so easily. "What were you planning on doing? Just give up?" She grabbed his face with her fingers. "Look at me…I asked you a question!"

She let go, and Harvey cried into his hands again. "I don't know what else to do. If I don't do as they say they'll tell my wife, and my sons. This'll kill my family."

"So you'd rather waste away, kill yourself, and leave your sick wife to cleanup your mess?"

Sniffling, Harvey shrugged his shoulders. "I don't have a magic wand in my pocket, Claire." He looked up with a pitiful expression. "What the hell am I going to do?"

Standing up and kicking off her heels, she paced back and forth, thinking back to what Esperança had told her. She glanced at Harvey; he was defeated, having already made up his mind. If he killed himself, and she knew he would unless she did something, it would mean the end for her, too.

He struggled to stay in a sitting position on the carpet.

"Harvey, I need you to focus." Claire spoke in a serious tone. "Get off the floor and sit on a chair. We need to figure this out, just like any other business deal."

He pulled himself up, meandered slowly to the chairs, and sat on the nearest one. "What can we do?" he asked, hopelessly.

Claire left the office, leaving Harvey alone for a few seconds, returning with a hot coffee mug. She handed it to him. "Drink. And from now on, I'm in charge of this ship."

Harvey sipped, as a small child would, and waited for her to continue.

"No more bullshit. And no more drinking! You hear me?" He nodded and watched Claire form her plan of action.

She chewed on the back of her pen. "Do you have a picture of her?"

Blinking, he gave a feeble smile. "Sure, she e-mailed a few to me. Why?"

"Don't ask questions. Just open your account and print one out for me." Harvey pulled his sleeves up and went to work. Claire waited by the printer and pulled up a nude print of the homely looking brunette sprawled on a bed. "This?" She was a repulsive creature. "Don't you have any with her clothes on?"

He looked the picture over. "Nope, that's it. I do have some with me in them, too."

In disgust, Claire shook her head. "You're an awful enough sight with clothes on, pal, never mind without." She pulled out a piece of paper and pushed it toward him. "Write down their names."

He looked confused. "What for?"

She slapped the back of his neck. "Just write the damn names down, and don't ask me why."

Harvey shrugged his shoulders. "Okay, okay, don't get your knickers in a knot, kid." He wrote the names down and passed the paper to her. She took a quick look, and folded it into a square. He watched her put the photo and paper into her purse. "You're not gonna put a hit on them are you?"

Claire studied the names, and then remembered the black candle, still sitting inside of her purse at home. "And if I do put a hit on them, are you going to have a problem with that?"

Breaking into a laugh, he chose his words carefully. "Claire, if you get me out of this and I come out smelling like a rose—" He stopped to consider what he'd do in return. "I'll make you partner." He downed the rest of his coffee as if it were a shot of whisky and smiled at her.

She thoroughly enjoyed hearing those words. It had been a long time coming. Claire replied in a strong voice, "I'm banking on it."

Nodding, he said, "You know what? If you'd only given me a chance way back when, I wouldn't be in this mess right now."

Claire rolled her leather chair over to him and stared into his face. "Harvey, I like you, and I don't often find myself able to say that about anyone. And there was a time when I actually had respect for you."

Fully conscious of his foolishness, Harvey exhaled soberly.

She took both his hands between hers. "Now, I've done a lot of bad things in my life, things most people would consider shameful. But the one thing I've never ever done is mess with my money. And unlike you, I never shit where I eat."

"I got your point."

Claire turned off her desk light, and slipped on her shoes. "Now, I must be off. And I should let you know, I may be going to Brazil soon."

Dumbfounded, Harvey asked, "Did you say Brazil?"

"Yes, and I could care less if the weather is lovely this time of year." Claire pointed to her new painting. "We all need a little Bliss from time to time, even if it means going into the jungle to get it."

24

The Rocking Chair

ack home, Claire pushed in the security code numbers and let herself into the house. She hung up her heavy black coat and slipped out of her shoes. Her eyes darted past the several bouquets of roses Jonathon had brought home the past few days and stopped at a single white rose which lay across the foot of the stairs. She studied it carefully before picking it up. Claire shook her head at the game he'd planned. She hated flowers. They reminded her of death—of the dark hole into which her mother's body had been lowered and the countless roses on top of her casket.

Climbing the winding staircase, Claire counted a dozen roses on the way to the empty room. She stepped reluctantly onto the upper level, leaving the roses where he'd placed them, and stopped finally at the closed door. Her breathing quickened, along with her heart rate. She hated surprises, especially those waiting in empty rooms.

From behind her, Jonathon emerged and wrapped his arms around her. "You ready?" He kissed her tenderly on the left cheek.

"I hate surprises," she whispered sideways into his lips.

He kissed her and turned her around to face him. "Surprises are meant to be sweet. I'm being sweet."

She leaned into him and pulled at his pajama drawstrings.

Jonathon's pectoral muscles flexed, and goosebumps speckled over his smooth skin. Claire nibbled at his collarbone. "You smell good."

Jonathon pulled away from her, took her hand, and opened the closed door. "Not so fast, I have something to show you first." He opened the door and guided her in.

"This better be good." Claire's voice ricocheted off the bare walls. Instantly, she detected the strong scent of wood varnish.

Jonathon flicked on the light switch and pulled on her hand, leading her toward the surprise.

After her eyes had adjusted to the sudden brightness, she recognized the dreadful cherry-stained rocking chair which sat by the bay window.

Jonathon walked closer and gave it a slight push. The chair rocked with a slight creak. "I asked Vince if he could replace the broken leg, and he even restored the wood."

Claire was silenced, stunned to her core. The astounding emotion caused a lump to form in her throat, and her nose tingled.

Jonathon eyes were soft. "I know it belonged to your mother. Rebecca told me it means more to you than it does her."

Claire stood, motionless. A flash of heat passed through her and then settled into her stomach where it twisted, tormenting her. The rocking chair did indeed mean more to Claire because Rebecca had apparently forgotten its significance. The chair had belonged to their grandmother, a handmade gift from grandfather to celebrate the birth of their mother, Connie. Claire's grandmother had passed it on to Connie, and after her death, the chair was bequeathed in her will to her eldest daughter. But Claire had insisted on storing it at Rebecca's house indefinitely. It was old and broken-down. It made her uncomfortable.

Claire walked with caution to the chair.

Her expression was unlike anything Jonathon had witnessed before. He watched her eyes soften as she took her finger and delicately traced it along the arms and the curves of the wood.

Claire looked up in defeat. "Why?"

Jonathon sat in the old rocker and took her hand, pulling her toward him. She fell into his lap just as she had fallen into the lap of her mother so many years ago. "I didn't mean to upset you."

He caressed her cheek and spoke in a calming tone. "I wanted to give you a piece of your mother to share with our baby." He rocked back and forth gently, in hopes that the rocking would calm her. "I know it's something she would have wanted."

Claire rested against his bare chest and listened to the beat of his heart. She closed her eyes, allowing the moment to send her even further into memories of "love time" Claire had shared with her mother. Those memories gave her strength when all else failed, when things got too difficult and the only thing that could save her was maternal love. Damn him. Why the hell did he have to think of this? Just when Claire thought the weak woman inside of her was buried, he had to go and dig her up.

"You shouldn't have done this." Claire pulled herself up and walked to the door.

"Claire, wait."

But she bolted out of the room, leaving Jonathon to sit alone and contemplate his next step. Rebecca had warned him that her sister might not be receptive to the gift. Claire had never offered much information about her childhood. The most he knew was that her mother had died in an accident when she was thirteen and her father had died of heart disease many years later. Aside from Rebecca, and an aunt that lived in England, she had no family. Rebecca had filled him in on a few more details during their occasional in-law "talks." He decided that Claire needed to face her demons and although the rocking chair was merely an old heirloom, for Claire it might be the beginning of a spiritual healing. He wanted that for her and, more importantly, for their future family.

Jonathon got up from the chair and walked into the bedroom. He found Claire staring out of the window, clutching Lady in her arms. "You okay?"

Claire nodded, placing Lady on the floor. She seemed to have recovered from whatever it was and began undressing. "I'll be even better after I've had my bath."

Jonathon watched as she carefully folded her clothes and left them on the side of the bed. He reached over to the door, passed her robe over, and helped her into it. "Hey," he lifted up her chin with one finger in an attempt to reach her with his eyes, "let's talk about it."

Claire pulled her chin away. "Not right now."

"Yes, now. Sit…please."

Claire sat on the edge of the bed, while Jonathon shared the edge with her. "I can't help but wonder if maybe we need to rethink having a baby. I just feel that the stress is taking a toll on our marriage."

Claire's tone was clipped. "Is this about the chair?"

"No, it's not the chair, it's everything. There are things that come automatically with being parents. Kids need love and warmth. I just don't think being a mother is something you'll be able to handle." Jonathon reached for her hand.

She snatched it away.

He knew his choice of words hadn't been the best. "You're mad now, right?"

Claire laughed at his question, "I'm not mad. I just can't believe all this has to do with my feelings about the chair." She turned to face him. "You can't expect me to get all sentimental over a tradition my mother tried passing off. It's bullshit; it means nothing. I don't need some stupid chair to prove I can be a mother." She was lying, but she couldn't bring herself to tell him how much it really meant, or *what* the chair really meant.

"I know that."

"But…" she pressed.

"But sometimes I wonder if the only reason you want a baby is to…keep me."

And now Claire was surprised again. He had formed a conclusion and happened to be correct.

Claire pulled herself up. "Having your child has nothing to do with keeping you. If you want to go, go. I'm not stopping you." Claire challenged him, but all the same, she kept her expression vacant.

His eyes softened and his jaw relaxed. "I'm not going anywhere. I'm simply saying that having children isn't the most important thing to me anymore."

Claire forced the question. "What is important then?"

Jonathon stood up to face her and wrapped his hands around her waist. "You are. And the only reason I questioned not having kids is because I don't want to force you into it. I don't want to fight with you. I love you. And we'll always have the twins and Olivia."

Claire cringed at the very idea of Olivia replacing a child of her own, a child she could give him. It was clear to her that to conceive his child was more important than ever. She was as capable as any woman who was able to bear children. "I may not be a sap like Rebecca, but that doesn't mean I'm incapable of being a mother."

"I know, Claire."

"It also doesn't make me a cold bitch because I'm not ecstatic over my dead mother's chair."

Jonathon held her close. "Look at me." He traced her lips with his finger. "I would love nothing more than for you to give me a little girl of our own."

Claire smiled sheepishly. "A little girl? Are you sure?"

Jonathon drew her in with his eyes. "I only hope she's half as beautiful as her mom." He kissed her on her nose. "With your pretty, tiny, nose freckles."

Claire laughed. "Freckles?"

Jonathon kissed both of her eyes. "And those beautiful green eyes."

Hanging on to his waist, she teased, "You're not so bad yourself, you know."

He picked her up and placed her on the bed. He stared into her face. "Seriously, though, I'll be happy with whatever happens, as long as I have you."

"You're sure about that?"

Jonathon nodded, "Without a doubt. I love you, Claire. More than I ever have."

Claire rested her head against his chest. She enjoyed listening to the sound of his beating heart. At least something was real. He caressed her tenderly. It was true that things had changed; she had him exactly where she wanted him. Things were perfect—too perfect. But she couldn't risk it. His love of children would cause him to view Claire as a failure for not providing him with one of their own. And she never failed.

"I can get rid of the chair if you want," he said, interrupting the flow of her thoughts.

Claire pulled herself up and accompanied her stretch with a yawn. "Nah, it flows with the room. We'll get a matching crib."

Jonathon gave her his boyish grin, his jaw shadowed with late evening stubble.

"I was thinking of the name Chloe for a girl."

"Chloe? Sounds like a perfume."

"You don't like it?"

Claire was too tired to argue. "Let's make a deal. If we have a girl, Chloe it is. If we have a boy, I get to name him."

"Let's work on making Chloe."

She pulled away and giggled. "I'm tired tonight. I just want to take my bath and hit the sheets."

"Want me to scrub your back for you?"

Claire shook her head. "Go to sleep. I need to reflect."

The early dawn roused Claire gently. Her bleariness moved slowly into consciousness. Eyes closed, her senses alert, she felt Jonathon's fire rise behind her. Gliding over her breasts, his hands lightly caressed her nipples in slow circular patterns. Claire moaned into her pillow, and felt her insides tighten with anticipation. His hands moved with quick precision, groping every inch of her nakedness. He stopped at the warmth between her legs.

Claire kept her eyes closed and slightly parted her legs, allowing him to penetrate her even more. His mouth moved in steady, meticulous vibrations. It was unlike anything she'd felt. He had found the spot that lay hidden behind the smooth hills of flesh. Claire's breathing quickened, and her body released in ecstasy, along with the rising sun. Wetness moistened the sheets beneath her.

She opened her eyes, thoroughly satisfied, and glanced at Jonathon. "Well, that was different," she whispered into the scruff of his cheek. "Jonathon?" She touched him lightly on his back to get a response from him.

He muttered something, and then turned over on his other side, in deep sleep.

"Son of a bitch!" Claire jumped out of bed and slipped into her robe.

It was back.

Claire darted quickly into the hallway and saw Lady scratching on the outside of the 'baby's' bedroom door. "It's all right, girl." She placed her hand on the doorknob and prepared herself before turning it.

Lady escaped downstairs.

The empty room glowed as the morning dawn poured through the floor-length bay window, and the vacant, cherry-stained chair rocked steadily with a slight creak.

She closed the door behind her. "Look, asshole, don't try that again!" She looked directly at the chair and waited for a response.

The rocking stopped, and the chair stood still. Claire shook her head. "And stay out of my mother's chair."

After she left, she closed the door behind her and listened in. The creaking resumed behind the bedroom door.

25

The Monster-Girl

The stairs to Claire's personal hell in Castle Hill confronted her again, only this time there was warmth radiating inside her which, oddly, reminded her of returning to the safety of home. Arrangements had to be made before she could depart for Brazil. On the upper landing, she rapped at the door and waited for Esperança to open it. Then, checking her watch, she realized she was a few minutes early.

A cold breeze blew in from the bottom of the stairs. She looked down the steep stairwell and watched while Patience struggled with a large cardboard box. Claire's upper lip turned up, causing her nose to wrinkle. *Oh, just what I need,* she thought, as the girl dragged the box with a slow and awkward pace. Her heavy breathing and crooked posture made her outward ugliness all the more horrible. Claire suddenly regretted not having stopped for coffee at her favorite shop before leaving New Jersey. If she had, she wouldn't need to deal with this crap. What she wanted right now was to disappear into the old smoke-stained walls.

Patience met her at the top landing and tore off her woolen hat. Her few strands of hairs stood up at attention, sparked by static.

"It wasn't so heavy until I reached the last block," she explained while shaking water droplets off her hat.

Claire edged away while Patience reached for a single key attached to a shoelace around her neck.

"Grandma's not back yet I guess," she said, unlocking the door.

The door swung open, and smells of evil welcomed them like an eager dog licking its owner. Claire sensed the wickedness envelop her like a protective shawl—she loved it.

"Would you mind helping me get this into my room?" Patience asked, seeming not to have noticed the invisible dark spirits, or perhaps choosing to ignore them.

Shrugging her shoulders, Claire made a weak attempt to help move the box.

Silently, they stepped into the other half of the house where Claire had never entered. The beaded curtain swayed, making clicking sounds, as it welcomed them through. It was exactly how Claire had pictured it. Pungent smells of long-ago cooked food, rotting walls, and corroding pipes forced her to hold her breath. Every space was stuffed full of items, from large bags of rice to canned goods stacked one on top of another. It was divided into sections by makeshift walls built with boxes and bins.

Claire stood still as she watched a rat move from a small space between the boxes, then scamper to the other half of the apartment. Esperança and her grand daughter were hoarders, sharing their living quarters with rodents.

"It's good here," Patience said. They set the box down outside a bedroom door.

Claire made an effort not to connect with the girl on any level and avoided eye contact. Instead, she followed the red-velvet, flowery-patterned wallpaper and stopped to take in several black-and-white framed photographs which hung on the hallway wall. A single bulb dangled from a wiry fixture, creating moving shadows all around them. One photo revealed a strikingly beautiful golden-colored man and woman with sharp facial features and dark hair. They stood relaxed and scantily clad, uncannily poised. Taking a closer look, Claire found the woman to be outlandishly appealing. Her long dark hair twisted and rested over her beautifully exposed breast.

"Those are Grandma's parents," Patience informed her.

"Her mother, in blood only."

"Happy couple," Claire said with disdain, without turning away from the photo. "Did you say in blood only?"

Patience simply smiled as they moved to the next photo. She pointed at the yellowed photo of an older man who held a large snake around his neck. "That's Grandma's grandfather."

"In blood only," Claire added, whatever that meant. Looking at the aged photo, she found herself intrigued again. He was a lean man with a washboard stomach, surprisingly fit for a man his age. Staring intently, she tried to determine where the photo was taken.

"It's in Brazil, in the place where my grandmother was born," Patience answered the unasked question.

On to the next photo they went, and the familiar dark, cold eyes of a little girl posing in a string of flowers caught Claire's attention. "Is this Esperança?"

"It is."

Claire studied not so much the image of Esperança as the typical tribal setting that surrounded her. In the past, she'd seen a few documentaries about natives in the wild, and now she wanted to prepare herself for her own visit. Large trees loomed in the background of thick foliage. Her eyes strained, looking for any sign to indicate this as a place where miracles happened.

"It's called The Valley of Souls," Patience spoke softly, "where souls are exchanged for the miracles you're hoping for."

Obviously the monster-girl could read minds, but unlike her grandmother, Patience was of no use to Claire. Beside her, she felt shamefully exposed.

Glaring into her face Claire said, "I didn't ask for your opinion, and I don't need your negative energy!"

"Negative energy?" The girl shook her head knowingly. "You're walking right into it."

Returning her focus to the old photographs, in an attempt to divert her attention, Claire soon discovered that her mind wandered back to what Patience had said. Putting aside the comment, Claire used her mind to purposely visualize the revolting girl locked in a cage as a palm-reading circus freak. She smiled shamelessly, hoping that Patience had read and was hurt by this exaggerated image of her.

Unnerved, the girl sighed.

Almost hypnotically, Claire looked over the photos again, and she felt a pang of terror whip through her chest. The idea of being in the middle of the Amazon sounded exotic, but the reality of where she was going and what she was about to do there worried her for the first time.

"It's one of the most beautiful places on Earth," Patience spoke. "And one of the deadliest, if you don't know what you're doing."

Turning to confront her, Claire said, "I know what I'm doing, and I don't need you sliding in your two cents."

Patience tilted her head to the side and read the fear in the pretty redhead's eyes.

Claire pulled away from the girl's stare and forced herself to focus again on the photos.

"You're afraid," Patience said, as she began to shuffle toward her bedroom. Dragging the deformed leg slowly, her black, rubber boots creating an eerie sound on the worn linoleum flooring, she struggled with the box. After several attempts, she was finally able to force it through the small doorway of her room.

Still viewing the photos, Claire searched each one for some kind of reassurance that her trip to Brazil wasn't anything she needed to fear. But the warning Patience had given her had left an indelible impression, and her head was full of uncertainty. Fuck it, she finally concluded, giving it no further consideration. Rather than knocking and waiting to be invited, she walked into Patience's bedroom.

It was as if Claire had entered the magical doorway of a different world, and she quickly drank in every inch of the bedroom. The freshly painted white walls gave the place a serene and spotlessly clean look. Although the girl's single bed was too small for her large frame and long limbs, it was neatly made. Her perfectly folded pajamas lay by her pillow. Several books sat on the end table beside her bed. Claire read the spines and noted that one was the Koran, the other the Tanakh. On the top of the short stack, was a black Holy Bible with gold edging. Tiny slips of pink paper poked through the closed pages. A hint of lovely flower fragrance lingered in the air. Patience's room was small but immaculate.

The attraction Claire felt for this tiny room brought to mind the closet she'd hidden in as a child. She'd discovered it shortly after her family had moved into their home, when her mother was pregnant with Rebecca. It was an old Victorian style house with high ceilings and a winding staircase. On the fifth floor, Claire had discovered that memorable room behind a hidden doorway. Over the years she had spent much time hiding alone there and daydreaming. For whatever reason, Patience's room brought to her a similar peace, a kind of coziness.

Having taken off her winter outer clothes, the girl stood at the window wearing a long, brown skirt topped with a yellow knit sweater. In her right hand, she cupped a small, wooden ball, no bigger than a softball. She turned around to face Claire.

"One of my students, he's ten, is fascinated by nature. See?" Patience balanced the perfectly chiseled ball in the palm of her hand.

"I don't get it." Claire walked over and snatched it brusquely from her hand. "It's just a wooden ball."

Patience exhaled and shook her head with a smile. "He calls it, 'a handful of secrets.'" She reached delicately to retrieve the ball and placed it back in her palm. Unfazed by Claire's abruptness, she touched its surface lightly with the fingers of her other hand and spoke lovingly. "I was teaching my students about nature, and how a tree's rings can tell us how old the tree is." She pointed to the dark lines on the carving. "Here, you can actually feel the rings."

Claire glided her finger along the curve of the ball. "This ball was made from an eighty-three-year-old tree when it was chopped down. Carlos, he's artistically gifted, saw this as something more. He saw that the tree had eighty-three years of secrets and wisdom to share, and that we just have to feel it to understand." Patience laughed to herself. "It's real hard not to play favorites as a teacher, and I really do have a soft spot for him."

"I suppose it's like any relationship, some parents favor one kid over the other; they just never admit it." Claire peered into the cardboard box of trinkets.

"My students prepared a care package to send to Africa. We had some marvelous news this week," Patience said, showcasing her crooked teeth with a full smile.

"Our school has been working quite hard, over the year, with our church, to raise money for an orphanage in Africa; a place where blind babies and children will have a chance at life. And because of some kind person, who wants to be kept anonymous, those babes will have a chance."

Claire felt her face fluster, this was not something that she wanted to bond with the monster-girl over. "Well, I'm sure that anonymous person will use that donation as a tax write-off and probably wanted to be nameless for a reason."

Claire eyed Patience directly, hoping she didn't have to say more.

"Those anonymous donors are the most generous of givers, when you give with your heart without wanting recognition."

"What about the rest of the world, the ones who don't have an orphanage or schools that care? It's scarcely enough," Claire challenged.

"But it's a start," Patience said. Claire knew by the warmth in Patience's eyes that she was talking about her.

"Look, let's cut the bullshit. I know that you know that I was the one who donated that money. So just to be clear, this isn't some after-school special where I'm going to have this amazing epiphany, make my peace with God, and you and I are going to be crocheting mitts and scarves for the homeless."

Patience let out a laugh, not a condescending one, but one that lightened the mood. "I can't picture you knitting, Claire, but I do know that you, having a say with the orphanage, will be the kind of leadership this project needs. That alone is enough. You and I don't have to be friends. I'm in awe of you, that's all."

Claire lifted a brow. "God isn't doing anything about it."

"And their suffering brought out the compassion in you," Patience said, pleased with the conclusion. "And you acted on it, did the right thing. You did it without wanting any kind of recognition. And it made you happy."

"Happy?" *happy*? Claire summoned a deep breath, to battle her unease. She gave Patience a penetrating gaze. The monster-girl's eyes were soft, very beautiful, shaded with perfectly arched brows. She considered her response carefully and thought, *why not? This should be good.*

Patience shifted, putting her weight onto her good leg. Claire had her full attention.

"When I was eleven, we had a pool. A nice sized kidney shaped pool with a diving board. My sister and I loved it, spent a lot of time in it that summer. And I remember that day in August so clearly, because it gave me that same feeling I had when I donated to that cause of yours."

Claire caught the anticipation in Patience's eyes. "There I was, in my inner tube, sipping on a cherry coke, when in the middle of our pool was this bee: a little bee, fighting for its life. Its little bee legs were paddling, its wings were heavy, stuck to the water. This tiny, unimportant creature was battling to live… battling against a mighty ocean, not wanting to die. So much spirit. But you see, Patience, I had the power. I was the difference to this little, insignificant creature's survival. And all I had to do was reach over and save it.

So I did. I held it on the tip of my finger and watched as the sun dried up its wings, and it fluffed its bristles. Its antennae were feeling around, and its little legs were clinging to me. It was so monumental. And I remember how it looked at me, with those big, round bee eyes. It just stayed on the tip of my finger and relaxed like it was grateful or something. Then after about five minutes it flew away. I thought about that bee for months, and I often wondered if it thought of me too."

Claire narrowed her eyes on Patience, and said in her most menacing tone, "You want to know why I really did it? Why I even bothered with the orphanage? It was no different than what I had felt when I saved that bug. Because I shit you not; there was this moment when that little bee—that tiny seed in the wind—looked right at me as if I was God."

For a long moment, Patience simply stared at Claire, her eyes devoid of any emotion. Then a strange expression crossed her disfigured face. Patience covered it with her beautiful hands, her long fingers splayed across her cheeks. Patience bowed her head and her shoulders shook convulsively.

Great, Claire thought, now she made Esperança's granddaughter cry. Having to ease Patience would be like having to use the toilet at a gas station.

A gasping sound from Patience made Claire even more uncomfortable. She took a step backwards when Patience lowered her hands and lifted her chin. Her face was flushed and she laughing. Laughing whole heartedly. It was the kind of delight that reached those rich, brown eyes.

The monster-girl had read Claire like an unlocked diary and knew that she was just joshing her.

"Smart-ass," Claire quipped, then turned her attention back to the window. In the busy streets below, Claire spotted Chino and his boys, but beyond the bustling city, there were hungry, blind children that some asshole took a picture of. They didn't even know what a camera looked like. But the fact remained that they were smiling on an empty stomach, covered in flies.

When Claire had looked into the situation online, something about the faces of the children distressed her; but it also evoked a memory to that day when she had saved the bee's insignificant life. It was the last time she remembered feeling innocence, feeling at peace.

It was before her father's cheating, before her mom's drinking, before her mom's death.

Patience joined Claire at the window but kept quiet. Despite Claire's efforts to dodge credit for her charitable gesture, she whispered without turning her head.

"What's sad is these poor kids were smiling for the cameras—paddling in the mighty ocean with this incredible will to live. And the irony is that these blind kids in Africa are no more significant than that tiny drowning bee." Claire looked to her right and saw the understanding in Patience's eyes. This was not supposed to be happening. She and the monster-girl would never be friends.

Uncomfortable, and needing to change the subject, Claire scanned the opposite side of the room. She observed numerous creatively colored paintings taped and tacked against her wall, turning it into a modern day shrine. On some the paper had turned yellow and the edges had curled, but others looked like they had been recently hung. From the corner of her eye, she noticed the wooden ball in Patience's hand.

She held the ball up to the light. "Carlos has an amazing way of expressing his vision, and yet he was born blind. Can you imagine? To be able to show what you see inside of you without ever being able to see it with your own eyes?"

Claire took the wooden carving and looked at it again briefly, "And this is supposed to go to Africa?" She passed it back to her with an absent grace. "What they need is clothing, food, and wells for clean water."

"That is true," Patience said. "But the children felt it was inspirational to show other blind children what they have seen in their hearts, to let them feel that they are not alone." Patience noticed her stare. "Pretty remarkable, aren't they?"

"Remarkable? That word should be reserved to describe people such as Beethoven. He created musical masterpieces even after he'd gone stone deaf." Placing her forefinger lightly on her chin, Claire said with considerable zeal, "Now, he was an artist. I remember reading somewhere that after he conducted the first public performance of his ninth symphony, he turned around, witnessed the glorious uproar of the audience, and cried." Claire walked close to the bedroom wall and looked over the students' paintings. "I doubt any of these would cause a glorious uproar." Claire felt the need to challenge her. What she wanted was an offensive answer from Patience, a reason to end their conversation.

Ignoring her disrespect, Patience kept by her side as she observed each painting. "I often wonder what the world would be like if we were all blind and had to live without sight."

"That's a ridiculous thought," Claire scoffed.

Patience smiled. "I believe that the gift of sight has simply produced more temptation."

Claire lifted her green eyes to meet Patience's brown ones. "You mean vanity."

"Among other things. Just think about it. These children are blind; therefore, they have no need to want what they can't see. Instead, they see by using their instincts. They make decisions based on their needs, not their wants."

Although, to a degree, she agreed with her, Claire concluded that the girl was amusingly simple-minded. "You have an unusual thought process."

"Then you get it?"

"I must say if I'd lacked sight I could have saved a shit-load of money." Claire paused to consider what she was saying.

"But I do love nice things."

"Define nice," Patience replied, without stalling the even flow of exchange.

"Well, for starters, I have a nice house."

"And what price do you have to pay to have a nice house like the one you live in?"

"Listen, I've worked hard for everything I have."

"I didn't say you didn't work for it," explained Patience, "but at what price? I don't mean money. I know you work in real estate. How many people did you tempt with things they may have wanted as opposed to what they needed?"

Despite the gap which ran through her upper lip and into her right nostril, she had an angelic smile. Patience strutted over to her Bible and picked it up, not opening it. "Do not love the world or the things in the world. If anyone loves the world, the love of the Father is not in him. For all that is in the world—the lust of the flesh, the lust of the eyes, and the pride of life—is not of the Father but is of the world. And the world is passing away and the lust of it; but he who does the will of God abides forever."

Staring into the face of the young woman whom she had underestimated, Claire remarked, "Well then, I guess our sense of sight works in Satan's favor."

"I guess it does," Patience answered. "But you know, without it, we would miss the gifts which God so generously gives us—gifts that cost us nothing to appreciate."

"Enlighten me," Claire challenged her and found herself enjoying the debate.

Placing the wooden ball on her bed, Patience swaggered back to her bedroom window. After a moment her face took on an even more relaxed expression as she watched the setting sun. "Well," she said to Claire without turning around, "for starters, when we watch a sunset, we have to take notice of the miracle of life. Without the sun we couldn't exist. We'd perish." Patience stared, past the low rooftops, into a bank of fluffy pink clouds in the distance and blinked once before speaking again. "I never get tired of watching a sunset. It's a true gift for the eyes." She turned to face Claire. "It doesn't matter who or what you are, or what your station in life is. The sun shines and sets for everyone."

"Too easy," Claire replied dismissively. "Everyone can appreciate a sunset, even me."

She joined the girl at the window and found herself in awe, not only of the sunset but also of the passion which Patience showed over a simple act of nature.

Following a long silence, Patience turned to face her.

Claire took in a quick breath when she locked eyes with her. Whatever tranquility Patience possessed, she managed to drape it over Claire like an invisible blanket of peace. The girl appeared virtuous, and despite the layers of ugliness that covered her, there was an unexpected trust that made her feel safe. Patience reminded Claire of her own mother.

"You say you can appreciate it, but do you really? Have you ever stared long enough to understand the greatness of what you're looking at? The glorious miracle that our world circles." Patience whispered gently, "How can you witness it and not believe in God?" Magnificent rays hit the window and a spectrum of warmth, dappled their faces.

Undeniably moved, Claire turned to her right and stared into Patience's rich brown eyes—light shone directly into them, and her long lashes softly framed the kindness in them. Wishing she could continue to scorn this creature instead of feeling whatever she was feeling, she shook her head. She tried to identify the emotion. Was it empathy, or mercy? Or was it…shame? That was it, Claire felt ashamed of herself. Biting on her lower lip while she came to terms with herself, the shame she felt both surprised and confused her. And it made her angry.

Claire scanned the room trying to pinpoint reasons to dislike the monster-girl. Instead, her attention was caught by a collection of diplomas and awards neatly displayed on the dresser. It was also very clear that Patience had concealed the dresser mirror with paintings and Braille-written notes. Of course, Claire told herself, sensing her advantage, *she hates looking into the mirror. I can't believe I let her mess with my mind like this.* She looked back at the window, ready to challenge her again.

"It's all scientific, referred to as Rayleigh Scatter," Claire said, avoiding her eyes, "after Lord Rayleigh." She spoke in a condescending manner, delighting in taunting the girl. "He discovered that as light travels through air, a fraction of it is scattered through dust and nitrogen and oxygen molecules. The shorter wave-lengths, blue to green, scatter more easily. That's how you get these ranges of color."

Claire paused, placing her palm against the cool window and recalled her tenth-grade science class lecture. "I remember it, even though science wasn't my favorite subject. So, there you go, a sunset is nothing to get emotional about."

Claire's reply and the expression on her face were at odds. Because despite having given her scientific explanation with confidence, Claire's eyes betrayed her. They yielded to the ever-changing horizon and a hint of awe had etched its way into them. Taking a quick breath through her nose, her lips pressed together, Claire watched, motionless, for many long minutes as deep clouds were flooded in fiery violet hues.

Neither did Patience move. Both women waited in silence until the horizon became a thin veil of soft gray, heralding the starry night.

Pick a star, Claire thought. Gentleness strengthened its grip on her as she recalled the lullaby her mother sang to her as a child.

Patience watched her from the corner of her eye. Claire was calm. Pulling the tune from her memory, and evoking "Song of Innocence," made a tranquil softness escaped her green eyes. Transfixed by the moment, Claire's lips surrendered, forming the shape of a brilliant smile.

Claire felt undeniably at peace. She looked out of the corner of her eye and saw a single tear trickled down Patience's face.

Patience wiped the tear away lightly, her eyes not leaving the changing sky. Her soft voice cracked the ice, "You have your mother's smile."

Claire could not repress the shiver than ran through her. Had the girl really seen her mother? She did indeed have her mother's beautiful smile. In fact, as the years had passed and she'd developed into a woman, people had often compared Claire's beauty to that of her mother's. Connie had been a breathtaking vision. And her smile was what Claire missed most.

But the way Patience had said, "You have your mother's smile," meant more. Patience had somehow sent the following message to her: "You could have been just like her, the finest aspects of her, before her heartache."

Claire blinked at the statement and saw something celestial moving through Patience's eyes. It was almost calming, a luring energy that was reaching for her.

"That's a gift worth seeing, worth remembering," said Patience. "And science hasn't explained everything," she added, stepping closer to whisper. "There's times, when the ones we love, try to reach us in other ways. Maybe your mother is trying to say something to you."

"What is it you know? Tell me," Claire whispered.

"I've seen what you've seen. I saw into your memories." She extended her hand. "Your mother's and yours. I can show you, if you'll let me."

There was something so tranquil about the monster- girl. Claire offered her right hand, and Patience gently took it in hers.

Claire's body surrendered to the strange magnetic pull of Patience, and an inexplicable energy surged through her mind. She soon saw herself, very clearly, hiding in her secret closet when she was eight years old.

Tears covered her little girl face. She caught her breath and clutched her favorite stuffed bear, which she'd named Mr. Wiggly. "I wish she never came," she whined. Then she whispered into the bear's ear, "We can stay here forever. We don't need anybody else."

The closet door opened, and light seeped into the dark space, exposing Claire's wet cheeks. Mommy wore a red, knee-length skirt and white cotton blouse.

"Sweetheart, please come out." She smiled radiantly, her red hair in large curls and pinned into a loose bob. She bent down to face Claire. "If you won't come out, then I'll have to come in with you."

Claire shook her head fiercely, and her red pigtails whipped around her face. "Not coming out! Not 'til you take Becca back!" She clutched her bear even tighter.

"Fine then, scoot over." Mommy pushed her way into the narrow opening and shared the small space with her. "It's going to be tight in here, but we'll make do. I thought we could bake some chocolate chip cookies today, but I guess we're staying in here."

Claire loved baking with Mommy. "We could still make some," Claire suggested. "Then bring them back in here."

Mommy laughed. "That sounds good."

She rested her head on her mother's lap. "Okay."

"That's my best girl."

"I'm not your best girl anymore," Claire whimpered into her mother's skirt. "You have Becca now."

Stretching her legs, Mommy scooped Claire into her arms. She whispered tenderly, "Enough of this, now," and carried her out of the closet.

Claire's tiny legs clung to her mother like a spider monkey, and her little head rested on Mommy's left shoulder. Mr. Wiggly dangled on her right.

"I think we need love time, Claire."

Sitting on her mother's lap in the gently swaying rocking chair, Claire's crying faded.

Mommy stroked her brow. "You will always be my best girl—my first best girl."

"Forever?" Claire looked up at her.

"Yes. You'll be my first best girl forever, and nothing will ever change that." Her mother kissed her forehead. "One day, you'll be my first best girl to get married. And after that, you'll be my first best girl to give me my grand-babies." She twirled Claire's red lock of hair around her finger. "You'll always be my first; never, ever forget that." Mommy stopped rocking and stared at Claire. "You're in Mommy's heart, and one day you'll be rocking your own little girl just like I'm rocking you now."

Mommy placed her soft, warm hand against Claire's cool, tear-stained cheek. The scent of lilac and honey, which Mommy often creamed her hands with, calmed Claire. Mommy always smelled good. Claire peeked up. The joyful smile on her mother's face looked down at the eight-year-old Claire. But she was now tumbling back to the present, and Claire compared her experience from over thirty years ago with the woman she had become. There was a burning in her chest as she pulled her hand back.

Gasping, Claire leaned against the wall and looked to Patience for an answer, "How did you do that?" Her breath caught, emotions racing. "What have you done?"

Patience stepped forward and put a tentative hand on Claire's shoulder. "I told you Claire, I've seen into you and your mother's memories."

Feeling that she might fall down, Claire sat on the edge of the bed. "I'm dizzy." She paused and spoke under her breath. "It was so real, like a movie. She was so beautiful."

Patience sat with her. "Yes, she was beautiful, and she loved you very much." She took Claire's trembling hands into her own.

It had to be shock, why Claire exchanged a genuine smile with the monster-girl. It lasted for six, healthy heartbeats and as swiftly it had come, it was gone. When Claire caught herself being susceptible to her gentleness again, she drew her hands back, and Patience's smile was instantly chased by a quivering, cleft lip.

A toadstool, Claire thought, *an underestimated fungus, which had its use after all.* "Esperança teach you a few tricks?" Claire joked, simply to mask her vulnerability.

Patience hung her head low and said nothing. Hating herself for being cruel, Claire snapped, "I didn't ask you to do that, and why the hell are you interfering with my life?"

Patience pulled her head up, "You need to know what you're opening yourself up to. Demonic forces. Eternal hell. I can't stand by and do nothing when I know what you need. And Claire, it's not this."

Because the girl's statement struck her so hard, she could think of nothing to do but laugh out loud. "This is some serious bullshit," she finally replied, ripping the elastic from her hair, smoothing back the loose hairs, and reusing the elastic to secure a thick ponytail. "I mean, Esperança has this voodoo shit down to a science, and now you have this 'Praise Jesus' thing going on. I mean, damn it, talk about being in a tug-of-war!"

Looking into Patience's eyes, Claire saw that sadness had glazed over them. "Okay, tell you what. You tell your God that you've done your due diligence, and yeah, I get it. But I've decided. And to tell you the truth, I'd rather go to hell in a Louis Vuitton bag than fall for his crap ever again!"

Patience took a deep breath, and then exhaled slowly. "What

is it you're looking for, Claire?"

There was no answer.

"Why are you here?"

Claire rose from the bed, tucked her blouse into her skirt, and walked to the bedroom window. Watching and feeling nightfall creep through the streets like an energy breaking through the cracks in the road—hellish energy seeking its prey in the night— she felt the cloaked powers and was at ease in their presence.

Still, she pondered the question Patience had asked. The short answer was obvious enough: she wanted control, a child in order to maintain that control. But the underlying reason was different. "All right, I'll tell you." She turned around to find Patience behind her. "Happiness, okay…I want happiness."

Patience smiled. The word "happiness" seemed magical, as if the answer allowed her to continue her lesson. "So you see, what you seek has been within you all along. You don't need to go through all this ugliness to find it."

Patience nodded, with a gentle understanding. "Now I know it won't be easy. I'd be lying to you if I said it would be. Let's work together and take it a step at a time. If you give me the chance, I know I can teach you, help you to understand your purpose, just like the orphanage. This is something you're good at; you're strong and you know people in authoritative positions. You, Claire, can make a difference. And in time everything can fall into place for you, that happiness you're searching for."

"You'll teach me? Oh, now this takes the bloody biscuit." Shaking her head in pity, she asked, "Are you happy, Patience? Can you practice what you preach when you look the way you do?"

Flinching, Patience turned her head, ashamed of her outer ugliness.

Claire pointed to the mirror she'd covered up. "You can't even look in the mirror and see what God has made you into, and you expect me to buy this happiness within crap."

Patience regarded her camouflaged dresser mirror. "I'm only human, Claire. But I do have a chosen path. I cover the mirror with the children's letters because it helps me not to become distracted…so I can remember the reason I'm here."

"Bullshit!" Claire charged at her with venom. "Admit it, you hate what you see."

Patience's lip quivered.

"Say it, and then I'll know you're not full of shit!"

Shaken, the girl nodded. "It's true. It isn't easy for me sometimes. But God has a plan, and he has a purpose for why I'm here." Patience stopped to tidy the few strands of hair that covered her otherwise bare scalp. Her hands trembled as she spoke again. "But what you're doing is denying God, turning your back on him and accepting Satan. You're surrendering your soul...selling it for eternal damnation in exchange for false promises." Patience used her eyes to plead with Claire. "If you want happiness, you'll have to find peace first."

Claire scoffed. "I'll tell you what I know about happiness... it comes with a price. Because as soon as you feel that glimmer of hope, that bubbly good feeling where your heart feels like it's going to explode, God comes in and takes it away. He gives it and takes it...he gives it and takes it. So the only peace I'm going to make...is with myself. God forgot about me, he forgot about my mother, and, judging by you, darling, he forgot about you, too."

"He didn't forget, Claire. God loves us all. If only you'd allow yourself to see, to have faith again—"

"—Right," Claire cut her short, "I know all about it. If your faith is as small as a mustard seed, blah, blah, blah." She stopped to open her purse and pulled out a tube of hand cream. "Cream?"

The girl shook her head no and watched while Claire vigorously rubbed the cream into her own hands.

"You see, Patience, I have my own theory. I think God gets off up there on the shit he has you and the rest of his followers believing." Claire stuffed the cream back into her purse while muttering to herself, her wrath swiftly picking up speed as she slammed her purse back down.

She shrunk back when Claire rounded her and released her barrage.

"I mean can you honestly tell me you believe God loves us all? What fucking moron believes such shit? Do you sincerely believe that God loves these sicko pervs that get-off on children? These creepy men holed away in their dens, pulling their puds over little boys, while their wives are in another room preparing them ham and cheese sandwiches!"

In spite of herself, Claire's anger increased. Her words chasing after each other in a violent rush.

"What fucking God could love us all and idly watch while babies are being raped? People dying of hunger? Just like those blind babies born in Africa, starving to a slow death. I mean, have you read the statistics? It's a shame, a crying fucking shame. What kind of God could fix it and do nothing! What kind of a God uses starving babies to force people into submission?"

Patience's enduring nature only enraged her more. Claire was now pacing like a madwoman, and her ears had turned red.

"He's there, floating around on some fucking cloud, swashbuckling in his glory, dangling salvation from his righteous fishing line. All the while, he's watching us trying to claw our way out of this bloody hell hole!"

Claire stopped pacing and gave Patience a searching look, but the girl remained calm, even tolerant of Claire's tantrum. Ashamed for losing control, Claire pinched the bridge of her nose with her fingers and closed her eyes, while taking several deep breaths.

"At least with Satan," Claire said, opening her eyes on the fifth exhale and feeling strangely composed, "it is what it is. He gives you what you want, without the begging and the constant stroking. At least with Satan, I've seen miracles. I can't say the same about God, can I?"

"Satan gives a taste, a lie." Patience argued. "You have to keep feeding it, hurting innocent people for it. Satan will give you exactly what you want; he'll reward wicked behavior. Don't you see? You're helping to build Satan's army with evil and corruption."

"Don't." Claire faced her. "I'm warning you, don't you dare try and use your brain on me again."

Patience shook her head in frustration. "You think it's right to call in forces to make your husband love you, to manipulate him?" Passionate wrath boiled over Patience's usual gentle exterior. "Do you think that it's right to take souls from innocent people so you can conceive a child of your own? Think about the consequences!"

The only thing Claire heard was 'husband' and it enraged her. She came at Patience, speaking through twisted lips. "I own my husband! And there is no way I'm letting another woman reap the rewards of my hard work."

Patience picked up the carved, wooden ball she'd introduced earlier to Claire. Her eyes remained closed as she rubbed the carving against her cheek.

There was silence.

"Did you hear me?" Claire pressed. "I'm talking to you, answer me."

"What you're doing is unnatural," Patience said. "It goes against God, against everything sacred. Satan found you when you were at your most vulnerable and desperate. You were prepared to do anything to keep from losing your husband, even if it meant lying and manipulating to have him believe you'd conceive a child for him."

Patience shook her head, spoke quickly, racing to convince her. "Don't you see? Had you been honest with yourself and with Jonathon, Satan wouldn't have been able to reach you. These demonic forces are dragging you into something unholy, something that will end in a very bad way."

Claire's lips parted as she prepared to challenge Patience, but her rebuttal lodged in her throat.

Patience took Claire's delicate hand and cupped it in the warmth of her own, gently rubbing it, causing Claire to succumb to her tender voice. "When we go against God, we're going against nature...the nature of what is right, of what is meant to be. The natural rhythm of life must go on." Taking Claire's soft hand, Patience glided it gently over the carved, wooden ball. "You see, when we go with the grain, then it's smooth. Natural." Patience dragged Claire's finger gingerly against the grain, against the rigid rings. "Can you feel the difference, the bumps?"

Claire nodded.

"When you manipulate something, force it to be something else, then those bumps will always be there. Consider it a reminder...it shows that what you're doing isn't the way it's supposed to be. Eventually it will all go back to the way God intended it to be—except you'll be lost. Lost and forgotten. Satan will take your soul. And I promise you, if that happens, you'll wish you had allowed God to carry you. But it'll be too late. Your soul will be damned."

Touching the carving and caressing the smooth grain, Claire's shoulders felt heavy.

"If you go to Brazil and go against God's grain, the little girl that will be sacrificed will pay a huge price. She will suffer so that you can have the girl you need, just to keep your husband. Innocent people will suffer. Is that what you want?"

Claire looked amazed. "Girl? You mean it's true? I'm having a girl?" She smiled, but it quickly vanished when Patience's words penetrated in Claire's mind. A little girl would die in place of Claire's bequest. "I didn't make the rules, Patience; I'm simply doing what I need to do to hold my family together." Claire was torn, though still leaning toward going to Brazil. She wished Patience hadn't said anything. In this case, ignorance was easier.

"You're not listening to me. This isn't a good thing, Claire! It's an atrocity against God. You'll pay for it and so will an innocent child whose soul will be sacrificed. You have no idea of the evil you'll bring into this world. It may look and sound like a child, but I swear to you, when it arrives it will destroy everything sanctified by God."

Not blinking an eye, Claire said in her most poised tone, "I noticed your choice of reading material," referring to the other bibles. "There's a Golden Rule, an ethic of reciprocity that is found in almost every religion. It's the most concise and general principle of ethics." Claire raised a waiting brow, but Patience remained silent. "Judaism and Christianity—You shall love your neighbor as you love yourself; Islam—Not one of you is a believer until he loves for his brother what he loves for himself. I mean it goes on and on. The same principle. But you know I have my own principle of ethics. Now you may not agree with them, and I'll give you a gold star for trying to break me, because I am not an easy person to spar with. But what I learned a long, long time ago—hurt me once, shame on you, hurt me twice..." Claire shook her head, with a tut-tut. "You know the rest and I'm sure Satan would agree."

Claire went to reach for her purse, "It's been a slice Patience, but I have to jet." That was when Patience seized a powerful hold of Claire's hand.

"I need to show you what your mother was thinking in her last hours." Patience held Claire's eyes with her own. "She wants me to."

The room spun around her like a kaleidoscope. Claire wanted to run, to escape the very thing that had broken her so many decades ago, but her body fell numb.

"She thought about you," Patience whispered.

A flash of heat spiraled down Claire's spine and settled into her legs, as if cement had been poured into them and quickly dried. She no longer controlled what was happening; her awareness dissolved into the murky past. Somehow peering through Patience's eyes, Claire watched her mother's final hours play like a convincing motion picture.

Bloody and motionless, Connie's body lay twisted and mangled behind the steering wheel. The gaping wound on her forehead had crusted over, and her red hair was matted in dreadlocks, saturated with blood. Her eyes were swollen and bruised. She opened her left eye, and summoning every ounce of strength she had left, she somehow brought her hand down on the car horn.

Outside the vehicle a full moon glowed above freshly fallen snow, while the faint sounds of Connie's painful whimpers could be heard by no one.

She had finally accepted her final hour of living. She mumbled indistinctly through broken teeth and split lips, before saying her last prayer. "Jesus, meek and humble of heart, make my heart like unto thine." Connie drifted off again as her mind floated between consciousness and unconsciousness. "Most sacred heart of Jesus, convert sinners, save the dying…" She nodded off again and slept for a few minutes, then fought her way back into reality. She completed her last words.

"Sacred heart of Jesus, thy kingdom come. Deliver the holy souls in Purgatory. Dear God in heaven, my sweet Jesus, and the angels above, please watch over my girls, especially my first best girl, my baby Claire. She's not going to…"

Connie muttered unintelligibly and her breathing became

greatly labored. In her right hand, a crumpled piece of paper was covered in blood. The heading, written in pencil, was titled, My Mother, the Brain of a Blue Tit Bird.

"Don't let Claire blame herself, don't let this ruin her. She's not strong enough. She's weak and needy...keep her safe, in your hands."

She inhaled three quick breaths and died at exactly 3:23 a.m. The beautiful snow continued falling, covering the family car, which had now become her coffin.

Claire pulled away from Patience. She fell onto the bed and fought desperately for air. She was rocking herself, while mumbling incoherent words into the mattress. "No, no, no...Mommy, no," she moaned over and over, while rocking herself in a state of shock. "No, please, I'm so sorry, Mommy...no, no, no."

Watching in silence, Patience could do nothing, but wait it out. She knew that Claire would take it hard, but it was more important for Claire to know that her mother wanted God to remain in Claire's life, and that she did not blame her for her last and final drinking binge. It was her dying wish, and it needed to be communicated. But as Claire managed to slowly pull herself together, Patience began to view Claire as an injured animal, a dangerous animal with rage enough to kill.

Moments later, Claire rose to a sitting position. Her eyes remained wide and completely alert as she sucked quick breaths, her emotions morphed from grief into a lethal rage.

Patience sensed Claire pushing her pain down, while her long-suppressed rage began to mount. Until now, the anger from deep within had spewed forth in tiny intervals of fury. But this was the core, the seed from which it had grown. Patience took careful steps backwards, knowing what was coming.

Jumping up from the bed, Claire drove herself toward Patience, slamming her fist into the side of the girl's jaw. Patience fell hard onto the floor, as Claire continued to pounce on her, ramming her fist into her mouth. Blood warmed Claire's knuckles, but Patience didn't fight back; instead, she remained limber, allowing Claire to exhaust herself. But not once, did Claire shed a single tear.

"Enough!" Esperança stood in the open doorway, a joint dangling from the side of her mouth.

Even in Claire's violent frenzy, the sound of Esperança's voice brought her back to reality, and she became aware that she was holding a fistful of Patience's sweater.

"Let her go," the voodoo priestess said in a calm, steady tone.

Claire opened her mouth to speak, but words scrambled around inside her head in a muddle. Mechanically, she opened her hand, releasing Patience's sweater.

Patience hurried to her bed, gasping for air.

"I know, I know," Esperança intensified Claire's confusion all the more by reading her innermost feelings with her taunting gift. "Patience can be very stubborn," Esperança said, feeling unease at the sight of blood splatter over Claire's blouse. She glanced at Patience, making sure that she was all right then inhaled masterfully on the joint before blowing the smoke scornfully in Claire's direction.

The smolder surrounded Claire as she inhaled the sweet scent that fogged her brain, turning the scene into slow motion.

Esperança gave a sinister grin, but it fell short as she studied her distraught granddaughter. The girl sat quietly on the edge of her bed, fiddling with her sweater and attempting to adjust the stretched fibers over her exposed breast. Her lower lip burst with a blister of oozing blood. She lowered her head in shame.

"Clean yourself up," the old woman ordered, while stubbing the leftover joint into her palm and pushing it into her jeans pocket.

"Yes, Grandma," Patience answered without looking up, but she made no sign of movement. With purse in hand, Claire made a quick dash, exiting the room without looking at either woman.

"Take a seat at my table and don't move," Esperança told her, without taking her eyes off Patience. Then, free from Claire's earshot, she limped over to her granddaughter, and stood before her.

"When will you ever learn, dear one?" Esperança said, raising Patience's chin with her index finger. Tears coated Patience's thick lashes, and fell across her cheeks. Using the bottom half of her white T-shirt, Esperança dabbed lightly at her blood and tears. "This is not a war that I want you to fight. I keep telling you that, but you never listen." Esperança attempted to comb over her granddaughter's hair, then fussed with her stretched sweater. "And now look at you…you're a mess."

"I know what you're trying to do, and it's not going to work. They always choose Satan," Patience said. "You give them an out, free will, and they always choose wrong."

"I think this one's different. I just need more time with her, get her to see," Esperança pleaded.

"Time's running out, and they're going to hunt for one, 'catching darkness' they call it, so that Satan can use Claire as a vessel. I saw her, Grandma, the little girl. She's God's divine and they're going to catch her," Patience whispered. "You're playing both sides, feeding one fire to help the other. But they'll kill the child in the process…they'll take her from her mother."

Esperança felt queasy. "And if they do, she'll go to a better place, to God's house…to be with others just like her. It's a beautiful thing. Really…it is."

Patience grabbed Esperança's hand firmly. "I know that you don't truly mean that. And I know that you can't do this alone. Please, Grandma," Patience begged in a whisper, while insisting with her eyes, "give Claire to me…let me make things right for her. Let me help her."

Esperança shook her head. "You know how dangerous this is. I might as well send you back to God myself."

Patience remained quiet.

"What is it about her that has made you so foolish? I've never seen you this bad before." Esperança paused with a sad smile that darkened her eyes, while waiting for Patience to respond. "You know that I cannot read your thoughts. Tell me, child."

No response.

"You won't tell me?" Esperança implored. "Is it because you see something in her, or have you seen what I've seen?"

"I know that you see yourself in her, Grandma," Patience replied. "I also know that you saw her future long before you even met her. Satan had his hold on her already, and you're using your powers to manipulate her into the other direction. You led her in, got her husband to love her again to keep her close to you, and now you're hoping that you can get her to see the truth before it's too late. But she doesn't scare easily, Grandma. She's too angry, too vengeful. She's not ready." Patience shook her head in sorrow, tears spilled over her cheeks. "But I also know that Claire is your redemption, your last redemption."

Esperança's arms fell at her sides. "And what about you, child," Esperança counteracted, but not denying the truth. "What is your reason…or reasons?"

Patience relaxed her jaw enough to gulp her answer back down.

"The light in my darkness…I would do anything for you." Esperança lightly stroked Patience's cheek. "You are the only good thing left in my life. Just tell me why…why Claire?" She cupped Patience's chin.

Patience swallowed hard, trying to contain her mixed emotions.

"It's because…" Patience began, pushing Esperança's hand away, "…because she weeps." She looked at her grandmother with a stricken look on her face.

"She weeps inside for her mother, and her mother weeps for her."

26

The Last Redemption

Esperança slipped slowly between the beaded curtains into the room where Claire sat, slumped over and listless. She limped toward the table, never taking her eyes off the redhead. She sat down in her chair and placed a small plastic bag on the table. Reaching inside, Esperança pulled out a plump, aromatic marijuana bud and inhaled deeply. Then she went to work cutting it into tiny flakes with a small paring knife. Finally, she spoke, without looking up. "You put your hands on my granddaughter."

Weary and confused, Claire raised her head and parted her lips to speak. Her lips quivered. Not a sound escaped.

Taking in a deep breath, her nostrils flaring, Esperança announced firmly, "I'll give you a pass this time. But don't think I won't fuck you up if you ever try that shit again!" She stabbed the knife into the wooden table. "One free pass," she quietly repeated, while sprinkling the leaves onto the rolling papers.

Again, Claire opened her mouth to speak, but the words in her head piled up on one another like a traffic jam. Wondering what was going on, she worried that she may have had a stroke, or worse: that she might remain a vegetable for the rest of her life.

Esperança read the terror both in Claire's eyes and inside of her. She proficiently licked the sides of the paper then rolled a perfect cone shape. She twisted the end of the joint, her eyes fixed the whole time on Claire. "Take your time," she finally advised her, as she bit the tip of the joint and spit it in her direction. "Don't force yourself yet. Let your body and mind come together again. Give it a few minutes."

Remaining mute, Claire observed Esperança light the joint with a match.

The voodoo priestess sucked in greedily. The tip lit up, casting a dim red glow throughout the tiny dark room. On her exhale, smoke leaked through Esperança's small mouth and nose, evoking the image of a shimmering Halloween skull.

The ordeal of watching and hearing her mother's last words had smacked Claire the way a window stuns an unsuspecting bird in flight.

A blue tit bird.

"Patience didn't mean to hurt you," Esperança said, reading the anxiety inside Claire. "She wanted you to understand your mother's dying wish, that's all. She didn't want her death to ruin you."

Claire closed her eyes, and the delicate skin above her eyelids creased tightly into wrinkles. She appeared childish, as if she believed that holding her breath might erase the image repeating in her mind—her mother's contorted corpse.

Esperança's free hand grabbed hold of Claire's chin. An unexpected mix of apprehension and understanding formed in the old woman's eyes. Her voice strange and shaky, her lips trembling for control, she said, "Let her go. Release her from your thoughts…remove her from your mind. She's gone, and nothing's gonna bring her back to you. Not in this lifetime or any other."

Several moments passed. Claire did not respond as she stared back.

Esperança's eyes were less intense, and her lips returned to their usual thin, creased lines. She released Claire's chin and stroked her right cheek affectionately. Her voice became soft and soothing. "I know you loved her, and she loved you." Then, pulling her hand away, she said recklessly, "But she's gone—like a fart in the wind."

A shade of a smile formed on Claire's face. It amazed her

how Esperança always managed to put her foot in her mouth.

Lightly slapping the redhead on her cheek, Esperança said, "Good. Very good. We have work to do and a baby to make. Isn't that good? You get to go to the Valley of Souls and spend time with the devil and his chosen?"

Claire eased into normal deep breathing. The voodoo priestess was making perfect sense. It was time to let her mother go. Patience had unknowingly given Claire closure by showing her how much Connie had loved her. Now Claire could move forward. Her eyes open wide, she focused on the old woman with renewed energy. Her vile friend was now a clear vision.

Esperança exhaled another deep stream of marijuana smoke through her wrinkled lips and gaunt cheekbones, blowing the smoke in Claire's direction again.

Claire's mind and body finally began functioning normally again, and she simply felt relaxed rather than disconnected. She was grateful that the drug erased the tension she should have been feeling after seeing her mother's death.

"You're getting high," Esperança grinned at her. "It's a small room, and this is really good shit. Straight from the crops of Mexico."

Before she could check herself, Claire released a slow, exasperated breath. "You are a sight."

"But you love me anyway." She motioned for Claire to lean closer over the table.

As if by reflex, and to her surprise, Claire did so. Esperança opened her mouth and released another lazy trail into the air toward her client.

Breathing in, Claire relaxed even more. She was surrounded by a vague and dreamy mist. "I think I'm floating."

After giving a deep, throaty laugh, Esperança followed up with a bout of coughing and choking. She spit phlegm into her T-shirt.

The revolting gesture did not shock Claire. But the sight of blood that drenched her blouse made her remember the swift thrashing she'd given Patience. "Can I wash my hands?" Claire asked.

Esperança placed her joint down and pointed to the small sink in the corner. Claire stood with a wobble and proceeded to the corner while Esperança departed through the beaded curtain and returned to her chair. Claire made her way back too and sat across from her again.

Esperança passed a tube of antiseptic cream to Claire. "For your knuckles."

"Thanks." Claire began the treatment. The raw, open cuts were painful to touch. If her own hands were this bad, she could only imagine the damage Patience received. Claire passed her the cream back in exchange for a plastic bag that Esperança had offered.

"You can't go home like that," Esperança said, referring to Claire's blood-soaked blouse.

Claire pulled a yellow T-shirt out of the bag and held it up. "Not this, anything but this." Claire was referring to the SIT ON A HAPPY FACE design.

Esperança let out a laugh, a full-blown, choking-on-her-own-phlegm type laugh. "What? Five for ten dollars; I bought them off this street vendor. It's new, never been worn," she promised.

"I have a feeling you knew this was coming." Claire turned around, while she removed her blouse. She muttered to herself, and pulled the T-shirt over her head. "I look like an asshole," Claire said, facing Esperança again, smoothing back a loose strand from her eyes.

"A *happy* asshole," Esperança added.

They both shared another laugh, but Claire's own amusement fell lost at the sight of her blouse placed in her lap. Esperança was touched at what she was seeing inside of Claire: a glorious sunrise, casting a ray over a darkened crevice. And inside the crack, a lone flower bud was reaching for the light. Some souls are savable, she thought to herself.

Claire looked up with a soft expression. "Is she okay? I mean…I didn't break anything, did I?"

"Why do you care?" Esperança's brows lifted, in silent scrutiny. She continued to see something blooming in Claire's eyes. But Esperança needed to be vigilant in choosing her words, words that would help the delicate flower bloom. "Patience will be fine; she's a big girl," she said, without a hint of empathy.

Claire was quiet, and even a little disappointed in Esperança's lack of compassion. "That's a bit cold, and she didn't seem fine to me. She didn't seem fine at all."

Esperança heard the snarling demons underfoot. *"No reverse physiology. Free will, you know the rules."*

"Patience knew what she was getting herself into," Esperança said, giving Claire an excuse to hold a grudge. "Your reaction was unavoidable."

"Still..." Claire bowed her head in shame. She remained silent for a moment or two. "It was wrong," she said, looking directly at Esperança.

Yet there it was, Esperança saw. The flower of conscience, blooming in total darkness, aided by the ray of dawn. Claire's eyes were empathetic; she blinked hard a few times, and shook her head in deep remorse at the thought of what she'd done. But Esperança remained quiet. Observing.

"I didn't mean to hurt her," Claire explained. "Perhaps you can tell her how sorry I am."

Esperança shrugged. "Sure, I'll let her know." *Close, so very close.*

Claire passed Esperança her blouse. "Please get rid of this," she added.

Esperança twisted the blouse into a ball and pitched it into the corner before settling back into her chair. They were quiet, both watching the flame between them.

Esperança picked up the joint and relit it with the candle's flame. She drew in a pull. "You don't have to do this, you know," Esperança informed Claire, while creating perfect smoke rings in the air. "We can always undo the work on your husband... let the chips fall."

"And then what?" Claire pressed hazily, while breaking apart the rings with her index finger as a child would.

"Nothing." Esperança took several more pulls, then stubbed the remaining embers of her joint into the table. She focused her full attention on Claire. "Just allow nature to take its course."

"You mean go with the grain," Claire added.

Esperança concealed her reverence with the term and furthered, "God's grain."

"Does Patience do that with all your clients?"

"No. Only sometimes. Patience saw something in you, and sometimes she'll give people an out before they sign on the dotted line. Sometimes, but it makes no difference once people's minds are made up..." Esperança was whispering now and wearing a poignant expression.

Without warning, the harsh reality of the decision rang through Claire's mind like a railroad-crossing alarm. Patience's words had left behind some unexpected strain on her conscience.

"What will become of me?" Claire whispered. "If I choose not to do this, I mean?"

Caught off guard, Esperança replied, "You'll live."

"But my husband will leave me."

"I told you before…it's one or the other. You can't be in the middle. Yes, if you choose God, then the work on your husband will fade. But you'll live. If you want, Patience can help you fight your demons," Esperança whispered. "I'd understand, and we could still hang out."

"What?" Claire asked, "I didn't hear you." Her ears were popping, and she was incredibly thirsty.

Esperança knew that the fallen angels were in the room with them. They were hovering, listening to every word. Yet she asked the question. "Are you sure about this?"

"Yes."

Pointing her finger directly at Claire's face, the old woman said, "You're absolutely sure?"

"Yes," Claire answered, without hesitation. She had come this far. "I'm absolutely sure."

"So, we move forward." The priestess gave Claire a searching look, then veered away, her gaze focused on the beaded entry.

"I guess it's baby time," Claire said. "Esperança?"

But the priestess had yet to answer.

"Hello, I'm talking to you," Claire tried again.

"What?" Esperança turned to her. Her deadpan face gave nothing away. "I didn't hear you."

"Is everything okay?"

Esperança's eyelids twitched. "Yeah, why wouldn't it be?"

Claire lifted an eyebrow, catching something in Esperança's eyes. "What's wrong? You're not your usual self."

"It's…" Esperança's words died on her lips. She gave Claire a long look before speaking again. "It's just the weed. It brings out the pussycat in me."

"Ha. You, a pussycat? More likely a panther," Claire countered.

Esperança's eyes were downcast, as still as the rest of her.

"Okay, what's going on here?" Claire pressed. "Are you worried about Patience?"

With a slow rise, Esperança stood up. She hobbled to her special shelf, fiddled about and produced an almost empty bottle of rum. After pouring a full gulp into her mouth, she walked back to her chair. Unlike marijuana, alcohol added fuel to her fire. She sat down and slammed the bottle hard, making the table shake and the candle flame flicker. "I promised Patience I'd quit drinking."

"And so you switched to a recreational drug?"

A cold, sinister look painted Esperança's dark eyes as she raised her head to face the ceiling. In a dreadful, tranquil tone, she said, "Sometimes I wish I could send her back." The room remained quiet for several minutes, save for the sounds of rum sloshing in Esperança's mouth whenever she took another swig from the bottle.

Clearly the rum was affecting Esperança. Claire measured each word with caution. "Send her back where?"

"Send her soul back to God."

"You mean kill her?" Claire whispered, but Esperança wasn't paying attention. Heaviness weighed down her eyelids, and she took another slow drink. Esperança had said she wished she could kill Patience. So what stopped her? And what had she meant by sending her back? But a surge of thirst overtook her curiosity. "My mouth's dry," Claire whispered.

Not saying a word, Esperança rose again from the chair and left the room through the beaded curtains.

A full minute had passed. The room became stone-still. Something was very wrong. Claire murmured between unmoving lips, "Esperança, there's something wrong."

The beaded curtain began moving again, clinking back and forth, and then a soft breeze swept through the room. Uneasiness crept into her, as her subconscious was warning her to run and never look back. But Claire's body remained grounded as if in temporary paralysis. Her eyes darted back and forth taking in every inch of the tiny room, a room filled with forces so strong they seemed to buzz all around her, whispering and laughing. From somewhere unknown came the sounds of a crying child. The candle flame rose three inches, then the room plunged into darkness. Claire clutched her thighs, bracing herself against the fear she felt. Someone or something had blown out the candle. From the extinguished wick, smoke circled Claire, teasing her nose, making it tickle. In her head, she ran and screamed for help, but outwardly she remained motionless. Her wide, horrified eyes adjusted slightly to the dark and scoped every shadow and every shape that lingered.

"Looks like we have company." Esperança's voice had shot through the dark, breaking the force that reached for Claire. The flicker of a match sparked the black room as Esperança limped in and relit the wick. "Here," she said, handing a bottle of water to Claire.

"C-company?" Claire stuttered, her hand shook as she took the bottle and looked at it warily.

"It's clean, potion free."

"Thank you." Claire's head tilted up until she'd swallowed the water to the last drop. She lowered her head and came eye to eye with Esperança.

Esperança spoke without taking her eyes off the redhead. "There was a real party going on in here, lots of visitors."

"I couldn't move." Claire tried to relate the encounter. "It was like they were holding me down or something."

"Hmm…" Esperança listened in on the voice in her own head. "My granddaughter dug up some helpers."

Gooseflesh climbed up Claire's spine and then spread across her arms.

"They're gone now. All but one anyway." Esperança gestured with her eyes to Claire's right side.

"One what?" Claire whispered, looking next to her.

"One helper. It's someone you've already met, Esperança teased. "Someone who makes you feel very, very good," she added, with an impious gleam in her eyes.

For all her fear, Claire's face flushed, and she snapped, "You should have warned me about that before!"

"Me? No, no, no. Don't blame me," Esperança chided,

"That's all you. Interesting, it's the first time my father ever did that with one of my clients."

Nervously, Claire uttered, "Father? You mean your actual father?"

"Yes," Esperança replied calmly. "My father in this last life. Actually, it was my sister in my first life who became my father in this last life. It's not unheard of for one of Satan's Chosen to bring a member back into the world, although my mother was simply a woman in the valley where our tribe is situated."

Claire was intrigued. "What are you, reincarnated?"

"Something like that."

Claire crossed her arms, trying to repel a sudden chill. "All of you?"

"Yes, all of us. We're reborn in the valley, and, if not by our immediate members, we're brought back by families that have nothing to do with Satan's initial selection. And by the time we enter into the world, the fallen angels will let the other Chosen know of our births, or even conceptions. It all depends. But we never refer to our new families as such, mothers are simply vessels."

"In blood only," she repeated Patience's words, with a new appreciation. "Patience mentioned something about it. So you mean to tell me that the tribe you and your siblings were born into just keeps returning among the living."

"That's about the measure of it."

"And in the middle of the Brazilian jungles no less, but why are you here, in The Bronx?"

"In the seventies, the Chosen were ordered to spread Satan's word. New York was one of the first places, along with New Orleans," Esperança explained. "New York has a very strong mix of energy. It's a very influential city...one of the reasons they call it The Big Apple. New York has the most temptation in the entire universe."

"I remember reading somewhere that it was a phrase used by jazz musicians, in reference to playing in New York, the big time," Claire said. "But I suppose temptation would make sense. And New Orleans?"

"New Orleans has very active ley lines, like sphere openings," Esperança schooled Claire. "You ever see the elaborate markings of a crop circle?"

"Sure, mathematical geniuses."

"In some cases, yes. But along the ley lines, it's most likely very playful angels, shaking up the rest of the world, with signs that the end is coming."

Bewilderment rendered Claire speechless, only because she valued what Esperança was saying.

"And that, my bony-assed friend, is a brief lesson about Satan's Chosen."

"It's like a family business," Claire commented, completely engrossed. "But let me ask, how many of you are there? Chosen I mean."

"There's many families across the globe. But in our circle, there's seventeen of us, including my sister—you remember meeting her—or rather, my father."

Claire's cheeks flushed.

"Don't be ashamed," Esperança teased her. "He…I mean she…was a good lover, a real hot tamale."

Shaking her head in disgust, Claire balked, "You are…appalling!"

"It's your fault. You have that sexy thing going on." Esperança leaned over the table to face her. "It's not something you learn, it's something you're born with. Like a power."

"Power?" Claire thought for a second. "The only thing powerful about it is the orgasm. Apart from that—"

"—Why be so modest?" Esperança interrupted, slanting her head slightly. "There's something more in you, something that makes men go crazy—even the dead ones."

A satisfied expression grew on her face. Claire nodded, "Some women just have it."

Esperança recalled her first encounter with Claire, how she'd never met a woman like her in any of her lives. And aloud she spoke, "Satan was the Perfect Beauty, too. The fallen angel…"

Citing from Sunday school the many names for Satan in the Bible, Claire began, "Angel of Light…God of this earth…"

"I know." Esperança held the heel of her right hand over the flame. "He was God's chosen angel, the anointed cherub and the model of perfection." A slight grin on her face, Esperança looked at Claire. "Satan couldn't accept being second best, so he rebelled against God."

"And two-thirds of the angels followed him," Claire added, almost hypnotically.

"And he became God of this world," Esperança concluded, a mischievous look in her eyes. With a playful smirk, she added, "Why can't we all just get along?"

Claire tried to figure out what Esperança meant. The drug had stolen her mind and now shuffled her thoughts around quickly, like a dealer reordering a deck of cards. She forgot about the old woman's strange comment and envisioned clearly the church she'd attended as a child. Father Riley had been a pudgy, gray-haired man who loved to be invited over to his parishioners' houses for home-cooked meals. Claire saw herself as a child sitting at the dining room table. Mom was not yet an alcoholic, Rebecca was in her high chair with meat and gravy on her cheeks, and Dad was engaged in deep conversation with the priest.

After a second serving of mashed potatoes and meat loaf, Father Riley spoke keenly. Claire repeated aloud what he had said. "They say this world is a believer's hell and a nonbeliever's heaven." Esperança nodded silently, her playfulness dissolving quickly, leaving a vacant and sorrowful expression in her dark eyes.

The flashback of her childhood gone, Claire chose her words carefully. "In other words, you and I are in heaven." She looked at the voodoo priestess for a response.

The remaining sparks of life drained into the blacks of Esperança's pupils. Like the last bit of water swirling into the bottom of a sink, she was gone.

She had completely zoned out Claire's rambling. Again Esperança thought about Patience, pondered the pain she was in, the pain that she herself had caused her. Biting down hard on her lip, she let her teeth tear into her flesh until she tasted blood. Her lip began to throb. Pain, she coached herself. Don't think about her.

Except for the crackle of the candle's hot wax, the room was completely still. Claire's mind zigzagged from one thing to the next. Another flashback. She was ten years old. Mom and Dad stood together, while Rebecca, as a tiny child, slept in Mom's arms. Father Riley was at his podium, adored by the congregation that packed the small church. In Claire's paranoid recollection, he spoke directly to her. His sermon was about God's mercy and his capacity to forgive: how even the most heinous sins could be forgiven if the sinner begged for forgiveness from a faithful heart.

Claire pulled herself away from her memory. In a loud voice, she said to Esperança, "They say there are rapists in heaven, and preachers in hell. What do you think?" It didn't surprise her when Esperança said nothing, but she couldn't fathom the blood around the old woman's lips and the vacant expression in her eyes. "You never know," Claire said, eyeing the bloody flesh between her teeth, "maybe if you ask for forgiveness, God will make room in heaven for a murdering voodoo priestess who wants to kill her granddaughter."

She waited for Esperança to strike. Red flames danced in the reflection of her eyes. Claire was not used to being left waiting, and she was losing her cool. "No offense, lady. And I don't care if you get pissed off at me for saying this again, but you sure are hypocritical at times. You espouse the cause of Satan, and then your actions say otherwise. I mean, shit, which side are you on?"

Once more, Claire mulled over what Esperança had said about Patience, remembering the warning she had given her after the beating. "First you protect her, and then you could care less if I hurt her. Plus to make matters even more bizarre, you confide in me that you wish you could kill her. I don't get you at all."

Esperança sat perfectly still, with her head bowed, hands folded in her lap. Under the light of the burning flame, her eyes appeared glassy and tormented. She sighed wearily and slowly lifted her head to meet Claire's glare. She licked at the blood with her tongue like a cat after a fight.

"I asked you a question. What did you mean when you said you wish you could send her back?" Claire demanded.

Heavy despair hung over the tiny room. "Just what I said," Esperança said quietly. "Send her back to her God. Send her soul back to where it came from."

"But why would you want to send her back?"

Esperança scratched at her nose and nervously ran her fingers through her hair. "She interferes too much, risks her life. I can't afford for that to happen again."

"Again?"

Following a lengthy pause, Esperança began to dig up secrets she'd buried long ago. "I had a daughter once." She stopped briefly, thinking of the daughter whom she had tried to forget. "I gave birth to her in the fifties, the Valley of Souls. The same place where I was born." She avoided Claire's eyes.

Knowing there was deep significance to this story, Claire stilled herself, not wanting to interrupt her in any way at all.

The voodoo priestess stared straight beyond Claire's head at the wall behind her, squinting, as if she could see the memory of her daughter's birth being played out. "She was perfect—tiny, but strong. Very strong. But her soul…" Esperança stopped and gave her head a shake.

"Her soul was stained, stained by the print of God's hand and blown with the breath of his divinity," Esperança added.

Claire pressed her lips together and then asked, "What exactly does that mean? The breath of his divinity?"

"They're chosen by God, to watch over the meek and to protect God's grain. Humans that walk with God's angels. God's Chosen."

"Let me get this straight," Claire said. "If you're Satan's Chosen, then that would have made you your own child's mortal enemy."

Esperança was still lost in her thoughts. "I should have sent her back as soon as she was born, but I couldn't. I couldn't do it." She met Claire's questioning eyes.

"It's easier to give them back as soon as they're born," she confided. "You get less attached. But she was divine and so, so beautiful…" Her recollection faded with her voice.

Claire contemplated damnation. Was it considered the worst of all sins against Satan to love a child born with a soul "stained by the print of God's hand." And if so, how many God-fearing families had loved and cared for a child with a soul kissed by Satan? The parallels between Satan and God made it clear to Claire that a war between heaven and hell was very real.

"And her father had a stained soul," Esperança added, without elaborating.

"Sorry?" Claire interjected.

"I said her father had a stained soul. He wasn't a divine be-ing, but someone who leans toward God's grace, someone like your husband. Someone who would never deny God if given a choice. A person that would never, ever choose Satan over God." Esperança bit her lip again and did not flinch. "I should have known. We were warned against going outside of our kind, but…"

"But what?"

"Forget it." Esperança stretched her small legs in her seat and forced a yawn. "It's a long story. I'd have to start from the beginning."

Claire's pulse raced. Esperança was back to her old self and she didn't want to lose the opportunity of learning more about the old woman's past. Not understanding why, she was com-pletely captivated. "I have time."

"Not tonight," the priestess said.

"Oh, come on," Claire urged in a frustrated tone. "You know every secret about me. All my private thoughts. It's only fair."

Esperança laughed and parroted back, "Fair?"

"Yes, fair. I mean, shit, your own father or sister, or whoever the hell it was, got off on me. It's the least you could do."

Esperança's eyes lit up even more. "I think you're the one who got off. You should thank me for showing you a good time and giving you the best orgasm of your life."

When Claire smiled, it was a sad and lonely one. Noting the emptiness within her protégé, Esperança realized that perhaps now was as good a time as any. She'd never told anyone what she was about to tell Claire, and she felt a measure of obliga-tion. But even more surprising, this was no longer just about Esperança's own redemption. This was now personal. She hes-itated, then shrugged.

"Fine, I'll tell you."

27

In The Beginning

Esperança reached into her pocket and pulled out the tiny plastic bag containing the last marijuana bud. "Shall we?"

Nodding, Claire reasoned, "If it'll help you remember the story."

"What story?" Esperança snickered arrogantly. "I was there."

"That's right, you're…reincarnated. It's fascinating to think you lived in this tribal bubble and you keep coming back. Do you get to choose your blood mothers? Because I saw her picture in the hall earlier…she's quite the beauty. Of course, I can't imagine who would have taken the photo; your people obviously have connections with the real world. I personally would have asked for something better than this," Claire said, referring to Esperança's apartment. "No offense."

Esperança considered the negligence Claire exuded. How carefree and comfortable she was learning about Satan and his Chosen. Had she no respect for her mother? And after everything Patience had tried to get Claire to sway, it all had made no difference. Patience was correct: Claire didn't scare easily, and time was of the essence. Frustrated, Esperança felt herself losing her patience with her. She was certain that Claire was close, but regardless of her developing empathy, Claire was still nowhere near to seeing the light of God. At this rate, Esperança was thankful for the bud she was about to smoke.

"We're gifted with specific obligations," said Esperança. "Just like my granddaughter was able to communicate with your mother's spirit from the dead, I too, can pull the dead into the living. But the dead that I pull in come from an entirely different place." Esperança prattled on, speaking slowly so that Claire could understand her. "Reincarnation you say…or better yet, entering the flesh again." Opening the pouch, she held the sticky green bud between her fingers. Without looking up, she continued. "And I have entered into many different kinds of flesh. I've seen the world through nine different sets of eyes." She used her fingers to break through the bud, still using the same tone.

"I saw the new world rise, and I watched the old one crumble." Esperança looked Claire dead in the eyes, abandoned the drug, and grabbed a hold of her chin. "But most importantly, Claire, I've lived in the in between–the middle that separates the living from the dead. And I am not a voodoo priestess. I am the Chosen, the chosen messenger that speaks to the living," Esperança released Claire's chin and looked to her right, as if there was someone standing beside Claire, "and to the dead."

Claire was silenced.

Esperança pulled her hand away and said in her singsong voice. "I thought you could handle yourself better than this. You know, Claire, you of all people shouldn't be so surprised at what I am. What did you think?" she asked, brows raised. "I did a little voodoo, Tarot cards, read your tea leaves? I'm the real deal." Esperança licked the residue off her fingers before reaching for her paring knife. "Nothing but the best for Claire… isn't that right?"

Claire felt herself fluster as panic set in. All the while, Esperança kept a keen eye on her. "That's right, deep breaths, nice and slow."

"If you're going to make it in Brazil, then I suggest you learn to accept what this really is. There's no ancient grandmother who passed down some bullshit recipes or magic. This isn't Santeria, Hoodoo, or some witchdoctor who mixes the Bible and the devil." Esperança raised her voice and the vein in her temple bulged as her anger increased. "This is the real fucking deal,

Claire! Lucifer's own angels, sent down to build his army and destroy God's work!!" Esperança pointed toward the door, her nostrils flaring, her eyebrows furrowing, but her voice dropping to a coarse whisper. "If you can't take the heat, then I suggest you get the fuck out of hell's kitchen."

Esperança's harsh warning put all the defiance out of Claire. It wasn't so much that she feared Satan, it was that getting closer to him was somehow getting God's attention. It was so final, no turning back. Claire nodded, swallowing several times, as she listened to Esperança's counsel.

"But if you think you can," she said, dropping her hand and looking straight at Claire, "then I suggest you'd better hold on. Because once you let them in, they're not coming back out."

Finding her voice and her anger, Claire cleared her throat and, without batting an eyelash, said, "I don't give one shit about who you are, just get the job done." Moistening her lips and smoothing the hair out of her eyes, she added, "And for the record, voodoo priestess, the Chosen, or whatever it is you call yourself, don't bring my mother into this. I'm done with her. I get it. I'll never see her again, and that's something I've accepted. I've made my peace with it."

Esperança's features softened, as if she was astonished. "You really want that?"

"Yes, I do. I have no choice, do I?" Claire asked, feeling regret.

Tread lightly, Esperança thought to herself. The bloom in Claire's eyes had returned, but if she suggested God to Claire, she might see right through her game. "And if God came down and gave you back your mother…what then?" Esperança said instead.

Claire noted the enamored look in Esperança's eyes, as if Claire's answer had something to do with the priestess herself. "If God wanted to give me my mother back, he knows where to find me. Look around," she said, turning her head left to right, "I don't see her, do you? Like you said, God made it snow, the biggest snow storm in years. The least he could have done was killed her on impact and not have made it a slow and cruel death."

Claire scratched the tickle at the tip of her nose. "I suggest you stop wasting time, Esperança, or whoever the hell you are, because I'd like to hear the rest of your story." Regarding the bud before them, she added, "And I'd like to smoke another blunt."

Esperança laughed, her eyes locking with Claire's. "We're talking over three hundred years ago, three centuries of family history." She began cutting the bud. "Hearing is one thing, but seeing it was an entirely different thing."

Esperança licked the paper before filling it with the remaining leaves. After rolling the sheet into a perfect cone shape, she resumed speaking. "I used to love the sounds of the jungle." She bit the end of the joint before lighting it. "The sound of the river…when it rained."

The insatiable greed with which Esperança drew in another drag from the joint made Claire feel that there must be a lot more to her than she had let on. Clearly, many things were eating away at her, causing her to self-medicate.

The old woman's face grew murky in a smoky haze as her gravelly voice continued. "I used to believe those were the best sounds in the world."

"What do you mean, used to?"

"Used to, as in, 'used to doesn't count anymore…it just lies on the floor until they sweep it away,'" Esperança said in a detached tone.

More secrets, Claire thought. What did she see now that she didn't see before?

With Esperança concentrating on taking deep pulls of the joint, Claire's mind used the time to wander further and without detection. Although she had never met a person with such great power, there was also vulnerability inside the old woman. It had something to do with a child she had killed and a monster-girl whom she loved and wished she could kill. But what made her want to kill her granddaughter?

A hoarse, hacking cough pulled Claire's focus away from her thoughts. Esperança fought to maintain control while her shaking hand held the joint she was trying to inhale. The old woman looked like a hopeless mess, a jittery addict. Strangely, Claire realized she had a soft spot for her. Being around Esperança was easy and required no work, no false pretenses. Staring across the table at her, in her stained clothes, with her greasy hair, Claire was reminded that her new friend was feral. You can take the savage out of the bush, but you can't take the bush out of the savage, she recited the old adage and shook her head in a kind of regret.

When she offered the joint to her, Claire said, "Just blow the smoke toward me." She wasn't about to trade saliva with the old woman, no matter how fond of her she had become.

Following another deep pull, Esperança exhaled the drug to Claire who sucked the concoction through willing lips.

In a matter of minutes, the drug fueled Claire's mind again and her thoughts spilled over. Her thoughts were on Esperança again. Her life here in Castle Hill, the Bronx, had to be considered a luxury by comparison. Nothing could be worse than the Amazon region, where she was born, with its deadly snakes and human sacrifices. "I guess having running water and being able to wear clean clothes has made it hard for you to go back...I mean, you know, to live in the jungle. I can't even imagine." She closed her eyes in a show of compassion.

Esperança smiled innocently enough. "I guess I traded one jungle for another. But yeah, it's good to have a bath when I want and to take a shit in a shiny porcelain toilet instead of in a hole."

Determination swept over Claire. "Once I'm there, I'll dig my own damn hole. In fact, I'll try not to eat so I won't have to shit at all." Claire looked up with a serious expression. "You know what I find absolutely amazing though?"

"Yes, but you'll tell me anyway." Claire was so high that Esperança found it very entertaining.

"I was thinking about all the people who take having a toilet for granted...I mean just think about it, all the millions of people who take shits all day long and just flush it away. I mean really, can you imagine? All those millions of turds floating around. It's quite fascinating," Claire said, nodding.

Lowering her head to the tabletop, Esperança laughed hard. Raising her head again, wiping tears from her eyes, she said condescendingly, "And this from the mind of a genius. Maybe you should become a reporter, set up a team of shit-head investigators to find the floaters. Wait...I have a breaking story for you..." Esperança leaned to her right, and let loose a burst of flatulence.

A stunned expression crossed Claire's face.

"That's so disgusting." Claire pulled the T-shirt's collar over her nose. "Put-out the joint before you blow this place up."

"I'm an old lady, what can I say?"

They were both laughing now, like two deranged women. Claire was hanging off of her stool, cupping a hand over her nose, while Esperança balanced the joint in one hand and held on to her stomach with the other. Once they exhausted themselves and the laughter dwindled, they managed to pull themselves together. It was a brief pause, both staring across at one another with tired smirks. Claire hadn't laughed that good in years, maybe even ever. Esperança shared in that sentiment but would never let her know.

"Will you tell me this story already? And leave out the shit holes, if you don't mind," Claire requested, sitting straight and smoothing out the lines in her skirt.

Esperança nodded. "Okay then, we'll start at the beginning. Brazil, the late sixteen hundreds." She stubbed the remaining joint into the table, saving it for later, and rose from her seat.

Growing impatient, Claire asked, "Where you going now?"

When she got to the other side of the room, Esperança answered, "Need some visual aids."

Straining her eyes, Claire tried to fix on what Esperança was doing. She returned with a long, coffee-colored cylinder, like the ones architects use. "Move this crap off the table." Claire quickly transferred the few items onto the floor. Popping the top off the tube, the old woman slid out a large roll of white paper. She hastily spread it over the table. "Put the candle in the middle."

Setting the burning candle dead center, Claire stared in confusion. Besides a series of red, circular pen marks and lines, the entire sheet was blank. "What's this?"

"A map of Brazil, in Braille." Esperança glided her fingers along the top, closed her eyes, and worked her way down. Her fingertips became her eyes.

Then Claire saw that Esperança's left index finger was severed above her knuckle. She wondered how she'd never noticed this before.

Esperança's gruff voice cut into her thoughts. "This here is the Amazon river. And this," she traced her fingers to the right of the map, "this is Bahia."

Claire copied Esperança, moving her fingers along the map. "It just feels like a bunch of dots and lines."

"Not so easy, right?" Esperança opened her eyes and gave a strange look. "My granddaughter, she ordered a map especially for me. She's a very good teacher."

Touching the raised bumps on the surface, Claire looked up playfully. "It's bizarre."

A smile hooked the corner of Esperança's lips. She fished around in metal box beneath her before pulling out a thin, black marker. "See, wasn't that a good idea?"

"Indeed. You were saying, Brazil, the late sixteen hundreds?"

Esperança licked her lips and took a quick drink. She placed the bottle on the floor next to her. "It was a time when slaves were picked out like a pair of oxen, or a team of work horses. When the slave trade was just another day at the market." She used her teeth to pull the cap off the marker. Pointing to the top right corner, the voodoo priestess wrote the word 'Bahia.'

"My story starts here." Below this, she wrote 'Mato Grosso.' "And it continues there." She looked up with a vacant expression. "Then there's the stuff in between. You ready for this?"

Claire shifted in the chair. "More than ready. And don't leave anything out."

Eager, Esperança traced her finger along the map, pointing to the word Bahia again. "What do you know about Brazil?"

"I know that in the 1500s Brazil was discovered by accident when a Portuguese expedition to India swung too far west. I can't remember the explorer's name, but I remember the original inhabitants were forced to work as slaves. They brought in slaves from Africa. Mostly Mozambique and Angola, I recall. The triangular trade."

Esperança shook her head with pity, causing Claire to lose her train of thought.

"What, did I say something wrong?"

"You know, I really hate when you act like that, like you're above it all. It's not what you said, but how you said it. No feeling. You're…desensitized, like a talking robot," Esperança scoffed. "Original inhabitants, slaves from Africa…"

Claire exhaled in frustration.

"I'm serious," Esperança said in a tone that brooked no argument. "You only know the stuff they taught you in school, the things they allowed you to know. You have no sense of how ugly it really was. You live in your own world. You wake up each day, run your miles, do your hair, paint your face, make your millions, and nitpick when they fuck up your espresso or if your nail appointment gets canceled. You have no idea what suffering is. At least you knew your mother, no matter how horribly she died. At least you know where you come from, where your blood line begins and where it ends."

Claire crossed her arms and leaned back. "And? What's your point?"

"The 'original inhabitants' had their land stolen from them, thanks to the white man. They stole their will and even their blood. A few centuries on, the blood of slaves was mixed so much with the white man's that their skin became lighter, their hair a little straighter, and it didn't matter that they lived and breathed because they didn't matter. They weren't even on the same level with animals. A slave was considered a piece of farm machinery. Not human."

Esperança picked up the leftover weed and soon placed it between her lips. She spoke while balancing the joint in her mouth and striking a match.

"Even a goat got to be a goat." She finally lit the tip and blew smoke out the side of her mouth, her eyes never leaving Claire.

Claire bent her head, unable to look Esperança in the eyes. She felt horrible, and she truly didn't know what to say to make up for her aloofness. It was no wonder she had no friends, so many rules.

Following an uncomfortable silence, apart from the inhaling and exhaling of the drug, the old woman spoke, silk coating the steel in her tone. "Anyway, doesn't matter anymore, does it?" She smoked the rest and dropped the leftover joint onto the floor and stepped on it.

Claire shrugged her shoulders, and her fingers fidgeted across the map.

Apologetic for her abruptness, Esperança reached out and pulled Claire's hands toward Bahia and lightly guided her fingertips across the word. "Two brothers, Manuel and Christopher. Two very different brothers who were born in Lisbon, Portugal and later set sail for Bahia, Brazil. Their plan was to build the largest sugar plantation in the northeastern part of Brazil. And they did but, not without a price," Esperança said, looking up and giving Claire a reassuring smile.

At ease, Claire sank into her seat and tuned in to the soft and raspy hum of Esperança's voice.

"There was a girl, because without the girl there would be no story. There's always trouble with two brothers and a girl in the middle." Esperança studied her protégé for a moment. "Who do you want to hear about first? The girl or the brothers?"

"The girl," Claire answered, without hesitation.

"Yes, the girl, of course," Esperança whispered, her concentration lost yet again. Her reluctance showed in the wild look trapped behind her eyes. As if the ghosts of yesterday were imprisoned in her head, waiting around the fire in Brazil to hear their own truths and Esperança's version. "It's not a 'nice' story, and there's no glass slipper," she cautioned.

"Go on," Claire urged her, "I never did like the happily-ever-after stories anyway."

Esperança's gaze was focused on the candle's flame. Claire watched it as well and counted nine flickers before Esperança continued with her narration. The tone of her voice remained calm and even. The look in her eyes—merciless.

"When a child is born into slavery, it isn't a child at all. A male child is seen as a bull is seen, built for hard labor, mindless work, under the blistering heat and sun. You can whip a bull into submission, and after a while, it'll do whatever you want. Every now and then, a bull will go off, lose its mind, and that's when it's beaten to death. Same thing goes for a male slave. Now, a female child…"

Esperança shook her head with disgust. "A female child is seen as a cow is seen. It reproduces to add more laborers, and it also does mindless work. It never ends. But what the white man loved most about the female slaves was found between their legs. Being born beautiful was her curse. It was even more of a curse to be a prisoner in your own skin and belong to everyone else but yourself. A piece of beautiful property. And the girl I speak of was exactly that. She was also unlike any girl that any of the men had ever seen."

"The girl was a slave?"

"Bingo. But of course, in the late sixteen hundreds those slaves who were born into slavery were comfortable in their own skin. They knew who they were and who their mothers were. But their fathers could have been anyone. The girl's father could have been any of the wealthy white men who passed through Bahia. Her own master might have been her father." Esperança reached for her bottle and wrapped her hand around it.

Claire caught herself nodding.

"Can you even imagine, Claire? Being born into slavery, never knowing anything else, not finding it wrong to be born a meaningless human being?" Esperança's grip tightened on the bottle.

"The girl you want to know about was born beautiful at a very ugly time. But her mother died right after giving birth... she went into shock and bled to death. The child was left alone. Never had a chance to feed off of her own mother's breast, to feel her mother's arms around her, or hear her mother's voice. So, the child was raised by the other tigers. They named her Filhote." Esperança put the bottle to her lips and managed a mouthful. She read the confusion in Claire and added, "Filhote means pup or cub. Like a tiger cub," she clarified.

Claire blinked at her description. "Oh, you mean they were half tigers, like werewolves?"

"You've been watching too many vampire movies," Esperança replied, setting her bottle down. "They were the slave women who took care of sanitation in Bahia. And I can assure you this, there isn't anything more bloodcurdling. You can't make this kind of stuff up."

"I don't understand. Why were they called tigers?"

"Back then they didn't have toilets, no indoor plumbing. The tigers had the job of collecting shit and piss from the white man. They had to balance containers of human shit and piss on their heads, walk a long ways to where they would empty the buckets. Along those walks, the acid would always spill over and run down their faces. A few years of this, they developed light-colored stripes across their cheeks and upper bodies. Like bleach marks. So they called them tigers," Esperança explained, running a hand across her face.

Claire swallowed. "Oh."

"But Filhote didn't stay long enough to earn those stripes, no she didn't. The men of Bahia had different plans for her." Esperança stared at Claire with an odd look.

"What?" Claire asked, shifting on her chair. But Esperança kept staring, her dark eyes flickered with a question.

Esperança cleared her throat and picked at something inside of her nose and flicked it away. "I feel weird when I smoke weed," she finally said. "It's like déjà vu, and somehow I was thinking about you and Filhote."

"Me?" Claire was more intrigued than ever.

"You and Filhote are very much alike. Filhote was unbelievably beautiful, so beautiful, and just like you, people noticed Filhote, too. You both shared that same appeal, that draw. But you also shared the same bizarre fate. Both angry, both broken. But I have a feeling, that if a flightless bird dropped into your lap, you'd nurse that bird wouldn't you?"

Claire didn't know how to answer that because once again, Esperança had that faraway expression in her eyes.

"Anyways," Esperança explained, "that anger came from somewhere, and for Filhote, the seed was planted when her mother died in childbirth...then later, because of Filhote's beauty, she was a target, susceptible to all kinds of evil."

"She was really that beautiful?" Claire murmured.

Esperança nodded. "You truly need to appreciate this child's beauty. Picture it, a girl-child born with two races and only the most beautiful pieces were passed onto her. Her mother was said to be average looking, a tall negro woman. Filhote was just as tall and slender, built in all the right places. They would say that looking into her eyes was like looking into the waters of a deep lagoon—blue, green, passed down by her white father. A reminder of the robbery they'd committed. The Gold that colored Filhote, darkened by the roots of her African mother. Because of her rare beauty, some men feared Filhote, said she was the daughter of the devil. God didn't make women like that.

That she was a product of their sins. But not all men felt that way. By the time she turned twelve, she'd been used, raped, and beaten. She became wild. By the time the Silva brother bought her, she was filled with rage, but she was also dead on the inside. That makes for a very deadly combination."

Esperança's voice lowered in level if not in fervor. Her gaze veered away from the table. "But Filhote was tough, very resilient, even in those times. Filhote never cried and not because she saw it as a sign of weakness, but because she knew that if she started, she would never stop. It was the one, the *only* thing she had control of."

Claire raised her head from her comfortable position. "I would have liked to have known her." .

"I think she would have liked you," Esperança replied, her black eyes fixated on Claire's face. "A couple of bad-ass bitches you two would have been."

A smile brushed Claire's lips. "Tell me about the brothers," she said, resting her chin on the heels of her palms again.

"The brothers couldn't have been more different. Christopher and Manuel were born into a very wealthy family in Lisbon," Esperança explained. "They owned one of the largest vineyards in the region, and the boys learned the business from the ground up. Christopher Tavares Silva was the youngest of five brothers. He was smart and very kind. He never drank more than a glass of wine at dinner and spent most of his free time studying God's word. He often considered becoming a monk. Later, he said he heard God's voice telling him he was chosen, and that one day he'd understand God's will. He never told his family about the visions or the voices. At times, he was convinced he was going mad. But of course, he wasn't." Esperança stopped to take a quick gulp of rum before continuing. A sneer lifted the corner of her mouth.

"Manuel Tavares Silva was the oldest, and his father was ashamed of him. He gambled, spent his nights drinking, fucking, and squandering his family's money. He got into brawls all the time, and his brothers would search for him in the early mornings to find him drunken, bloody, and asleep in doorways and alleys. Silva senior decided to send Manuel to Brazil, probably hoping that the relocation would fix the dirty ways of his oldest son. Christopher was terrified when his father insisted that he go with Manuel. He knew his father sent him to watch Manuel and secretly hated his brother. Christopher wanted to stay with his mother and siblings, but he also understood that if anything really awful happened to Manuel, he could take over. He didn't want the king of Portugal to have a bone to pick with his family, and in those days, only noble men were given land in Brazil. The brothers were big-shots, noble...because of their family's connections with the king."

"So that's it? Just like that...that must be awful, having to leave your home and set off into a new world," Claire sympathized.

"It was. Christopher was barely sixteen, and Manuel was in his early twenties when they left for Brazil. Manuel left behind a young wife and two infant sons. You see, men who set sail for Brazil didn't bring their wives or children with them. It would be years before they would see their families again, but for someone like Manuel, that was no problem."

"Is this when he found Filhote?"

"Not that soon. She came into their lives years later. But in the meantime, things happened very fast for the brothers. They settled quickly in Bahia. Miles of land needed to be turned and worked. Slaves, of course, made it easier. By the first year, they'd built the main house and, of course, the slave quarters. Manuel worked them brutally hard. He used to say slaves needed three things: a cloth to cover their private parts, some scraps of food to eat, and a whip for punishment. It can take anywhere from a year and a half to two years before the cane's ready. The slaves worked from early dawn, sometimes twenty hours straight, with little sleep, little to eat. It starts with the planting of seeds. All the slaves, including women, that'd just given birth, their babes strapped to their backs, little boys and girls, lined up and moved from row to row, planting seed stems. And all by hand. Then the harvesting. These hungry and abused human beings worked in the hot sun. Cutting the stems and stacking the bundles onto carts. From there, the bundles got transfered into the sugar mill.

"Christopher worked alongside the guards, while his brother oversaw the entire operation from the inside of his mansion. Manuel watched from a room where he entertained the wealthy men who came to do business. Mirrors were carefully placed on each of the walls. The mirrors reflected off one another, so he saw everything and everyone on the outside. Nothing got past him. He was an ugly man who demanded complete control. The guards who worked for him were ordered to whip any slave to death if they couldn't keep up with the work. For those slaves who were no longer of use, Manuel instructed that they be tied and whipped sometimes for nine days at a time. He even had his men rip off the mangled flesh then pour salt and pepper into their wounds. If Manuel got bored, he'd single out certain slaves and have them shackled and tied over ants' nests. The sound of their pain gave him a hard-on, and once he was aroused, he went on to abuse and rape the women. Most slaves lived only a few years."

Esperança moved the bottle toward her mouth. "When he was running low, Manuel just went into town and bought more slaves." She took a long swig and placed the bottle down gently. "He loved buying slaves as much as you love buying shoes."

"Just stick to the damn story."

"All right then, let's talk about the loose packing system," the priestess continued.

"As in?"

"As in, the captains of the ships, which transported the captured slaves from Africa to Brazil. You see, sugar was like cocaine. Everybody wanted a piece of the sugar pie, so Portugal moved fast, colonizing the land in Brazil for more plantations. At this point, they needed more slaves, strong slaves, that could fight off bugs—viruses that the original natives of Brazil couldn't. This was when the captains of those vessels created systems…the loose packaging system."

Needing some levity, Claire joked, "Don't you mean loose meat?" She regretted her words as soon as she'd said them.

The priestess instantly bristled. "Not the same thing! Loose packing meant the captain carried fewer slaves than his ship could carry in hopes of reducing sickness and death. The other system was tight packing. Captains who used this method believed many of the slaves would die anyway, so they carried as many as the ships would hold. These voyages took months, and the poor people were chained below deck from sunup to sundown. Can you imagine? The torture, the filth and vomit, the rotting flesh. Sometimes, after these long voyages, a vessel was so contaminated, so unbearable that they had no choice but to burn it, or abandon it all together.

"New shipments of slaves were taken to Salvador. Christopher went there once with Manuel, but never joined him again. He was traumatized after watching what was done to them. Men like his brother stood around sizing up the slaves while they were called out from a line. The slave had to stamp his feet, shout, and prove his strength if he didn't want to be killed. Then the women…"

Esperança said nothing more for awhile. Her neck was bent forward and her eyes were closed.

"Go on…what happened next?"

Esperança lifted her head and met Claire's gaze under hooded eyes. "The more money that sinful bastard made, the more wicked he got. For the slaves he purchased, he designed his own branding symbol. It was burned into the backs of their necks so that if they escaped, his ownership of them was clearly visible. Manuel bragged that his emblem, a crescent-shaped serpent coiled in thorny vines, represented half of the circle of life because he deemed the slaves to be only half-human. He said the other half was evil and that once slaves shed their skin, a serpent lay underneath.

"Christopher was horrified and wrote his father and begged him to let him come home. Manuel was now successful, and the king was pleased, so Christopher argued that he was no longer needed. Instead, Christopher's father ordered him to start another sugar plantation. It was intended to be almost double the size of Manuel's. Since Silva senior's plan had the blessings of the king of Portugal, Christopher had no choice in the matter.

"He spent many days and nights wandering through the streets of Bahia. For hours, he sat in the churches, the same churches built by the hands of slaves, looking for answers— needing answers. Nothing made sense to him. But as much as he wanted to leave Brazil, a voice, as loud as my own voice is right now, told him he had been chosen. And that this was where he needed to be. He said it was the voice of God's angel."

"What did the voice say?"

"That Christopher was a divine being, chosen to watch over the meek and to protect God's grain."

"That's why Christopher was hearing voices, because he was God's Chosen?"

"That's right, the voice also told him that his purpose was to save the 'slaves' souls, to teach them Christianity," Esperança answered.

Claire was astonished. "You mean God wanted Christopher to buy slaves just to teach them Christianity?"

"Exactly," Esperança said.

"Was this even possible?"

"Of course, slaves were being baptized on the vessels that carried them, and the law in Brazil was that all slaves had Christianity forced on them by their masters. Christopher was just following through with the king of Portugal's orders and, most importantly, God's."

"What about Manuel?"

"Manuel could have cared less about the well-being of his slaves. Anyway, slaves had their own ideas about God. They believed in voodoo worship, black magic, and elements of the earth. Especially on a full moon," Esperança explained.

"I always thought voodoo and a full moon was just a story."

Esperança gave her a wary look, "A full moon and voodoo is not a joke, my friend. I've seen both sides of the coin, where a full moon is concerned. I've seen souls being ripped out by the roots; I've seen souls pulled through sphere openings. I've even been washed under the light of a full moon's rays and seen the thin layer between the living and the dead. Not just heard it, but seen my actual fallen angel."

None of this fazed Claire. "That's a trip."

"A trip to hell."

Out of respect for Esperança, Claire curbed a smile. "And Christopher? How could one man fight against so much power, regardless if he was a divine being or not?"

"Christopher realized that in order to spread Christianity, he needed to do it with a gentle heart. He had set out to build an empire and send the king his share. But Christopher decided that the profits would be used to help the slaves. They'd work the land and live as they chose on the land. They would live in peace and raise families. He needed men he could trust. He chose carefully, hiring men who spoke several African languages. He hired priests who lived in accordance with their Christian beliefs. Using his instincts, he also relied on the voice to guide his decisions. And the closer he came to doing what God wanted of him, the louder and clearer the voices got."

"So your people answer to the fallen angels," Claire verified. "And Christopher and other divine beings answer to God's angels."

"That's right," she said, with a growing serious tone. "As I said, the angels that led Christopher were ones sent by God above." Esperança scratched at her scalp. A loose strand of gray hair fell in front of her left eye. She tucked it behind her ear and stared across the table.

"One man, aided by an army of angels. And for the first time, Christopher was at peace with what had to be done. He had more than enough money to begin his project. Within six months he built the main house and bought slaves, selecting those that other slave owners shunned…weaker ones, including the sick and the pregnant women. He had the slaves gather on his plantation and greeted them personally, one by one. He would actually embrace them and speak softly. He told them that this land was now their home and that God wanted them there…that he wanted no harm to come to them. Before long, the sick were nursed back to health, and the pregnant women were free to become happy and loving mothers. These slaves were given materials to build their own houses on the land, cultivate it, and grow what they could. One year afterward, Christopher had over three hundred slaves working the land during the day. At night they assembled, curiously and joyfully, to learn about Christianity and God's will. Soon, Christopher became, to them, an earthly version of God in heaven. It didn't take long before all of the slaves abandoned their satanic worship. I imagine that Satan wasn't too pleased about Christopher's intervention, because Satan had somehow reached so many souls, on so many different levels."

"Well, Satan was exiled to Earth," Claire added. "It was inevitable."

Esperança took another drink. She nodded her head knowingly. "Inevitable or not, God used Christopher as his means, kind of like a lighthouse, a moonbeam into heaven. And I believe Christopher was the reason for Christianity spreading throughout Brazil as quickly as it did. He did the impossible. But his compassion was great, and the fortunes of his plantation were too. You know, in just a few years, he was the wealthiest man in northern Brazil."

"Really?" This fact impressed Claire.

"The slaves worked with their hearts in exchange for the better life Christopher gave them. He was very secretive about his method and somehow managed to keep it under wraps. Christopher was a man among men, respected by all. But Manuel...he hated his brother, hated him with every fiber of his being. Then came the girl."

Claire perked up. "Filhote?"

Esperança nodded absently. "She was in the town square the first time Manuel saw her. In those days, slaves wore these license plates around their necks. Filhote belonged to a wealthy man. He owned many slaves, men and women. The women served sweets and food to the white man, took care of the sanitation and other mindless duties. Male slaves constructed practically all the buildings in Bahia, from cathedrals to colonial forts. They also served as the cooks, the shoemakers, the blacksmiths, you name it. They were everything, yet they were nothing. Except for Filhote."

"How?"

"Because she was different. And while many men were afraid of her wild nature, others lusted for her. The Englishman who first owned Filhote had also owned Filhote's mother. Like I said, he may even have been Filhote's real father. Who can say for sure?"

"The Englishman was a nervous man. Never could sit still, always shaking and waiting for God to strike Brazil down with lightning or an earthquake. He swore that the demons were walking the streets of Brazil and that he and the other slave owners would be swallowed by the earth and pulled into hell. Then he would drop to his knees and beg God's forgiveness. He was sickly when Manuel first approached him with his offer. He wasn't in his right mind and was selling his estate. He had a large family in England, and his plan was to die at home. Manuel came at the right time, offering to buy ten of his finest slave women. He'd already built an addition on the back of his house, preparing to pick and choose which slave he would fuck on any given night. The Englishman agreed to nine. But Filhote was off limits. He had plans for her…maybe he was going to take her back with him. No one knows for sure. Manuel insisted—her beauty made his pulses throb—but the ill owner said she was especially close to his heart." Esperança was staring off again. "But Manuel was good at getting what he wanted."

"What did he do to convince him?"

"It wasn't difficult, really. He stole her in the middle of the night and replaced her with his best milking cow."

"Are you fucking kidding me?" Claire leaned back and crossed her arms. "Her life was valued in comparison to a cow?"

"His *best* milking cow," Esperança reminded her. "As soon as he got her home, he raped Filhote and branded her. And after that, Manuel spent the next year of Filhote's life raping and beating her. After a while, he no longer chose the other female slaves. It was Filhote he craved. He got silk fabrics from China and had beautiful dresses made for her, hats to Match, and soft-leather shoes with silver buckles, too. Of course, she never stepped outside or had anywhere to go wearing these clothes. He also got special oils made from coconut and Brazil nut. He massaged them into her skin. Sometimes, while she was tied to the bed, he inspected every inch of her, kissed every part of her. He affectionately rubbed the creams and oils into her skin. And then he switched, just like a light. He changed into another person. He would say this to her, whisper it… in that cold tone of his, 'prazer adiado é prazer amplifica' …'pleasure delayed is pleasure amplified.'

"Manuel began smashing things in the room, beating her with his fists. Beat her till she could no longer cry. Sometimes Filhote would freeze, not move a muscle, faking unconsciousness so he would stop. But she still heard him, standing over her, breathing. He had a wheeze in his chest, the sound Filhote would listen for, because then he changed back, became nice. He cleaned her cuts, kissed her wounds. Manuel told her he was sorry, but explained that the half of her which was evil had brought it out of him, and he only did what had to be done. Sometimes, he suspended her from the ceiling like a side of beef and cut into her skin, draining the blood into a dish. He said he was expelling the evil in her. After a while, she felt she was losing her mind. She started hearing voices and seeing things. Eventually he took her down, cleaned her up again. And the next night, it was more of the same.

"His sick mind made him believe he loved her. The following year he had a room made up for her. It was unlike anything Filhote had ever seen, a room built for a queen."

Claire lifted a brow, waiting for Esperança to continue. For some reason, this part of the story captivated her.

Esperança spoke in a near-whisper monotone. "The wallpaper was hand painted…gold and red roses, vines that ran from corner to corner. One of Manuel's artistically talented male slaves had worked on it for weeks, painting each and every flower, bud, and thorn. One night, when this slave was extremely tired, his hands shook from the days he had spent painting the wall. Manuel barged into the room and beat him with a candlestick holder, smashed it right across his head.

Tiny droplets of his blood miraculously hit one of the walls in perfectly even dots. The slave had to finish each rose, using his own bloodstains on the wall as a guide. Manuel said that if the walls were not finished within seven days, he would hang the slave by his feet, cut him open, and use his blood to complete the painting. Instead, the slave made sure the walls were done in two days."

Claire and Esperança stared across the table at one other, each lost in her own thoughts.

"What else?" Claire murmured, even more fascinated.

"What do you mean what else?" Esperança asked. "The room? Is that what you're asking?"

Claire nodded. "You said that it was built for a queen. Tell me more…I've always loved the Renaissance period–the jewel-toned velvets, the silk damasks they used to make draperies, the textured, flocked and embossed wallpaper. But I especially love the chandeliers."

A stunned laugh escaped Esperança's lips. "You do, do you? Well this chandelier was made of quartz-cut crystals, and it had beautiful ivory candles placed in gold cups. At night, the light sparkled against the patterns on the wall, and the roses flamed to life. The painted vines moved like snakes. The room was alive, I tell you. And Filhote was so frightened of the walls. And then, there was the bed."

"What about it?" Claire whispered. She could picture this ornamented canopy with its elaborate patterns carved into the wood-posters, and a soft featherbed under the exquisite sheets.

Esperança bit back a scowl, "More like her coffin, and the only comfort she had in this four-poster bed was the cream curtain that wrapped around the frame. And it was no jewel-toned velvet or silk *dumbass* that you mentioned. It was her only refuge, this cream curtain." She crossed her arms and leaned back.

"Filhote imagined herself hidden and protected, because the curtain was the only thing that could keep the snakes away. It was the only way she could calm down enough to sleep."

Claire felt stupid. "Sorry. Please...carry on."

"One night, after Manuel finished raping her, Filhote used that cream curtain to hang herself. It didn't work. Some women slaves found her, and Manuel had the curtain removed for good. After that, there was no more sleep for her, and no more curtain to keep the snakes away."

"When did Christopher meet her?" Claire whispered, feeling empathy for this woman with a room built for a queen.

"After the incident with the mirror," Esperança said.

"What mirror?"

"The silver mirror Manuel had custom made; the full-length mirror he positioned in front of the bed. He wanted to watch himself raping her. He told Filhote that the vision in the mirror was evil and that if she stared long enough, then the evil would be caught, staying forever in the glass. She actually thought there was some truth to that. Maybe it was because she was so exhausted. But she looked anyway, and it terrified her. Absolutely terrified her. For the first time, it made sense why she was there in Manuel's prison. It wasn't because she was a slave."

"Because she was so beautiful," Claire said, with a strange understanding.

"So, she set herself on fire," Esperança said.

"No, you can't be serious."

"She believed the snakes were a sign, and since they could shed their skin, Filhote felt that she could also. Shed her curse.

Her hair went up in flames, fast. The first layers of her skin burned...she could smell her hair and burning skin." Esperança wrinkled her nose. "By the time the other women reached her, she had second degree burns all over her body. They rolled her around, poured water on her. But she was laughing. Filhote was laughing, hysterically. She was happy because she was finally free from her curse. She was now ugly. And Manuel would no longer want her."

A long silence prevailed. Claire could never imagine purposely wanting to be ugly. "What did Manuel do?"

"He spit on her and beat her until she was unconscious. Then he had her taken into the forest where she was left to die. The slaves from Christopher's plantation found her there, barely alive. They knew the right thing to do was to take her to their home, bring her to God, because only God would know what to do with her."

"You mean Christopher?"

"Yes, and he knew she belonged to his brother by the branding on the back of her neck. Months later, by the time Filhote had recovered, she and Christopher were in love. She was already pregnant, but with Manuel's child. So you see, Claire, Filhote's beauty, along with the fact that she was broken, made it very easy for Satan to take notice. And because Satan loves beautiful things, he chose her to be that child's vessel. And that unborn child was the chosen soul to enter the conception."

"Chosen to do what?"

The reply was long in coming. Finally, Esperança answered, "Chosen to destroy Christopher...and to crush Christianity."

28

Catching Darkness

The sweltering sun's breath reached through the trees and softened the skin of ripened fruits and nectars, sweeping their scent through the tropical rainforests. Their fragrance carried along the mighty Xingu River, then through the Kuluene, and finally, floated up the nameless river that the aborigines referred to as, The River of Tears. Legends said that the land was protected by the angels of God, and that they shed tears into the nameless river for those who broke God's heart.

Merely nine years old, the girl stood alone, barefoot, on soil which grew the ancient and splendid greenery surrounding her. Flashes of flora and fauna still fresh in her mind, she closed her eyes and reached her arms out to welcome the warm Brazilian breeze as it billowed her pale-yellow cotton dress and passed through her long black hair. She gathered her locks, working her tiny fingers quickly to collect the loose strands into a tight braid. She fastened the ends with a red rubber band hanging from her wrist.

Closing her eyes again, the child sensed the coming rain. The bouquet of scents was carried along the River of Tears and into the small, secluded area where the child and her mother lived. As soon as the sun set, daytime creatures would scamper away and nocturnal life would awaken in the Mato Grosso forest.

The child skimmed the terrain tenderly with her rich, brown

eyes. It was just slightly more than one acre, yet she loved and appreciated every rock, tree, and flower. Another soft breeze gently grazed her face, delighting her tiny nose with the pleasant smells from the north. She reminded herself how fortunate she was for the gifts this land had given them. "We thank you," she whispered, closing her eyes as she focused on her other senses. The air was thick and tacky, moistening her exposed skin. The breezes transformed into winds that rushed past her ears. The land's song grew instantly quieter, and creatures prepared to take cover from a torrential downpour.

A powerful wind moved through her dress, and the fabric pulled wildly around her waist, emptying the contents from her dress pockets. She moved quickly, gathering the bits of coconut shreds and mango that had fallen from one pocket and the small mahogany seeds that had fallen from the other. She picked through the long blades of grass where the small beads had dispersed and returned all twenty-one to her pocket.

Tamarind trees were stripped of their fruits. Just the other day, an enormous supply of savory pulp and mahogany seeds, encased in brittle, reddish-brown shells, had covered the branches. That morning, as Gabriela and her mother Anna prepared to work, they'd made the discovery. Someone had taken the precious fruit. Her mother was filled with rage. Although she had no idea what had really happened, she cursed the thieves for stealing and vowed that they would not get away with it.

Gabriela's father had disappeared before she was born. Anna was born and raised in the city of Cáceres, Mato Grosso, referred to as "Porta do Pantanal," the door to the marshes; she was one of eleven children born into poverty. She was raised as a Catholic and practiced her faith as an adult, along with Gabriela. Resilient and resourceful, Anna understood how to survive by utilizing every bit of her land, the fruits, the nuts, and seeds. She and Gabriela used seeds to make charms by hand and sold them to merchants where tourists bought them. The necklaces were keepsakes, trinkets which travelers took home and later tossed away or forgot about, but for Anna and her young daughter, the extra income provided them with such things as cloth for a new dress or a pair of shoes. Gabriela learned from her mother how to use the special seeds from the many different fruit and nut trees which grew on their land. Even the hard co-conut shells were used and sanded into distinctive centerpieces on beaded necklaces.

The girl looked north now, where a thick brush of tamarind trees grew and leaves rustled in the wind. Tamarind seeds were close to their hearts. The small mahogany seeds had a strong, thick exterior and a slick, smooth shine. Anna was taught to make rosaries out of them. Once a year, Anna and her daughter worked for days, stringing hundreds of rosaries in prepa-ration for the 'Humanity Festival,' which was tied in with the Easter Celebration. Each rosary Anna and Gabriela made held fifty-nine beads and a beautiful silver cross. Anna's brother, An-tonio, had a small shop in Cáceres and made the impressions there. The rosaries brought in the bulk of their extra earnings for the year.

Sighing, Gabriela thought again about the forbidden place where several nut trees, their branches full of woody seeds, wait-ed for their bounty to be picked, cracked, and roasted or boiled into fragrant oils. Countless miles of thick brush remained untouched by human hands. Hectares of unchanged land and fruits hid behind velvety green leaves and flower blossoms.

A familiar squawking sound focused her attention on the gold horizon. As Evening mist veiled the primeval forest, two bright yellow and blue hyacinth macaws took flight. They flew in the direction of the small girl. Their swift moving silhouettes flickered against the setting sun. It was a dance, a succession of moves, which the child followed with her eyes.

The birds landed in a nearby tree. "Hungry, hungry!" they called. She held out her pinched fingers, waving the coconut and mango she'd prepared earlier.

Hungry, hungry!" The two macaws squawked. "Hungry, yes you're hungry!" Gabriela reached over to the two brothers with the fruit in her palm. To them she was "mama," the human who had stopped them from starving since the day their own mother had never returned to feed them. Anna and her daugh-ter lived in a small three hundred-square-foot home, a typical residence made of stone, adobe mud, and other local material. In the eyes of upper class Brazilians, it was considered a pau-per's dwelling, but to Gabriela, it was the most beautiful place on earth and the only connection she had to her father, who had built the house with his own hands while her mother was carrying her.

The birds fluttered their wings, and Gabriela laughed with childlike wonder. She was ecstatic to find that a female macaw had laid its eggs inside a hole in the Brazilian nut tree she loved so much. The meaningful sight of macaws flying through the Brazilian heavens was a rare one. Gabriela feared that one day she might never see the species again.

Following the hatching of the eggs, the mother had never returned. The mother bird had been shot with a bow and arrow and its feathers used for a headdress by one of the local tribes. It was Gabriela's chosen duty to care for the abandoned and hungry babies. With constant love and timely feedings, they lived. Through the years, many animals of the thick bush sought and received refuge from her. Farmers had set fires and cleared the lands in order to make their domain suitable for cattle and other livestock. These fires forced injured animals to seek refuge on their one acre of land. In addition to injured birds, there were hundreds of other animals, from howler monkeys, to the most dangerous of all.

Gabriela was highly intelligent, and because she was so innately connected to the earth, she was intensely aware of her surroundings. By the time she was only two years old, Anna had made sure her daughter understood that she needed to love the earth and soil on which she lived. All life, flora and fauna, needed to be preserved.

"Hungry, hungry!" the birds squawked again. "Gabriela," she spoke her own name in a sweet voice. "Say,'Gabriela.'"

Instead, the birds nibbled on the coconut strings they'd taken from her hand. She reached over and gently rubbed the birds' heads. Their eyes relaxed to her soft touch. Gabriela looked again to the north. Yes, rain was on its way; God would see to that. But her senses suddenly sharpened because something else was also coming, something she was not prepared for, and not an act of God. The bird closest to her nuzzled her hand with his beak. She worried.

Checking her pocket again, Gabriela made sure the seeds were still there. She wondered how many tamarind trees stood in the nearby pastures, how many brittle pods were filled with the seeds. The forbidden place was less than a mile away on foot. Glancing at the two burlap bags by the doorway that she used for collecting, Gabriela contemplated her mother and her warning about "the dark ones." But she'd never seen them, so maybe they didn't exist? She peeked into her pocket again. Twenty-one beads weren't enough for even a single rosary. But two bags of seeds from the forbidden north would be ample.

Gabriela looked toward her house. She watched as her mother removed laundry from the line.

Perhaps another hour before darkness fell and the rain pelted down. Her rubber-soled slippers sat next to the door. She needed them if she were to run into the forest.

Sliding into her shoes, Gabriela swung the burlap bags over her shoulders. She took quiet steps past a row of white crosses fixed into the ground at close intervals, indicating the boundaries of her family's property. Her tiny heart pounded heavily. A quick bolt of lightning cracked. Once she'd taken her first feeble steps past the partition, the entire earth changed around her.

Like a pebble skipped into a still and mysterious ocean, Gabriela rippled through thick brush, as a wave of warning tried to whisper to her from tree to tree. She peeled away from gigantic cliffs surrounded by lush foliage that bordered the huge waterfalls below. From the steep crystal waterfalls, she paused to watch a pure-white bird emerge, followed by three more. The natural beat of the land stretched beyond the sandy mountains and grottos. By force of habit, she paid vague attention to her instincts for signs of unusual danger, but now she was lost in the rapture of strange life pulsing through the forest and in the reverberating crash of waters echoing around her.

Gabriela paused. Her sight had become blurred by the light mist that weighed down her thick lashes. She used the back of her hand to wipe at her eyes, and focused on a vibrant tamarind tree. The deeply rooted forty-foot tree stood majestic, its branches richly covered in brittle but healthy pods. She moved toward it. Along the trunk a collection of candles, a hairbrush, and a faded picture had been placed. It wasn't uncommon to find ritualistic displays in the most natural settings. Mother had told her that slaves from Africa were imported to work on the sugar plantations or other industries, such as mining. Their owners forbade them to practice their African religions and instead converted them to the Catholic faith. Although many of the slaves earnestly converted to Catholicism, others continued to practice their native beliefs, either in secret nighttime ceremonies/routines or during rituals.

But this was different. Gabriela froze on the spot, her eyes searching the dark earth. Rows and rows of trees had similar ritualistic displays. Some seemed as though they'd been placed recently, while others appeared weathered by the elements and the passing of time. The rituals were desperate, as desperate as the rows of crosses with which her mother had cordoned off their land. Fear.

After taking a deep breath, Gabriela resolved to keep her eyes open so the ghosts of yesterday would not awaken from their sleep and steal her soul. The 'dark ones' waited, lurking in the trees. Identifying them was next to impossible; they were invisible to the human eye and blended with their surroundings. But in this forest, where fruit hung in abundance, there was little life. No sounds of nightly creatures, moths, or even mosquitoes. Maybe the 'dark ones' had scared them away.

Lightning thwacked above a canopy of trees. The rain had yet to fall.

A white bird, swooped from the top branches and fluttered above her. Following its flight, she tried to feel the energies surrounding the creature, but nothing came. This white bird was not a creature of God's. It flew off into the distance and disappeared into the waterfall.

"Hungry, hungry!"

Gabriela looked up, delighted to see the blue macaws perched and nestled among the leaves of a papaya tree.

Then she saw him, in the next tree over, camouflaged in paints, blending in perfectly with the trees and bright colored blossoms. Emerald-green around his eyes, red-and-black stripes that spread across the bridge of his small turned up nose. He sat in an ancient tamarind tree on a thick branch closest to the ground, his legs dangling, sporting a pair of striking brown-leather, lace-up foot coverings. I wonder how old he is. Maybe eight, nine, Gabriela reflected. What could he be doing alone in a place like this? Behind the paint, he was cute, a golden complexion, and bright blue eyes that stood out beneath his mask. Was he even real?

"Hello," the angelic boy finally spoke. The boy's golden brown curls were moistened by the mist of the fog gathering around his face.

"Hello," Gabriela returned the greeting.

The macaws landed on the same branch as the boy. A ripened papaya rested on his lap, and he began cutting the fruit with a small knife. Juice and fragranced oils escaped the thick skin as his blade sliced into it.

"Hungry, hungry!"

The boy looked at her through a mischievous grin. "It sounds like they're saying they're hungry."

"They're not really…they think it's my name and it's the only word they know so far."

He took a piece of the papaya, stabbing the tip of the blade into the flesh. "Can I try anyway?"

Gabriela nodded. "If they'll take it from you."

The macaws used their claws to grab the pieces before chomping on them with their bright beaks. For a moment Gabriela felt a slight pang of jealousy when the boy took his attention away from her. She was immediately ashamed of herself for feeling this way, but it didn't matter; the macaws became nervous and flew off into the other tree, away from the boy and from their view.

"Are those your birds?" he asked, following their direction of flight.

"I raised them. Their mother never came back to feed them." Gabriela caught herself. She was normally an outwardly shy child. But she found herself now surprisingly curious about the boy, wearing a simple white covering that wrapped around his body, fastened by a leather belt. And how long had he been sitting alone in the very place she'd feared her whole life? She stared down at the marble handled blade he used to cut himself another piece of papaya.

He waved the knife toward her. The juicy papaya was still suctioned to the silver.

Gabriela accepted the fruit and slid it downward and off the blade. Her mother taught her to never reject God's gifts, and a gracious act was to accept the offerings. She bit off a piece and chewed slowly, then swallowed. "I guess they're attached to me—the birds, I mean." The flavor of the fruit exploded on her tongue. The papaya had a very different flavor, a sweet sharpness.

The boy severed another piece and offered it to her. She took the fruit and bit into it, chewing slowly.

He didn't take his gaze off of her.

Making a high-pitched kissing sound, Gabriela held out the remaining piece of fruit. The smaller of the macaws emerged from the leaves and hopped onto her wrist. She rubbed him gently around his neck, never taking her eyes of the boy. The macaw took the fruit from between her fingers with his claw.

The boy studied her. She amused him. Her way of thinking was simple, yet unexpected strengths surfaced through her deep brown eyes. They were thoughtful, astute. He finally challenged her. "It must be a lot of work to keep them alive. Why don't you just let them die?" It amused him, to toy with her morality. It disappointed him more when she genuinely forgave his crudeness.

"I could never allow a living thing to suffer," she answered. "People forget about other living things…they feel that they're better. Animals live by their instincts. Humans survive by learning through their feelings. My feelings, like compassion for example, guide me to do what God expects of me."

Gabriela rubbed her cheek against the macaw, a natural way of relating to an animal by mimicking its behavior. She laughed while the bird nibbled at her brow. The other macaw landed alongside the first. Gabriela reached her left hand and gently stroked the bird's bill. The boy studied her, and for the first time wondered whether or not she was who he thought her to be.

Her ring of laughter pulled him from his thoughts. "They're still young," she explained. "They mate when they're six years old, and then they'll have families of their own."

She is indeed the one, he determined. That she was aware of her inner guide, there could be no mistake. Her naiveté made her very vulnerable. It was too easy, almost unfair. A divine being. "You have a connection to the earth," he noted, "for flora and fauna."

Gabriela shrugged off the comment and for the first time in her life considered her abilities. It was true, like her father, she possessed an inexplicable bond with nature.

Gabriela's father, Karael, had been a warrior and was named after God's angel, who had the power to thwart demons. He fell in love with Anna when they were both quite young. He confessed to her that his people were said to be chosen by God to destroy the enemy that ruled earth. They had lived for centuries hidden in the ruins of Mato Grosso, and Anna always knew one day her only child would carry the cross her father had left behind.

He studied her even more intensely now. The child was human, but born into this world with special obligations. Still, she had yet to fully recognize them. A danger to his kind.

The boy used his inner guide to detect the energies surrounding her. She was the one; the voice in his head confirmed it. His prey was so close. Unlike the usual prey he'd been catching lately, she was not a stained soul or a simple dispatch. She was a righteous kill, stained by the hand of God, and blown by the breath of His divinity. The greatest duty of all. This would be his first, and presumably the last, for him in this lifetime. Prior to his present lifetime, he had sent back countless divine beings.

"How old are you?" he asked, jumping from the branch, and standing over her. "You look young and very small." He slid his knife into a brown, leather holster, which was fastened around his waist.

Gabriela swallowed and stood on a thick root in order to speak to the boy at eye level. "I'm nine," she answered. "I was premature. My mom went into labor two months early. They said I should have died." Gabriela held her breath, wishing she hadn't divulged such personal information about herself. She always struggled with the fact that she was small for her age and felt awkward about having to explain it. Gabriela was taught to give thanks to God for surviving at birth.

The boy held out his hand. "My name's Erebus," he said, not

removing his eyes from hers. He willed himself to investigate the true identity of her soul. She would become weak at the touch of his hand; his energy would draw hers in like a magnet.

She took his hand and shook it. It was at that very moment that Erebus knew exactly who she was; the only child of Karael, one of God's most divine and loyal servants. Eleven years earlier, after searching for over four hundred years, Erebus's tribe had found God's Chosen ones. The village had been wiped out, save for a few auspicious escapees. Karael was one of those who had escaped in an effort to protect his new wife, and unborn daughter. And here she stood, the last of her kind, fatherless, and unprotected. Unaware.

Gabriela was nervous but excited. Erebus was wild, and yet he was civil. Something was very wrong, but she couldn't bring herself to leave. She extended her right hand and felt awkward when she realized he was left-handed.

"I'm Gabriela," she blushed. She'd never shaken hands with a boy before, not someone who wasn't a cousin or a distant relative. She was enjoying his company. Gabriela began to retract her hand, but he took it back and calmly placed his other hand over hers. She felt light, almost intoxicated by the softness of his hands, the well-manicured tips of his nails, and the smooth edges of his cuticles. His nails were clean. Mortified, she glanced at her own hands, the dirt beneath her nails, and the roughness that he must have noticed while holding her hand.

Erebus looked deeply into her eyes and held his stare longer than she wanted him to.

A few seconds later, he released his eye-grip, and focused on the burlap bags draped over her shoulders.

"Can I help you?" he asked.

"No, it's okay."

"I want to," he insisted.

Gabriela blushed again, happy to have worn her favorite yellow dress today.

Working together in silence, combing the grounds for fallen pods, they sifted through the rotting ones and selected only the brittle, ripened ones. Small animals scurried about in the undergrowth.

She liked having Erebus help her. She also felt bad knowing

that his flawlessly fine hands were now as filthy as her own. But she'd made a friend, and in the most unexpected place of all. Gabriela's adrenalin was rushing, to the detriment of her caution. She had disregarded her mother's words of warning, and now she savored the company of her first crush. She could only hope the boy liked her in return.

Erebus pointed triumphantly to the burlap bags filled to the brim. "See, all done." He moved back to the ancient tree, pulling himself up onto the lower branch again. "Now you can tell me more about yourself and about your gift." He sat comfortably with his legs swinging beneath him.

Gabriela looked to the sky. "I should go. It's going to rain soon, and my mother's probably getting worried, wondering where I've gone."

Erebus revived the adrenalin surging within her. "Five minutes," he bargained, "and if you want, I'll walk you back and help you carry your bags."

She blushed again and smiled. "All right, five minutes."

"Hungry, hungry!" the macaws cried from a branch above them.

Not noticing that the birds had grown anxious, Gabriela pulled herself up to sit with Erebus on the branch. Her legs dangled alongside his, and their warm bodies pressed up against each other. She felt giddy. "Aren't you afraid to be here by yourself?"

"No, I come here all the time. I like to watch people, people like you." He leaned into her. "You were looking at the pictures and stuff that people leave by the trees. Why?"

She turned around to look at the tree roots. "I was thinking about the dark ones…and wondered if the story about them was true."

"The dark ones?"

An aggressive growl, followed by a second one was heard in the distance. Gabriela listened in. Worry filled her face. "Jaguars," she said. "They're in trouble."

"What kind of trouble?"

Gabriela closed her eyes and zeroed in on the sound. She spoke, with eyes still closed. "Hunters maybe." She opened her eyes. "Warning calls."

His upper lip curled into a sneer. "The jaguar's tongue is so rough it can peel the skin off its prey."

"I know," she said.

"You've handled them."

It was true. Gabriela had rescued hundreds of animals, and jaguars were no exception.

He spoke slowly and evenly. "I've seen a jaguar lick the skin clean off a human. Right down to the bone while he was still alive."

"Jaguars only attack humans if they're being threatened."

"I guess we have nothing to worry about then, do we?"

Gabriela looked at the ground. "I don't see any paw prints. I have a feeling they won't enter into the Devil's Web."

Erebus let out a mocking laugh. "Is that what they call this?"

"They say the dark ones wait in the web to steal people's souls," she said, her attention diverted by the troublesome sounds in the distance. Something was definitely wrong but for some reason, she couldn't remove herself from where she sat.

"I've heard the stories, too, but I don't think they're dark," Erebus said.

"Of course they're dark. They call them dark because they're evil…they take souls from those who are good."

The macaws flapped excitedly above them. "Hungry, hungry!"

Gabriela spoke fearfully before she could stop herself. "My mother told me the dark ones took my father from her before I was born. He came to her in a dream, while she was still carrying me, and he told her to never go into the north forest because the dark ones waited there to rip my soul from me. And here I am, not listening to her."

"You were thinking about helping her. That makes you a good daughter. But your mother is to blame. She's been keeping things from you."

The words stung her. Her mother was secretive. Anna had always been overly protective of her daughter. The family stayed put, except when they traveled to buy goods, and even then, Gabriela's uncle, Antonio, had to accompany them. Recently, her mother had been having frightful dreams. Anna was certain that her husband was sending her messages that the time was coming, the dark ones were closing in, and Gabriela needed to be kept safe. She went so far as to keep loaded shotguns in the house and never allowed Gabriela to leave the property.

As much as Gabriela loved her mother, this protective obsession of hers had been wearing her down. And of the few friends the family did have, many of them secretly told others that Anna had gone mad. Still, Gabriela felt it her duty to stand up for her mother in the face of the appealing boy. "I think she's trying to protect me from the dark ones."

"If you believed her, you wouldn't be here," Erebus challenged in a sharp tone.

Gabriela looked at the hundreds of trees decorated at the roots by the candles and photos. "How do you explain that then? There has to be some truth to it."

"Those are people who lost someone," Erebus said. "They think it'll help their souls find their way back home again."

"But if the dark ones don't exist, what is stealing the souls?"

Erebus bit his lower lip. "How do you know they're dark? Maybe they're not dark. Maybe they're as bright as the sun." He spoke with quick sureness.

"The eye is the lamp of the body," Gabriela explained with kindness, as she recalled her mother's teachings. "A person with a dark soul can live only in darkness, there is no light. Therefore he cannot see through God's eyes."

Her words brought a glare to his sky-blue eyes.

She continued, "My father believed that what you gave in this life, you take with you in death. So whatever light you bring to others in life, you'll take that with you to your afterlife. The dark ones will remain forever without the light and love of God."

"Did he explain that evil existed in order to bring forth a sacred outcome?"

A breath escaped her lips. Her mother had a written copy of those very words, and Gabriela's father had lived by them. She took a deep breath and responded. "My mother also told me that my father believed that a sacred outcome is to live with compassion for those who suffer. That is what living in the light of God is all about, Erebus. Don't you see how beautiful it is? To live as loyal servants of God."

"Hungry, hungry!"

Gabriela turned her attention to the sky.

Darkness swiftly rushed to the earth between the canopy of leaves, and a new darkness spiraled out from the black pupils of the boy's blue eyes. He had gripped her without touching her.

She felt weak.

"Are you a loyal servant of God?" he challenged her.

Pulling herself off the branch to face him, she said, "I am. I carry God's light, and I live in the eyes of God."

"Have you ever looked into a person's soul, Gabriela? Have you ever used your eyes to see the darkness you speak of?"

Shivering, she whispered, "No."

"Your mother never told you that you were born with your eyes open. That means something. Look into my eyes…I mean really look. Tell me what you see." Erebus knew that once she saw inside of him, she would see inside of herself. She would understand that they were mortal enemies.

She did as she was told. Then heaviness gripped her as she witnessed his sky-blue eyes change into two black portals, sucking her into a void.

"What is the earth whispering…child?" he asked her. "What is the voice telling you to do?"

"Hungry, hungry!" The macaws flailed above her head.

Goosebumps crept along Gabriela's arms. For the first time, she felt the warnings the terrain had been giving her, the warnings she had chosen to ignore earlier. Erebus wasn't a handsome boy who'd befriended her in the forbidden brush. He was what her father, from his grave, had warned her mother about. Gabriela knew her life was at risk.

The younger macaw perched on her shoulder. She still stood stiff, her legs grounded. She was like a rodent, hypnotized under the spell of the serpent before the kill.

She barely whispered, "The voice is telling me to destroy you."

His arms outstretched, Erebus said mockingly, "So here I am…do your worst."

Gabriela's legs felt detached from her body. She opened her mouth to speak but nothing came out.

"Your father had that same look just before we sent him

back to where he came from." He wished he didn't have to say that, except he wanted her to retort with words equally cruel. He wanted to hate her, so that he could enjoy the hunt. There was nothing gratifying about this. "You have his eyes."

Gabriela was quickly losing her strength. Her knees began to bend. "It was you who stripped our trees bare. You planned all this," she somehow managed to say.

He shrugged and confessed easily. "I didn't need to strip your trees to catch you…I just didn't want your mother to have to see it. It's not her we want. And I had no idea who your father was, or what you were. That was unexpected."

Erebus waited and whispered with absolute calm. "Yes, yes, I knew your father well." He spoke his words through lips that were no longer those of a boy. "You see, we are Lucifer's Chosen. We're cleansing earth, creating a balance, and sending all those disloyal to him back to God. 'Catching the darkness,' is what we call it."

Gabriela opened her mouth to speak, but found it impossible.

"Do not try to speak," Erebus said, placing his forefinger on her lips. "It was before you were born and before I was born into this body. I was a man, a warrior like your father. But I was the one who killed the dark ones, the souls of your kind. Over five hundred years ago, a tribe was born, God's Chosen. And much later, there was a man, his name was Christopher. They formed an allegiance to God, to destroy all those loyal to King Lucifer."

"Hungry, hungry!"

Tears fell from Gabriela's eyes and ran down the sides of her face.

Erebus attempted to clear up her confusion. "For hundreds of years your people, the tribe that your father was born into, had been hunting us, just as we had hunted them and others with a duty to God…"

Gabriela shook her head, uncomprehendingly.

"Did you ever wonder why you were so different? Why you heard voices inside your head. Those are God's angels guiding you, just as we are guided by the fallen ones. Your mother knew, and she tried to keep you hidden, because your people are the only humans on this earth who have ever come close enough to finding us. The key feature of your kind is that your senses exceed those of all other humans. Your connection to God's angels and animals has caused the deaths of so many in my family. A jaguar ripped into my flesh. I felt its tongue lick my skin to the bone. But my essence, my soul, moves like the wind. You can feel it, though you can't catch it. King Lucifer protects my people. What about you? Where is your God now?" He looked about. "The coward leaves you to die in the Devil's Web."

Gabriela struggled for air and said, "I live in the eyes of God, and your existence will soon see its final truth."

Erebus paced back and forth. He yelled, "How can you say that? He leaves you to fight alone…Your people have stood in the grace of a God who lies and plays with lives. When you say the dark ones are evil, you're really talking about yourselves."

A crack of lightning struck hard in the distance, and static sizzled over Gabriela's skin, lightly sparking the fine hairs on her arms.

"You have to see how wrong that is. He allowed your father to die. And now he'll allow the same for you." He shook his head in a show of compassion. "A bird without wings dropped in a cage with hungry lions. Your God could not be more unfair."

Gabriela swallowed with difficulty.

Erebus gently cupped her chin. "You know, young Gabriela, if you were to understand Lucifer's plight, perhaps switch sides, you would be of great value to us. Your strengths would be that of a hundred of Lucifer's Chosen. I myself am proof of that."

Gabriela pulled her chin away.

"There is no win greater than the win of an enemy's allegiance. A freedom of will," Erebus said with a soft tone. "It's not that I hate you or want to bring you any pain, but it's time you go home." He removed his hand, and using the back of it, he wiped the tears on her cheek. "Don't cry. Be brave, Gabriela; the heavens await you…and so do your people."

The macaw on her shoulder jumped to a tree branch in a loud state of panic.

She closed her eyes tight. Gabriela whimpered and thought of her mother. How she wished she had never crossed the barrier of white crosses. How she wished she was curled up in her bed listening to the familiar sounds of the rustling leaves and the songs of the night creatures humming lullabies outside her bedroom window as she had done all her life. And she prayed for all this to be a very bad dream. When she awakened in the morning, Gabriela wanted to smell a plate of freshly baked bread, and eggs. She wanted to sit at a kitchen table and tell her mother of the terrible dream she had and have Momma kiss her brow and tell her everything was fine.

It was a risk getting acquainted with the enemy. Killing her later made it that much harder. Erebus wanted nothing more than to have her adherence, but there wasn't enough time for that. Her death was ordered by the fallen angels. Erebus heard the faint rustle through the leaves, his reluctance to move in on Gabriela would cost her. There was nothing more he could do.

"Hungry hungry!"

She opened her eyes and followed the macaw, which flew to her, but his flight was ended by a golden snake who snapped its head out from behind a cluster of plush greenery where it had hidden. Paralyzed by the boy's gift, Gabriela stood and watched as her precious blue bird was swallowed whole. A single tear fell from her cheek and dropped to the ground, where the earth absorbed it.

Thunder rumbled, and the downpour finally pelted the foliage overhead.

He gave her a sympathetic smile. "A baby jaguar will one day grow new teeth. And those same teeth will be sharp enough to rip into flesh." He traced a half-moon crescent into her forehead. "Cut their circle of life short, and send them back to where they came from."

A complete understanding filled Gabriela. She was God's Chosen. God's divine being who was created to watch over the meek and protect God's grain. An overload of information began to rapidly penetrate her mind. She saw herself clearly for the first time in her short life.

"I am God's grain, and I am to be ground by the teeth of wild beasts…" Gabriela recited her tribe's words, for she knew that they would be her last. And as surely as the snake had devoured the bird, Gabriela knew the demon would kill her and devour her soul.

29

God's Alter Ego

A sharp knock on the door brought both women reeling into the present and left Esperança's history hanging in the room. Claire's heart raced hard and fast.

"I ordered New York's finest pizza for us while you were partying with ghosts." Claire's gaze followed the old woman as she shuffled hurriedly to the door.

Esperança fished into her worn-out jeans' pocket before producing a sweaty twenty-dollar bill. Then she swung open the door to reveal a small, weary man sporting a red cap embroidered with the words 'Brooklyn Slice.'

The smell of pizza wasn't enough to pry Claire's interest from what had happened next to the beautiful, dying woman named Filhote.

Taking his time sifting through his change, the deliveryman tried to put together seventy-three cents. "Keep the change," Esperança exclaimed, practically pushing the man out the door. She locked the door and walked back to her waiting client. "I had them bring paper plates and napkins just for you," she said, placing the steaming box on the table beneath Claire's nose.

"Here!" Esperança passed Claire the stack of napkins and paper plates, followed by a bottle of spring water. "Take."

Claire shook her head. "I'm not hungry."

"Bullshit," she challenged, while sliding into her chair

again. "That's why you skinny women are so miserable. You're hungry, but you never eat anything." She opened the box and yanked off a greasy slice. "You have no ass either, no curves." She took a large bite out of her slice.

"I'll have you know I have a wonderful ass," Claire said, straightening up with a backward glance, focused on her butt. "I don't understand this new craze, women actually wanting to have a mammoth ass. It's disgusting…not to mention having to keep it clean."

With a closed fist pressed against her to chest, Esperança let out an enormous burp then said, "Say's the woman with no ass."

Watching Esperança polishing off her crust and reaching for another slice, Claire considered her story at great length. The old woman, with oil-stained lips and sauce on her chin, still remained quite the mystery. Between her smacking and belching, it was almost unreal when she displayed bouts of decency, as though she herself was split in two. Here she was doing the devil's work, yet when she spoke of Christopher, and of God, she seemed so respectful, a completely different person. Claire thought back to the day when she had witnessed Esperança murder the man who wanted to kill his wife and children. Claire caught the old woman's glare.

"Why did you do it? Why did you kill that man instead of his wife and children?"

A pepperoni slid off the slice, landing on Esperança's lower lip. Reaching it with her tongue, she pushed it back into her mouth. "Because I could…because he didn't deserve them."

"I don't get you," Claire said. "You're hiding something."

"No one asked you to get me," Esperança said, with her left cheek full of food. "You want to hear the rest of the story or not?"

"You're avoiding my question," Claire challenged.

"Blue tit bird," Esperança threatened her, in a sing-song voice. "You wanna hear the rest, don't you?"

"Yes, I do want to hear the rest," Claire replied, not wanting Esperança to go there.

Esperança swallowed. "Only if you eat with me. Take it or leave it." She resumed her eating.

The revolting smacking sounds the voodoo priestess made while eating, coupled with the drug, sparked Claire's appetite. "Fine," she gave in. "At least let me wash my hands again." She stepped with a stiff walk to the small sink, grabbed the sliver of green soap, and lathered her hands generously in suds. "Damn woman," she muttered under her breath.

Returning to her seat, Claire watched Esperança reach into the box and set two slices aside. "For my granddaughter."

Claire opened her napkin into a perfect white square, placing it on her lap. She caught Esperança rolling her eyes. "What? You have a problem with etiquette?"

"Etiquette, shmetiquette," Esperança said, placing a napkin over the plated pizza, and dove back into her slice.

"I finally found your weakness," Claire said with a sly smile, her eyes on the slices set aside for Patience.

"What weakness?" Esperança responded, without looking up from her plate. "Pizza?"

"No. Your granddaughter."

Esperança chewed in quick bites before swallowing. "Congratulations, Sherlock." Then she thought it over a few seconds. "She takes care of me…she's a good girl. Eat."

Claire reached in and pulled out a slice onto a paper plate. "Was your daughter young when she died?"

Esperança plucked a pepperoni off the slice with her index finger and thumb, popped it into her mouth, and nodded. "Almost six."

"But since you have no other children," Claire pressed, "how can Patience be your granddaughter? Or is she your granddaughter from a previous life?" No longer able to hide her hunger, she bit into her piece of pizza. It was fabulous, no doubt the best pizza she'd ever eaten. Claire swallowed and waited for a response, which Esperança obviously dodged. "You never answered me," Claire insisted, taking a bigger bite. "How is Patience your granddaughter?"

The voodoo priestess became serious. "Blue tit bird!" she warned her again. "Don't ever ask me about her again, especially in the presence of the fallen angels."

Claire stopped chewing and gulped down the mouthful. "They're here?"

"You may not see them, but they see you. And they hear everything you think and say. Patience has nothing to do with this."

Taken aback, Claire resumed eating and mulled over the mystery surrounding Patience. Who was the monster-girl? And how was she able to do that thing with her hand? By the time Claire had wolfed down the entire slice, it struck her. Could it be that Patience was a divine being? Was Patience actually God's Chosen? Is that what Esperança meant when she said that she wished she could send Patience back?

Claire sucked in a breath when Esperança stood up, reached over and grabbed a firm hold of Claire's chin. She looked Claire dead in the eyes as their gazes collided. A moment passed, and Claire's expression softened.

"You will erase that thought from your head. You will never question what Patience is ever again," Esperança commanded. "Your focus will be on Filhote. Her story."

Claire blinked fast and hard. Esperança soon released Claire's chin and sat back down. "Where were we?"

Esperança took a swig from the bottle, arching her brows in silent scrutiny.

Claire was mystified, trying to recollect her thoughts, her mind was a complete void. "Shit, what happened?" The slight wrinkle between Claire's brows deepened. "I just had a mal-adaptive brain activity change. In layman's terms…a brain fart." Claire laughed at her own joke, then said, "Filhote! You said that Filhote was pregnant by the time Christopher saved her, and they fell in love. Tell me about that."

Esperança set the bottle down, wiped her lips with a napkin, and resumed her narrative. "Filhote was very sick when they brought her home. Christopher put her in an area of the house where other sick and beaten slaves were treated. But this was different."

"Because she was Manuel's property?"

"And for what he saw in her. He said later that when he touched her, he looked into her tormented soul. But there was also something more. Filhote could see between, the thin veil that separates the living and the dead. And that's why she saw things, like the snakes on the wall in her old room. Filhote's supernatural abilities were passed down from her dead mother's side, the deep African roots, black magic and so forth. The angels that hovered over Filhote were not God's angels. And because she was so damaged, she'd somehow tapped into the darkness during her darkest hours."

"Like me," Claire uttered.

"Like you, beautifully broken. Susceptible. Only the difference between you and her was that her curse was passed down. You, on the other hand, have a different kind of gift," Esperança said. "You have powers of manipulation...a genius, and your own worst enemy. You summoned the fallen through your actions." She took a pause and whispered, "Anjo em pedra."

Claire just heard her. "What was that?"

"'An angel in stone,' Christopher used to say. He said that there was a stone around her heart, a hardness, because of the way she had suffered. He wanted to believe that if he hammered away at it and gave her hope and faith, he could release her soul, give her freedom. He also told her that if she were to have faith in God, the stone that weighed her soul down could be lifted by the winds beneath the wings of angels."

Claire felt humbled. "It's almost poetic. It's like we all have an internal battle going on inside of us. And the hardness weighs us down, weighs the goodness down. The angelic part I mean. Anjo em pedra, I like that. But was he able to help her?"

"Sure, only his hammer was made of feathers. She saw him with a bird in his hands, a yellow-winged cacique. They're pretty birds, mostly blue and black with bright yellow stripes on their wings. Anyway, its right wing was bandaged up. Filhote watched him while he tended the bird and removed its cast."

Esperança's eyes were warm. "He was so gentle, so patient. He caught her watching him from the bed. And I'm sure that she had that look in her eyes...like she wanted to ask what he was doing but was too scared. So he brought the bird over to her and placed it in her hands. She loved the softness of its feathers, the way it nestled up to her for warmth. What Christopher saw in Filhote was a light radiating within. It was as if the love they shared for the creature brought her back to life. He knew it would take time, and she still trusted no one. But if he brought to her the love of God's creatures, the light inside her might grow. She nursed that bird night and day until it was time to set it free."

"Did the bird fly afterwards?"

"Yes," Esperança said, "but this meant much more. Christopher wanted her to feel compassion for a suffering being. He wanted her to understand that, like the bird, she also needed to heal."

Esperança's face took on a look of wonder. "He told her she was a lot like the injured bird. He said a bird without flight was like a person without salvation. And a person without salvation needs saving. While holding the suffering bird, she saw herself clearly, and for the first time in her life, she put her trust in the hands of a man."

Esperança stared down at the final slice and pushed it away. She had clearly lost her appetite.

"When did they actually fall in love?"

"Soon after."

"Even with…the scars all over her body?" Claire continued.

"Even with her scars." She reached for her bottle, her stare lingering into the golden liquid. She rocked the bottle back and forth. The sloshing sounds calmed her, and she spoke in a daze. Claire noticed how intensely into her story the voodoo priestess was delving.

"He nursed her for months, treated her burns, fed her, and cleaned her. In the beginning, while she was in and out of consciousness, Christopher was so respectful of her that when she needed a dressing changed or a bath, he had women attend to it. No one else had ever shown such kindness to her. He was a true gentleman." The old woman looked up with a fanciful expression. "She thought he was the most handsome man she'd ever met."

Claire challenged her with a smile. "Why, Esperança, underneath your gruff exterior lays a hopeless romantic."

Esperança fanned her off. "One night, after one of the biggest rainstorms had passed, and the others retired for the evening, Christopher asked Filhote if she would like him to recite Bible passages to her. Back then bibles weren't around, and Christopher studied in Portugal. He recited God's word like a poet, so much passion." Esperança's face softened more, and she inhaled deeply. "It was as if God himself meant for those words to be expressed to her. Like a Band-aid on her soul." She shook her head at the thought. "It was the first time Filhote cried, and the first time he'd ever heard her voice. And she really cried; cried for the mother she never knew, cried for the beauty that cursed her life, and for the men like Manuel who raped her because of it. And just as Filhote predicted, she knew that once she started crying, she would never stop. Christopher stayed with her until she was able to fall asleep."

"And that's when their love story began," Claire said, totally captivated after all.

A faint blush colored Esperança's cheeks. "I thought you didn't like happy stories?"

Claire shrugged.

"Yes, that's when the love story began. Every day, Christopher taught her about God. He taught Filhote as he had the other people he'd saved. He drew three circles in the dirt to teach her. One circle represented the human body. The circle inside was the soul. And the center circle was God, the center of our world. Everlasting life. The soul needed to be nurtured. It was the way he explained it, though. He said the circle on the outside was when the human body and soul were most vulnerable to evil, the most susceptible to temptation. And evil existed in order to bring forth a sacred outcome."

Claire nodded. "Like if there was no suffering, there would be no need for compassion?"

"You got it. He told her that without faith, there was only one circle. In order to reach the center, you have to work very hard and be very determined. There were lessons to learn in order to enter the center with God."

Esperança became quite serious. "Initially, Christopher was faced with a challenge. How could people be expected to find the center with God if they have no idea about Christianity? How could they be denied for their ignorance? When you think about it, natives, the uncivilized, well, they were in the dark. How could a compassionate God reject a soul based on its lack of knowledge?"

"That's right," Claire agreed. Christopher was a smart man. She had often wondered that herself.

"He then realized that it wasn't necessarily Christianity God wanted enforced, but rather, a protection from Satan. Christopher needed to have them understand, that there was only one God, and that the Heavenly father was that God. You see, a good person is a good person…compassion, love, understanding, patience. That's what Christianity meant to Christopher. But Satan had an advantage, reaching those without those tools and guidance, who were unprotected. It's no different than children being raised as terrorists; they see nothing wrong with the only thing they know. So Christopher struggled with this. He also knew he couldn't do it alone, so he trained foot soldiers. He knew the slaves he'd saved couldn't stay forever on his plantation. But he wasn't about to let them go until they were ready and armed—armed with faith that protected their center circle. In those days, slaves who escaped in Brazil and formed tribes with other men and women were called 'maroons.' They were also known as fugitives, runaways. The slaves Christopher saved formed settlements together, where they continued to live in freedom. Not only did they live in freedom, they also spread Christianity to the natives Christopher was unable to reach."

Claire shook her head in awe. "Incredible, he led by example."

"Exactly."

Claire wanted to hear more about Filhote. "Go back to Filhote. Did Manuel ever find out she survived? Did she ever regain her beauty?"

Esperança pondered before answering her question. "Not for a very, very long time. Her outer circle healed, her skin returned to what it once was, and her hair began growing in. She was healing on the outside, and on the inside, she was growing, feeding the light of God inside of her. When she was well enough, Christopher asked her to join him on his plantation. He introduced her to the others, the men and woman he had saved, and the children. They were so grateful to him; they loved him. Sick and dying slaves gathered, and she noticed how he treated each of them with dignity. Filhote and Christopher became a team. She was honored to walk arm-in-arm with him.

"Yes, they fell in love. Sometimes when the sun went down and the world turned quiet, she caught him staring at her with this lovesick look in his eyes. Other times they took long walks, and he pointed out his favorite flowers to her, explaining the different smells he enjoyed from the reds, yellows, and blues he loved the most. Of course, she'd known these flowers her whole life, but hearing him talk about them made her look at nature with new eyes, like she was seeing it for the first time. He had her doing things she'd never before done in her life. They behaved as silly children do, jumping into rivers and sitting along banks while water rushed over them. For hours they talked about everything and nothing."

Esperança looked at Claire with a peculiar smugness. "They had the kind of love you only read about, the kind that makes your heart go light, and the world just spins out of control. They were crazy for each other. They had this thing for climbing trees. Christopher believed that it was a way to get closer to God. There was this one kapok tree, which must have been a hundred years old and more than a hundred feet high. Its huge branches hung over the river overlooking the plantation. Christopher hammered wooden pegs into the bark so they were able to climb it. At night, they often sat on a high branch and watched fires burning for miles all over Christopher's land, where hundreds of souls lived. They could hear the laughter of children, singing and praying combined. All these people had hope because of one man."

Esperança inhaled meaningfully and nodded her head when she exhaled. "It was like witnessing a miracle. She felt unworthy to be in his presence, unworthy of being part of something so profound. But he was always very good at making her understand. He used the moon as an example. He told Filhote that the moon was God's gift to us. He said it was his children's candle in the dark night. God kept the light burning to guide us home; that is, if we wanted to come home. Looking at the moon through Christopher's eyes made a godly impression on her. She savored those moments on a high branch in the tree, watching the world with him. They were so happy." Esperança said, meeting Claire's enamored gaze.

"The other side of the coin," Claire said. Esperança stilled herself, her eyes set softly on her. "The moon, you were saying that there were two sides to it."

And although the comment went unrequited, Claire saw a glimmer of approval, bubbling to the surface in Esperança's bottomless eyes. The moment passed, and Esperança's face darkened.

"Sometimes goodness brings out the bad, and other times, badness brings out the good. When Filhote discovered that she was carrying Manuel's child, she wanted to rip the fetus out of her, wanted it gone. Christopher wouldn't hear of it. Instead, he asked Filhote to marry him. Because marrying her in a church was dangerous—word of their marriage might spread—he built her one."

Claire whispered, "Badness bringing out the good."

"He built her a small church on the plantation behind his house. Remember, his trusted priests lived as missionaries on his property. Christopher said it was God's house and everyone was welcome to worship in it. They married. Six months later she gave birth to Manuel's son which they named Christopher."

Esperança stopped speaking and reached for her rum. She placed it on the table in front of her and contemplated before continuing. "They both knew something was wrong, though. Very wrong. Then the snakes came back, like the ones on the wallpaper in that special room Manuel had put her in. You remember."

It wasn't a question, and Claire could think of nothing to do but nod.

The voodoo priestess grabbed hold of the bottle and managed two full gulps. "They're called golden lanceheads," she said, wiping her mouth with the back of her hand. "Color of wheat fields. But make no mistake, one bite and you're dead. Your kidneys stop working, you vomit, and if you're still alive your brain hemorrhages and blood seeps out your ears."

"These snakes are real?"

"Very real. The baby was less than two hours old when Filhote went to put him in his crib. There she found two snakes hiding under her son's blankets. They hissed at her as if they were preparing to protect the child. She called some of Christopher's men to help. They took the snakes outside and a good distance into the forest. But at night they hissed in the grass outside. Christopher said he couldn't hear them but Filhote could.

She knew they were watching. Watching and waiting."

"Waiting for what?"

"She sensed that it was only a matter of time before the snakes would return on Satan's command, and the baby would join them. Christopher moved quickly and had the child baptized, but the hissing didn't stop. It was then that Filhote sensed her son was a creation of Satan.

At first, she wanted to kill the baby, but Christopher wouldn't hear of it. He loved him. He believed the child's soul could be spared, and that their love would be enough to drive Satan away." Esperança looked up with a half smile. "And for the first twelve years of the boy's life, Christopher was correct.

"He was a beautiful child. He had Filhote's intense blue-green eyes and the Silvas' black hair and strong features. Still, he was no ordinary boy. He ran before he walked, sang before he talked. By the time he was six, he had learned every language spoken on the Silva Plantation. And in case you didn't know, there are many languages spoken throughout Africa. And the child spoke them all. The Africans nicknamed him Kamau, meaning 'silent warrior.' Soon, no one called him Christopher anymore. The child was much stronger than the other children. He was calm, rational, and extremely intelligent, dangerously perfect. At night, while Kamau slept, Christopher often placed his hands over his heart and he saw the most incredible light in his son's soul, but where there was light, there were shadows as well; shadows that existed only under the watch of the fallen. Naturally, he didn't want to accept what his wife had said all along. He didn't want to believe that his beloved son was a child of darkness." Esperança bit the inside of her cheek, contemplating.

"Kamau loved Filhote and Christopher as much as they did him. He adored his father, and they did everything together. Christopher taught him how to hunt, make wine from berries, and which flowers and plants were used for healing. But most importantly, he taught him Christianity. Strange as it seems, the boy took a special interest in the subject. He recited biblical passages perfectly. Sometimes, when Christopher was unavailable, Kamau spent hours preaching Christianity to the newcomers, but still the shadows hovered over him. Like an invisible predator, waiting, watching.

"On many nights, the three of them sat high in the tree watching the land by the light of the moon, and Kamau fell asleep against his mother's breast. If only she had pushed him off the branch while he was asleep, the hundred-foot fall would have snapped the boy's neck for sure, and all their troubles could have been avoided." She exhaled sadly. "But Christopher swore that he could save him, fight the darkness within him." Esperança paused and heard the question in Claire's mind.

Claire opened her mouth to ask it, then decided against it.

"You have something to ask me?" Esperança said.

Claire's head was bowed, her voice almost inaudible. "Do all people have that? Both light and darkness inside them?"

"Yes, they do."

Claire raised her chin and spoke through her lashes. "Even me, do I have a light inside?"

Esperança's eyes softened with some reaction Claire couldn't identify. "Of course, Claire. Apart from those souls that are too late, most have a light inside. You just have to know the difference. But then again, perception is everything. What one person classifies as evil, another person will say it's righteous."

"Such as al-Qaida's promise of seventy-two virgins," Claire suggested. "Human bombs."

"Exactly, for example, I have a riddle for you," Esperança offered. "Since you think you're so smart."

"Try me." Claire was back to her saucy self. She uncrossed and re-crossed her legs.

"What would you say is more evil, a soul that knows it's evil, or one that doesn't?"

Claire repeated the question once in her head and said without a hesitation, "One that doesn't."

Esperança concealed her marvel. "And how did you come up with this?"

"It's obvious. A person that would question his actions has conscience enough to know it's wrong. One that doesn't know would never yield, never see the pain it's causing," Claire explained.

"That's correct. You know, you're the only one that has ever answered correctly," Esperança admitted. "And I have asked many." After a moment's thought, she asked Claire, "And what about you, what evil would you fall under?"

"I'm evil knowing I'm evil."

"And this pleases you because it hurts God," Esperança stated.

"And what of you?" Claire countered, without skipping a beat.

"It's complicated."

"Complicated...because you know that you're evil, and it doesn't please you." Claire's rejoinder went unanswered. She knew better than to press the issue, but Claire asked the next obvious question. "And what of Kamau, did he know he was evil?"

"Smart question," Esperança replied. "But that's the beauty of perception, the difference between knowing that you're evil and not knowing when you are. At the age of twelve, Kamau's soul was no longer his own, and he began to understand his purpose, the reason for his summons. One night he disappeared for six days straight. Christopher went crazy looking for him, sending out teams of men to find him. When Kamau returned, he wasn't the same. His soul was under the shade of the fallen. And from that point on, whenever he touched his son, Christopher saw that Kamau's soul was overshadowed. The worst of it was when the boy went with his father to where the sick slaves were treated, those who had recently been brought in from Salvador. One slave in particular had been dying a few days before, but was now on the slow road to recovery. Kamau placed his hands over the eyes of that slave and apologized, and without a second thought, the boy wrapped his hands around the man's skinny neck and snapped it, killing him instantly. Afterward, Kamau spoke, and the words his son uttered drove Christopher to tears."

"So what did Kamau say?" .

"He said, 'I sent him back to where he came from.'"

Claire thought for a moment. "From heaven?"

"Correct. You see, it was of no coincidence that Kamau was chosen, because his soul was invaluable to Satan in his war with God."

"Invaluable in what way?"

Esperança gave Claire a penetrating look before explaining. "Understand this...when Satan ranks souls to lead to his armies, he doesn't choose just any random leader. He chooses souls that were once loyal to God. And because Kamau was a divine being of God's, that made it the best kind of win, a stronger win. God's Chosen, leading an army of Satan's Chosen."

Claire thought she'd misunderstood. "Kamau was a divine being?"

"Yes, born to watch over the meek and to protect God's grain. And there was no greater leader than one who understood his enemy, one that could communicate with God's angels as well as the fallen. You see, to turn God's Chosen into evil not knowing it's evil was the ultimate victory for Satan."

"But God's Chosen was Christopher."

"Yes. And what better than the son that Christopher loved and raised as his own, used against him? Two tribes, one to enforce Christianity, the other to crush it."

Claire took a moment to digest her words. "So Satan had plans for Filhote? He planned on sending Manuel to impregnate her and then leave her for dead," she said to herself. "And this because Christopher was interfering."

"That's what I said earlier, about Satan loving beautiful things, broken and beautiful," Esperança reminded her.

It was all making sense. "Poor Christopher, it must have killed him. He saved so many slaves, but he wasn't able to save his son. What did Christopher do that night when Kamau killed the slave?"

Esperança picked up the bottle and drank to the last drop before meeting Claire's troubled gaze. "He was too shocked and needed prayer, time to reflect. Anyway, he decided it was best to hold off until the morning before doing something rash. But Kamau left the next day."

"He left. Where did he go?"

"To his real father, Manuel, only nobody knew this at the time. And they weren't prepared for what was to come. Manuel and Christopher hadn't spoken to one another in more than a decade, even though less than eight miles separated them. Neither Filhote nor Christopher had ever told the boy who his real father was, but Kamau knew.

"And by this time, Christopher set thousands of slaves free so they could spread Christianity. God's work was being done, while on the other side, Satan was playing his card. And just as Christopher was chosen to train slaves as Christian foot soldiers, Satan was about to use Kamau to train loyal foot soldiers to defeat them. It was simply a matter of convincing Manuel to agree. Manuel had no idea Kamau was his own flesh and blood, or that Filhote was alive and married to his brother, and Kamau was not yet ready to reveal it. Instead, he told him he had made Christopher wealthy beyond belief, and that he could also do the same for Manuel. But the boy required free reign, and Manuel gave in to him. So this is where the real work began, and just as Kamau had helped train Christian foot soldiers, he was about to do the complete opposite on Manuel's plantation."

"Kamau was a threat to God," Claire concluded.

Esperança nodded, "A huge threat, because divine beings are earthbound, almost immortal, because they can return back among the living. But as I said, they have a straight line of communication with God's angels, as well as the fallen if they choose. Can you imagine? If Kamau was able to sway the other divine beings, and have them switch allegiances against God?"

"Just like Lucifer, when he took one third of the angels with him on his fall."

"Exactly!" Esperança replied. "So now you understand the difficulty Christopher faced."

"But what could have made Kamau turn against God in the first place?"

"Many things, Claire, but the most important fact remained, that Kamau believed, and he became evil not knowing he was evil. This was where Kamau was instrumental in training Satan's foot soldiers. Kamau believed that God wanted slavery to happen, that God was responsible."

"God didn't stop it."

"In this case, Satan had Kamau believe, that God purposely wanted Brazil to be found, as a lucrative lure, for the Christians to uproot the slaves from Africa, because they were lost in darkness, worshiping Satan and not Him. Pedro Álvares Cabral, was on route to India, and on April 22, 1500, violent winds, that Satan said, were sent down by God, blew them far to the west resulting in the discovery of Brazil, originally called, 'Island of the True Cross.' The beginning of the slave trade in Brazil, followed shortly and the intervention of Christianity, which was enforced on Slaves."

Claire's lips were quivering. "You're trembling," Esperança said. She stood up, and returned with an unopened bottle of rum, and two paper cups, and set them down. "A drink to harden the soul?" Esperança suggested. "Because there's more, and I think you'll need this." She sat back down.

Claire surprised herself when she gave her a nod of agreement. Esperança poured and slid the cup over to Claire. "I've never drank in my life," Claire said studying the liquid.

"Your first drink and last," Esperança said, holding her cup up. Claire touched her cup to hers, "here's to hardening the soul," Esperança said, before they knocked back their drinks. Claire made a sound of disgust, and pushed her cup away. "Definitely your last," Esperança said, taking another drink from the bottle itself.

Their silence stretched. Before them, the candle's wax had almost melted, the flame tall and eager, anticipating.

"Go on," Claire said, feeling warmth traveling through her. She felt calmer now, and somewhat equipped.

"The other reason that Satan was able to get Kamau's loyalty, was because Satan claimed: that he was God's alter ego; that when God created Lucifer, he simply created an extension of Himself...that this war was God warring with himself; and that soon, God would surrender to his other self. But in the meantime, there was work to do, and an earth to claim."

"God's alter ego," Claire whispered. "What do you think? You agree with this? Could it be?"

"It's a compelling argument, but then again, Satan is very good and a beautiful liar."

"So you don't believe it?" Claire pressed, but Esperança refused to give her a direct answer.

"Regardless of what I believe, Kamau believed it, and Satan had his full devotion. And as Manuel doubled his wealth, Kamau was successfully training Satan's foot soldiers and releasing teams of men to find the freed Christian foot soldiers, only to destroy them and send them back from where they came. Kamau developed a ritual, under the direction of the fallen, where he rounded the Christians up and had their throats slit before being burned to ashes. Kamau ordered the bones crushed into powder and then poured into cement blocks. Each brick represented a sacrifice to Satan. And each sacrifice was added to a wall that was being built at the back of the house. The wall of souls, he called it."

Recognizing this phrase, Claire knit her eyebrows together. "Patience mentioned to me something about the Valley of Souls, is this where the ritual originated?"

"It did…a burnt sacrifice. For those that walk the earth as enemies, shall leave the earth in smoke," Esperança replied. "Kamau trained soldiers and at night, slaves practiced voodoo and black magic by the light of the moon. They danced, called on the God of Darkness. Although it was later said that Kamau didn't agree with Manuel's vile behavior and the raping of women. He ordered that Manuel stop his behavior, that he needed to treat his slaves with kindness if he wanted to be as wealthy as Christopher. He wanted Manuel to understand, that Satan was a loving God, that there were two sides to the story, and that Satan needed to be worshiped and accepted. This became a problem, as well as a challenge."

Hearing Kamau refer to Satan as loving sounded erroneous, "And Christopher and Filhote?" Claire asked, needing to change the subject.

"When Kamau left, he took the darkness with him. Things on the plantation became lighter, less anxious. Filhote and Christopher were married for over thirteen years, yet she became pregnant again. She had so many miscarriages after Kamau was born, but this time she carried the child to term. They had a little girl that they named Fé."

Claire translated the name out loud. "Faith."

"Fé." Esperança repeated the child's name in a reverent tone. "She was a beautiful girl, filled with God's light. She, too, was a divine being. Meanwhile, Christopher was consumed in aiding God, knowing of what was happening. Small tribes were being wiped out. Kamau's trained soldiers were slaughtering the Christian foot soldiers he'd saved, and something needed to be done. Christopher needed more help from men who were driven by their faith in God and nothing else. This was when he began working with other missionaries, Europeans who spread Christianity to the infidels. Christopher heard of an exceptional tribe of people living in the ruins of Mato Grosso, who displayed a special connection to earth and animals. These people were believed to consist of the brightest lights of any humans, Christopher had been told. They were celestial beings, put on Earth to protect all creatures, as a part of God's grain. Christopher and his priest traveled out searching for areas where they could relocate their foot soldiers...a safer area, far from Bahia, and away from Kamau. On one occasion, the priest caught a virus and was dying of it. This tribe performed a miraculous healing, saving the priest's life, using these twelve stones."

"A real miracle?" Claire verified, "With actual stones?"

A smile quirked Esperança's lips. "An honest to goodness miracle. But even more miraculous was that this special tribe, living in Mato Grosso, was expecting Christopher. They said that the angels that shed their tears in their river, The River of Tears, told them that these miraculous stones were to be given to God's Chosen, and that this man would teach them God's tools and become their leader. They'd waited many moons for him and had a celebration in his honor. And as a commemoration of their unison, Christopher and his priest baptized the youngest children in their river. And that was the beginning of God's Chosen Tribe."

"Sensational," Claire said, in awe. "And just what kind of stones were these?"

"The Stones of Fire, the stones that once belonged to Lucifer, before his fall."

Claire was considering, recollecting the King James version. Stones of fire, stones of fire...when finally it struck her. "Lucifer's actual stones...you mean the stones, The Stones of Fire that were brought by Moses from the mountain of God?"

"Good memory," Esperança said in wonder of Claire's sharp mind. "You see, these stones can not only heal the sick, but can also summon God's angels...a very powerful gift, to Satan's enemies. And these twelve small stones were just the beginning of a unity between Christopher and God's chosen tribe. He became obsessed with his plan to teach them Christianity, in hopes that they would use their gifts to rid the earth of darkness. He left Filhote for months and lived in the ruins. He was so determined, so passionate. Nothing else mattered. He was in the war of his life, and somehow he unwillingly neglected his wife and child. Things were just spinning out of control, because Satan began using ley lines in his war against Christianity.

"Some of Manuel's raping of slaves resulted in unwanted pregnancies. Satan was pushing souls loyal to him through sphere openings, the ley lines I told you about, and these souls would scour the earth for pregnant women. Any children born, who were not approved by Satan, were sent back. They called it a balance, claiming the earth. 'Catching darkness.'"

"And how did Kamau determine this?"

"The fallen angels would communicate it to him, and on their command, the sacrifices had to be followed through."

"Oh."

"Manuel was such an idiot he had no handle on what was going on. He enjoyed the sport, but still thought of himself as a Christian. A thirteen-year-old boy was making him wealthier because of the control he had over the slaves. Manuel found entertainment in taking a child from its mother and watching her plead for it."

Esperança shook her head with regret. "One night, following a ritual, things went wrong. Manuel was enraged after watching Kamau and his men waste so many healthy Christian foot soldiers they caught. Manuel didn't understand that they were no longer slaves, but enemies to Satan. Manuel thought it was a waste to kill them and not use them on his plantation. He grew tired of Kamau and his demands and ordered him to stop the rituals. It was then that Kamau gave Manuel a choice. He explained that Manuel's loyalty to King Lucifer needed to be established; that labeling himself a Christian was an insult to the King."

Esperança now spoke close to a whisper. "Manuel refused, and the fallen angels ordered Kamau to reveal his identity to Manuel—that he was Satan's chosen, that he was also his son and that Filhote was his mother. That night, something in Manuel snapped, really snapped."

Esperança picked up the bottle of rum and took several

gulps, then set the bottle down. Her eyes downcast.

"Go on," Claire urged her. Looking up again, Esperança's eyes had a liquid sheen to them.

"Kamau never forgave himself for telling Manuel who he really was, because in the end, his mother paid with her life. Killed by Manuel himself."

"But Kamau was following orders, the fallen angels ordered him to tell Manuel that he was his son." Then, after a long pause, Claire added, "Or was that the plan all along? To hurt Christopher by killing the woman he loved? Son of a bitch."

"Ask me again if I could ever believe that Satan is God's alter ego," Esperança whispered, and without further delay, she told Claire the rest.

"The smell of freshly fallen rain and violet orchids hung thick in the air. A smell you can't bottle. The sounds of night you can't forget, the humming in a constant rhythm. When Manuel saw Filhote, for the first time in more than thirteen years, she was sitting on the swing of the long porch, her hair down just the way he liked it, breastfeeding his brother's three-month-old daughter. He could have killed them both right there, but he wanted to wait and savor the moment, in his own words, 'pleasure delayed was pleasure amplified.' He instructed his men, on his command, to kill everyone in the house. But Filhote and the child were to be saved as his kill."

"What about the hundreds of slaves in the back?"

"The main house was too far from earshot. Filhote was asleep when they came in. With her in the house were three men and two women. One screamed and woke her up. Christopher was expected home that week, but in any event he had made sure his family was protected at all times. In Christopher's heart, he knew that Kamau would never have hurt his own mother. Yet no one could have prepared for what happened. Manuel's men murdered Christopher's men first and then the woman who had screamed. Then they looked for Filhote and her child. But Filhote had placed the baby in the other woman's arms and helped her to escape through the window and down the stone wall.

Filhote begged her to protect Fé, run to safety, and not return until it was completely safe."

"Why didn't she leave with her daughter?"

"She didn't want them to be hunted together. She also believed God would save her."

"Which, of course, he didn't," Claire threw in.

Esperança opened her mouth to speak, in search of where to begin. Finally, she spoke with a slight crack in her voice. "Manuel cornered her in the bedroom. At first he stared at her for a long time. He had that crazy 'hurt' look in his eyes, and then he fell at her feet and cried like a pathetic fool. Kissing her feet, running his hands up her legs, touching her…and then he dug his nails into her skin, forced her onto her back, bit a piece of her lower lip off."

Esperança swallowed with great difficulty. In a low monotone, newly poised and strangely calm, she continued. "Manuel raped her. When he was finished with her, he kicked her over and over. She fought for her life, slammed an iron poker into his face. On his turn, she rushed to the window and jumped to the ground, broke her foot. Manuel and his men stayed close on her trail. She dragged herself to their special tree, the one by the river. It was too late. They got her before she had a chance to climb it."

Biting her bottom lip, Esperança finally said, "Then they raped her again. Six men taking turns, some went twice. God never came and Christopher's 'free' slaves never heard or saw anything. When it was over, Manuel stood her up against the tree and told her how great the moment was, that this was his greatest pleasure, drawing out her death. Amplified pleasure, prazer adiado é prazer amplificad. He actually thanked her for giving him a son and asked her if she had ever loved him. She told him that he would rot in the depths of hell, then she spit in his face right before he killed her. Killed her in more ways than one."

"How exactly did they kill her?"

"They used a rope and hung her. And during those final moments, Satan and the fallen got what they wanted, because Filhote renounced God and removed her Christian faith from her soul. She struggled for a few seconds, and then she shit herself."

Her adrenalin racing, Claire tried to moisten her cracked lips and dry mouth with her tongue, without success. "I have cottonmouth."

Esperança left the room but returned swiftly with two bottles of water. Both women cracked open the seals and drank all the water.

Placing her empty bottle of water on the table, the old woman resumed her narrative. "When Manuel returned home, Kamau was waiting for him. He didn't know his mother had been killed and that he was indirectly responsible. Manuel tried to avoid him, but Kamau stopped him at the foot of the stairs. He asked Manuel where he'd been. He simply said, 'I sent your mother back to where she came from, back to hell.' Kamau said nothing. Maybe shock, who knows. Manuel said he was tired and that in the morning they would get her body and add her to the wall of souls." Esperança shrugged her shoulders. "Manuel went to bed, leaving Kamau standing there."

"That's it?"

"No. While Manuel was drunk and asleep, Kamau cut into his skin, poured salt into his wounds, and had the slaves hang him upside down in a tree and covered his face in honey; his head was positioned over an anthill. Bitten alive, he hung that way for days, until he choked on his own tongue. Apparently it swelled and stopped his breathing."

"Didn't Kamau put Manuel's ashes in stone, along the wall of souls?"

"Manuel? That piece of shit? He could never be placed in the wall of souls! Only those loyal to God deserved such honor. Manuel was scum. No loyalty to God or Satan. And make no mistake, for those who are undecided, the only place for them is hell or in the in-between. Nothingness." Esperança's eyes narrowed as though she saw herself in a faraway place, removed from where she was. Perspiration glistened on her forehead.

"Imagine being lost between worlds for eternity with nothing but loneliness and pain. Like being lost at sea, holding on to a log, waiting to be rescued. But you know no one will come, and there's no escape, not even suicide." She gave her head a shake and finished the rest of the story.

"Kamau needed to finish what he started, what he was born to do. He gathered the slaves he'd been training and journeyed back to Christopher's plantation with golden lanceheads leading the way. Hundreds of snakes slithered though the brush, followed by Kamau and about fifty men and women. As soon as they arrived, he ordered the house to be burned down, and then the slaves' houses. The snakes lashed out with their poisonous bites, while Kamau and his followers slaughtered those who remained. In the end, nearly two hundred Christian foot soldiers were murdered." Esperança fell silent again, a flash of empathy flickered in her eyes.

"But when Kamau found his mother hanging, naked, bloody, covered in semen, shit hardened down her legs, he cried. I don't believe he had ever cried until that day. Not even as a child. He later explained that he knew he'd failed her, that he was responsible for her death. He wanted to remove the rope from around her neck and clean her. He wanted to put her in a pretty dress, lay her on a bed of her favorite flowers and give her a proper burial. The kind of burial meant for a queen. But there wasn't enough time for that. He knew he needed to move on, because he was now a fugitive."

"Where did he go?"

"He and the slaves traveled for months. The snakes led Kamau and a handful of men and women to an island offshore, south of Sao Paulo. It's known as Ilha de Queimada Grande, an untouched piece of land, but Kamau referred to it as King Lucifer's Island. They lived there for nearly two years, with the golden lanceheads."

"How does it translate?"

"Queimada means 'burn.' Interesting, no? That Kamau slashed and burned all the Christian slaves he could find on Christopher's plantation, and then he moved to an island that's named after what he'd done. But today people call it Snake Island because it's overrun with the snakes. And because golden lanceheads exist nowhere else in the world, the Brazilian government protects the island by not allowing people to walk it." She let out a soft chuckle. "They're a protected species."

Claire took in the story and carefully tucked it into her perfect memory. "I'm not going there, am I?"

"No, as I said, they lived on the island for less than two years. Our land is deep among the ruins of Mato Grosso."

"Mato Grosso? But isn't that where Christopher found that special tribe, the one by The River of Tears?"

Esperança gave her a nod.

Claire held Esperança with her gaze. "What about Fé and Christopher?"

"What?"

"Fé and Christopher?" Claire repeated. "What ever happened to them?"

"All was lost, hidden under the rubble," Esperança said, searching the table for the remaining joint. Surveying the floor, Claire pointed to two stubs. Esperança moved gradually, combing the polluted floor for them, eventually plucking four more from inside the ashtray. She picked apart the stubs with her fingers and created a pile of remains. "Searching through the remains of what was left," she whispered, as she filled the papers and licked the strip before rolling it into a perfect cone, "Christopher searched through hell."

Esperança lit the fat tip of it and inhaled deeply, taking several pulls, filling the small room with smolder. She blew the smoke through the side of her mouth, her gaze on Claire.

"There's a fog that covers the land at just the right time before the sun rises. Sometimes the fog is so thick you can't see two feet in front of you. If you add the smoke from the fire and the hundreds of slaves Kamau burned to death, you wouldn't see your own hand in front of you."

Esperança drew in another long pull. She held the smoke in her lungs, then released it through her nose. "When Christopher came in on his horse…the smell of burning wood…the stench of death…his home, of course, was scorched to the ground. He and his men searched for other survivors among fallen walls and rooftops, searching for Filhote and his baby. They found the baby crying but safely hidden beneath the floorboards inside the church, the woman who escaped with her, beheaded, her head placed at the altar, her headless body seated in the pew."

"Why didn't they kill Fé?"

"If you could believe it, Kamau hid her. He spared her life for Christopher and his mother, but a clean death was ordered to all those who denied Satan. Obviously, they didn't follow Kamau's orders. It was atrocious what they did. And when Christopher saw the heinous acts, he needed a few minutes alone to try and understand the horrendous evil that had happened in his absence. He walked to their tree…he found her there."

Esperança bit at her lower lip again. "Can you imagine what it was like for him, seeing her like that? He couldn't save his cherished one, the woman who made his life complete. He stood there for a very long time." She looked up and shrugged her shoulders. "He saved thousands of lives, touched so many souls, but without Filhote, it almost seemed pointless. He buried her by himself, next to their favorite tree. Afterwards he pulled out his knife."

"He killed himself," Claire murmured.

"If you'll let me finish," Esperança said. "He used the knife to carve into the bark of the tree, as if it was a headstone. He wrote: 'Beloved wife and mother, My Angel in Stone, may your soul be free.' And the sad thing was that she wasn't free. Even in death, she was cast into Nothingness, because she renounced God in her final minutes of life. As I said, they killed her in every way."

Claire shook her head with regret. "That's messed up."

"Christopher, he vowed that her death would not be in vain. So he took their daughter, his priest, and a few of his men, and they traveled back to Mato Grosso where he planned to live with the special tribe." Esperança's tone hardened and her eyes became glassy. "And his vow to God, and his promise to his wife, was to seek revenge and rid the earth of all evil souls, banishing them to hell."

A long silence enveloped them. Sounds of rain pelted against the window. There was something so sad about that sound.

Esperança's gaze was on the window too. "Pelting the world on pause…Patience says that the rain pauses the world. Slows it down."

"Patience sees much in the simplest of things," Claire said. "My mother used to say that snowflakes were gifts, frozen into sparkly packages. She said that the reason she loved snow, was because it snowed on the night that I was born. The first snowfall of winter." Claire's gaze veered off. "Said I was her gift." *If only it rained instead of snowed, then my mother would be alive, and they would have found her. If only I…*

"Claire?"

Claire spared her a glance. "Yes, Esperança." She knew

where Esperança was going. Claire felt a hitch in her breathing as she prepared herself.

Esperança's voice was low, her tone calm. "Sometimes bad things happen to good people. One of these days, you're going to have to forgive yourself. Make peace with it. You were just a girl, you couldn't have known. And you know what I'm talking about."

Claire drew a hand over eyes and bowed her head. "Not now," she said with a thick swallow. She dropped her hand and lifted her eyes to meet Esperança's understanding gaze. "Please? I can't do this tonight."

"The sooner the better, while there's still time." Esperança's gaze lingered on Claire's face and then settled on the lit candle. Relief washed over Claire.

They remained quiet, both staring into the flickering flame. Claire looked up from the firelight and caught the sadness in Esperança. She was calm and very still. Her dark eyes were soft, and under the golden flame, Esperança looked almost radiant. Claire recalled the beautiful woman's picture hanging on the wall again, Esperança's mother by blood. She had lovely, long black hair, and great bone structure. It made Claire curious. Who was Esperança in her other lives?

What did Satan see in Esperança, that God didn't?

"And when did you enter the family?" Claire whispered. For some reason, she didn't want to leave. A part of her yearned for something, but what that something was, was unclear.

"Not long after the relocation."

"What was your childhood like?"

"Another time." Esperança removed herself from the table and returned with a sheet of paper. She handed it to Claire, and stood over her. "Your instructions. You'll need to book a few flights to get there. And you'll be escorted by a trusted member of our tribe."

Claire looked over the paper. "Mato Grosso?"

"Welcome to the jungle, baby," Esperança said softly. Then she stopped, as if she remembered something. "By the way, where's your boss's info? The pictures?"

"Harvey? Oh, yes, I forgot about that." Claire reached for her purse, pulled out the folded pages, and handed them to

Esperança. She opened the pages and took her time, glancing through them.

"Your boss, he's a nice guy. But for some people, it's just too late," Esperança said, pointing to Macarena's photo. "Her and her husband have been doing this a long time, hurt a lot of people. Spreading depravity. Their souls belong to Satan." She passed the pages back to Claire. "Did you remember to write what you want in the wax?"

But Claire's thoughts were elsewhere, thinking about the night that Esperança had killed the man, with the crisp, white collars. Esperança had uttered those exact words, right before she'd killed him. 'For some people, it's just too late.' Was it too late for her? Would Esperança kill her, the way she'd done so with the others?

"I thought it was never too late."

"That's correct. But that doesn't apply to those souls that have slipped through the cracks of hell, just to wreak havoc on the earth. For those souls, it's just too late."

"I see." Claire folded the pages into her purse.

"Well?" Esperança said, setting a hand on Claire's shoulder. "Did you remember to write your commands into the candle's wax?"

"I was going to, but I wasn't sure what to write."

"Write what you want." She gave Claire's shoulder a gentle squeeze. For some reason, her touch brought Claire comfort.

"I can write anything?"

"Anything. For all I care, you can get the angels to have them join the circus. You should go now."

Claire asked, "Is everything okay with us?"

"We're good," Esperança assured her. "I don't plan on killing you just yet," she added with a smile. But that's where her smile settled, never reaching her eyes.

Claire was thinking about Esperança's daughter.

"Come back on the eighth. A week from Friday. I'll finish telling you the rest of my story," Esperança said, reading Claire's thoughts. "In the meantime, I want you to think about what I said. About making your peace."

"If you say so." Claire rose from her seat and felt her legs, stiff from sitting for so long, begin to loosen up. She stretched and dusted off the crumbs from her skirt, picking up her purse at the same time. But Esperança said nothing and walked with her to the door and opened it.

Claire stepped out the doorway and turned around, "You all right?" She didn't feel right leaving her; something was off. She was genuinely worried about her.

Esperança gave her a tiny nod. "I'm fine, just tired." Claire studied her for a moment, then turned around. Esperança shut the door and walked back to the table.

The candle had liquefied to a small puddle, and the fire danced with its last spark of life. Esperança took her wrist and hung it over the flame without wincing, until her skin sizzled. Tears welled up in her eyes, as she let out a long sigh of despair.

"Deuces, Kamau," she said, as burnt skin and hair filled her nostrils. She kept her wrist hovering over the flame until it blew out on its own. Esperança inspected the damage and carefully poked at the developing blister.

30

Against the Grain

Claire walked into her front foyer still dazed from her visit with Esperança. Instead of rehashing the awful visions of her mother's death, Claire felt closure, knowing that her mother wasn't lost, caught in Nothingness like Filhote was. Connie had died with God in her heart. She was with the angels in heaven, maybe she was even smiling again.

It was a bittersweet situation because Claire used Filhote's sorrowful life as a comparison to her own. Claire's own story now paled in contrast. She removed her shoes and took her time while hanging her coat in the entrance closet.

"Where were you?"

"What?" Claire turned around and was taken aback to see Jonathon sitting on the last stair, a crazed look on his face.

"I was in a meeting…it went on a little longer than we planned," Claire explained.

Jonathon stood up and looked down at his wristwatch. "It's almost midnight…I've been calling you like a crazy person."

"Oh, my cell phone died, see?" Claire pulled her phone from her purse and raised it for him to see. In truth, Jonathon rarely crossed her mind lately. Her newfound friendship with Esperança had become a fabulous diversion.

Looking into the face of her suddenly possessive husband, Claire found herself at odds. This was strange, not something she'd ever seen him do. She walked over to him and playfully traced her finger from the curve of his neck down the smooth and naked planes of his muscled stomach. She stopped at the drawstring of his pajama bottoms and tugged at the waistband.

"If I had known you were half naked, I would have rushed home sooner." Claire remembered the open cut on her knuckles and immediately concealed them by resting her hands at her sides. Jonathon didn't notice; he was too enraged with jealousy.

The corded muscles in his neck and shoulders were tense. "I'm not playing with you…I need to know who you were with, what you were doing." He had a demented look in his eyes. "And what in hell are you wearing, it's disgusting," Jonathon said, pointing to the T-shirt. "Really, Claire? What were you thinking wearing this in public?"

"Oh," Claire said, remembering the absurd T-shirt. She had completely forgotten about it. But judging from the rage on Jonathon's face, he would not soon forget.

The muscle in his jaw twitched. "Well? You mind telling me what the hell you're wearing?"

Claire stared at him with a blank look, and, to his chagrin, a laugh escaped her lips. "You think this is funny?" Jonathon pressed.

For whatever reason, Claire couldn't help but find the whole thing comical. She tried hard to remain solemn. But standing in her front hall, wearing a hideous 'sit on a happy face' T-shirt, tucked into a pencil skirt was incomprehensible. And watching Jonathon standing half naked, his hands on his hips and wearing furry slippers, caused her to finally break into a hysterical bout of laughter. She was snorting now, crying tears. It was insane and completely out of character. Where was she? And what was she wearing? How could she tell him that she'd spent the evening with a monster-child and her grandmother who sucked back rum by the case and blew her boogers into her shirt? Her double life was hitting her hard; sheer insanity was taking over.

Jonathon looked on, appalled that his normally composed wife, who seldom found anything entertaining, was now amusing herself into hysteria. Her entire face had turned a shade of red, and her continuous outburst caused tears to run down her face and her nose to run.

He was strangely afraid of her.

"Have you been drinking?" Jonathon asked grabbing her chin and forcing her to look up. "Look at me. I asked you a question."

Finally, after a full minute of laughter, Claire managed to pull herself together. "No, I wasn't drinking, but I was celebrating," she replied.

A mystified expression crossed Jonathon's face. "Celebrating what? Are we pregnant?"

"No, silly, Harvey has finally asked me to become a partner with the firm," Claire explained and pointed to her shirt. "I spilled coffee all over my blouse, and Harvey found a street vendor across from the pub we were at. It's slim pickings, but I had to take what I could get, or go home wet."

The look of confusion dissolved and after a few seconds he finally said, "Oh, that's great…so I guess you're happy."

Claire wrapped her arms around his waist and buried her mouth in his neck. "I am happy…life's good."

Jonathon returned the embrace, then pulled away to have another look at Claire. "Harvey smokes around you?"

Jonathon was annoying her, but Claire concealed it well. "I let him get away with it tonight. It was a cigar though—Mexican, actually."

Jonathon studied her for a good moment until he finally relaxed, satisfied by her answer. "I made a cheese plate and a fire for you."

"Tell you what, I'm going to take a long bath, and when I'm done, I hope that you and that cheese plate are still there."

Following the bath, Claire felt numb. She pulled her wet hair into a loose knot on the top of her head and wrapped herself up in the soft, full-length pink robe that Jonathon had recently bought her. He loved her in pink, and it would be an effective way of getting him to forget her most recent outburst.

She slipped down the dark hallway and slipped into the 'baby's room' without turning on the light. She found the room much colder than the rest of the house and detected a faint scent of varnish. She pulled her robe high around her neck and, without a second thought, eased into the chair. The slow rocking and creaking of the wood ricocheted off the bare walls and empty floors. Generations of women had found solace in the old wooden rocker. Important decisions and life-altering plans were contemplated while simply teetering back and forth.

With her toe, Claire lightly rocked the chair and mindlessly touched the arms, feeling the grain of the wood beneath her fingers. The grain that Patience had referred to was the grain of God, and going against the grain was her turning her back on nature and on God's intended plan.

But regardless, Claire had made up her mind.

She stopped rocking and thought again of her mother. Following her visit to Brazil, things would change. The fact was, once Claire had made her allegiance with Satan final, she would never be reunited with the mother she adored. She needed to say good-bye to Connie and let her memory remain buried under the snow that had taken her so long ago.

"Good-bye, Mommy," Claire whispered. Connie was condensed into one very beautiful memory of a mother who loved her child without conditions. She inhaled deeply, and glided the tips of her fingers against the grain of the chair. Following one last stroke against the grain, she let her mother go.

Jonathon slept naked by the blazing fire. Claire gently invited herself beneath the blankets and lay behind her husband, with his buttock touching her stomach. She inhaled his soapy scent and kissed him gently on the back of his neck, her hot breath waking him up to a full erection. After a few minutes, he turned around to face her and began planting deep and lustful kisses over her mouth. She thrilled in the sensation and felt her insides tighten.

"I want you," she whispered over his lips.

Jonathon moved with an even stronger force than usual. He became lost in the act of lovemaking and was now ravishing her. He moved quickly, opening the pink robe, and leaving her sprawled on her back and exposed in front of the fire. Her legs open, Claire moaned into the moistness of her hair, which had now come undone and was spilling in waves of red ribbons around her neck.

"I was thinking crazy thoughts today," he whispered into her soft flesh and painfully sucked each of her pink nipples with an erotic passion she'd never seen him display before. He pulled Claire's face up to him while hovering over her nakedness. "You are so beautiful."

"Take me,"she moaned, before Jonathon plunged his hardness into her. Following several hard and painful thrusts, he exploded all his pent-up frustrations into her.

A full five minutes passed before Jonathon, was still planted inside his wife. He rose from where he lay into a sitting position. He was staring at her, resting against two bunched pillows.

"Do you remember our first date?" Jonathon finally asked. Claire rose from the blanket and sat close to him. The flames spread warmth over her naked back.

"Sure, I picked you up at the shipping dock and you took me to that hole in the wall," Claire said.

He reached over and threaded his fingers through her hair. "You pulled up in your Diablo, all black and shiny with the windows down and your hair all wild." He drew his hand back and gazed at her. "And I remember how you walked over to me, wearing that really short, black lace dress." He ran a slow finger along her inner thigh, never taking his eyes off of Claire. "Legs for days."

"I threw my keys at you and told you I wasn't driving in no van," Claire joked, only to mask her discomfort.

Jonathon cupped Claire's chin and pressed his thumb into her lower lip. "You took care of me...you were giving, made me the man I am today. You believed in me."

I wanted to own you, Claire thought. But apart from his obvious appeal, she did see something in Jonathon. He was kind, although a problem arose when he was kind to anyone other than her. It enraged Claire, made her jealous, and created tension in their marriage. While staring into Jonathon's beautiful face, she was thinking about Christopher.

"Sometimes, you can be so mean," Jonathon began explaining. He had a flush in his cheeks. "Lately, I can't stop thinking about you in that dress, that feeling I had. It's like I fell in love all over again. I can't get you out of my head."

The compliment felt like a dagger slicing into her conscience. Was that the voodoo? Or had he ever really loved her? He pulled Claire close, her head resting on his chest.

Two people couldn't have been more opposite. They weren't meant to be, and Claire felt tremendous guilt for what she'd done to him. Jonathon was cut from a different cloth. A white cotton fabric in its purest form. Claire, on the other hand, was an intricate, black lace with delicate, alluring designs. A crafty piece of fabric which she had placed over her husband's eyes when she pulled up in her Lamborghini. If she was stupid she would remove her lacy spell, let him go and be happy with Nicolette. How could she though? The ramifications would destroy her.

Jonathon brushed his lips over her forehead. "Don't tell your sister, but I set Vince up with a hot stock. It's gonna go, make them a lot of coin." Claire angled her head on his upper arm so that she was able to see his face. She found herself in admiration of him. He gave her his smile, that imperfect grin, splitting his perfect face. She nudged his chin with her nose.

"It's a bit premature but he's already making plans. He said that when the time comes, he's hiring you to find some property, a rebuild. 'Tara.' Vince is hoping that he can count on you."

A sincere smile grazed Claire's lips. "Of course."

She thought back to the New Year's Gala. How quickly the months had passed. "How did things work out with Vince and Walter Ross?"

"Good. Real good. You have people like Patrick and Walter singing your praises and you've got it made. Vince made an impression that's for sure. He has enough work to keep him and his crew busy for the next four years. Good thing too, Vince just got the news that the pain in his hands turned out to be the early stages of arthritis. There's going to be a time when he won't even be able to hang up a picture."

Whether Jonathon had meant to or not, his words had found their mark, landing heavily on Claire's heart. She peered up at her husband and caught the tail end of his frown. He gave her a lazy wink, followed with thin smile.

"Rebecca never said anything about Vince having pain in his

hands."

"Yeah, well. You know your sister, she hates to burden people with her problems."

The troubled look in his blue eyes gave her pause. Poor Rebecca, always the selfless one, leaving herself for last.

"Are you certain about this investment?" Claire said.

"Don't worry, I would never lead him in the wrong direction. You know that I have their back."

And Jonathon did.

Despite Jonathon and Rebecca's painful childhoods, they turned out to be good people. Without 'fuckage,' as Esperança would say. Claire had wasted so much time not appreciating how fortunate she was to have these two people in her life.

She sat up and faced Jonathon, just staring at him until something shifted inside. She jerked back a little, slowly taking him in. She could hear the soft sound of his breathing, feel the intensity of his eyes on her, but she couldn't pull her gaze away. It was like looking at a holographic image that changed when you tilted it. Maybe he'd always been this way—good to the core—and much more than just a designer purse.

Claire's eyes journeyed over his face. She smiled to herself at those familiar parts of him that felt like home to her. His hair was a little too long and curling at the ears; his strong jaw was shadowed with evening stubble. Her gaze settled on his azure blue eyes. She looked so deeply that she was able to see the flecks of copper that ran through them. His eyes were soft, almost pleading, as she reached up and lightly traced the scar below his brow. *How terrified he must have been*, she thought, *having his mother abandon him in a hospital.* Claire wished she could hold that child... comfort him.

"Did that hurt?"

He gave her one nod.

They continued to stare at one another, as husband and wife. As friends.

"Sometimes bad things happen to good people. One day you'll have to make your peace with it." Claire cupped a hand beneath his chin and placed a slow kiss over the scar, then faced him again. "Am I making any sense?" She was looking directly into his watery eyes.

His brows furrowed in bewilderment. "Yeah."

With her hand still holding his chin, she rubbed his cheek with her thumb, then resumed her position on his chest.

After a long silence he said, "You've changed." He ran a hand through her hair. "Only I can't put my finger on it."

Yeah, Claire thought. *You drank the Claire Kool Aid.*

"These last few..." Jonathon paused. There was a persistent tapping outside their bedroom window. "You hear that?"

"I do." She got off of Jonathon and slipped back into her robe.

Jonathon stretched his legs and got up. He moved toward the bay window. After drawing the curtains open, he was surprised to see a pigeon tapping its beak against the glass.

"What is it?" Claire asked, without turning away from the fireplace. She picked up the poker, and pushed in a new log. The hot flames felt great.

"It's a pigeon, and—you're not going to believe this—it sees me, and it's not stopping. Looks really creepy." As Jonathon rambled on about the bird outside, an unexplainable feeling came over her.

She stood up and watched in horror as the male dove, whose partner's heart she'd swallowed weeks before, tapped his beak on her window. The iron poker slipped from her grasp and made a crashing sound against the stonework. Jonathon's lips were moving but she couldn't hear him. The pounding of Claire's heartbeat in her ears drowned out all other sounds.

"What?" Claire said.

"I said he has a message tied around his leg. They used to send pigeons out to do that. Think it's hungry?"

"Forget it. Let it be!" The sound of the beak tapping at the glass was more than Claire could take. As if at any moment Jonathon would get the paper and see, in Claire's own writing, what was attached to the bird. "Get him away from the window. I mean it!"

Laughing at his wife's fear, he chuckled, "It's just a little bird." He turned around with a full smile. "Is this the bird you meant...the one that killed the coyote?"

He was laughing now, his cheeks glowing as he opened the window and held his hand out. Instead of the pigeon moving away in fear, it flew directly through the window and moved toward Claire. Flapping wildly around her head. Her erratic screaming and flailing caused the haunted dove to fly directly into the open fire. He was squealing, squawking in pain.

"Do something, don't let it die!" Claire begged.

But Jonathon just stood there.

Without realizing it, Claire pushed her hands into the wild flames trying to save what she deemed to be Jonathon. She looked up at her husband who still stood silent, as cold wind whipped through the open window. A pungent odor and black smoke filled the room, and the pigeon was completely blackened. The bird lay lifeless without his partner while the fires of hell consumed him, and Claire's handwritten message to King Lucifer, until there were just ashes left.

31

Mato Grosso, Brazil

Claire worked from home that morning and decided to take care of some pressing details that needed to be arranged before her flight to Brazil. However sure she was about her decision to go, a new revelation had presented itself. The dove that had somehow found her was no longer just a bird. There was an inexplicable connection, as if the dove were human, as if it had come to warn her against going.

The stench of burning wings and flesh still lingered in the air, and Claire's nausea went unrelieved. It was a smell she would not soon forget. Ghostly sounds of the dove's cries echoed throughout the quiet house, while the vision of the flames that consumed the bird played and replayed in her head. How very close Jonathon had come to reading Claire's own handwritten note to Satan, and how quickly the forces prevented the bird from letting him. The grisly sequence of events left Claire with even more questions about the power of Esperança's family which, by her own admission, were handpicked by the devil himself.

Still dressed in black, silk pajama pants and matching long-sleeved shirt, Claire sat at her computer and confirmed her travel plans to Sao Paulo, Brazil, along with the several connecting flights that followed.

She had to fight the urge to Google information about the region where Esperança's family had lived for the last three hundred years. The part of Claire that had no fear was now being dominated by her other aspects. She was afraid, and genuine paranoia was setting in. She ran her hand through her knotted red tresses and began nervously twirling a curl. Her gaze settled on the package, which Rebecca had left with Jonathon. A blue velvet jewelry box, containing their mother's beloved pearls. Tapping an apprehensive finger on the box, Claire turned her focus back to the computer.

Contemplating, she went back and forth as to whether researching her destination was a wise thing to do or not. She understood that breathing life into her fears would only cause her more anxiety. Still, she keyed in the words 'Snake Island, Brazil.'

"It is home to a species, fer-de-lance, the golden lancehead, which is one of the most venomous snakes in the world; local legend claims that there are five snakes to every square meter. The golden lancehead is the only species of snake on the island, yet it is considered in danger of extinction since it has no other habitat and might be wiped out by wildfire. The Brazilian Navy bans civilians from the island, though scientists sometimes receive waivers...."

Claire's hands stilled over the keyboard. "Shit." She'd read enough and didn't need any more convincing. Esperança was many things, but she was not a liar.

She almost wished that she were.

Claire's hands moved as if they were detached from the rest of her body and keyed in the words 'Mato Grosso,' the state where she would be spending a week with Esperança's very own, and the very place where family rivals have been at war for over four hundred years.

"Thick Woods" was the first translation of Mato Grosso. It didn't surprise her to read that Esperança's place of birth was considered "the Thick Brush." Esperança lived in the most civilized place in the world, yet her shit-hole of an apartment was something Claire could only handle for a few hours at most. One could only imagine what her childhood home in the jungle looked like, with its tribal setting and straw huts.

Claire skimmed past some images of greenery and thick,

plush forest and paused at a photo titled Natives of Mato Grosso. The image was scantily clad men holding spears in their hands. "Some of the Indigenous peoples, known as lost tribes, are peoples who, by choice, live or have lived without significant contact with the connected civilizations of the world."

Claire's eyes darted back to the photos of the tribe. This was what Esperança was, where she came from, where she herself was going. It would be a hard few days, like camping on the edge of the Grand Canyon. She continued reading.

"Located in central Brazil, the Mato Grosso dry forest is part of the Alto Xingu. This is an echo region of an unusual diversity of plants, animals, and indigenous peoples. The region constitutes an intermediary area between the Amazonian moist forest and the cerrado flora.

Blah, blah, blah...."

Impatient, Claire went back and scrolled down to a piece that dated back to 1925: a mystery surrounding an explorer who went missing after entering into Mato Grosso. Her first piece of shocking fact was about an explorer by the name of Percy Fawcett. "Percy Fawcett, and his elder son, Jack, and Jack's friend, Rimmel, entered into the region in 1925 for an exploratory expedition and were never seen again. Percy Fawcett had studied ancient legends and chronological records and was convinced that a lost city existed somewhere in the Mato Grosso region, a city Fawcett named "Z." Fawcett left behind orders stating that if the expedition did not return no rescue mission should be sent for fear that the rescuers suffer his fate. Fawcett chose only two companions, so they could journey light and so they would draw less notice with the tribes of the jungle, some of whom were hostile toward explorers; many tribes at the time still had not come into contact with white men. On April 20th, 1925, his final mission departed from Cuiabá. In addition to his two principal companions, Fawcett was accompanied by two Brazilian laborers, two horses, eight mules, and a pair of dogs. The last contact from the expedition was on May 29th, 1925, when Fawcett telegraphed his wife that he was ready to go into uncharted territory with only Jack and Rimmell. They were reported to be crossing the Upper Xingu, a southeastern tributary of the Amazon River. Nothing more was heard of them..."

"Fuck." Claire sat in deep deliberation and remembered Patience's words of warning. "It's also the most dangerous."

What if something were to happen to her?

From the information, Claire gathered two very important details: one, Mato Grosso was truly the most dangerous place she would ever travel to; and two, her visit into the most dangerous place could result in her own death.

"What am I doing?" Claire leaned back into her chair and lightly rocked herself. She mindlessly reached for the jewelry box and opened it. Instantly, she felt at ease. In one hand, Claire cradled her most valued memories. She lightly touched the ivory pearls, enjoying the cool feel beneath her fingers. She set the box down, reached for the cordless and dialed Rebecca's house.

"Hello," Olivia's voice, caught Claire off guard. The last time she'd seen Olivia, she had reduced the poor kid to tears.

"Hello, Olivia. It's your aunt Claire."

"Hi...you want my mommy?"

"Sure, but before you go, I'd like to apologize to you. I said some things that were inappropriate." Claire paused, and summoned a breath to battle her apprehension. "I was very mean and I'm sorry."

"You called me a *stupid shit*," Olivia said, drawing an unexpected laugh from Claire. The kid was as sharp as a tack, and Olivia reminded Claire of herself as a child.

"Yes," Claire admitted, trying to remain the responsible adult. "It was very wrong and I won't let it happen again."

"Okay." Olivia's tone was carefree. "My mommy's coming inside now."

"Hey, stranger," Rebecca said, out of breath. "Just unpacking the car, we went grocery shopping."

"Sounds like fun."

"Not really, but someone's gotta do it," Rebecca replied with a laugh.

How could she laugh, Claire thought. Her entire future was hanging on by a thread. *Vince's hands.* "Why do I have to hear from my husband that Vince has arthritis?"

"I—"

"—Is this what it comes down to? You can't even turn to me!" Claire snapped.

"Why are you yelling at me?"

"I'm not!"

"You are. And since when do care about Vince?"

It was a fair assessment, one that made Claire truly think. She didn't search for strategic words, nor did she want to dismiss her sister's feelings. She ran a hand through her hair and nervously twirled a lock between two fingers.

"I don't even know what I feel. But I do know that Vince would do anything for you and your children," Claire admitted, dropping her hand into her lap. "Regardless, you should be able to come to me, especially with something like this. If Vince can't work, what would happen to you guys? Talk to me, we could figure something out." She felt her cheeks flush. "And where's your plan B? You used to be a book keeper. *I* know people...I could set you up, and you can work on a part-time basis. You need to have a plan, and that's what pisses me off about you. You take things so lightly. You have this naïve way of looking at things..." Claire's words trailed off.

She pinched the bridge of her nose, collected her thoughts, and tried again. "I'm sorry. I'm trying here, and this isn't easy for me." Claire's gaze fell on the jewelry box. It took her a few moments to find her courage.

"We're sisters. You're all I have left. And these pearls," Claire explained, fingering the velvet box. "It wasn't your fault that our mother..." The word *died,* died on her lips.

Dead silence resonated on the line for a moment. When Rebecca spoke again, her tone was gentle. "It wasn't anyone's fault, Claire."

If only you knew. You would hate me if.... "Everyday," Claire uttered instead. "I think about her everyday."

"What?"

"You asked me a few months back if I think about our mother, and I lied to you. I wish I could forget, but I can't. I think about her all the time. And these pearls...I *wanted* you to have a piece of our mother. Please, for me." Somewhere Claire found her voice and added, "I haven't always been there for you."

They both lapsed into another silence.

On the other end, Rebecca's response was barely a whisper. "You weren't the easiest person to deal with, but I get it. You had to raise me. You were just a kid too."

"You don't know the half of it," Claire stated.

"You must have resented me for it," Rebecca said, in a questioning tone, as if she was reaching.

"When you were born, I hated you," Claire admitted.

"You...you hated me?"

"I did. I was so mad. For so long it was just mom and me. I don't know why they waited so long to have another child. In any case, I had our mother all to myself. I couldn't warm up to the idea that there was a baby growing inside of our mother's tummy." Claire's tone lowered in level if not in honest passion. "I hated you before you even came into this world. When you were five months old, and mom was napping, I came into the room and took you out of your crib. I hid you in the laundry hamper. Threw a bunch of towels over you. Mom woke up and found you missing."

"Oh, Claire...that's awful."

"Yeah, it was. Our mother was frantic—searching the house for you—calling 911. By then, I knew I had to put you back. And when I pulled the towels off your fuzzy hair crackled with static cling, and I guess it made you giggle. You had this big, gummy grin. You loved it. Like it was a game. Just like now, you just breeze through everything. Even then."

Claire breathed out a laugh. "Just a fat baby, with this toothless smile. After that, I didn't hate you anymore. I guess I realized then, that I loved you. Always have."

"Yeah?" Rebecca said, with optimism in her tone.

"If you could believe it, I even changed your diapers. Lucky for you, I didn't color your face in with blue ink. I hated dolls."

Rebecca sighed, then said in a wispy voice, "I wish I could remember something?"

"Our mother really loved you. She did. She loved you, in the way that you love your children. And we were really happy. We truly were. We had a great house. The Victorian that dad sold shortly after mom's funeral. It had lots of stairs and great hiding places. Even a dumbwaiter. You and I would hide, and mom would look for us. Other times, mom would hide. Dad too. It was great. The best the days of my life. But after her death, we never played the hiding game again."

Claire cleared her throat, and forged ahead. "When our mother went missing, you didn't get it. You lit the candle with me for three days, but you didn't get it. You thought she was hiding. You went looking all through the house, searching in all the hiding places, and you didn't understand that she was gone and wasn't coming back."

"That's so sad," Rebecca's voice wavered. "And it breaks my heart."

Claire knew that she was crying on the other end. Her sorrow filtered down the line, and Rebecca had enough tears for the both of them.

"At the funeral, you wanted me to take her out of the coffin. You thought she was hiding."

Claire clapped her hand over the mouthpiece so that Rebecca couldn't hear her awkward breathing. On the other end, Rebecca's sobs only intensified.

Claire's eyes remained closed, recalling that dreadful day. It was Olivia's voice that carried through the phone. "Don't cry mommy."

"Mommy's okay," Rebecca coddled her. "These are good tears. You go and comb your doll's hair. I'll play with you soon."

"Here, drink my juice," Olivia offered. "It puts apples in your cheeks."

A small smile tugged at Claire's lips. Olivia was truly charming, and maybe even had a photographic memory.

"Okay, Livy. Thank-you." Rebecca blew her nose, and took several swallows, gulping her emotions.

Rebecca came back to the phone, her tone composed. "We should take turns."

Claire's eyes were closed, and for the first time, it was Rebecca who took the lead.

"I think today was hard. Very hard, but necessary. We do have a lot to talk about. But about our mother's pearls, I think we should take turns with them," Rebecca decided.

Claire's mind continued to swim in memory behind closed lids. She pictured Rebecca as child, smiling up at her, that cheeky smile and those blameless green eyes. She soon saw Rebecca in the oversized hat and gloves, their mother's pearls strung around her little neck.

"Well, what do you say?"

Claire's eyelids fluttered open. "Take turns?"

"Sure, we'll make a pact."

"A pact?"

"It's tradition," Rebecca said. "In honor of mom."

"Fine," Claire agreed. "But we'll need hats and gloves to match. I don't suppose you and Olivia own any?"

"No, not like that."

"Then we'll have to go buy some. I'd like to take my baby sister and charming niece, hat shopping." Claire un-locked her desk drawer, placed her mother's pearls inside, and quietly re-laxed.

Moreover, if for only a moment, Claire felt at peace.

32

God is in the Details

T he devil's lair," Esperança said to herself, while taking in the visitor's room inside the Metropolitan Detention Center in Brooklyn. The room was cold, smelling of pine cleaner, and the florescent lighting made it impossible to relax. The shock of brightness made Esperança miss her candlelit room, because the shroud of darkness mollified her. It covered all the harshness that put strain on her eyes. Looking around in the whitewashed room, there were many ugly things to see.

She, along with a handful of others, was the first to visit for that day. It was a sad display: children dressed in their best, waiting for their mothers to be escorted into the cold room, sisters, a brother, and even a lesbian lover waited with eagerness to visit with her light-fingered girlfriend.

The first inmate was escorted in, a thin black woman with cornrows, swimming inside of her beige jail clothes. She slid into her seat and sat across from a young girl and toddler, the inmate's children. Her daughter picked up the young boy, placed him onto her lap, and pointed.

"See? It's momma." But the boy wailed, turning away from his mother and clawed at his sister to escape his own mother. He was petrified of the woman who had given birth to him. The inmate didn't seem to care much. She scratched at her scalp, looked underneath her nail bed, and flicked what was there. Esperança had to look away; it made her stomach churn. She hadn't eaten anything that morning, which was nothing new, but had managed a half a bottle of rum and several mints that followed, prior to her admittance. Maybe it was the mints, or maybe it was being there, inside the hell, that made her want to retch. But looking into the eyes of the terrified boy, she knew the reason for her sudden queasiness.

More female inmates filled the room, taking their seats. So many broken wings, Esperança thought. So many damaged souls: prostitutes, drug addicts, thieves. All mothers, all daughters, sisters, some even wives. A husband broke down into tears at the sight of his crack-addicted wife, while holding a drawn picture of their three children in his hand. A man who was addicted to his wife, just as much as she was addicted to the pipe. He was a good man, and he lived to save this woman. She strolled into the visiting room, cold and stripped of any empathy. Her brown, silky hair was cornrowed, her pants rolled up. He gave her a piece of paper showing a house with stick people all drawn in crayon. She barely looked at it. She would never change, Esperança saw. A sickly pale complexion, rotted teeth, and cold blue eyes. This woman was a prisoner to the pipe.

Another detail into which the devil insinuated himself.

But one child in particular got Esperança's attention. A beacon of light that commanded over this dark room. She was no older than five with large blue eyes and a head of blond curls.

In her hand, she clutched a blond Barbie she'd named Alexandra—her mother's name. The golden haired babe was accompanied by her grandparents. They were older than their years, aged by the wear and tear of their daughter's choice of lifestyle. From what Esperança could determine in her father's sad Russian eyes, Alexandra was charged in conspiracy to murder, along with drug racketeering with organized crime. What the father had failed to understand was that the devil was in all of the details, and it didn't matter where you lived, he'd find you if your wings were broken.

Esperança kept a watch at the door, in search of the woman she'd come to visit. She was in protective custody and was being personally escorted by a mannish-looking jail guard with short blond hair.

Jocelyn Boudreaux, inmate number A673, a thirty-three-year-old nurse, arrested in the death of her three-week-old son. The news reported that she had bathed her son, taken a pillow, and smothered him to death. She then wrapped him in a blanket, walked into a police precinct station, and turned herself in.

Jocelyn looked younger than she did on television. Her sandy brown curls were swept up, held by a red rubber band. Her ivory complexion and thin face made her large, brown eyes more pronounced. Jocelyn reminded Esperança of a white deer before the slaughter.

"You don't look like someone from the church," Jocelyn said, taking her seat across from Esperança and crossing her thin arms. She was angry and no doubt bitter.

"And you don't look like the mustached tamarin monkey, the species that often kill their own offspring," Esperança blurted out. To her surprise, Jocelyn didn't turn around and bolt.

"You forgot demon mother, and the other labels they've called me, too ugly to repeat," Jocelyn explained, lowering her gaze to the table.

"And little do they know," Esperança said, "that while the devil is their details, God was in yours."

The statement made Jocelyn pull her head up and her hardened expression dissolved into an encouraged one. She chewed on her lower lip, a habit which left it raw. "You're not from the church."

"No, and you haven't called Cynthia Jennicks, nor have you taken her visits," Esperança clarified. "So you left me no choice but to come in myself." Esperança listened in on the different thoughts that shuffled through Jocelyn's head. Her first, was that she and her husband could not afford Cynthia, the second was why would Cynthia, a well-respected lawyer known as 'The Sleeper,' have anything to do with a washed-out vagabond. But her final thought was that she and her husband were intent on sticking to their truth.

Jocelyn sighed, "Infanticide, postpartum, insanity. I'm not doing this anymore. Three lawyers and all of them want me to play their game, pretend I'm still hearing voices, that I'm a schizophrenic. Not going there, not when I know the truth."

"The truth," Esperança countered, "was that you smothered your three-week-old son first, and then you bathed him."

Jocelyn's mouth quivered, she underestimated the old woman after all.

"You bathed him because you wanted to cleanse him from the evil that touched him," Esperança said. "The truth is that you don't belong here and if you don't accept my help, you'll end up an old lady, locked in the devil's lair. Is that what you want?"

"What choice do I have?" Jocelyn stated softly.

"The choice to play by Cynthia's rules so that she can get you off and out. You wanted someone to believe you, and I do. I know what happened and so does God."

Jocelyn nodded, looking Esperança dead in the eyes. "Your name, you didn't tell me your name."

"Esperança," she mumbled.

"Hope," Jocelyn said, translating Esperança's name into English. "And you're here to give me that? I don't see how," she added in a whisper.

"Stick to your truth and you'd be surprised by the sway Cynthia can have on a jury of twelve. You're a nurse; you know that certain levels of chemical imbalances within the brain can make a perfectly sane person make irrational decisions. Brain tumors can cause impulsive and violent behavior. Lots of things we can do, but you have to call her…illusion I can do, the work has already started. But the rest is up to you guys," Esperança counseled.

"We can't afford her," Jocelyn explained, without a second thought about what Esperança had said. "We've depleted all of our savings over the last six months."

"You tell your husband that you'll have New York's best legal team working pro-bono, and that we believe you," Esperança stated flatly.

Jocelyn nodded through her captivation.

"And let him know that he should make preparations to sell your property, the cars too. Everything. You'll need to arrange yourselves, and start over. Go wherever the wind takes you." Esperança pulled a card from her shirt pocket and slid it over to her. "You call Miss Cynthia Jennicks. Let her know that you've agreed to allow her to be your attorney. And once you're acquitted—which you will be—you and your husband will make arrangements to relocate somewhere far from here. Somewhere in the world where nurses are needed, where you can continue healing the sick. I have a hundred thousand dollars in an offshore account set aside for you. Your lawyer will see to the details."

"Who are you?" Jocelyn asked. "Apart from a hope in hell."

The comment caught her off guard, almost to the point of laughter. No words were truer. "I'm the sister of the voodoo priest you allowed to read your palm in New Orleans," Esperança said, not wanting to waste anymore time.

Jocelyn narrowed her watery eyes on her. "You look nothing like him."

"And your son looked everything like you but was nothing like you," Esperança said. "But those unimportant details mean nothing at the moment. I know what I know, and I know what happened on the night you met the man I call my brother. I know that when Valerian laid his black hand over your belly, gave you the details only you would know, that it made it very easy for him to get close enough."

"Did Gaston tell you this? How—"

"—I'm not here to convince you of my skills as a priestess," Esperança explained, "but I'll tell you what I know. I know that you and your husband go to New Orleans every year, Mardi Gras."

"Gaston and I met at Mardi Gras during college break; he has family in Chalmette, Louisiana…we go once a year…to celebrate."

"And you went, eight months pregnant, and saw the voodoo priest in a cafe. And you let him in, after your husband told you not to, you allowed him anyway. You allowed him to put his hands over your belly."

"He said that my son was special," Jocelyn said, her voice trailing off. "He knew that it was our first baby. He knew things…he knew that we wanted to wait for the right time… the voodoo man knew so many facts about our lives, I couldn't help myself. And that night when we went back to the hotel, we knew something was wrong."

Esperança nodded. "Of course you did, a mother knows," she added, looking down at Jocelyn's breasts which were still lactating.

"Gaston and I would sing to him, an old song my grand-mother taught me—'Lavender Blue.' She sang it to my mother, and her mother sang it to her." Jocelyn closed her eyes and gave Esperança her own rendition of the song. Her voice was weak and off tune, carrying into the room like nails on a chalkboard.

"Lavender blue, dilly dilly, lavender green, when I am king, dilly, dilly, you 'll be my queen. Who told you so, dilly, dilly, who told you so? 'Twas my own heart, dilly, dilly, that told me so…"

Jocelyn's eyes were closed, tears ran down her cheeks, but she kept singing, spewing out the words to the song in insane speed. Being isolated and locked away with only her pain to keep her company had taken its toll on her. If she were to stay imprisoned, she would truly go mad and become the schizo that bathed her three-week-old son, and then smothered him with a pillow.

"Call up your men, dilly, dilly, set them to work, some to the plow, dilly, dilly, some to the fork, some to make hay, dilly, dilly, some to cut corn, while you and I, dilly, dilly, keep ourselves warm. Lavender green, dilly, dilly, I will love you. Let the birds sing, dilly, dilly. I will love you. Let the birds sing, dilly, dilly, and the lambs play…"

Esperança felt ill, unfazed by the curious eyes that wondered what the murdering mother was doing. The blond-haired lit-tle girl smiled over at her. Esperança couldn't stand to look her in the eyes. Instead, she turned her attention back to Jocelyn, whose breasts were lactating even more, creating a small wet spot through her beige jail shirt. Jocelyn opened her eyes, used the back of her hands to wipe her face.

"My husband and I were singing this song to him since we found out that I was carrying. Every time we sang the words 'dilly, dilly,' he would kick. Every time, without fail. We sang it every night before falling asleep. But that night—"

"—That night he stopped kicking," Esperança finished. "And you knew that he was gone. Did you feel it?" Esperança asked. "Did you feel the shift inside your belly, like you knew something had pushed him out and your ears were popping? Both you and your husband felt it."

"Yes."

"And you heard things, didn't you? Like the sounds of wind, catching the tops of bottles, like—"

"—Like someone blowing over an open wine bottle, quick and faint," Jocelyn described.

"He didn't move for three days and we made an appointment to have an ultra sound. They said he was fine," Jocelyn said. "But I knew. *We* knew. And we never felt him kick to our song again. Ever!"

"And when he was born," Esperança said, "you knew that this was not your son. You knew that if you didn't kill him, that one day, when he was old enough, he would bomb seven churches on Christmas morning…one after the other. A brilliant mastermind, it would have only taken a simple press of a button. Thousands of innocent people. Men, women and children, would have died at the hands of your son."

Jocelyn nodded and hugged herself to conceal her trembling hands. "I worked as a nurse in pediatrics. Held so many newborns in my arms, and never had I had the visions that came on the day that they put him into my arms."

"Nero, Pol Pot, Hitler, Manson, Idi Amin Dada, their own mothers knew, but unlike you, they weren't brave enough to do what needed to be done. But you did."

"And what next? Where do we go from here?"

"You'll keep singing that song," Esperança advised, "'Lavender Blue.' Same time as before. Keep your son's soul close." Esperança pointed to the milk spot by Jocelyn's breasts. "That's why you're still lactating; he's waiting to come back, and he will…within two years from now. Just keep singing him close to you."

Jocelyn burst into a sob, mumbling into her hands. "I knew it; I could feel him, my boy." She was weeping hard now. Esperança searched for the clock and noted the time. She craved a drink and felt as if the walls were closing in. Again, her gaze fell a few tables over: to the little blond girl, milk-white skin, and her golden spirit that lit up the entire cold and colorless room. Jocelyn's cries tapered off, and she became quiet, internalizing. Esperança rose from her seat, wanting nothing more than to leave. Jocelyn grabbed a hold of her wrist, holding her back.

"And what about you?" Jocelyn begged. "How did you keep your child's soul close?"

"I never said anything about a child of mine," Esperança replied, prying her wrist away. The look on Jocelyn's face was both confusion and anger. Esperança also read her thoughts and saw that Jocelyn knew that she wasn't being honest with her.

Jocelyn seized Esperança's wrist again. "You're lying."

Esperança's eyes were swimming with tears. "I'm...I...didn't..." Her words trailed off into a jumble of tangled syllables.

"You're going to deny it," Jocelyn said, with a strange understanding. "It doesn't matter because I can read it in your eyes...'grief steals their light' my husband says."

With her hand still wrapped around Esperança's wrist, Jocelyn offered a squeeze along with a sympathetic look. Esperança stared back with wide and glossy eyes, beseeching Jocelyn to stop.

"I know because you asked me all the right questions only a mother that killed her child would know. I've been interviewed a hundred times over, psychiatrists, doctors, police, priests. You're the only one who knew what to ask," Jocelyn said.

"I'm a reader of souls." Esperança wrenched her wrist free and wiped at her eyes with the flats of her hands. "It's what I do."

"No, there's more. I was a nurse; I saw sickness every day. Your yellow skin and eyes. You have jaundice; your organs are failing. You should be bed ridden, and yet here you are, the sister of a demon who stole my son's soul and replaced it with evil. You're self-medicating, because you can't stand yourself. I can smell the rum, the mint on your breath, see your trembling hands. You're trying to save me because you're trying to save yourself." Jocelyn narrowed her sad eyes on her. "I read between the lines, and my instincts are almost never off. So tell me, please. How did you keep your child's soul close?"

Esperança felt her knees buckling. Overcome with exhaustion, she answered Jocelyn.

"Unlike you, I was never blessed to be able to keep my child's soul close. Because where God was in the details of your actions, the devil was in mine."

33

Miracles

Claire walked along the pedestrian walk on the Brooklyn Bridge, above the roaring traffic, and made her way to her favorite spot where she had a perfect view of the city. Dressed in her black velour, Juicy Couture tracksuit and matching woolen toque, Claire waited for the sun to bleed out into the world below.

She took a slow and careful sip from her steaming foam cup, enjoying the brew. The flavors of milk and honey, along with her caffeine fix, were exactly what she needed.

A moment alone with her thoughts.

The mesmeric backdrop seduced her. It had been a long day, and the diversity of life that continued below made her feel even more alone. The millions of people whose emotions whirled throughout the legendary city made her feel so small, so insignificant.

But as the sun's breath was just reaching the earth, casting a sparkle over the East River, its luminescent warmth touched on something deep inside of Claire.

She thought about Patience and wondered if she too was watching the sunset. If she was, her rich brown eyes would have softened at the prospect. A true gift for the eyes, she would say.

Claire relaxed as the sun's rays washed over her, and in that very moment, she no longer felt alone. With her eyes closed, she thought about the blind babies in Africa, the ones whose eyes would never see such a vision but would no doubt feel the warmth of God's love against their skin. While surrendering, a dread filtered into Claire's consciousness. How did God creep into her thoughts? Her eyelids snapped open, and she focused her attention on the silvery waters below. What was happening to her?

In just a few days she'd be in Brazil, ready to take part in human sacrifice so that she could be given the gift of conception. Why did the thought of God enter into her quiet moment of reflections? Was she making a mistake?

"It's a sight," a voice said, cutting into Claire's deliberations. She turned to her left and saw that a tall and muscular black man was sharing her spot on the bridge.

"You mean the sunset?" Claire asked, unable to turn her attention away from this stranger's face. He was strikingly handsome. With a strong jaw and thick, smooth lips. He smiled and jerked his chin to the magnificent backdrop. The golden hues of the sunset reflected back in his black, catlike eyes.

"I meant you," he said, in a strange yet alluring accent.

"That's a bit presumptuous of you," Claire replied. The man laughed with an open mouth; his red tongue in contrast to his dark skin reminded Claire of a chocolate-covered strawberry.

"It is a bit conceited of you to think that I was referring to something inappropriate," he explained, pulling his gray hood off, wearing a gray toque underneath. "What I meant was, it's a sight to see a person so connected with their inner self, appreciating a simple moment."

"Oh," Claire felt her face flush, "I didn't mean to come across as rude, I was just so caught up."

"Valerian." He pulled off his glove and extended a massive hand.

As if by reflex, Claire pulled her own mitt off and shook hands with him. "Claire, nice to meet you."

His mouth quirked into a near-smile. "Would you mind sharing this spot with me?"

The warmth of his hand relaxed her. "I don't own the bridge, and somebody recently reminded me that the sun rises and sets for everyone," Claire joked, drawing her hand back and slipping her mitt back on. Shaking a perfect stranger's hand was something she never did, unless it was business and as long as she had her hand sanitizer. For some reason, she felt unguarded.

They both shared in the scene, remaining quiet. After some time, Valerian said, "So many sad and hungry people in the world, so much suffering. It makes a man wonder how a God that created the world in a few days, pulled the moon from behind the mountains and the sun from the oceans, could do nothing to stop the anguish."

"I often wonder that myself." Valerian was methodical and handsome. Claire turned her gaze back to the panorama. Someway, the view had lost its appeal.

"Miracles, and this is as good as it gets." He reached over and pulled a strand of hair caught between Claire's lips. His touch ran a shiver that ghosted from the nape of her neck to the small of her back. He gave Claire a clever wink and set his foot up onto a bar to tighten his laces before slipping his glove back on. "Back to my running, enjoy the miracle."

She watched him jogging away and felt her phone vibrating in her pocket. She checked the display; it was Harvey. "Hello," Claire answered, still fixated on the fading jogger.

In his all-business tone, Harvey said, "We need to talk."

"Now? I have somewhere to be," Claire replied. "It can't wait?" Claire would have to cancel her time with Esperança, and she was leaving for Brazil the following day.

"Trust me," Harvey replied. "You'll want to cancel whatever it is you have planned. This can't wait."

"Close the door," Harvey said. He was standing next to his aquarium and nursing a glass of ice-water.

Claire took a seat on the chair in front of Harvey's desk and made herself comfortable. Pulling out her tube of lotion, she squirted some into her palms. Looking around while massaging the cream into her hands, she was immediately impressed with the changes in him. His office was clean and fresh, his salt-water tank was bubbling clean water and, from the looks of things, there were additions to his tank. Bags of newly bought fish floated in the tank.

"You gotta let them get used to their new home before releasing them," Harvey explained, without turning around. "PH shock can kill a fish."

Claire took in Harvey's new look. He was shaved, groomed, and dressed in a crisp, dark suit and polished shoes. He even had a blue, silk handkerchief tucked into his suit jacket.

The old Harvey was back.

He took a seat across from Claire, keeping a steady gaze on her. "Well?" Harvey leaned forward and set his glass on the polished surface of his desk. "You have something that you want to tell me?"

Claire's focus was on his drink. She watched as the moisture collected on the outside of the glass, and dripped onto Harvey's ebony wood furniture. She reached over, lifted the glass, and used her sleeve to dry the surface before placing a file under it. She caught Harvey's questioning grimace. "Cooling water vapors increase the rate of condensation. You'll ruin the wood."

Harvey clamped his capped teeth over his bottom lip. After a moment of reflection he said, "You always do that, throw out useless information when you want to dodge a question, or when you're feeling uneasy."

Claire snuffed a laugh. "I do?" She stopped to consider Harvey's observation. Maybe it was true, maybe she did like to manipulate the conversations by diverting the topic. But this time was different, she thought. Harvey's glass truly captivated her. In fact, the whole world around her felt off, as if she was seeing it for the first time. "What was your question?"

Harvey leaned into his desk, "It was about that thing you did." He raised his bushy brows as if he was trying to send her a clue. Claire noted the happy playful flicker in Harvey's blue eyes. "Sounds like a dance," he added, then leaned back into his chair, rocking himself while he waited for an answer.

"I'm not following," Claire said. She had done a lot of 'things' lately.

Harvey narrowed his eyes on her, a slight smirk tugged at the corners of his mouth. His hand slipped inside the top drawer of his desk. He removed a sheet of newsprint, slid it across to Claire, and then waited.

Claire moved the page closer to her and read it without picking it up.

"Holy shit," she said, with a victorious laugh. She had asked, in writing, that the fallen angels sway Macarena to kill her husband and herself with witnesses present, so as to avoid speculation regarding foul play.

"Holy shiznit is right," Harvey whispered. "Macarena shot her husband in the tub, and went on the front lawn, naked, and killed herself. Sweet mother of pearl, she did it in broad daylight, right in front of a bunch of kids coming home from school. Poor kids are going to need therapy for the rest of their lives."

Claire's smile dissolved, as uncertainty held her lips together. She turned her head away from Harvey and considered her extraordinary dilemma. She needed to choose her words carefully. She stared off into the fish tank and tried to come up with a suitable answer, one that would protect Esperança's identity as well as obligating Harvey to make good on his promise and make her partner. While she watched the curious fish poking the angelfish trapped inside the bags, she found herself admiring the striking, new additions. Her vision became a blur. Claire reflected back to how quickly things can change. The tank, which not too long ago was a morbid ruin, now appeared so peaceful.

She pulled her gaze from the tank and met Harvey's questioning eyes. A lie made no difference when the truth was even more unbelievable. "I know a little old lady who drinks Bacardi 151 by the case and has a magic wand in her pocket," Claire finally stated.

Harvey processed her answer and folded his hands onto the desk. It was obvious to Claire that he wanted an answer, and she wasn't going to go there.

"Don't ask, Harvey...just be glad that it's over." Claire hoped to reassure him.

"Over," Harvey whispered to himself, while he twiddled his thumbs for quite some time.

He stopped twiddling and looked up with glassy eyes. "It really is over."

"I would say so," Claire said, taking a quick glance at the clipping.

Harvey rolled his chair back, stood up, walked over to Claire, and pulled her up, planting a big kiss on her mouth.

Claire laughed. "Germs, Harvey." She wiped her lips with the back of her hand. "After you had your mouth on her, it's like kissing a Petri-dish."

Harvey's eyes were still soft. "Thanks, Preston."

"You're welcome."

"I owe you, and, as promised…I'll arrange for that partnership we spoke of."

Claire patted him lightly on the cheek. "Sounds good. And I'd like a tank of my own, if you don't mind. And no clowns… just angelfish."

"You got it."

"How's Libby?" Claire asked.

The question made him smile. "She's doing real good. Got the boys staying with us. Grandkids always lift her spirits."

Claire looked Harvey in the eyes. "No more cheating or I'll hire that same old lady to chop off your dirty pecker and stuff it into your mouth."

Harvey let out a boisterous laugh and knocked her cheek lightly with his knuckle. "Tongue in cheek, Preston." His laugh vanished while they locked eyes. "You're a good egg, Claire. You really are. I'll always be glad for that day when you walked into my office dressed to the nines and not a nickel in your pocket."

"I was wearing a skirt…it had no pockets," Claire remembered. It was her mother's skirt.

Harvey let out a laugh. It was good laugh, a mixture of relief and exhaustion. They both fell into peaceful silence. Life was good.

Claire pulled her gaze away and found herself rereading the clipping's header: **SLEEPING WITH THE FISHES HUS- BAND KILLED IN TUB.**

"And get rid of that clipping before somebody finds you with it," Claire advised.

"Okay, boss." Harvey embraced her in a brotherly fashion again. "Let's you and I grab a bite, I'm starved. We'll do Ku- dos's, it's casual and quiet enough for us to discuss a few details about our partnership. "

"Why not," Claire agreed, while Harvey held her a little longer than she normally allowed as she mulled over the sequence of events.

Jonathon loved her again, and Nicolette was history; Harvey was off the hook, his blackmailers dead, and she was going to be a partner as a result of this.

But lastly, Brazil. Claire's final challenge would soon be fulfilled, and she would give Jonathon the daughter he wanted.

Miracles.

34

Lua da Flor

A deafening quiet filled the stone-still room. As Claire searched her way through the dark, her heels echoed with each step. Tacky sounds came from the soles of her boots on the sticky, vinyl floor. She stepped over hundreds of names that had been etched in markings and blood, faded by wear and the passing of time. The countless people whose life's problems and desires had been solved in a room where candles burned, and demons listened with soundless heartbeats. Pathetic souls unburdened over a weathered, wooden table that wobbled from a slight unevenness.

The whole room teetered over an invisible abyss, while alliances were made with fallen angels with broken wings and axes to grind.

But tonight there was an ease to the silence, a hint of weightlessness; as if the power that once had hung over the grimy room no longer remained. It felt like the last days of summer had been overtaken by the cool shade of fall.

Or is it the other way around?

Claire didn't know how to identify the feeling. She was split in the middle. She stood dead center, listening for sounds of life. Something was dreadfully wrong.

Claire was guided to the corner of the room where a faint moonbeam shone a trail of light directly through the window from the clear, starry sky. A ghostly light danced over a crumpled figure. The shape sat on the floor, its back to the corner, legs bent and parted. She moved closer to see who or what it was.

The once sadistic woman who had commanded a room was now reduced to a wilted version of her former self. She wore only a loose, white garment that hung off her bony shoulders. In the moonlight, slivers of scars where her breasts had once sat told a story of brutal butchery and grisly torture; her arms were equally mutilated. Esperança had fresh wounds covering her forearms, open lesions that looked more like self-inflicted burns. They were infected and looked very painful. Esperança looked up wearily, through a mane of greasy and unkempt gray hair.

The light of the moon captured her aging skin and the pronounced shape of her skull. Through her stony stare, she acknowledged Claire, then stared back down at something she held between her fingers. For the first time, Claire saw that Esperança was caressing a blade with what remained of her left index finger. Her hands trembled.

"Are you ill?" Claire's voice reverberated in the emptiness. Following a full minute of further silence, Esperança began humming a soft and gentle tune. The song's words, lost with the hoarseness in her weak voice.

"I asked you a question. Are you ill?" Claire now regretted canceling her time with her the night before. What the hell happened? Esperança continued to trace the blade against her fingers, one by one, still humming through unmoving lips. The sound seemed to stir the sleeping spirits from below the ground, and life began to slither at her feet, moving up along Claire's calves.

"What's wrong with you?"

The answer came in a broken whisper. "You were supposed to come last night," Esperança said, without moving her attention from the blade. "You weren't supposed to see me this way."

Claire sat alongside her, not concerned at all about what lay beneath her, or on the wall she leaned against in her Barguzin sable jacket. Following another long pause, Claire carefully lifted Esperança's wrist up for closer inspection.

"What did you do to yourself?" Esperança pulled her arm back and passed Claire the knife. "Those are burn marks, Esperança, a knife wouldn't do that." Claire took the blade and placed it far from Esperança's reach. Claire was afraid of this woman, especially now that she could see the self damage she was capable of. Claire's eyes narrowed in on the deep scars that lined Esperança's small frame, and a memory flashed, the memory of a dog that had been run over by a lawn tractor when Claire was nine. Although he had lived, his body was mangled and scarred, the blades leaving his skin with lacerations that went right into the muscle.

"What happened to you?" There was no way Esperança would have cut her own breasts off. Or was there?

Esperança's focus was on the window, her hands trembling incessantly in her lap. She spared Claire a glance and said, "I don't hear them tonight…it's so quiet." A smile flitted over her lips. "I wish it could have always been like this." She moved the hair from around her face, still mesmerized by what she was looking at. "I do have to wonder, though, when all this is over, who'll get the moon."

"What?"

"The moon," she said, turning to Claire. "I was wondering if God would take back the moon after the war with Satan is over…" Esperança turned away, brought her legs up beneath her gown and wrapped her arms around them. With her head resting to one side on her knees, she went on in a childlike whisper, fixated on the window again.

"Sometimes I think about the millions of people who share the moon…the good and the evil. Sometimes I'll stare at it for hours, trying to remember where I was, in what century and how many times I'd done the same thing. Just staring and staring. Wishing I could go back. Change things. And the circle starts all over again but the moon just stays the same."

Baffled by Esperança's alter ego', Claire listened with short breaths as Esperança went on. "The moon has many secrets… it's watched the world beginning from the alpha. Watched it change for thousands of years, just taking it all in and waiting. Waiting like all the rest of us for the omega."

Esperança turned her sad eyes fully on Claire. For the first time ever, Claire was truly worried. Esperança's hands went on shaking. This was the result of going 'cold turkey.' Claire remembered the bottle of rum she'd brought for her in her purse. It sloshed as she pulled it out of her bag and placed it on the ground before them.

"Your body can't take the shock, that's why you're shaking," Claire explained. "You have to wean yourself off, and I doubt you can do it alone."

Esperança turned her gaze back to the moon. Claire pulled the elastic from her own hair, allowing the tresses to fall free around her face. She reached out toward Esperança. "Here, let me get your hair out of your eyes."

Esperança remained still, allowing Claire to fuss over her. Undaunted at having her hands touching something unclean, Claire ran her slender fingers through the matted and greasy strands. "You really do need a bath...I could help you if you want. It'll calm your nerves." Claire used the elastic to secure a limp ponytail.

In that rare moment of affection, Esperança held Claire's gaze with an unusual expression. The old woman's eyes appeared sad, but appreciative; although her eyes had changed somehow. She turned her attention back toward the window. Claire pushed the bottle forward, reminding Esperança that it was there. Esperança spoke without turning again to face her.

"If I drink that," Esperança said, her voice cracking, "it'll make me forget her, and I don't want to tonight. I need to feel this. I need to remember her."

"Remember who?"

She turned around to face Claire, her eyes so full of vulnerability. "Lua da Flor," Esperança whispered respectfully, as if the name were connected to the most precious part of her existence. She seemed both unchained and hindered.

Claire stared long into her face, waiting for her to continue. Esperança's once deep-set and angry eyes, like reflective black circles wrapped around twin bottomless pits, were soft. Claire couldn't identify the change in them. *Lua da Flor,* she thought back to what Esperança just said. Was this the child's name?

"Moon Flower?"

"The child I killed," Esperança clarified.

Her words hung in the air, leaving behind a resonant silence, and then the beaded curtain began to move. The beads clinked back and forth, as a gentle breeze swept through the room. The air smelled clean, almost like the ocean. Claire caught movement from the corner of her eye. She turned her neck and saw that fine, white feather danced inside of the moonbeam with them. Claire kept her gaze on it as it stirred in quick and sporadic moves, disappearing into the darkness, then reappearing inside of the light. It was almost a metaphor, the battle that was going on inside of Claire. She was that tiny feather, going back and forth, struggling to choose between right and wrong, good and evil, darkness and light. Claire remained motionless, not wanting to sway the tiny dancer as it gently tumbled inside of the moonbeam and landed on her thigh.

"Today's her birthday," Esperança said.

Claire carefully pinched the feather between two fingers and blew it into the darkness.

"She would have been forty-seven," Esperança said. "She would probably have gotten married, had a few babies. Today's also the deadline."

"What deadline?" Claire asked, but her question went unrequited. Esperança looked at the bottle and gestured for Claire to open it for her. Without a second thought, Claire cracked open the seal, eager for her only friend to return.

"I'd probably be a grandma," she whispered.

Esperança was hurting, and Claire was at a loss. She knew Esperança had loved this child, but there was also her granddaughter whom she loved. "You do have Patience," Claire said.

"Yes, but if I had my Lua, things wouldn't have turned out like this. And Patience wouldn't be here."

Claire held her breath as Esperança took the bottle with trembling hands and downed her first big gulp. A flicker of life began to glow in her eyes, and Claire felt that the heart of the room had begun to beat. The tension began to ease as she plied Esperança with the alcohol. Claire exhaled.

"Drink more, you'll feel better." Seeing Esperança so weak terrified her. It was cruel to want her drunk, but seeing her in pain was even harder.

Esperança shook her head in amazement. "It's amazing how

quickly it happened, as if I'd loved her my entire existence…as if my soul came alive when I first held her in my arms."

Esperança took another big gulp, her gaze still drawn toward the moon. "Sometimes the lies you tell yourself become the only thing you want to believe," Esperança began, gripping the bottle with both hands. "And then you drink the truth down so deep that the only way it stays down, is by drinking the real hard stuff."

The silence was infiltrated by the sound of liquid snaking through the opening of the bottle and slithering onto her tongue and down her throat. She swallowed hard, leaving droplets of liquid dribbling down her chin.

"And all you're doing is trying to keep it from floating back up." Esperança looked to Claire and gave a sad smile, then turned away.

Esperança needed help, just as Claire's mother had needed it. "When I get back, maybe we could get you some new clothes…better food, get you some help…to get off the sauce. This shit is going to kill you." Esperança let out a weak laugh and placed her hand over Claire's. She jolted back; the old woman's hands were icy cold. "Well?" Claire pressed, rubbing Esperança's bony shoulders. "What do you think…how about letting me help you?"

Esperança shook her head with a pitiful expression. "You want to help me?"she said, without looking up.

"I do," Claire said, feeling guilty about feeding her the alcohol. "You're my only friend," she mumbled under her breath.

"I'm no friend." Esperança took another slow swig.

"But you are. You've been very helpful to me…it's the least I can do," she said, still rubbing Esperança's shoulders.

Esperança let out a soft laugh and smiled to herself. "If I was," she said, the smile vanished when her eyes met with Claire's, "I would have told you the truth about why I sent for you. I would have been able to get through to you. And now time's run out. The deadline…on Lua's birthday."

Claire dropped her hands into her lap and studied her grave expression. "Where are you going with this?"

"I promised that I would tell you about my daughter."

"That's right, you did."

"What I have to say might make you change your mind about me being your friend. I've been keeping things from you, things you should hear," Esperança cautioned. "Still want to know?"

Claire nodded.

"Okay then, but first…I'll need a favor from you."

35

Midnight Flower with Morning Dew

The favor was not one Claire had expected. The instructions were simple enough, though bizarre. The cake was pre-ordered: a three-layer vanilla cake with vanilla cream icing. The top of the cake was adorned with flowers with white petals and tiny yellow centers. Intricate green leaves of sugared vines weaved between each flower, and the yellow inscription read simply: HAPPY BIRTHDAY LUA DA FLOR.

Esperança had cleaned herself up by the time Claire got back. She was seated at her usual place with an ivory candle placed before her, burning an even, calm flame. She wore a pair of white cotton pajamas with a faded violet flower pattern, her pant legs tucked into a thick pair of thermal socks. Her hair had been washed and combed back, her expression soft, and a sad smile tipped the corners of her mouth.

Claire set the cake down before her and took a seat. Esperança opened the box and peeked into it. She was serious. "Good, very good." Her eyes were alert now. "Plates?"

"Oh, right." Claire placed the bag on the table, wondering if now was a good time to ask questions about the bizarre task.

"Every year, I order this exact cake. And it has to be exactly the same. Vanilla icing with eleven moonflowers."

"Why eleven?"

Esperança closed the lid and mumbled, as if in shame, "She held eleven moonflowers in her hand on the night I sent her back."

"Oh." It was not the answer that Claire had been expecting.

"Lua always wanted a party, the real kind, surrounded with children wearing party hats, presents wrapped in shiny bows. The kind of parties she saw in her picture books. Of course I could never give her that. We were all alone in the world," Esperança whispered.

Esperança pulled the bag of paper plates apart and took out a few. "All we had was each other," she said, carefully taking the cake out of the box and placing it to one side. "She was a very curious child, always asking questions. Questions about the sky, questions about the sun, the stars…"

Esperança stood up with a slow and cautious rise, her posture bent, as if she fought against physical pain. The rum hadn't helped. She picked up a silver knife from the table, wiped the blade on a napkin, and cut into the cake. "But her favorite was always the moon," Esperança whispered. "I made a promise to her that one day we would go there. That the moonbeams would take us to the stars and we would hop them, one by one, until we got close enough to jump up onto the moon." Esperança took the piece, put it on the plate and set it to one side. With the knife still in hand, she added, "She believed me about everything…right to her last breath." She set the knife down and gave a sad nod. "Happy birthday, my child."

Claire shifted in her seat, watching Esperança as she carefully pulled her knife through the cake and plated another slab. "You picked up the milk I asked you for?"

"Oh, yes, I left it by the sink."

A crippling pain seized Esperança when she stepped away from the table. She gripped the back of the chair for support and waited for it to pass.

"I'll get it," Claire offered.

"No," Esperança held up her hand to stop her. "I'm her mother…they won't stop me from doing this. She shuffled over to get it, and returned with a quart of milk and a stack of plastic cups. Esperança eased into her chair with a grunt and handed

Claire an open bag of plastic cutlery. She plucked a fork from the bag and held onto it.

"Who are they?" Claire asked.

With a shaky hand, Esperança pushed the plated cake over to Claire. "You weren't invited, but I'll be insulted if you don't eat. It's Lua's party and only right."

"No no, I'll have some and, of course, some milk to wash it down."

Esperança overfilled her cup and slid it over, leaving behind a trail of white. Claire took a generous morsel of cake into her mouth, followed by several gulps of milk. Esperança stared back at her with heavy eyes.

"They," Esperança whispered, watching Claire, as she enjoyed Lua's cake, "the ones who wanted my child dead, are the voices I can no longer hear."

The firelight of the flame washed over Esperança's gaunt face. Claire was able to look deeply into her eyes. The eyes staring back at Claire were not the eyes she'd met a few months back. Not only were Esperança's eyes soft, but her irises were a warm, golden brown, almost hazel. "Your eye color, it's different. It used to be black."

Esperança's weary expression congealed around the comment. "When the Chosen are under the watch of angels…the dark angels I mean, it's no different than being in their shadow. Your eyes adjust to blackness and pupils naturally dilate. There's also a scientific reason. It has to do with that part of your brain that gets stimulated while under the angel's watch. Our brains function at a hundred percent, and we can do things that no normal humans could ever do. As the Chosen, we also develop certain skills that increase the ability of our brains. After a few lifetimes, you acquire abnormal control."

"Like when you killed that man by having him walk into an oncoming truck," Claire suggested.

"That's right. His mind was not his own, and the angel simply manipulated the man's mind, forcing him to do what I wanted done to him."

Claire asked, "And you know your angel personally?" She gave Claire a single nod. "Can you see it?" Claire furthered.

"Only in the in-between, when the dark angel Lahash, would

pull my soul back among the living, in search of a vessel. You can't see them directly, but you know that they're there. My angel was known to interfere with divine will, its specialty. That voice I used to hear was the voice that got inside your head, and then inside of mine. These angels know your every secret, your every thought. But once the angels are gone, the darkness goes with it and our pupils relax, go back to their own natural state."

"And you're free of them?"Claire asked.

"I am."

A creeping shiver traveled the length of Claire's spine. She was scheduled to leave for Brazil in the morning. "Is there something I should know? Or better yet, what have you done?"

Esperança tittered softly. "I did a lot of things. I'm just surprised I've lasted this long."

"And this has something to do with Lua?"

Esperança's sorrow spread into her smile. "Yes and no. But mostly yes." She closed her eyes, her smile dissolving. "Do you know, that even after all these years, I can still see her so clearly. Just the sound of her name, and I see her golden curls, her big, peacock-blue eyes."

"Sounds as if you really loved your little girl," Claire said, not knowing what to say, or what to think.

"I do," Esperança said, opening her eyes. "But I don't deserve to."

Claire felt a sensation come over her, as if something unseen was slithering up around her ankles and up her calves. It was as if the fallen angels were reaching out to Claire, compelling her to aid Esperança in whatever it was she'd done.

"You can feel them, can't you?"

"Yes," Claire replied.

"You've opened yourself up to them, but it doesn't have to last. You…" Esperança's voice trailed off. She was panting and doubled over. Claire got up from her seat, and knelt down before her, placing her palm against the old woman's cheek. Esperança was extremely hot.

"You're not well, something has to be done." Claire blotted her forehead with a napkin.

Esperança pulled herself to a sitting position, and managed a breath. "They don't want me to tell you the whole story. But as long as I am breathing, I'm going to tell you what you need to know."

Claire backed off, dropping her arms to her sides. So that was it, the moment Claire had been dying to know about. Yet, as much as she wanted to know the truth, a part of Claire understood that what she was about to hear might be enough to change her mind about going to Brazil. Claire shrank back into her seat and stared longingly at her. Esperança was in no condition to be up and about. Her skin was sickly yellow, the whites in her eyes looked as if they'd been colored with a mustard colored crayon. She was being wrung from the inside out, and Claire knew that Esperança was being punished.

"That's right Claire; we'll start from where we left off last time. About the night I sent my child back and what followed after. What you need to know."

"All right," Claire agreed. "You were saying something about the moon, why don't you start there," she suggested, running a plastic fork through her cake. "What was it with Lua and the moon?"

"Lua knew I loved the moon best," Esperança said, taking shallow breaths, a slight wheeze in her throat. "She always knew we were running from something, and she thought we would be safer there…that we wouldn't have to hide anymore." Esperança swallowed hard and paused. "Funny thing is, in the end, it was the moon that finished her."

Confused, Claire put her fork down. "How?"

"Without a full moon, the soul cannot depart as fast. Without a full moon, the pressure needed to extract the essence from a body will leave the soul wandering the earth, to transmigrate into another vessel. The full moon pulls the soul by the roots and ensures that it's given back to God."

Esperança became zealous and seemed stronger. "The soul is the most valuable thing you can ever take from a person. A soul guides the human body, governs the heart and mind. These are lessons that I've learned over centuries, I've seen the soul leave the body with my own two eyes." Esperança noted the fear in Claire's eyes. "I know it sounds a little crazy, but you should hear the rest. And if you still plan on going to Brazil, you should know the whole truth."

Claire nodded, pushing her plate to the side, resting her chin on the palm on her hands. She had grown to love the sound of Esperança's voice.

"There are fragments of a soul's essence, unique characteristics. Kind of like a person's fingerprints. What makes them different. Gifts. Things that guide us on Earth. Make us who we are. Some essences are stronger than others. Some essences are creative, healers, musical, while others are dangerous, wicked and corrupt. Meant for destruction. The earth holds many souls, and Satan has worked very hard to collect his and send those that deny him back to God. But what a full moon does is enable the circle to be broken. That's why I ask, who will get the moon? And how is it that the very thing God created to help guide his children through the dark, also helps Satan in his war? But then it occurred to me, a few centuries ago." Esperança paused to take a small morsel of cake into her mouth, with a trembling hand.

"Souls that were created by God were also used against Him. Just as He created Lucifer and was betrayed. Souls like mine were taken at our most vulnerable and used by Satan in the war against God. Our weaknesses become Satan's weapons. Just like the moon. It was created for good, and yet Satan was able to find the one thing that served him, and he used it against God."

Claire nodded.

"The pressure of the full moon causes so many things to happen. The moon and the earth are attracted to each other. On a full moon, it works like a magnet. It pulls at the earth, wanting to bring it closer, like the oceans. So we get these beautiful tides. High tides, low tides." Esperança stopped, and in her mind's eye recalled a memory. "My little girl and me, we used to watch the tides for hours, we would count them as they came in. Count the smaller tides, then count the bigger ones. I told her the story about the moon and how it sent down the angels. We called them water-angels. We would close our eyes, feel the mist against our faces as the waves washed to shore." Esperança chuckled amiably to herself as if she, once again, was sitting by the water's edge with her child. "She would laugh and say, 'Momma, the angels are kissing us.' And while we were enjoying watching the waves by the full moon, my own people used it to destroy God's most divine souls."

"And I suppose, this is the reason why you drink?"

Esperança nodded, and then said without animosity "Sometimes we fight demons with demons. Sometimes the pain can be too much, and in order to battle these demons, people do what they have to do. And in my case, it was amplified times two. I've been fighting demons for a long time Claire, fighting myself in the process."

Claire gave her a searching look.

"You cannot hide the truth from the heart. Yes, you can cover it up with anger, malice, revenge, but you can only hold on to your anger for so long. And soon enough, that bottom will drop, and that's when you have no choice but to look at what's left."

Claire swallowed the anxiety building in her throat. "And what's left?"

Unbuttoning her pajama shirt, Esperança whispered back, "This."

Seeing the scars again made Claire squirm, while she forced herself to look.

Esperança fought through the shame, and despite wanting to quickly cover up her wounds, she left herself exposed. "You asked me what happened, and I'm going to tell you." She slowly buttoned up her shirt, never taking her eyes off Claire. "People worship what they fear. And, as much as gold may glitter, all that glitters is not always gold. In my case, it made no difference because even though I knew better, I was trapped, trapped and young on the outside, centuries old on the inside. I was a girl of twenty-beautiful and young."

Claire remembered the photo of Esperança's mother in blood only, it was possible that Esperança could have once been a beautiful Hispanic beauty.

Esperança surmised, "I guess you can say that I'm the storm before the calm. Funny, though; it's taken me nine lifetimes to admit out loud what I've always believed all along." She gave her head a shake and smiled. "Our worlds are in chaos, Claire. Like one of those snow globes: the ones with the picture inside and the crazy blizzard all around." Esperança used her hands to form a small ball.

Claire nodded. The simile was so appropriate her case, and she understood perfectly.

"We have good against evil, Satan battling against God. There's natural destruction: floods, earthquakes, wars. And in all the commotion, people are caught up and taking sides, trying to find the answers, searching for inner peace, but in all of the wrong places. New religions, new gods, new age promises. But one day the world will become still, and once the dust settles, the answer will remain. My own answer was always there, waiting for the right time, but I was a coward and too afraid to fight for it."

The tone of Esperança's narration was quiet and steady. "We're approaching Armageddon, and Satan is moving at a rapid pace, pushing toward the end. There are several kingdoms of his on the earth. The family I was born into lives in one of them, Mato Grosso, in the Valley of Souls."

She wiped the sweat from her upper lip and winked through her words. "In all of my lives I knew I was different. I'd struggled with that part of my existence. That change. When a soul is reincarnated and transitioned into new life it doesn't always start smoothly. From the time you're born, you possess certain strengths that make you different from normal children. People often refer to them as 'old souls.' They're quieter, composed, and almost unnatural. Sometimes a reincarnated child will live without knowing who or what he or she is until six or seven years of age. By then, it all makes sense and the work begins. The fallen angels take over, and from that moment on, their souls are not their own, their lives are not their own. We're just vessels, bodies used in the battle against God.

"You asked me about my childhood the other night, what it was like. And all I can tell you is that it I never had a childhood because I had no innocence. I was created for murder, reborn in The Valley of Souls. When Kamau took his people off of Snake Island, they relocated in the jungles of Mato Grosso. By the mid 1700s, my family had established a strong allegiance with Satan and the fallen angels. We were a very powerful family, sending back as many as twenty souls a week, sometimes thirty. We would take the enemy, rip their souls from them, and then burn them into ashes and dust. 'Holocaust' comes from the Greek. It means, 'that which is completely burned.' When translated into Hebrew, it means, 'that which goes up in smoke,' a burnt sacrifice. I told you about that the other night, any soul that is not in complete allegiance to Satan shall be removed from the earth. They would say that those who walk the earth as enemies can only leave in smoke."

"A balance," Claire whispered.

"A balance, a game. You see, Satan plays the sport better than God. He'll create other versions of God; any other God will do, just as long as it's not the Heavenly Father. And for those who worship these other versions, they too end up in Nothingness, with no place for their souls to call home. If Satan can't have their loyalty, neither will God. So then he'll reach these lost souls who've either been caught in the in-between, or even in hell, and give them an out: loyalty, in exchange for a human vessel. A chance back among the living."

"And you, what was it like…being reborn…knowing what you were, where you came from? Where were you? Hell or Nothingness?"

"I was in Nothingness," Esperança admitted, her eyes cast downward. "The loneliest feeling you could ever imagine. It's not easy to explain. But to answer your question, when you're in spirit form, you have all the memories, all the emotions that go along with your history. But once you enter a body, the spirit relaxes because other things take precedence, like survival, hunger, cold, exhaustion. And as the soul merges into the body, it takes a while for the brain and vessel to morph as one. Sometimes shock will make that transition ride out longer, other times it'll happen almost immediately. Some of my siblings have merged by the time they're three, but I always took the longest. I suppose my soul wanted to forget because I never did fit in." Esperança shook her head. "I fought against it, rebelled, and was often called a deserter by the others. But Kamau always favored me. And despite all the trouble I caused him, I was always given another chance by the fallen angels and reborn back into the family."

Esperança looked up with heavy-lidded eyes. "By my ninth life, which is the life you see before you, I'd become a liability to my family. I was eighteen when the trouble really began. Of course I understood that my loyalty had to be with Satan, but knowing that they were sacrificing human souls took a toll on me. I would become sick, unable to speak for days. It just got to a point where I needed to get the voices to go away." Esperança cupped her hands over her ears. "In my head, every minute of every day, the constant noise that made me crazy." She dropped her hands into her lap. "But in order for me to be allowed to live and not be sent back into Nothingness, I needed to do Satan's work. I needed to feed his insatiable hatred of God."

Claire's mouth became very dry.

"I was so far in. On the one hand, I understood the consequences. On the other, I hated myself for being what I was. I was known for letting souls escape. And other times, I'd hide by their prisons, bringing them food; and doing whatever else I was able to do to make them comfortable. It was very difficult. And it drove me to self-medicate through drinking, partying in Rio, then sex. Sometimes I would drink so much just to make the voices go away. Keep moving, keep drinking. Reckless behavior and men. Lots of men." Esperança ran her fingers through her damp, thin mane.

Claire's gaze darted to where Esperança's breasts once had been.

"I spent a lot of time in Rio and Salvador, the capital city of Bahia, and that was the year that I met my daughter's father, David. His family was Dutch, with a long family history of earning their livelihood as fishermen. They owned some property along the coast of Salvador, where they ran a lighthouse. David had no interest in becoming a lighthouse keeper, but he was nice. A nice young man who was good to his mother. I liked that about him."

Esperança nodded almost to herself before focusing her attention at Claire. "I always said, if a man is good to his mother, then he's half-way there, worth getting to know. Anyways, the sad thing for me was that I didn't get the chance to know him more. He was killed by a madman who poured kerosene on him and set him on fire. I know that Satan had something to do with it. And that was just the beginning, because I soon discovered that I was pregnant." Esperança's stopped speaking.

"And what did the others say, about the pregnancy?" Claire

asked, bracing herself.

There was a hint of steel in Esperança's tone. "Kamau was uneasy when the angels informed him of the life I was carrying. As Satan's chosen, I was to procreate in the valley, where I could be under the protection of the fallen. Satan would choose a soul to enter into the homunculus. I was merely a vessel, a body for the souls he chose to come back. And regardless of what soul was in the fetus, it didn't mean anything. As long as a woman is pregnant, that soul could be pushed out at any time. All we could do was wait."

"When you said the other night that your child was stained by the hand of God, you meant that she came straight from heaven?" Claire verified.

"She was more than just a soul stained by the hand of God. God had blown his divine breath into her, and she was born with obligations and gifts. She walked with God's army of angels."

"Did you know, while you were carrying her, that she was the enemy to your kind?"

Esperança smiled and regret replaced it. "In a way." She plucked a sugar moonflower from the top of her cake. She balanced it on the tip of her right index finger. "I remembered a struggle during my last trimester. My ears were popping; the fallen angels were battling something that I couldn't see. Something that was going on around me. I could hear a faint sound, like breaths of air passing over an open wine bottle. Quick and light. Of course I didn't know my child was divine at that point, but the moonflowers, they're very beautiful. I'd never seen one until that night."

Esperança paused briefly, staring down at the flower. She placed it on her plate.

"It was soon after that strange sensation, the battle you can call it, when I discovered them. Vines had grown and circled around our territory and hills. The alabaster-white flowers bloomed beneath the light of the moon. They looked like tiny stars that had fallen from the sky and rooted themselves in our land. They had this glow, like moonlights. The Chosen discovered that they were poisonous after some of our animals ate them and became very sick and died. We'd never seen them before, but now they were everywhere. And it didn't matter what we did, they kept coming back, for no particular reason." Esperança nodded at her own realization. "But you know, there's always a reason," she affirmed, looking directly into Claire's eyes. "My daughter was born a few months later, and I then understood the reasons for the moonflowers."

Claire caught herself nodding.

"In all the hundreds of years, not one of us Chosen had ever given birth to a child with a divine soul, chosen by God. Not one."

"Until you?"

"Until me. What I said earlier, about Satan choosing what souls entered into our kind, was exactly what should have happened with me. But for whatever reason, my child's soul battled against all the souls combined, against the fallen, so that I could give her life. I'll never know when she entered during my pregnancy, but I do know that there was a battle, and she won."

She stared at Claire intently and held her with a strange look. "You need to understand what I mean. A pregnant woman is very vulnerable. There's a fight that goes on in the world between the living and the dead. The dead want to get back among the living. And an unborn child is their vessel to achieve that. It should have been impossible for Satan's Chosen to give birth to a divine soul of God's. Impossible. I mean there were other women in the valley that sometimes gave birth to souls not approved by Satan. But never one of Kamau's chosen children, much less the birth of a divine being. Not ever!"

Claire gave her head a quick shake. She was undeniably unnerved. "Is that what happened with Janice? Her son's soul? Did Satan give him a choice?"

"Janice? No, Satan had no interest in her boy. James was too green, too good. He died a quick death, drug overdose. His soul was caught between the living and the dead. Eventually he would have found the light, but Janice was so broken over his death, so torn over the fact that his soul was lost. Of course she wanted to save him."

"But she got him back, Janice told me."

"That is true. But first, Janice needed to get pregnant, which was the easy part," Esperança said. "Once that happened, Satan chose the evil soul that entered into the child's fetus, the child that Janice was supposed to bring back into the world. That's where I would feed one fire to help the other. The hard part was finding her son's soul, then having him battle his way back into the world. But he did, and somehow, I managed to make it happen."

"And Satan's fine with this?" Claire asked.

"I'm a charlatan, remember?" Esperança said. "Feeding one fire to help the other, fighting demons with demons. I think it all started when my baby girl fought her way into my life. Like she left her own imprint coursing through my veins, a gift of some sort. Because over the last three decades or so, I realized that I could do anything as long as my actions were motivated with good intentions. But I still have yet to know why God wanted me to be the mother of a divine being. Why me?"

Esperança's lips trembled before her upper lip curved into a sad smile. "Oh, but she was beautiful, and just like the moon-flower, she was perfect...alabaster-white with golden hair. Lua was born with her eyes open."

"Is that normal?"

Esperança gave a nod. "All divine beings are born with their eyes open. And her soul was miraculous, the most beautiful thing I'd ever seen. The fallen angels sent word to the Cho-sen, said that I'd given birth to the enemy, and that she was as poisonous as the moonflowers and needed to be destroyed and sent back to where she'd come from."

"No," Claire whispered under her breath. Their gazes met, both grief-stricken.

"She was born at a little after midnight. They called her a midnight flower with morning dew, an abomination to the King," Esperança said, dropping her head in shame. "It would be years before I would uproot my child from the earth. And for years my midnight flower rooted herself in the madness of my existence. You see, she was a slight to Satan. But to me," she shook her head with her neck still bent forward, "to me, she was the love of my lives." Esperança finally looked up, her eyes plagued with the recollection. "And because she was a divine soul, a full moon was needed in order to rip her from the earth." Esperança stopped speaking.

Claire swallowed hard. "And that's what you meant by the moon ending her."

Esperança nodded.

"And a full moon is needed every time?"

Esperança coughed something up into a napkin. Claire spied what looked like blood. "Only for God's divine beings," Esperança clarified.

"Your own child was your greatest enemy," Claire said, beneath her breath.

"A divine being. And I brought her into the world. *Me.* How did the most beautiful flower in the world, grow from such poisonous soil, from this very body?"

"I don't know," Claire answered. "Only, I don't understand why the full moon is used only on the divine?"

"Because, a simple kill is just a simple kill," Esperança replied. "Even a stained soul isn't a threat to Satan, because they're not earthbound. They'll go straight to heaven, no detours. Divine beings are bound to battle God's war with Satan and the fallen. They're bound to the earth. And for those caught between worlds, the simple kills, Satan had use for them: their alliance for a chance back. A divine being would almost never form an alliance with Satan."

"Therefore," Claire surmised, "a divine being is Satan's biggest threat. So what you're saying is that a stained soul is someone like the Christian foot soldiers Christopher trained."

"That's right, straight to heaven. Those stained by the hand of God, souls that lean toward his grace and human compassion. Those that would never choose any other God ."

"And the divine beings are earthbound and reborn just like Satan's Chosen," Claire ensured.

"Souls that bear his stain and have direct contact with God's angels, souls that have lived on the earth before, earned God's trust by watching over the meek and protecting his grain; souls that will stay on the earth and come back among the living to fight God's battle."

"Just like Christopher," Claire added.

"Just like Christopher was. There are places on earth which have certain mystic powers. You combine these fields with the force of a full moon, and…and it…" Esperança stumbled on her words. "It's like…"

"Like a magnetic pressure." It was all making sense, all these scientific explanations.

"That's right," Esperança said, "like a magnetic pressure." The words trailed along with her thoughts. She was thinking about her Lua, pondering the same question that had eaten away at her for decades. Was Lua earthbound? Was the pressure of the full moon enough to send her back to God? Because it was the only place Esperança wanted her to be, in the heavens with God and his angels; not lost, waiting to return, with the heinous memory of what Esperança had done to her.

"But because Lua was a divine being," Claire affirmed, "that couldn't have gone well. What was God thinking?"

"I won't pretend to guess. But it's true; it did cause a greater rift. But that rift was already there. When my child was born with a divine soul, it just confirmed it; I wasn't one of them. They wanted to destroy her, but a full moon wasn't due for a few weeks. And in order to keep her from dying, she needed to be fed, kept alive, to ensure that her soul wouldn't be left to wander. They couldn't take the chance of having her soul return. Of course, Kamau knew that I wasn't like the others, and there would be the risk of having me become attached to her. He wanted Lua to be fed by a wet nurse. But when the time came, I couldn't do it. Instead, I asked for more time. At first, an hour, then two. And by the time I'd given her my breast and watched her cling to me for life, I was so taken by her, so at peace with her that could actually feel her love. I mean, really feel it. I'd had children before in my other lives, but this was different. It cut to the core of my soul, brought out things in me that I hadn't felt in centuries.

"Kamau came to me; he demanded that I release her. It was time. Instead, all I wanted to do was leave. Take my child and run."

Claire closed her eyes, beginning to comprehend how painful Esperança's life really was.

"I took what I could from my family's safekeeping. And once we got out of Mato Grosso, I traded what I took for some cash. It was enough to get us on our way, and the man who had bought them made sure that Lua and I had transportation. Following a few weeks of sleeping in different places, we settled in

Rio de Janeiro and I managed to find a small room to rent, paid in full, five years worth, the cost of a few stones. Those uncut stones I took lasted a long time, it was enough. I needed very little, anyway. As long as I had food to eat, I was able to breastfeed her." Esperança touched her flattened hills. "I was her mother, and for whatever reason, that was all that mattered to me—that and protecting her."

Claire considered the sequence of events; uncut diamonds were of no surprise, considering that the Mato Grosso State was one of the major diamond producing areas. Although to run through such danger, carrying a newborn, was a bold, yet desperate decision. The sickly woman, hunched over and holding onto her chest, was as deep and mysterious as the Amazon itself. Claire could see that Esperança was in pain, both physically and spiritually. Her skin had become a deeper, sickly shade of yellow, and the circles under her eyes darker. She looked like a rotting banana. With a trembling hand, Esperança put the bottle to her lips and drank slowly. She placed the bottle down gently and put both her hands in her lap.

"It's strange how the centuries have passed so slow, an agonizing stretch, and yet with Lua, the years went by so quick, like a flash forward, in just a few blinks. She grew so fast. If there was only a pause button, I would've spent the rest of eternity frozen with her. She was my morning glory, my sunset, my moon. Sometimes I watched her sleep; the way she pulled her tiny mouth as if she was still nursing. Or the way her little fists clenched into small balls when she was in a deep sleep. The little sounds she made, the way her eyes twitched when she was dreaming. Other times I would watch her sleep just to make sure she was still breathing…that Satan didn't take her soul from her while she slept. I was so afraid for her.

"Early on, in the first months of our escape, I became aware of something. For centuries, I had been guided by my fallen angel. I would hear the words in my own voice. Words that were not mine, commands. Directions of what needed to be done. Who the enemy was and what souls needed to be taken. But for the first time ever, the world was quiet. And the only voice I heard, wanted to hear, was my child's. And the first time she called me mama…" Esperança squeezed her eyes shut. "You'd have to be a mother to understand what that word means. It means, 'I trust you, I need you…I love you.' And I was her mama; I was all of those things."

All Claire could offer was a nod.

"Those were very interesting times, peaceful times." Esperança continued, with watery eyes. "And a three-year-old made it all the more interesting. As I said earlier, she was a very inquisitive child. Always had questions. Why was the sky blue? Where did clouds come from? Why did the birds have wings? Where did they fly with their wings? But when she asked me why I'd named her Lua da Flor, I was surprised. She understood perfectly well what a moon was and what a flower was, but for whatever reason, she insisted on knowing why I'd named her that. It was then that I also realized that there were no moon-flowers anywhere about, not the kind that grew on our land. They were spectacular, that glow I told you about. Like lit candles."

"Bioluminescent," Claire whispered. *What a vision.*

"Brazil has some of the most beautiful flowers in the world," Esperança explained. "Yet I couldn't find the very flowers that connected me to my Lua. We were always searching for them. Searching for pieces to a puzzle that explained the reason why God wanted me to be her mother. For my child, the search for the flowers was an innocent game, but for me, not finding moon-flowers anywhere else became confirmation that I was right all along, and that she was put into my life for a purpose. I didn't deserve her, and she didn't deserve to have to live on the run."

Esperança stopped speaking and held her hand to her chest. Perspiration dotted her forehead. She seemed very frail and weak. "You can stop you know, if it's hard for you," Claire suggested, all the while hoping that Esperança would continue.

"No. I need to do this, and you need to know." Claire nodded and passed her a napkin. Esperança reached for it and wiped the perspiration off her face. With trembling hands, she took the bottle off the table. Then she began speaking again.

"When she was close to reaching the age of five, Lua had become a very spiritual child. I'd never mentioned God to her, for fear of riling up Satan. But she understood who he was and what was expected of her. She was a compassionate child. We would see kids running in the streets, begging for food. Homeless, dirty. She would cry for them, want to help them. And yet here we were with very little ourselves. She would wrap her arms around me and tell me how lucky she was to have me for a mother, how much she loved me…She never once complained that we, too, had very little. We found happiness in the simplest things. Every once in a while we would go into the town and look in the shop windows.

"Sometimes I would read to her right in the stores. We would pick the book and find ourselves a place to sit, and I would read to her. Some store owners would pretend to not see us, while others would get angry, forbid us to come back…At night, we would talk about the stories we'd read or the pretty pictures inside." Esperança elaborated further, "I ended up getting a job at night, cleaning one of the stores, shelving the merchandise in exchange for food. It was ideal, and I could bring Lua with me. I would never spend a minute without her, for fear of losing her. And aside from the rent, which was soon due, I had no other means to support us, and I'd run out of diamonds.

"But life was good. And our walks were always the best. We would take a blanket and lie on our backs and watch the moon. I would tell her our plans and how we would get there. The stars…in Brazil you could see them so clearly then. You could almost reach up and touch them. They became an obsession of ours. Like searching for gold in the dark. I explained to Lua how the moonflowers only bloomed by the light of the moon and how very special they were. Often at night, instead of sleeping, she would keep me up wanting to hear the story about the moonflowers and how beautiful they were. I would snuggle up to her and twirl her golden curls around my fingers. I would tell her that her beautiful spirit was the center of the magical moonflowers and that she was my most precious angel. I don't know how many times she heard that story, but she loved it all the same. Looking back now, five quick blinks, I remember how much I savored every moment with her. I never wasted a day, never wasted even a second, although things became hard. The man who owned the store had died. The store closed its doors and we were left homeless. No money for rent, no money for food. I was truly afraid for us, and of course, we had no one to ask for help. Then Lua said something to me:

she said that we needed to go where the light was, the same light that shines on the waters."

"What did she mean by that?"

"Lua's grandparents, Lua's father's parents. Remember, they were lighthouse keepers."

"Wow, just like that."

"Just like that," Esperança said. "So out of the blue. Go where the light is. Now I understood that they had no children apart from David, and Lua was their only grandchild, so that alone was a good reason. But I knew that I needed to do it; I needed to listen to Lua, that God's angels were guiding her, sending her there. I—" Esperança doubled over, gasping for breath. Claire stood up, but Esperança held her hand up to stop her. "Sit down," she said.

Claire took her seat, picked up her purse, and began rummaging through it. "I have some pain medication for my migraines. It's very strong."

"I'm fine, Claire, just give me a second."

Claire looked up and knew by the sweat which glistened over Esperança's face that she was lying. "Have it your way." She set her purse down.

Esperança puffed out several quick breaths and steeled herself against the pain. She fearlessly continued where she left off and managed to articulate every word.

"I remembered the lighthouse in Salvador. I also knew they were heartbroken over the death of their only child. I didn't care about me but I was hoping that, for Lua's sake, they would be welcoming, even consider giving her a bed to sleep in, food to eat. But I never expected that they'd be so kind to me as well, offer unconditional love to complete strangers."

Claire felt inspired by this.

"It was night by the time we got there. The rain came in, and we were soaked. Lua fell asleep on the bus, and I had to carry her the rest of the way. We found their lighthouse along the coast. Lua's father took me there once; they lived in a small house beside it." Esperança smiled with a peculiar look in her eyes.

"Edith was David's mother, Lua's grandmother. She must have remembered me, but when I woke Lua up to meet the nice lady, I didn't even get the words out that Lua was her grand-daughter. She took one look at her and cried. Wouldn't let her go. She was a dead stamp of her father you see, had the same peacock-blue eyes, and the same golden hair. So did Edith. It must have been a shock, seeing their dead son in Lua. Of course they welcomed us to stay, to live with them as long as we wanted."

Esperança and Claire shared in the moment together. "That was nice of them," Claire said, thinking of her own mother's reaction if it were her grandchild. "I imagine Edith was over-whelmed with happiness."

Esperança agreed with a nod. "David senior, Lua's grand-father, cherished her just as much. Oh, they had a unique rela-tionship. Lua was his little helper, as he called her. He said that she brought life back into the old lighthouse, that her bright eyes made the beams of the lighthouse shine brighter. But I think he was really talking about himself. He loved her very much. Then there were the walks by the ocean." Esperança's eyes lit up, as she recalled a memory. "David senior believed that all the world's mysteries would wash up along the shore, and some-how, the ocean would answer life's unanswered questions. We just had to look inside ourselves. Lua searched that shore for the moonflowers. We all did. It was a silly thing to do and we never found them of course, but it was our special thing to share with them. David senior did something very special for Lua one night. He placed a row of jars, filled with lit candles, all along the beach. He said that if they couldn't find the special moon-flowers, these would do for now. And it worked. Lua was so happy; I remember how she ran to the top of the lighthouse just to get a better view. She stayed up there until the candles burned out. Lua's grandparents ensured that those jars were refilled with fresh candles. But we did have our little tradition though," Esperança said, with a weak laugh. "We only used wooden matchsticks, because Lua said that God grew the trees which were used to make them. And only one matchstick was used per candle. Each candle was special, and with each flame Lua would say a prayer. But the prayers could only be made for others, or it didn't count. She was very serious about that part."

Esperança took a long pause, and caught the softness in

Claire's eyes.

"Thank you," Claire finally said, "for sharing that with me." Claire meant it; she felt almost honored, even unworthy, knowing this precious part of Esperança.

Esperança gazed at her in stony silence, until her expression turned thoughtful. "You're welcome, Claire. I suppose it's only fair that I let you in, since I am your friend. But you know," Esperança said, "somehow, what David senior said was true. All my answers were right there on the shores of the beach. I had everything I needed. We were a family and lived a very simple life." Esperança paused and lowered her voice. "We even went to church together."

"Church? Isn't that an abomination to Satan?"

"Lua was a divine child of God's. It was never about me. Oh, but Lua loved that lighthouse," Esperança said, not allowing Satan to ruin her reminiscing. "She helped her grandfather trim the wicks, wind the clocks. Sometimes he even let her clean the lenses. She was so intrigued by this way of guiding the ships safely into the harbors. Her grandfather had an interesting way of explaining it. He told her that God was the very essence of light and that just as the lighthouse guided its ships home, God's light guided his children home."

"That sounds like something Christopher would have said," Claire commented.

Esperança gazed at Claire with sad and tired eyes. "It does, doesn't it? But we always ended up on the shore, waiting for the ocean to wash up the moonflowers, the pieces of our puzzle.

"Edith and David senior came to me one night and asked if we could talk. They knew I had no family and hoped that I would agree to become their daughter. Legally. They wanted me and Lua to be taken care of if anything were to happen to them. Of course Lua loved the lighthouse, she was a natural, and it was a part of her family's legacy. And it made sense; we had no intention of ever leaving. This was where we wanted to be. Of course I said yes." Esperança closed her eyes. "I just wish it had lasted."

Claire's heart began to race. "Why didn't it last?"

Esperança opened her eyes. They were glassy and tormented. "Lua was reaching the age of six. She was looking forward to her party. Her grandmother had made her a real pretty dress—white ruffles with flowers and ribbons. She was so excited and couldn't wait to have balloons and cake. She wanted her cake to be all white, with pretty moonflowers all around." Esperança stared thoughtfully at the cake she'd cut into earlier. "But the party never came because Lua would never see her sixth birthday, or her grandparents again.

"We had been together for almost a year when her grandparents disappeared. By the second day, I knew they were dead. I knew without a doubt that they had found them—found us. It would be only a matter of time before they would return. By then, I'd become very sick. It got so bad that I completely lost the use of my left arm. Eventually, I had almost no feeling at all on my left side. I had lost so much weight, and I could feel my bones shrinking inside my skin. I began to lose my hair. It fell in clumps by my pillow and eventually my nails began to fall off, one by one. Lua would light those candles on the shore. She wanted to believe that I'd get better and that her grandparents would return if they saw the flames. She spent many days up in the lighthouse, waiting, praying. Weeks went by, and I think even Lua understood that our time was running out. And there was nowhere left to run."

Esperança stared at Claire with a blank look. "The voices came back, and they told me." The stillness was thick, settling over them like a shroud.

Claire hesitated, then asked, "Told you what?"

"That I was dying."

Claire felt the escalating tightness in her chest.

"I knew Satan was punishing me for not sending her back, and worse, my baby would be left alone and motherless. They would come for her…"

Esperança shook her head, trying to convince herself. "I didn't know what else to do but go back to the valley. I knew that if they got to her first, it wouldn't be as easy on her as if I were the one to do it."

"Do what?"

Esperança swallowed hard. "Send her back to God.

Promising the Moon

I got us as far into Mato Grosso as we could get with what money I found in a small tin that David senior kept hidden along the crack of the lighthouse's foundation. The rest of the way, we used the rivers and were aided by fishermen and other locals. It was dark by the time we reached the forest that my people's land was connected to. The guards, who protected our lands, never asked any questions, never said anything really. It was as if they'd been expecting us, as if the fallen had warned them of our return. They carried us the rest of the way. I was too sick and delusional. By the time we made it back, I was worse…I had these sores forming all over my chest, all over my breasts. I needed to stay alive for another day because there would be a full moon, and without it, my child's soul could have been left to wander. I couldn't have that…I needed to be sure that she got home.

"I remember very little about what followed on the day of our return. But I do remember clearly that when I came to, I could see my Lua standing over me crying. The lesions on my chest and around my breasts were now open blisters filled with black fluid. I could actually feel teeth biting into my skin, tearing into my flesh. I remember my family gathering around the place where I slept, speaking in whispers, and all I could do was watch my Lua left uncared for, without comfort. I could barely lift my hands up to hold her. Tell her I would be all right."

"What was it? The lesions, what were they?" Claire asked.

Esperança hesitated. "Necrotizing fasciitis."

"Oh my God, the flesh-eating disease."

Esperança slammed her hand down on the table, causing Claire to flinch. "God had nothing to do with it!"

Esperança looked down at where her breasts once had been and looked up. "God would never be so pitiless, so vengeful. The very thing I gave my child life with, Satan destroyed and took from me. Every time I saw these wounds, I would remember his wrath. And I would pay.

"Kamau asked the fallen to spare my life. He told them that I'd come back to set things right. We all understood that I was there to surrender my child's soul and that I had only a day left with her. I needed that, for her, but more for myself. I needed to scrape together whatever strength I had left in me so that I could send her back without terrifying her. That would be the hardest thing I had ever done in any of my lives.

"By the end of that day, the teeth had stopped chewing into my flesh. When they'd stripped me of my clothes, my skin had literally scraped off with the cloth. Deep, black holes filled with blackened rot were all that remained. And all this time my poor child was pushed to the side. Ignored. All except for Kamau. I later found out that he fed her, spent time with her while I slept, was very kind to her. That's what I meant earlier about him, he had a kind heart; the tools Christopher had given him remained somehow, or maybe it was because God had created Kamau first, as a divine being. Regardless, I was always grateful to him for that, this gentleness about him. It was nice, seeing him with Lua, even for a spell." She smiled at the memory. "When I woke up, she was wearing her party dress that her grandmother had made for her. Kamau must have found it in my things. Lua looked clean, taken care of. But I prayed anyway. I begged to God in heaven to give me enough strength so that I could spend some more time with her, send her home with a soul at peace. I didn't want her to remember me sick and dying."

Esperança stilled at the recollection, then spoke with a mother's pride. "Lua's divinity. It bloomed right before my eyes, before Kamau's eyes. She understood her purpose, to watch over the meek and to protect God's grain. Lua placed her tiny hands over me, over my wounds, across my heart, and she stopped me from dying. Stopped the pain. And if only for awhile, I was able to be her mother." The edge of sorrow in Esperança's voice made her words almost inaudible.

"I brushed her curls and braided her hair the way she liked it. I led her by the hand and showed her all the places I'd been as a child: my tree, the river where we swam." She paused. Her shoulders rose and fell with a deep breath of regret. She continued speaking in a dreamlike gaze.

"But I'll never forget, as the sun went down and the full moon took its place, I was finally able to show her what a moonflower was and where her name came from. We sat, as one, by the second river's bank, tranquilly watching as countless and countless of glowing angels lit the land of darkness. There had to be hundreds of thousands of them. I was gone for almost six years, and in that time, the moonflowers spread into the entire valley. We watched them from where we were, and they opened all at the same time. Like a wave of light. Lua was so quiet, so still in my arms." Esperança bent her head forward. "She had tears in her eyes."

A long silence prevailed, then she looked up and stared into Claire's eyes, both of them reflecting on the long awaited moment.

"That had to have been so beautiful," Claire said, faintly. "So worth the search."

Esperança nodded, looking down into her lap. "It was, it really was." She paused to envision the memory in her mind. "Sometimes I'll replay that very moment, over and over again. Do you know that I can still smell the night air, the sound of the water moving through the valley? I remember how peaceful everything was. So quiet, like we were the only people left in the world. We were silent for a very long time. I held her in my arms, kissed her eyes, and smelled the sunshine in her hair. I kissed all nineteen freckles on her nose, telling her I loved her and that one day I hoped she could forgive me. She never asked why," Esperança said, returning her attention back to Claire, with a bewildered expression, "or pressed me for explanations. All she said, through her baby's breath, was that she loved me too and that I'd been good to her.

"We were saying good-bye on the banks of the second river, although it was never actually said. I remember how she held me by the hand and led me over the hills. She hummed a song that I'd taught her as a baby, while she picked eleven moonflowers. When she was done, she looked at me and saw the tears that were running down my cheeks. Lua named them. She reached up, touched them with her tiny fingers, and called them moondrops. I'll never know what she meant by that, but I named each of my tears after her."

"Oh, no…" Claire said, forcing her face into her hands, but Esperança forged on.

"I smiled at her through the hardest pain I'd ever felt. I tried so desperately to be strong, to do what needed to be done without frightening her. How very strange it was, counting the minutes, understanding that in a few hours I would never get to hold her in my arms again. I didn't know how to tell her what I needed to say. How could I? How could I tell her that I was going to be taking her life from her in just a few hours? How could I tell her that she needed to trust me, to allow me to put my knife to her throat? A knife was the only way, it's quicker than a bullet, or a pill or poison. It pulls the soul upward, and draws it from inside of the heart. But how do you do it? How do you tell your child that?"

"I…I can't even imagine," Claire said, fighting the urge not to sob into Esperança's dirty table.

"I said nothing at that time. I guess a part of me was hoping that God, in his infinite wisdom, would send down his angels and save her from what I needed to do. But the angels never came. At least not then.

"When the moment came, I had her in my lap, her head rested against my heart, against the wrapping where my breasts once were. We were alone, and to her, it was a strange place, but she never asked any questions, not one word, almost like she knew. I told her that it was time, and that we needed to go. I told her the only lie I knew she'd believe. I told her that if she was good and listened to what I was telling her, that once we were done, we'd be on the moon."

Tears, like full drops of dew, shivered on the edge of Esperança's lashes. "I told her to close her eyes real tight, keep them that way. I promised her that it would only hurt for a second and that when she opened them again, we would be walking on the moon and that her Grandma and Grandpa would be there waiting. I promised her that there was a lighthouse up on the moon and its beams would guide us safely up."

The tears plunged down Esperança's cheeks, weighted with heavy despair.

Eyes down, Claire couldn't bear to see any more.

The old woman's voice quivered, her body trembled. "I promised her the moon, the moon! I used the thing she loved, to get her to listen. She shut her eyes closed and I took this blade…"

Her hands trembled excessively as she held up the knife. "I cut off my own finger so that when the time came to send her back, my own agony could distract me from the pain I felt when I needed to end her life."

Claire gasped in regret, a hand clapped over her mouth, only stealing occasional glances.

Esperança continued to purge herself. She wouldn't stop—couldn't stop. She needed to say what evil she'd committed against her child. She believed that by saying it out loud, it would somehow free her.

"After I cut off my finger, I said to her, 'Keep your eyes closed, my child, and don't move. And she said, and I'll never forget, 'Momma, do you promise that we'll get to live on the moon?'

"What could I say? I had no choice but to lie to her. It was that, or let them do it. *Me* she trusted. I'd never lied to her, never even raised my voice to her. She believed me, every word I said." Esperança let out deranged laugh. "Do you know that she smiled and promised to be brave?"

Claire wanted to say something, words that would divert the topic, but the growing lump in her throat wouldn't allow for any sound. Esperança began to unravel at a swift pace. She looked almost dangerous and on the brink of madness. Her yellow eyes were wide, haunted by the memory of what she'd seen, the memory of what she'd done. Esperança began rocking herself back and forth; her mouth was open, her lips quivered, as a faint groan rose from her chest. Claire could see that she was struggling for a full breath, struggling with her own heinous admission. Saliva soon dribbled from her lower lip and stretched into her lap. She wiped it with the back of her hand, and addressed Claire again.

"She did, Lua said, 'I'll be brave then, Momma. I'll close them and I won't move. See?' And my baby shut them closed…"

Esperança held the knife in her trembling hand and dropped it onto the table, no sound passed through her lips. She tried to speak, searching inside of herself, blinded by her tears. They fell, collected at the base of her chin, and dripped as she pulled at Claire's hands in search of strength. Her dark eyes were begging, drawing courage from Claire, as she prepared herself. Claire was still, her hands in Esperança's. She was mesmerized. The most powerful woman she'd ever known was gone.

"My baby struggled, fought for her life—wanted me to stop. And she had this look, a look I'd never seen before. Her eyes were open; she was terrified of me. Sweet God, they stayed like that. Wide open and lifeless."

Esperança ripped her hands back. "Oh, my poor, poor child. So limp in my arms. So limp and gone." She continued to rant, her voice cracking. She began explaining, her eyes still wide and terrified, while holding up her stump and rocking back and forth in her seat. Claire wanted to rise from her seat, hold her friend, but couldn't bring herself to move.

"I needed her to have a piece of me. You know? To know that I loved her, wanted to be there with her. I sent her to the only place I trusted, to a God who loved my child as much as I did, and to a God who gave me the only peace I'd ever known." Esperança wiped her tears with her hands, shaking her head. The truth of what she'd done penetrated deeply inside of her mind.

The visions of her dead and lifeless child tormented her to the point of insanity. Esperança began slapping her own head with a full open palm; all the while, her eyes remained closed. At one point, she slapped herself in the face, and her nose began to trickle blood all over the table and Lua's cake.

"Esperança, don't!" Claire collected napkins and threw them at her.

Blood continued to pour from her nose. She began rocking again, back and forth in her seat. "Oh, dear God, what have I done? What have I done, what have I done, what have I done? I'm so sorry, I'm sorry, Lua, my precious child. What have I done?"

Claire was traumatized, hearing her repeating the words over and over.

To Esperança, Claire was no longer there, no longer important. She continued to unload centuries of suppressed agony. Her body heaved continuously, with bouts of uncontrolled sobbing. As if the poisonous pain exited through every cell in her body; as if all the years of suppressed pain had finally escaped the prison within.

Claire's ears began to pop, and heaviness fell over the room. Under hooded eyes, Claire studied the flame as it began to weaken and darkness descended on them. But, just as the flame quivered its last sign of life, it began to rise from the dead, higher than she'd ever seen it. Blackness crawled into the edge of her vision and she saw distinct movements to the right of her.

Without turning her head, she looked through the veil of her hair and saw a moving shadow along the wall; while before her, the candle's flame, guided by an unknown something, began to bend itself, pointing directly at her then slowly changing its direction, pivoting to Claire's right. Moving with a slow caution, she heard herself whimper, once she understood what it was.

It was Lahash: Esperança's second voice, the angel that interfered with divine intervention, the voice that Esperança no longer heard.

It was a shadow so clear and so obvious that Claire could discern it from its demon hooves to the tips of its wings. It was a massive shadow, hovering over the entire room. Its wings were opening and closing, like a vampire bat selecting its prey from a herd of cattle. Its tail flickered from side to side, with the tension of an anxious cat waiting to pounce on its target. Claire did not fear the angel. She felt as if she knew it, was accustomed to its presence.

The beaded curtain made a soft clinking sound, and a light breeze swept through the room. The heaviness lifted, leaving nothing apart from a knowing feeling and, playing inside the glow of the calm flame, was the white feather. It danced in the still air above them.

So small—yet so significant.

The shadow was gone.

Claire looked over at Esperança and saw that she had exhausted herself, covered in blood, with bits of cream from the cake in her hair. She was now mumbling her words in a peacefully crazed tone, taken to a different place, in the recesses of her mind. Esperança was now ready to acknowledge the damage she'd done.

Claire sat perfectly still, her quivering fingers pressed into her belly as she witnessed the final surge of Esperança's insanity.

Esperança was completely removed, facing her maker and confessing her truth. She saw herself, that night by the river, sitting alone without her child. On bended knee, with her hand to her heart, she was watching the moon, looking for signs that her baby girl was home.

She began whispering, the words spilling effortlessly out. Claire listened intently from across the table.

"I'd seen the world over and over, centuries of it. And still, I'd never seen it the way I'd seen it when I was with her. I felt light, unburdened for the first time. Even as a child myself, there was a constant ringing in my mind, reminding me that my time to enjoy the world around me wasn't yet to be. There was work to do, things left undone. That my centuries of sacrifice would soon pay off. And the war between God and my new maker would soon run its course. That our rewards were close and in our reach."

Esperança blinked once, her stare lost again in the memories she'd folded and tucked neatly away, in a drawer left forever closed. Her voice became soft; her eyes gentle as if her ghost child once again snuggled into her lap and rested her head between her phantom breasts. "And yet here she was," Esperança said, looking down at the remains of her breasts. "A tiny life driven by nothing more than the need to feel my love, hear my words, my voice. She lived every minute of her five years, eleven months, sixteen days, seeing the world through my eyes, just as I had lived those years seeing it through hers."

Esperança lifted her head, only a hint of life left in her eyes. "I promised her the moon…and then she was gone."

Rivers spill mysteries into the ocean,

and the ocean washes the answer to the shore.

37

Blue Tit Bird

How could you!" Claire slammed her hands down hard. Esperança's head was hung low, and she was sobbing into her hands. "How dare you drag me into this shit and then fuck my head up this way. I'm leaving...in the morning, and you lay this shit on me now!"

Esperança pulled herself up, held the palm of her hand to her nose, and gathered what strength she had left. "I'm sorry," she finally replied, between deep, exhausted breaths, tears glistening down her wrinkled cheeks. "I was trying to keep you close...I thought I'd have more time with you."

"Time! What in hell's name is that supposed to mean? What are you saying...what kind of game have you been playing with my life?"

"Please, Claire, let me explain, give me that," Esperança begged. "You'll see that I've been trying to save you, no games, child. Please," Esperança held out a bloody hand, "as a friend, hear what I have to say."

Claire eased herself onto the chair and waited for an explanation. It was the only thing Claire could do, considering her quandary. By this time, Esperança's dark circles had intensified in contrast to her yellow skin and eyes. Sheathed in a film of sweat, she held herself up, slumped over the table. The blood and cream that dried over her cheeks and chin made her look even more ghastly. Claire pitied her, but not enough to concede.

"Before I met you," Esperança explained, the wheeze in her chest increasing, "the fallen angels had sent for you. You wanted a child to keep your husband. But what I never told you was that Satan had an interest in you long before. He was waiting, biding time, as your misplaced hatred of God was increasing."

"Misplaced!" Claire screamed.

"Misplaced. Please, child, let me finish," Esperança pleaded. Claire crossed her arms and waited.

"Do you remember when I told you about Filhote? How Satan chose her to be a vessel? How because of her beauty, and the fact that she was broken, he picked her to bring his chosen leader into the world, to crush Christianity?"

"Yes, and what of it?"

"He chose you, Claire. The child you plan to give your husband will simply be a host to bring evil into this world. Something unholy, something so wicked. A beautiful host, a baby girl, with a force so deadly and so depraved. With Filhote, it was Kamau; with you, I can't even imagine…the world on the cusp of the Armageddon. I was trying to save you, get you to see, because if I don't, Satan's Chosen have already found you. You've been chosen, child, chosen by Satan himself."

Claire was internalizing, but not afraid in the least. "And so what? Is that really so bad?" Claire felt empowered by this news. She was chosen, and for the first time, she was in complete control. Although, seeing Esperança's pain-stricken face ruined Claire's good disposition. Esperança shook her head in remorse, mumbling to herself. "What about Brazil, Esperança? The reservations I made. I leave…in the morning. What of that? Was all that a lie?"

"Free will, child, it was the condition," Esperança replied, in a voice akin to a whisper.

"What condition? Explain yourself!!"

"Feeding one fire to strengthen the other. I was given time in exchange for the magic, so I could keep you close, so that the others wouldn't interfere. The condition was that I give you the proper flight information in exchange for more time with you, to save you. But this is it, free will. If you take the journey, you will not only be given the gift of conception, but you will also get to keep the gift of your husband's love."

"And if I don't take the journey?" Claire countered.

"Then the control over your husband will fade. There won't be a pregnancy. At least not with you. You'll have to be honest with him, work at your marriage. Make sacrifices. But you'll save your soul," Esperança said. "And there is no greater gift than that."

Claire was silenced, not in any way undecided. "I made up my mind a long time ago. I've chosen Satan." The decision caused Esperança to weep. Her body quivered, her head hung low. "What?" Claire snapped. "You said yourself that I've been chosen. Do you understand what having that kind of power would mean? It's what I've dreamed about, it's a gift, and you expect me to take the latter? It's my soul!! I'm going, I made up my mind, and I'm sorry if this isn't the answer you wanted."

"You were my last redemption, and I failed you," Esperança said, with soft, half-stifled sobs. "I failed you, and I failed your mother."

"Don't bring my mother into this!" Claire snapped, anger rearing its ugly head. She no longer cared about her friendship with Esperança, nor did she care that Esperança was now trembling even more; her body still draped over the table, sweat dripping from her brow. "I made up my mind, I'm going. And now you want me to change my mind, walk away from the greatest power I've ever witnessed?"

"That's right, walk away; make your peace with God and save yourself." Esperança garbled the words in a voice that sounded as if someone had their hands wrapped around her throat. But Esperança forged on. "The soul is the most precious thing you can ever own. Money, vanity, a man…it means nothing, Claire. My gift to you is the truth, so that you can use what I tell you. I, of all people, know, because you and I are very much alike. Angry, hurt. But I get you. My God, do I get you. I understand how it feels to be alone, to feel forsaken by God. That anger you feel and the sorrow you swallow…you try so hard to keep down. And you grab on to that darkness, and that darkness grabs on to you." Esperança was pleading with her eyes. "But God has not forsaken you. You have forsaken yourself."

"You can't make me believe that. I can't. I won't."

Esperança said, "I went to church the other morning."

Claire let out a gasp.

"That's right…I walked right in, dropped to my knees, and prayed for God's forgiveness. I cried like a hopeless beggar. Cried for hours and hours. I stayed down on my knees until I lost all feeling in them. I implored God to have mercy on my wretched soul. I begged God to forgive me for the thousands of his most divine beings that I helped slaughter. For the wall of souls that I helped build, for the people, like you, who I used just so that I could be spared.

"I don't know how long I laid there on the church floor, but I do know that when this young priest came in and helped pick me up from off the floor, the sky outside was black." Esperança laughed blithely. "He asked if I wanted confession. Can you imagine?" she asked, shaking her head. "Confession…"

Her eyes were wide with horror. "If I let him hear what I had to confess, the demons might have found a way to hurt him. I couldn't let them do that. He seemed so kind, so young. Instead, I thanked him for his kindness and warmth. Then he insisted that I come back, that God's house would welcome my return, and he placed a quarter in my hand. Said I could light a candle, so I did." She smiled, with a look of peaceful madness, the wheeze in her chest deepening.

"Then I saw them, Claire. I did. Thousands of them. Angels, surrounded by lights so bright that I was blinded. I couldn't see, I couldn't hear, but I felt something like the hands of God removing the black stain that has shadowed my soul for hundreds of years, as if God had used a magnet and drawn out all the blackness from inside me. And I didn't care if I spent the rest of eternity in Nothingness again, because I would never again have to go back into hell. I'd never have to hurt another soul and subject them to Satan's wrath."

Esperança stopped and searched Claire's face for a response.

Claire's stern expression didn't waver. "You're sick, fevered. You probably needed a drink."

Esperança shook her head in absolute refusal. "It was God. I know it was God, because from that second when I felt the darkness leave me, the voices were gone too."

Claire was eyeing her skeptically. "On my shelf," Esperança said, "you'll see what the angels left behind...you'll see what they put in my hand."

Claire moved to the back of the wall and felt among the many candles, bottles, and other strange relics before touching what looked to be a single, white flower placed in a small vase. Claire pulled the flower out and studied it. It was not much bigger than a tulip and while holding the hard vine between two fingers, Claire felt as if the flower was alive, as if there was an electrical current running through her hand. And almost immediately, a faint glow illuminated through the golden center, the heart of the flower. It almost looked artificial, but it was real, a glorious example of the truth Esperança had spoken.

"It's a moonflower, exactly like the flower I named my child after. See how beautiful?" Esperança said, in the most reverent tone, while straightening up in her chair. Claire walked, holding the flower at a distance from herself, and passed it to Esperança's reaching hand. She was as radiant as a child who had a magnificent secret. She held onto the flower, cradled it, as if it were her baby. All the angels had spoken and delivered an answer. Esperança was heard.

Anger quelled the sorrow which had crept into Claire's heart, and she stood still, staring down at what she deemed an enemy. A simple white flower that meant so much; she had just witnessed a miracle. Claire was both rapt yet cautious; God's angels had made it past the fallen, past the enemy lines, and laid a single affirmation into the hands of a lost soul. God had heard her. But rather than concede to this miraculous gesture, Claire bent low and spoke just inches away from the old woman. "You can't hear my thought, can you?"

"No," Esperança answered, with a look of sheer joy. But as quickly as Esperança embraced her freedom, fear set in. Claire moved in on her, meaning to wound.

"You know I hate you. You're a drunken, selfish slob. You're a traitor, a weakling. You're ruining everything."

"I know the reason why you've been split in two," Esperança went on. "You're not angry with God, you're angry at you. That night of your mother's death, it wasn't your fault; she doesn't blame you. That paper you wrote about her, that—"

Claire covered her ears. "—Don't. Please don't make me say mean things to you."

"Life's tragedies change us, make us hard. Your mother's death stripped you of so much. You're just a little girl who never got over her mother's death, a little girl whose mother spoiled her too much—the same little girl who lit a candle for three days and waited for her mother to come home, then blamed God when she didn't. It's not God's fault, Claire. I told you, sometimes bad things just happen to good people. I don't know why, but they do."

Claire felt as if the room was splitting down the middle. "You don't get it." Her emotions caught between elation and despair. "I'm happy. I am actually happy. And I can sleep now. Do you have any idea what it's like to be woken up unable to breath? To have panic attacks, to feel out of control? *You* did this," Claire stood rooted, sifting through the last few months. "I owe it all to you," she said, nodding. "For helping me to see, for helping me find Satan."

"No child," Esperança said. "You've been finding that inner peace. You're healing. It's because you've been finding God."

Claire shook her head, rejecting the words, but the words covered her like an invisible net. Her response was almost muted. "No, it can't be."

But it was.

For a moment Claire simply stood there, breathing shallow and letting the silence run over her. She was trapped and had no choice but to accept the truth. It *was* God. A wave of uneasiness surged and Claire felt her stomach bottom out. She turned away from Esperança, her face partially hidden by shadows.

Claire's voice wavered with emotion. "Did you even like me, or is this about your redemption, your way of punishing me?"

"I more than like you," Esperança said. "A punishment would have been to give-up."

"You playing me again?"

"Playing?"

Claire's voice caught. "Whatever you do, don't press the big, red button. You tricked me. You used reverse psychology on me. You beat me at my own game."

Claire faced her again, combative and defensive; her green

eyes stripped of any warmth.

Esperança extended her hand toward her. "It's not a game. If you weren't savable, you never would have opened yourself up to God. I had no choice in the beginning. I didn't know how else to do it. I had to think like you, calculate like you. But only for a time. The rest was all you. There's hope. It's not too late for you. Can you —"

Claire bit back a scream, when Esperança fell from her chair and landed hard on her side. The chair made a loud crashing sound, and Claire dropped to her knees and hovered over her. "Oh, no." She got closer, grabbed a hold of her cold hand, and saw that there was blood saturating through Esperança's pajama top. It seemed to be coming from her chest, as if the old wound had reopened.

"Are you…" She leaned in. "Are you dying? Here? Right now?" Tears began to form in Claire's eyes, and her vision was blurring.

Esperança was composed, flat on her back. She reached up, and placed a hand over Claire's cheek. "Why do you do that, fight the tears?"

"Please don't go," Claire said. "I didn't mean what I said. You were right that day, anger is a cover-up for hurt. It's also a cover-up for guilt. I don't like hurting you."

They locked eyes, while a torrent of tears continued to fall on the sides of Esperança's cheeks. From outside the window, a trail of moonbeam washed over Esperança's sickly complexion. Claire soon smelled a foul odor and saw that Esperança was urinating. A small puddle collected around them. The old woman's eyes had a childlike expression, as if she had no grasp of how grave the situation was.

Sorrow rose, relentless as the scent of death that rose around them. And it was right then, in that exact, still, and unforeseen moment, that Claire realized that she loved Esperança. This drawn, decrepit woman covered in her own urine, this breastless tragedy. Claire loved her for the same reasons that she should have hated her. Because beneath the rum that excreted through her pours, her crudeness, and self-mutilation, was one of the most gentle though damaged souls she had ever known. Instead of deserting Esperança, she stayed on the dirty floor, moved even closer, and carefully placed the old woman's head on her lap. Claire could feel the heat coming off of Esperança, through the fabric of her pants.

"Why do you hold your tears back?" Esperança insisted on knowing. "Is it because you know that once you start, you won't be able to stop?" Her neck was still tilted upwards.

Claire forced herself not to look down at her dying friend. There was a constant pressure behind her eyes and inside of her throat. She mindlessly began stroking Esperança's hair, while staring straight ahead, keeping her eyes wide and fighting the tears. When she felt that the tears had dried out, she glimpsed down and whispered, "You're really dying."

A sad smile shaped Esperança's blood-cracked lips. "I've been dead a long time, dear-heart." The blood was now flowing through the cotton at a swifter pace.

"You can't go, not yet…tell me what to do…there has to be something that can be done," Claire pleaded. "There ha—"

Claire had to swallow the sudden wash of nausea, when a foreboding feeling overcame her followed by a warm prickle on the back of her neck. It was a breath, a voice, close to her own although akin to something nonhuman, said, "She has the stones, the stones for her life."

"Stones," Claire proclaimed. There was hope after-all. "You have stones."

Esperança's eyes awakened. "I do, twelve stones that God once gave to Lucifer, his appointed cherub no longer. The very stones that God's divine used to save my life. She lost her life by The River of Tears, trying to save mine."

"The Stones of Fire? The stones God gave Christopher, you actually have them!" Claire whispered. Her own hands were trembling now, knowing their deep significance. "Oh, Esperança, they'll kill you for them. Surrender them, I'm begging you, as a mercy for your life."

"I don't want Satan's mercy. I never asked for it," Esperança said through her raspy breathing. She remained perfectly calm, though keeping a turned-up eye on Claire.

"Do you remember that day…when I told you about Filhote and Christopher and how we all have a light inside of us?" She raised her eyebrows with a hopeful expression. "Do you remember, Claire, when you asked me if you had that light inside?"

"Yes, but what does that have to do with the stones?"

"You have that light," Esperança said, staring right through her. "I can see it."

The breathless catch in Esperança's voice made it difficult for Claire to remain focused. "No, you're wasting time. I need you to pay attention and listen to me. How did you get the stones? When and who gave them to you? Tell me."

"The day that I first met you, I saw both…But I see it now, your light is stronger, that part of you that makes you so beautiful." Esperança swallowed. "Wouldn't you like that…to see her again? Your mother, because you can, you—" Pain struck Esperança, causing her to moan in agony. She turned to the side and began vomiting and coughing something up. The strain in her throat sounded excruciating. Claire was drowning, unable to think clearly.

When her heaving had stopped, Claire gently rested Esperança's head in the crook of her left arm. "It's okay, I've got you, I'm not going anywhere." While cradling her, Claire's gaze skittered around the candlelit room: the chair she sat in, the wobbly stripped table where they shared laughs and ate pizza together. The dirty room, where Claire had smoked her first joint, drank her first real drink…made her first real friend. She looked down into Esperança's sweat-covered face, and searched for the right words, but her heart spoke in place of her brain. "I more than like you, too," Claire whispered. "I guess we're a lot alike after-all. Like when Christopher found Filhote. An angel in stone, he called her. But isn't that us too? Angels in stone, both hardened, both hurting?" She swept a strand of hair out of Esperança's eyes so that she could look into them. "I owe you my story. Would you like that? But I need you to listen, to stay with me…okay?"

Claire took a hold of Esperança's cold hand. It was difficult; the hardest thing she ever had to do, next to burying her mother.

"Blue tit bird," the forbidden words spilled out of Claire's mouth so suddenly. To her relief, a light flickered in Esperança's eyes, her lips parted, and her neck was turned up even more. "That's right, so pay attention, because you won't get me to do this ever again. That said," Claire inhaled deeply through her nose and pulled her chin up, "where do I begin? Maybe the beginning, or maybe I should just...Oh, what can I say," Claire said. "I killed my mom. I killed her; I'm the reason she's dead."

Claire's voice turned wispy with her recollection. "On the night my mother crashed her car, she had a meeting with my eighth-grade teacher. My teacher had called her in about a thesis I'd written. The topic was about human development, addictions. And while the other kids wrote about smoking and other unhealthy habitual traits, my paper was titled, 'My Mother, The Brain of a Blue Tit Bird.'" Claire looked off into the corner of the room, unable to look down, ashamed. "They're little chickadees, a pretty blue and yellow. In hindsight, I should have used my father's sex addiction as a topic; but sex and a class of thirteen-year-olds—in comparison to the latter," Claire admitted, "seemed like the wiser choice. Oh, I got my A plus and used my mother's addiction as an analogy...I compared my mother's loyalty to my father as a mimicking behavior, a wife who had no goals, no life of her own, and lived for a man. I wrote that she was mimicking the other wives, addicted to love; and at her own expense, she became a drunk who needed a drink in order to continue mimicking this behavior."

Esperança gave Claire's hand a faint squeeze. "It was so cruel." She began stroking Esperança's hair with her other hand. "So incredibly cruel. I remembered reading about these chickadees one summer; Grandma Preston always kept these thick encyclopedia type books around." Claire's tone became gentle and engaging, as if she was telling her a bedtime story. "In Southampton, England, in the nineteen twenties, they used to deliver milk in bottles, and they'd leave it outside on the doorsteps. The cream would collect at the top of the bottle," Claire explained, looking down. Esperança blinked a few times, she was listening, her eyes alert, although her lips had now turned a light purple.

"And these blue tits, these chickadees, created the idea to poke holes in the soft cardboard tops, with their beaks and suck out the cream. This went on for years, and it wasn't that the birds were intelligent, you see; they were simply mimicking one another. But the sad thing is, in doing so, some poor blue tits ended up drowning in the bottom of the bottle...just like my mom," Claire said. "In trying to get the cream out of her life, and in her need to mimic these stupid and brainless housewives, to keep her family together, she ended up drowning at the bottom of her own bottle—a sixty-ounce bottle of vodka, which she most likely picked up on her way home from my school. They found her car three days later, my paper covered in her blood. I found it with my father's things. Belongings that were recovered in the car. "

Esperança coughed something up, wanting to speak, but couldn't. However, her weary eyes spoke for her. *Don't be stupid, she was saying. You were just a girl; you couldn't have known.* Claire also read the sympathy in them; the understanding that only a true friend would have. Claire's only friend.

"Three days, my mom survived with my paper to read. Three days. To think that my mother died never knowing how much I loved her, needed her. She was my world, and I killed her," Claire confessed. "Because of me, her face was destroyed. A closed casket. I never even got to kiss her goodbye. How I wished I had that chance." Claire blinked hard at the memory.

"And poor Rebecca. My baby sister grew-up without our mother. Has no memory of her. I think it was post-traumatic. After my mother died, my father sold our house, the same house that Rebecca was born in. And after we moved, Rebecca stopped crying. Completely forgot her." Claire stared off, her gaze fell on the rum bottle still placed a few feet away on the floor.

"As for me, I think a part me drowned in that bottle with her…and now you." Claire was now looking down into Esperança's eyes. "What am I going to do without you?" she pleaded, unable to forfeit her true feelings toward her, unable to tell her that she loved her. Esperança continued to stare up, her mouth was opening and closing, like a fish struggling for air. "You got the last laugh, didn't you? Because you finally broke me."

In the circle of Claire's arm Esperança was dying with dignity for what she believed in, and was gracefully accepting her fate. Claire was in awe of her. She used her thumb and gently swept away the bits of cream that had dried above Esperança's brow. "Lua's cake." Claire caught the appreciation in Esperança's longing eyes, for she knew how much Esperança loved hearing her child's name. A few feet over, the moonflower lay inches away from the stream of urine. Claire stretched her arm out, picked it up, and positioned it over Esperança's heart. It gave off a dim, bluish light, illuminating her chin. "I'm so sorry about Lua. Don't hate yourself. You would have died and she would have been left alone. You were very brave, sparing her from the Chosen, and my mother would've done the same. She would never have allowed me or Rebecca to die at the hands of a stranger. Not like that. You lied to spare her, so that she would go along with her own execution. You're a good mother."

Claire thought about Lua, and the vision of the moonflowers, lighting the land of darkness. *She held eleven moonflowers in her hand, on the night of her execution,* she thought. Thinking about the child set something off in her; a fusion of emotions swept over her, in defeating waves. A sob ripped its way up, throbbing, full, stealing her breath, and draining Claire, to the point where she almost caved.

She battled her inner turmoil and uttered, "Although you had to have known the risk you were taking…even an animal knows to kill its weak young as soon as it's born." Tears welled up in Esperança's eyes and ran down her cheeks. Claire reached over and tenderly wiped them with the back of her hand. "I can't help but wonder if this idea of me going to Brazil is the wrong choice to make. But then again, I get this nagging feeling that there's more, and I'm not talking about keeping my husband. I mean that part of me which died in the bottle with my mom…maybe it's alive somewhere else, fragments of my essence, which Satan is nursing. Maybe, but I have to know for myself. I need to find me, find the pieces of my own puzzle, just like you had to with the moonflowers." Claire felt the light tremor coming from Esperança. She was weeping again only this time her tears had tapered.

Pure regret continued to consume Claire as she thought of her mother and now Esperança, who fell ever so still, dying in her arms. Again, she had to open her eyes wide to keep from giving into the sensation to cry. Once she regained her self-control, she looked down into Esperança's yearning gaze. "You want to know why I hold my tears in?" Claire said, in a stronger voice. "It's because I choose to. Just like I'll choose to be evil, knowing

I'm evil. I choose power over pain, control over tears. And yes, Esperança, I hold my tears in, because if I start, I'll never stop. Because once I do, it means I yield, and I choose not to."

A low, gurgling sound rose in Esperança's throat. "Don't," Esperança begged, her voice muted by phlegm. Instantly, she detached, fell limp and heavy, her eyes rolled back in her head, and she began convulsing as though a low-level seizure had overcome her. Claire's voice came out in a wail. She screamed for Patience; Esperança's head was still on Claire's lap. It was as if someone else was screaming the word help. Claire screamed it over and over again. The sound of her own shrieking voice terrified her.

Esperança's body vibrated in a convulsive tremor, her feet kicking up, knocking over the bottle of rum, its contents spreading around them. The fumes and stench of bodily excrements were overwhelming, but Claire was unwavering in her concern for Esperança.

Patience burst through the curtain and fell to her knees. "Oh, Grandma, no!" She wept, cupping Esperança's face in her hands. Esperança was still shaking, her eyes still rolling in the back of her head.

"Make it stop!" Claire screamed. "Make it right!" Patience continued to hover over her grandmother, with her arms stretched out, as if she was stopping whatever it was. Claire felt an electrical static, which sparked the hairs on the back of her neck, followed by a soothing weightlessness. There was a soft breeze, and the air became clean, like after a fresh rain. Esperança became still again. Her eyes were wide and startled. Claire affectionately removed a strand of hair that was caught between Esperança's lips.

Patience looked up through her tears. "She's dying, Claire. Please, let her go in peace."

Claire looked down at Esperança's stony, blank expression for a while and waited, hoping she'd snap back. But she was gone…as if in a coma. Claire nodded and shifted back, before placing an unrushed kiss on Esperança's hot forehead. She leaned into the curve of her neck and whispered, "Good-bye, friend," and then carefully placed her head onto the floor.

There was nothing left to discuss.

As Claire began to amble away, Esperança regained consciousness, only to be struck by an invisible blow, as if serpents' fangs had been plunged deep into her. She screamed, squirming in excruciating pain. Patience placed her body over Esperança's like a protective shield hovered over her until she lost awareness again. There was a reprieve, and all was still, apart from the beaded curtain, which swayed back and forth, clinking in the gentle breeze. Claire swallowed the swelling knob in her throat before reaching for her purse, by Esperança's table. She looked back at Esperança for one last time, her eyes locked with Patience's.

It was a jolt when it happened, like a shiver that cut right through Claire's spine. It was a frisson that caused her knees to almost bend.

A light shone through those rich brown eyes, an indescribable grace transfigured her entire being. What Claire was seeing, was that Patience was no longer Patience. She was dark haired being, with a gentle beauty, surrounded by a bluish glow.

God's Chosen.

Claire stood there, her eyes still locked with hers. How did this unsuited union between Satan's Chosen and God's Chosen come to be? Claire remembered Patience's words from a week before, 'God has a plan, and he has a purpose for why I'm here.' *Was this God's plan?* Claire thought. *To create a monster, that only Esperança would love?*

That's it. Claire shuddered at the revelation. She was standing in the presence of God's divine. She pulled her gaze away, and spotted Esperança's box of wooden matches, alongside the lit candle. Whatever possessed her to take them was unclear, but as she made her way toward the exit, Patience's words made her pause.

"Is this what you *choose* to worship?"

Claire said nothing.

"May God grant you mercy, Claire."

"I never asked for mercy," Claire said, slipping Esperança's matches into her coat pocket. She placed a trembling hand on the doorknob and turned it.

Claire spoke without turning around. "Don't let her suffer any more than she has to."

She opened the door and closed it behind her.

The Stones of Fire

There were few moments worth remembering, Esperança believed, but this was something she would savor for those dark days ahead. It was a calm evening on the shores of Salvador, Brazil. The waves came in at peaceful intervals, lacking in their usual power.

She shared in that sentiment, while watching the waves as they neared the shore. A comforting sequence she'd grown familiar with. The ocean had many moods, but tonight, the ocean was at rest, taking slow, easy breaths. Each wave rose, crested, and then dissolved. A thin veil of white water swept across the sand just inches from her toes.

Carrying a large smooth stone in her hands, Esperança made her way back up a small hill and walked toward the direction of her lighthouse. It was always intimidating, standing in the shadow of this great, white structure. There was a small crack along the side between the fourth and fifth window which somehow had never spread. Inside that space, she'd hidden a few keepsakes wrapped in plastic. *So many things to hide*, she thought. *So many things to bury.* It was such a paradox: that this same lighthouse and shore, that had brought her the most happiness, could also bring her the most sadness.

A short set of stone stairs led Esperança down into the lower level of the structure. It was a good place to bury such things;

the dirt floor was easy enough to dig, but dry enough to never uncover her secrets.

"Avó, olhar," her granddaughter said, seeing Esperança coming down. Her chubby-cheeked granddaughter was beaming in her pink, ruffled bathing suit and covered in dirt.

She had a small, red shovel clutched in her right hand and pointed to the hole she'd made.

"Avó, olhar," Patience insisted, with a gleam in her brown eyes.

"Grandma, look," Esperança said, teaching her granddaughter the English translation.

Patience's warm brown eyes were serious. Patience crossed her legs and sat thoughtfully, while her tiny lips formed around the strange words. "Gamma, wook," she finally said.

She reached over and gently dusted the grit off of Patience's cheek. "Grandma," Esperança corrected. "But you will learn, dear heart. America is very different, but it is also very much the same. You will learn," she explained, placing the stone down with a grunt and sitting across from her. Esperança learned the most valuable lessons centuries ago. The English language was just one of them. It was the language of change, her people had said. Yet it made no difference what language Esperança spoke, for the devil knew them all.

Esperança pulled a small, brown leather satchel over her head, placed it into Patience's reaching hands, and waited.

The child blinked once, and the glimmer in her eyes dissolved instantly. Following a long moment of reflection, Patience looked up with an almost frightened yet reverent expression. "Grandma, look," Patience said, holding the full pouch up between two palms.

"Yes, I see," Esperança said. It was fascinating how serious Patience had become. She couldn't possibly understand what was inside.

"Grandma, look," Patience said again.

"Drop it in, dear one," Esperança instructed, flicking away the dark strand of hair that tickled her nose.

"Está bem," Patience replied. *Okay,* Esperança thought, wanting to teach her the English translation, but the moment was stolen. She was too fascinated by her granddaughter's little hand as she set the bag inside and looked up, waiting for her Avó to tell her what to do.

"You cover it with dirt now," Esperança instructed in Portuguese. Patience's small eyebrows knitted together in confusion.

"They belonged to God's divine. She saved my life with them. Her name was Asmodel." Esperança wiped her eyes with the back of her hand. *My payment in tears*, she thought.

Patience nodded and began pushing the dirt into the hole. Esperança spit out bits of sand and watched her granddaughter. The child was methodical, packing the dirt, pressing her weight down with her palms. Esperança reached behind for the gray stone and placed it over the filled hole.

"Souls weighed down in stone may be carried by the winds beneath an angel's wings," Esperança whispered. But the man who'd said those words never did specify if it were God's angels or the Fallen ones that could lift those burdens.

The sound of feet clanking down the metal lighthouse stairs pulled Esperança from her enthrallment. She left Patience alone, using her shovel to add sand around the stone, and joined Oliver by their rock along the shore. It was a perfect place to say good-bye to her only friend. He waited, sitting comfortably, holding two small glasses, with a bottle of cachaça placed between his thighs. Oliver's best was saved for days like this.

As Esperança neared him, she could see he was tormented. She and Patience were leaving for the United States the following morning, and he was struggling. As she approached him, it was as if she were seeing him for the first time, knowing it would be her last. He'd aged some over the last decade. The once unruly black locks were still dark but had thinned out. *A sequence of parallels*, Esperança thought, watching the defeated waves as they thinned upon the shore, the veil of foam disappearing across the sand. And as he gazed across the ocean, Oliver's eyes reflected back the same color of kind blue. He regarded her with a smile while watching the ocean in deep thought.

Esperança liked staring into those kind blue eyes, and she had come to learn that there were many ways to describe the eyes in comparison to an ocean. There was the quiet blue, the eyes of the unpredictable, the quiet before a storm. There was a cold blue, for the unforgiving. And a mysterious blue, for those eyes she couldn't read. *Truths dropped to the bottoms of the oceans,* someone had once said.

Before Oliver had come into her life, the only blue she'd ever loved was peacock blue.

"I know," Oliver said, putting a brotherly arm around her, sensing her sorrow. In his right hand, he teased her with the small glass. "A drink to harden the soul?"

Esperança took the glass from his hand and held on to it. "In awhile." She knocked her head to his.

"I like you like this," Oliver said, referring to her openness. She was normally not one to get too close, and she would have squirmed away at anyone's touch.

"I always like you." Esperança turned her head away. Oliver and Esperança's relationship had never gone further than what it was. In Rio, she was the voodoo woman, who loved a strong drink. In Salvador da Bahia, she still loved a good drink; however, here, she was the lighthouse owner and Oliver its keeper. They had their rock, their drink, two glasses, and an ocean view.

The silence was treasured beneath the rays of the setting sun. Patience finally emerged from inside of the lighthouse and toddled over the rocks and onto the sands. She eased herself down, her chubby legs stretched out as waves gently washed over them. Her chin was turned up, as her warm, brown eyes took on a wondrous expression.

"She's been doing that for a while now," Esperança explained. "I can't imagine what she's thinking."

Oliver cracked open the bottle and taking a whiff. "You can't read her soul?" He'd always wanted to know more about her gift to read and when he asked her, she made it clear that it was a curse rather than a blessing.

"For some reason I can't." Esperança wondered if it had anything to do with the fact that Patience was born to one of her infertile clients, a child born through evil. The mother was horrified when the doctor placed her newborn babe in her arms. A monster, they called her. A child even her own mother couldn't love. The mother wanted Esperança to kill her, but Esperança could never, ever bring herself to do that.

Now, Patience was her sunshine. And Lua, forever her moon.

Oliver's eyes softened even more. "You were good to love her...at least she'll have you."

He meant it. Despite Esperança's childlike frame and pretty face, there was no one stronger or more intimidating. Patience was in good hands.

"Until she understands what I am," she said, holding out her glass, "and then she may resent me for it." Oliver poured, filling her glass to the rim. The golden liquid made her mouth water; its fumes filled her nostrils. Esperança held the glass steady in her hand.

"One day you'll be giving Patience the keys to the lighthouse, and she'll sit in that very spot and hopefully have at least one good thought about me," Esperança said, still staring into her glass. It was not a premonition, but a wish.

Oliver smiled. "I have no doubt that she will."

"You're the only person that I trust with this lighthouse," she said, still staring down into the glass. That much was true, and it made no sense to leave the lighthouse empty when she had no option but to leave. "I only hope that the United States shelves a good drink, or I'll have to return."

Oliver laughed at this. He'd never met a woman who could drink him under the table and still hold herself together. *I could drink you over and under*, she'd say.

"Here's to you," Esperança said, holding out her glass.

"And to you," Oliver said, clinking his glass to hers before swallowing. Oliver refilled her glass and then his. After some consideration, Oliver spoke. "Tell me, do you see a woman in my future? Someone to fill in the loneliness maybe?"

Esperança let out a boisterous laugh. "Yes, my friend...and she'll wash up along this shore naked as the day she came into this world, with breasts the size of jackfruits, and you still won't get it up."

Oliver laughed at this, but his laughter dissolved into a sad smile. Her crudity would be missed.

After some time, Esperança turned to him and said, "What would you say is more evil, a soul that knows he's evil, or one that doesn't?" Oliver's thick brows furrowed in thought.

He wasn't the brightest man, but he was the most honest she'd ever known.

"A soul that knows," Oliver replied. Normally he'd have taken a drink, but this puzzle sidetracked him.

"You would say that. I don't wrong you, because one would have to know evil to understand it. The answer to my question is: a soul that doesn't know he's evil. You see, a person who has the sense to question his evil, understands that his actions are wrong. A soul that has no understanding how evil it is, will never question his actions. He will fight with more vigor against his enemies, believing what he feels is true."

Oliver was quiet, mentally reiterating Esperança's answer. It made no sense to him. She touched her glass to his, slung back the drink, and held out her glass for another fill. Oliver slugged back his own before topping up their glasses again. "It'll be a good night," he said, looking at the bottle of rum, "but a bad morning."

She let out a laugh. "Not for me, I'll be on the wings of a seven forty-seven, enjoying the bar." Perhaps those were the wings that would lift the stone off of her soul, she thought. The drink was setting in, and it relaxed her enough to consider idle thoughts.

"Can you image the world, years from now? I've had premonitions, too many to count. I saw more babes being raised as terrorists, forming armies to destroy the innocent," she explained. "Little boys, not much older than Patience, holding guns to the heads of men and women and children alike."

"Evil, not knowing it's evil," Oliver added, understanding the answer to her riddle. "That's a frightening thought."

Oliver's face reddened, and it wasn't because of the rum or the setting sun. Esperança swallowed hard and looked over to her right, where Patience was still captivated by the sunset.

"I saw a blood-demon entering into the veins of humans. A demon transferred through sex and needles. It'll be known in the eighties, this virus, a killer of humans. More cancers, more terror. So much terror. Bombs and bloodshed; buildings blowing up, people trapped inside. People terrorizing their own countries. I see giant waters, destroying cities, flooding streets and killing people; thousands of birds falling from clear skies; millions of fish washing up dead along shores. I see so much lately," she whispered.

Oliver was silenced by the horror, still nursing his drink.

"The evil is swallowed by the fires of hell then spit back out like embers of fire. Those embers settle around the unsuspecting like a poison. And it just keeps going. In and out, in and out. The heart of evil, pumping its poison." She paused, and shook her head with regret.

Oliver cleared his throat and found his voice. "Will you be safe, where you're going?"

Esperança nodded with a smile. "No safer than I am here. My people want to spread out, broaden Satan's word." She paused, squinting her eyes against the backdrop and spotted a ship in the far distance. At one point in history, a vessel would have docked, transporting captured humans from Africa. A lighthouse would have guided those ships safely into the harbors, only to guide tortured slaves to their own dooms.

"You and I have a great deal in common, my friend," Esperança explained. "Because as you'll spend your years guiding ships and souls into the harbors, I, too, will do the same. And though some souls counting on us will be both good and bad, you'll do it regardless."

"Whoever loves his brother lives in the light, and there is nothing in him to make him stumble," Oliver said, reciting the words etched above the lighthouse door.

"As I said, both good and bad," Esperança said, holding up her drink. "Some souls are savable, while others—useable."

Oliver touched his glass to hers and said, "And we'll wear our armor to do so."

Esperança turned around to spit before facing Oliver. "Here's to fighting demons with demons."

And they both drank to that.

39

Angel in Stone

When Esperança came to, she was resting on her bed, covered in a heavy quilt. Just a few inches away from her pillow, the moonflower was carefully placed, the white petals spotted with her own blood. She opened her eyes but her vision was blurred. Feeling around, she found Patience kneeling by her side in prayer, her arms crisscrossed over her chest. Esperança gently grazed her hand and touched her granddaughter's cheek.

Patience lifted her head. "Grandma."

"I dreamed of you. You were just a little girl, and you were wearing your pink bathing suit."

Patience slid over to the bed and sat on the edge, taking hold of her grandmother's cold hand.

"You loved that shore," Esperança whispered.

"I did...because you loved it."

"Always my sunshine...the light in my darkness. You were..." Pain ripped through Esperança's chest, forcing her to take several short breaths until the throbbing eased. "It's happening so fast this time, she said, opening her eyes, blinking against the light and distorted shadows. "Everything's so blurry."

Patience gave her hand a gentle squeeze. "Just listen to the sound of my voice. I'll be right here."

"Claire...I tried to stop her, I tried everything I could."

"I know, Grandma, but we came close."

Esperança nodded and gave her hand a slight tug. "Come close, child…there's no time. I need you to hear me." Patience leaned in and Esperança positioned her hands on either side of her granddaughter's face, then placed a trembling kiss on Patience's forehead. "Did I love you enough?" Esperança blinked hard at the blurry vision before her.

Patience let out a sigh of despair. "Yes, Grandma, you loved me enough."

"And even after everything I've done," Esperança pled, "Will you think kindly of me when I'm gone?"

"I will always think kindly of you, despite everything that you've done." Patience bent over and slowly kissed each of the dying woman's eyes. She hovered just inches away from Esperança's face and waited. "Try opening your eyes now. You'll be able to see."

Esperança's eyes fluttered open and focused intently on Patience, who was smiling sorrowfully through her tears. The old woman placed a hand beneath her granddaughter's chin. "Don't ever think that you're not beautiful."

"I won't, Grandma," Patience promised.

Esperança blinked back her tears. "My sweet girl, I will miss you." She removed her hand from under Patience's chin and used her fingers lovingly to arrange the thin strands of her hair over the severe balding areas. Esperança paused, tucking a limp curl behind Patience's ear. "When you were a little girl, you used to let me put ribbons in your hair."

Patience managed a weak laugh. "I wanted them all over… to hide my bald spots."

Their eyes met, and Esperança said simply, "A beautiful light like yours should never have to hide. You…" As she spoke, awareness dawned in Esperança, and, miraculously, she saw her granddaughter clearly for the first time. "You're God's most divine being. I've always known it, but I was scared they'd come and take you away." She cupped Patience's face with both hands and stared. "But I do know you, don't I?" Esperança looked intently into her eyes. "From a long time ago."

Patience brushed her tears with her fingers. "I'll take your payment in tears."

Esperança dropped her hands. "It's really you."

"Of course it's me."

Esperança was mesmerized. "I see you."

"And I see you," Patience answered in her kindest tone. "And it's very beautiful."

"I had no idea it was you. Dear God, how could I have not known…Of course, it all makes sense now. I have something of yours, the lighthouse—"

"—Don't," Patience said. "I know exactly where they are. I used my red bucket and shovel. I remember it well."

Esperança's eyes combed the room, before she spoke again. Her voice was low, her tone guarded. "You will use the stones to summon God's angels. The Valley of Souls…do you remember how to find it?"

Patience nodded. "The map…you asked me to teach you braille. I know exactly where it hides. I'll summon the help of God's army to destroy it."

Relief washed over Esperança. "I didn't know how else to show you. But you understood."

Patience swallowed hard. "I always understood. God understood."

Esperança's lips drew back in what started as a tired smile but turned into a grimace of pain. Shudders, more aggressive and prolonged this time, swept through Esperança and her lips were deep purple, from lack of oxygen. Fevered and slipping in and out of awareness, she summoned every ounce of strength within to ask Patience the one question that had been eating away at her for decades. She grabbed a hold of Patience's hand and begged, before it was too late.

"Did she make it? My little girl, did she make it home?"

Patience looked down and nodded. "Yes, Grandma, Lua made it."

Esperança let go of Patience's hand, then settled back onto her deathbed. She opened her mouth to speak, but stammered in search of the right words. "D-does she. Lua…"

Patience rested a soothing hand over Esperança's cheek and gave her a hopeful nod.

Equipped, she uttered in a childlike voice, "Does Lua forgive me? Please…tell me she forgives me."

Patience continued staring down at the woman who loved her unconditionally. Muted by grief, all Patience could offer was a simple nod. *Yes.*

The old woman surrendered into defeated sobs. "Please tell me, I know you know. Why me? Of all the souls, why did she fight so hard for me to give her life?"

Patience leaned in and placed a slow kiss on her grandmother's forehead. Tears filled Patience's eyes and spilled down her cheeks. She remained that way for several heartbeats, her lips pressed against Esperança's skin, already grieving the loss of her.

Somewhere, Patience found her voice. She whispered into Esperança's yearning ear. "My angel in stone, may your soul be free."

In her delirium, Esperança blinked several times, wondering whether she'd heard correctly. "My beloved Christopher?" she whispered, shaking her head. "But ...How? Why me?"

Patience cupped Esperança's chin, tilted her face up until their gazes met. "Oh, Grandma...why do you even have to ask?" And with tearful smile Patience added, "It's because you were worth saving."

40

The Winds Beneath the Wings of an Angel

At around 6:30 in the morning, Esperança was given her final surge of energy. The angels of God had come to collect her soul and guide her into the next transition. She had suffered into the night, her organs failing at a rapid speed, and once the toxic shock set in, she fell into a partial coma. Before the final surge of strength, Esperança's eyes were cloudy when she regained her senses. Her breathing a labor and her lungs congested, but her final rush was sufficient for her to speak her last words.

"Patience?" Esperança called.

"I'm right here, Grandma." She'd been holding her hand, though Esperança had no feeling left in her limbs.

"I had another dream. But this one was of Lua...I saw her, Christopher's tree. Our tree." Esperança caught her breath, her lips puffed out on her exhale.

Patience forced a smile. "Sounds beautiful, Grandma."

"You will spread my ashes along the shores of Salvador. The lighthouse, it's yours. Our special place," Esperança said.

"Okay."

"Promise me, child...promise that you'll finish what I start-ed," Esperança begged. "And the child that Claire will bring into this world, you will destroy it."

"I am God's Chosen. To watch over the meek and to protect God's grain. That is what I do, Grandma, and I will finish this," Patience vowed.

This is what Patience was chosen for, yet she hadn't been prepared for how painful losing her grandmother would be. This woman loved her when her own birth mother had wanted her dead. Esperança had been there for all of her milestones, wiped her tears when children were cruel and threw rocks at her for looking the way she did. Esperança believed in her, told her she was beautiful, sat proudly and sober in the audience for Patience's school plays, then later at her graduations. Suddenly, Patience felt very alone and couldn't let her go.

Patience felt the wings of the angels, like a gentle breeze on the back of her neck. "It's time to go home, Grandma."

"Home," Esperança repeated. "My soul's free." She closed her eyes, slipping closer to death. "I can hear them, see them," Esperança said in a gentle whisper, her lips barely moving. "Like wind chimes in a field of sunshine. I hear them, child. It's so beautiful."

Patience held both of Esperança's hands as Esperança took two deep breaths. Her hands fell limp in Patience's own, and her soul moved on to her other life. The angels hovered over them, in a shielding light.

"Let her go, Asmodel," the angels said to Patience. "She's free."

Patience pleaded. "Please, not yet. I need to see this. I need to remember this."

For so long, Esperança had lived in darkness, born the daughter of a tiger, a slave who died in childbirth. *Filhote* (puppy), a name given to a baby girl seen as nothing more than an animal; a cub raised by other tigers who wore the lines of human excrement on their skin and human depravity that stained their lives. Esperança was the slave, caught between two brothers.

One left her for dead; the other saved her life, and almost her soul, and renamed her Esperança, meaning 'hope.'

Esperança was the beloved wife to Christopher, and mother to Kamau and Fé. She was raped and hung in her and Christopher's favorite kapok tree. And in her final minutes of living, she hatefully renounced God from her heart. She had lost her faith and ended up lost between worlds.

Her son, Kamau, the leader of Satan's Chosen, ordered the fallen angels to pull her from her oblivion, and she was reborn, only to live a life to serve Satan. In her ninth life, Esperança had given birth to a divine being of God, whom she named Lua da Flor, but it had been Fé's soul all along.

By the grace of God and his angels, Fé had returned to save her mother. But it only ended in sorrow. The golden-haired child, named after the glowing flowers, was later killed by Esperança's own hands. But the angels were not ready to give up, and Patience was sent to save her soul and set matters right, not only for Esperança, but also for the divine beings of God that were slaughtered in the ruins of Mato Grosso. Esperança was worth the battle, but it was far from over. There was still much to do.

Patience's spirit was caught between heaven and earth, the thin sheath that billowed in the gentle winds of harmony. It was magnificent. She saw Esperança, the woman she called Grandma, moving into the heavens, her soul unburdened, being carried on the winds of the angel's wings. For Esperança, her heaven was a field of moonflowers, her kapok tree, waves washing to a shore, and moonlight guiding her into the safe harbors in the holy lands. Heaven was her golden child, running through the pastures of white, glowing petals, running into her mother's arms.

"Lua," Patience whispered. "I see her…I see them." She laughed in pure and absolute joy as tears fell over her cheeks. "Take care of my grandma."

Lua and Esperança curled into one another in a glorious light, a peaceful, long-awaited sunrise and a glowing moon, with just the two of them. Patience remained inside of the spiritual realm until she could see them no more.

"Good-bye, Grandma." Patience let go of her hand, kissed her on the cheek and covered her with a several sheets. Outside, the sunrays hit the bedroom window; it was a new day. She thought of her grandmother's wishes, for there were a few.

The first was Claire.

Her last redemption had failed, and Claire was still lost in the darkness, destined to bring a child of darkness into the world. But Patience was enduring and loyal to the end.

She walked outside, without a coat. The morning chill eased by the warmth of the rising sun. Amid the pollution, the acrid smells that escaped from the sewers and encircled her, Patience turned her uplifted face to the dawn. It was a comfort, a gesture from the goodness above, which brought her strength to combat the ongoing war between good and evil.

The sunrays covered her broken spirit as a blanket would cover a cold child. Each beam that touched her skin was the hands of angels bringing her the tonic for the pain that had wounded her spirit.

Her mind fell into a calm state, and Claire crept into her psyche. Claire was watching a sunrise and thinking of Patience at that exact moment. Claire was hurting, missing Esperança and wondering if she'd survived the night.

In Patience's mind's eye, she soon saw a clear vision of Claire. Her green eyes looked tired and red-rimmed, her hair swept up and her hand pressed against a cool window. She was in awe of the sunset, but felt especially alone. Patience saw through Claire's eyes, and the image that Claire was seeing at that very moment was the light of the same dawn: flickers of pink and red, skimming over an endless blanket of swelling clouds. In the breaks of mist, golden shafts of light ran upwards, illuminating the continuous vision. And while Patience was looking up at the sunrise, Claire was looking down. She closed the blind and settled into her seat.

First Class, nothing but the best, and, as was her custom, Claire always took the window.

Turn a few pages for a preview of

Ashes in Stone,

the sequel to Angels in Stone.

Available Spring 2013

Blood from Stone
The third installment
of the Stone Series.

Release date: to be announced

Brazil Eastern Area

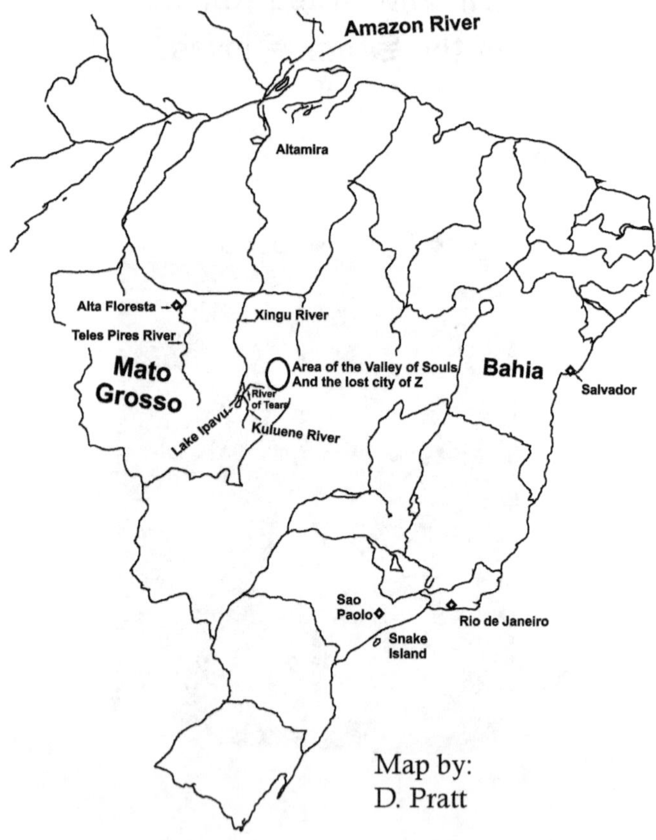

Map by:
D. Pratt

Ashes In Stone

BY

TANJA KOBASIC

Ashes in Stone

Prologue

Tudo could hear the bone crushers whispering while they sifted through the cooled shards. Bone crushers knew the law—No speaking in the presence of the soul's bones. Even Tudo never dishonored the law, although he was only a mute by choice.

The man sacrificed the night before was fat, with a lazy heart. His love of God had cost him his life. He was a sweaty man with a soft neck, who had strayed from his group. Tudo had watched him from the trees as he came into the Devil's Web in search of food and water. The fat man came from across the big waters, they said, with others like him, in search of tribes, to teach them God's word. That was when Lucifer's Chosen had found him eating gifts from their trees, this fat man with large bones that the bone crushers were now setting on top of the pounding stone.

Tudo moved from the top branch and slid down, ever so careful, to get a closer look. He considered himself as quick as a snake and as light as a bird. He wrapped his long legs around the strong branches of the tree and hung upside down; his long black hair caught in the thinner branches. Combining the strands with his fingers, he wrapped them into a knot before gently cracking off a thin twig to pull through the hair to keep it in place.

The bone crushers dishonored the law again when they smiled and showed their teeth—There was to be no pleasure in the presence of the soul's bones. Still, Tudo enjoyed watching them from where he was. He could see the tops of their heads and the way the sun made the younger bone crusher's golden hairs, those that covered his beating heart, shine like the wings of the flying dragons. He liked the way his neck pulsed, the way it flicked beneath his white skin pushing the blood into his heart. The younger bone crusher was healthy, his blood clean. Tudo was hungry, and the fat man's heart was too lazy, too fatty and hard to enjoy. The older bone crusher disciplined the younger one. He pointed into the fire pit and pulled out small pieces the other man had missed: the bones that ran up and along the fat man's back, the stairs that led to the fat man's head, the head held up by the fat man's neck. Around the fat man's neck had hung a silver chain and a medal that the bone crushers had not noticed. It was caught between two stones.

Tudo watched for a long while as the bone crushers worked away, pounding the fat man's bones into powder. The bone crushers were sweating, their water dripping onto Lucifer's gift. The older bone crusher picked up the watering pot and walked over to the third river, washed his sweaty face, and drank from cupped palms before filling the container. He walked with a limp, his back bent, and he had short and furry legs that reminded Tudo of the sloths that fell from the trees, unable to walk straight. He returned, and they were whispering again. Tudo watched as the bones were scraped into the mixing pot where the older bone crusher added sand to the fat man's bones. The younger man added the water from the third river, a little at a time, using the rod carved from the black trees to mix the bones into a wet, stone compound.

The older crusher added the fat man's teeth. Good teeth, Tudo saw, strong and white. Teeth that chewed the many meals that made the fat man's heart sad. Tudo could not understand why a man with a single pounding heart could be so unthinking as to eat even when his body didn't ask for it. Why would someone destroy such a gift? Tudo studied the bone crushers and saw that the last teeth were added into the mixture. Tudo knew what would follow: they would pour the wet, stone compound into the mold that would then be left in the sun to dry. Once the compound had hardened, it would be laid along the Wall of Souls by the stone setters, an honor given only to Lucifer's Chosen. A testament to the king, the Chosen said.

They thought they were done but they weren't finished.

Leaving the fat man's silver chain caught between two rocks was another law broken—Never leave a soul's possessions un-buried in The Valley of Souls, or he could remain earthbound. The bone crushers had begun filling the stone mold when Tudo decided to show himself. He pulled himself up and gripped the upper branch with his hands before sliding his way down the tree. He moved deliberately, as quick as a snake, as light as a bird, and then hit the ground with one swift motion. The bone crushers stood unmoving, just like the lizards that mimicked the dead in order to escape death. Tudo would spare them he de-cided. Tudo knew that the bone crushers understood that all he needed to do was to see into their eyes, and they would become immobile enough that he could rip their hearts out. He sensed their fear but Tudo would honor the law. He was promised the heart of God's divine, as well as those loyal to God, if he agreed to not eat the hearts of those living in The Valley of Souls.

Tudo stood before them in his nakedness. His hair came loose and fell across his breasts. Tudo knew he looked like a woman; they called Tudo beautiful, with eyes as striking as the glass stones that they chipped from the mines and hair as black as the stone coal that birthed those glass stones. Tudo kept his hair long only to hide his breasts for he hated the feel of cloth against his skin. Tudo also knew that his breasts aided him in his hunt for prey—men that ate fruit in the devil's web.

The younger bone crusher's sky-colored eyes were exploring, looking at his breasts. Men liked the roundness of his breasts but Tudo hated them and wished they were flat, with hairs that grew over the tops and shone in the sun like the wings of the flying dragons. He also wished that behind his breast he had a single heart. Tudo's blood pumped through several small hearts so that he could live longer should one fail. He never under-stood why Lucifer made him this way, with many hearts and the body parts of both the male and the female. The Chosen had named him Tudo for that reason. They said that he was the only one of his kind, both female and male, both mother and father. Everything. The Chosen should have named him Only.

The younger bone crusher's eyes and stance said that he enjoyed the sight of his breasts, but the crusher never once looked down. Tudo once again wished for a mate. Perhaps Lucifer would make him a wife.

Tudo walked to the fire pit and pulled out the silver chain that belonged to the fat man with the lazy heart that he couldn't eat. He held the fat man's possession between two fingers and walked toward the bone crushers. They stood still, afraid, but Tudo knew the law—No eating the hearts of those living in The Valley of Souls. Tudo dropped the silver chain—with the imprinted image now blackened—into the wet, stone compound and turned away.

He scaled the black tree until he was high enough to be hidden but low enough watch. Tudo wondered, if he was good and obeyed the laws, would Lucifer take away his breasts, and the woman's gift between his legs that hid behind the man's gift, and make him just a man. He also wondered how many hearts he would have to consume before his seven hearts could make one.

The bone crushers moved again and stirred the rest of the wet, stone compound into the mold. Tudo gazed across the land to where he could see the wall of souls shining in the sun's waves. So many souls, Tudo thought. So many testaments to the king. The king who gave him everything.

It was wrong of Tudo to wish for more, when there was a battle to win, and a Wall of Souls to build; the wall which ran for miles and stood twelve feet high. These souls had paid with their lives, enemies of the Chosen.

It was then that Tudo thought of the most vital law of all— Those who walk the earth as enemies shall be removed from the earth in smoke.

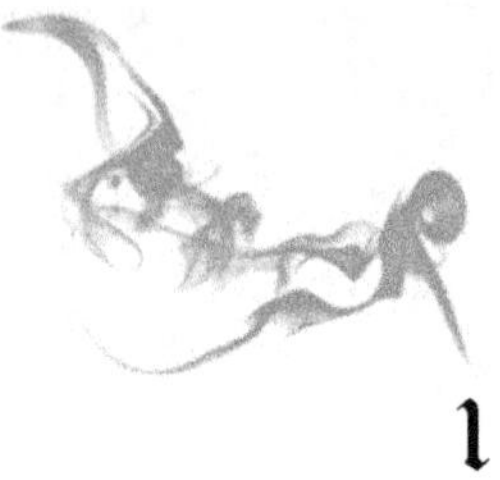

1

It's Just Wood

Somewhere between the coast of Sao Paulo, Brazil, and Queimada Grande, known as Snake Island, the preacher's daughter had taken her last breath. Pastor Byron Lansing, seated in the center of the small motorboat, held his daughter in his arms. When her trembling stopped, he gently shook her, waiting for a sign of life, but nothing came. It was then that he knew with certainty that his last-born child had died.

Miles ahead was an endless spill of blue with a cloudless sky and an ocean that ran a seamless line where land and water fused as one. In that absolute moment, Lansing felt as if he'd been swallowed alive, lost in an abyss of blue despair.

Summer Rain Lansing was just twenty-one summers old, born on the hottest day of July. Following her birth, it had rained for eight days straight. The loyal parishioners of Jefferson Parish in Louisiana called her a gift since her birth had miraculously ended an abnormal six-week drought. The desiccated crops were replenished as a result of the torrential downpour, and the local farmers' prayers had been answered. But those were the days when signs of God and righteousness were one and the same, when light was good and darkness was bad, when earth was heaven for those without faith.

But that had been years earlier. Now, when lightning struck

Lansing for the fourth time and in the exact same place, his faith had turned to ash, fragments like drifts of cinder dissolving into air.

Squinting against the bright sun, he looked at Lucifer's Chosen, seated at the front of the craft, guiding the boat's direction. The man, Valerian, was faceless, merely a silhouette through glaring sun and the tears that had welled over. Valerian pointed ahead to the tiny island, no bigger than a smudge, which bled through the blue pallet of water and sky. An island where miracles took place, where the soil would bring Lansing's dead child back to life, as Valerian had promised.

Stealing himself against the pain, Lansing found his courage and glanced down at his dead child. Summer's eyes were closed, concealing her chaste blue eyes, and her mouth was open, as if she tried to say something in her final moments. Whatever words Summer may have uttered were lost to the sound of the running motorboat pushing through crashing waters. Lansing felt a sob rising in his chest, rising up like the tides that rose from the ocean's own heart. He felt detached from the morbid nature of what he was about to do, as if he were plunging over a precipice and taking his baby with him.

His tears streaked sideways across his cheeks, forced by the same mighty winds that slapped him back into the present. He carefully pulled Summer's yellow silk scarf down, knowing she would have hated for anyone to see how bald she was, her blond tresses long ago destroyed by the chemo. Even her pretty, pale lashes were gone. He kissed the top of her head and looked across the ocean in search of some sense to this madness. Was her soul swallowed by the merciless waters? Or was it dancing over the blue stage, waiting to return? He lovingly covered her long, bruised legs with her hospital blanket, wanting to protect her skin from the smoldering sun. She would dance again, he convinced himself, remembering her healthy.

Summer had a natural grace but when he saw her dance the lead role of Princess Odette in Swan Lake, he was unprepared. As far as Lansing was concerned, ballet was a joke, people skipping in their tights and floating around in their step ins. But seeing Summer on that stage, was like watching an angel dancing on the head of a pin. He was so in awe with her love for ballet, with her utter giving of self for the dance, that Summer's magnetism brought tears to his eyes. His wife Ellen cried softly to his right, and his eldest daughter, Naomi, squeezed his hand to his left, while their boy, Jonah, stayed close to the stage, recording Summer's performance. She was happiest on that stage, so energetic, with a smile that always touched her eyes. Those were the days when God and righteousness were one and the same; when light was good and darkness bad, when earth was heaven for those without faith. Those were the days when lightning hadn't yet struck and Summer had danced the lead in Swan Lake.

Against the ocean backdrop, Lansing held his dead daughter a little tighter, keeping her close to his chest, sharing with her his beating heart, still fighting her battle. Summer felt lithe in his arms, so tranquil and departed.

A swan without feathers.

Lansing was a man whose faith in God was the keystone of his existence. In that keystone were four generations of preachers along with their families, devoted men and women who'd laid the bricks to that foundation. Byron Lansing was the fourth preacher, and his wife and three children were the last of the laid bricks. However, on that day when he'd had to tell his baby that it was over, that she had to accept God's will, something he'd never seen before emerged through Summer's chaste blue eyes, something very close to what he was now seeing in the emerging distance, a dark smudge rising through the blue. Snake Island.

Did Summer know something, while lying on her deathbed. A man with one foot in the grave has a spiritual advantage, over one who doesn't. A kind of physic knowing.

Lansing shifted the weight in his arms and looked down at her. "Did you know something?" His words slipped from his lips and fell to the bottom of the ocean. There was no one left to hear him.

But Summer did know something. He saw it in her eyes that day. Weeks before, she had pulled her own stone from their faith foundation, and the structure that had held together for four generations had collapsed.

Cancer had spread into Summer's marrow and blood; the

transplantation of bone marrow had failed. Summer had lain still, surrounded by fragrant flowers, stuffed animals and cards of encouragement. The private hospital room was filled with lifelong friends and family. He'd asked everyone to leave, needing a moment with his child. Once alone, he cupped Summer's hand and searched for words that did not come. She was heartbroken. She was Princess Odette, falling off a cliff. But there was something else, something he'd never seen before, something he'd never forget.

That dark smudge

"It's just wood daddy," Summer said, when Lansing had strung a wooden cross around her neck. She was feverish, drugged up and speaking gibberish.

"No," Lansing insisted. "It's Olive wood. This cross was made from an olive tree, the same tree that was chopped down in Bethlehem. Brother Favreau wanted you to have it." He carefully placed it over her hospital gown.

"It's just wood. It can't do anything," Summer said again, looking up at Lansing. He saw it then; those blue eyes that were once as clear as rainwater were tainted.

She was a sickly gray and perspiration dotted her forehead and upper lip. Seeing her so close to death set something of in Lansing. He couldn't do it anymore, pretend that things would get better. He sobbed into his hands until he felt her cold fingers touching his face, prying his hands apart. "Do you remember the story of Swan Lake?" Summer said in a gravelly voice. "Do you, daddy?"

Lansing nodded *yes,* his voice muted by anguish.

"Do you remember how the evil sorcerer, Von Rothbart, turned the other girls into swans, and the same lake was formed by the tears of the weeping parents?"

"Yes, I remember the story," Lancing replied. Where was she going with this? But somewhere in her state of madness, there was reason; like picking sense out of nonsense.

One foot in the grave.

"What if God is like the evil Von Rothbart? And what if black is white and white is black? What if light is really darkness and darkness is really light?"

"What are you saying, child?" Lansing took her tiny hands

and warmed them into his own.

"I'm saying; what if just like Princess Odette had to jump off of a cliff, and come back to life, I have to too? Remember, when we did missionary work in Brazil…remember that island we heard of, where the soil is a miracle. The soil that cures the sick?"

"Those were just natives talking. They're legends. They're not true," Lansing said.

"Find it, daddy. Or you'll be adding more tears in that pond," she added, turning her face away, speaking in a tone so removed that it brought him shivers followed by a cold sweat. He'd made peace with three other deaths and now, in this fragile moment, he couldn't bring Summer the comfort or the peace she needed to ease her into the next life. Summer Rain Lansing had lost her faith and he, a lifetime man of God, shared in that sentiment.

His wife, the mother to his three children, had died of an aneurysm in while he was preaching his sermon. Two years later, Jonah and Naomi were driving home following a football game. Jonah lost control of the car after the front wheel came loose, and the car overturned, killing both children on impact. Summer Rain was all he had left.

In the quiet hospital room, where he fought both his grief and Summer's disillusionment, Summer's eyes were closed, and a single tear fell across her cheekbone, where her last blond lash quivered. Lansing carefully reached over and captured the lash between his two fingers, not willing to drop it. God help him, he had his reason, yet he hadn't made his mind up until just then, until the sign had shown itself, a tiny pale sign that he wrapped in a tissue.

Now, far from that sorrowful room where the only future was death, a cool mist touched his cheeks and he lifted his head and narrowed in on the nearing island, a vision of vibrant green that declared life. This was where miracles happened, from dust to flesh, molting and rebirth. Valerian steered the boat until they were only yards away from the island, where they were to transfer onto a smaller vessel. Rocks surrounded the island, and rowing was the only way in. There were others coming to get them, Valerian explained. All they could do was wait.

Valerian was a strong black man, tall and strapping. The first time Lansing set eyes on him, in a red-lit room, he'd thought Valerian looked tougher than a two-dollar steak.

"I can't say that I've ever eaten a two-dollar steak," Valerian had said, reading Lansing's thoughts without giving him a second glance. The voodoo priest remained seated, keeping a cool disposition. "I won't be needing her eyelash, shepherd," Valerian said in a deep alto voice, "contrary to what you thought."

Lansing had taken a reluctant seat across from him, clutching the tissue containing Summer's eyelash. But the voodoo priest had been preoccupied. He simply returned to the task before him, gorging on sugar cookies dipped in steaming milk flavored with honey that he continuously stirred in. He ate slowly, dunking one at a time, enjoying every bite.

Valerian was known in New Orleans as a voodoo priest who worked out of a small shop along Bourbon Street in the famous French Quarter alongside dozens of voodoo priests and priestesses, shamans, psychics, palm readers and mediums as well as countless little shops where tourists flooded in with curiosity. Inside the red-lit rooms was an excess of masks, rattles, dolls, candles, bracelets, offerings, statues, books, beads, tarot cards, jewelry, oils, and incense. One could cast a love spell simply by using a certain oil or rid himself of a curse by laying the hair of a monkey over a running river. But despite all the hoopla and knickknacks, Lansing quickly discovered these people who called themselves healers and such were as useless as buttons on a dishrag.

But inside Valerian's little shop there was simply a wooden table, a single lit candle, and a small television blaring the local college football game, a welcome distraction for Lansing. They watched in silence, cheering for the same team. It was a weird thing, sitting in that small room, watching a game with a man who had a close connection with Satan. This man was a preacher's mortal enemy, a snake in human skin. Lansing studied the voodoo priest up close, under the lit candle. The man's hair was shaved low at the sides, and the center was corn-rowed into a thick braid that ran down the back of his neck. He paid Lansing no mind as he sipped his milk between fleshy, dark lips.

It's fixin' to come up a bad cloud, Lansing thought. Because behind the candle's flame was a man whose eyes were as black as ink oil, with a smile that was suspiciously warm and as unsettling as the gathering clouds before a hurricane. Valerian picked up his remote, shut off the game, then addressed him.

"Look, shepherd, I know what you came here for, and I think it best if we get on to what needs to be done," he advised. "Because from the looks of things, your little girl has but a few days left."

He spoke in a heavy accent, words served with a thick tongue, a mixture of Cajun and something Lansing couldn't quite put his finger on. In search of a reply, he blurted out, "You worship the devil, son." He stood up, pushed the tissue containing Summer's lash into his jeans, and proceeded to the door.

"You're as nervous as a long-tailed cat in room full of rocking chairs," Valerian said.

Lansing stopped. He wouldn't be made fun of by a servant of Satan.

"Have a seat, because I have a story for you," Valerian said with a composed urgency. "A story that ends with a question that will be your answer. You want your child to live, to dance again. That right?"

"You have something on your mind?" Lansing said, with a backwards glance.

"I got your mind in mine. And I know what you want."

Lansing made his way back and settled into the chair. "Speak your peace, then, if you think you have an answer for me."

Valerian leaned back with his arms folded and smiled. A tiny crumb hung on his lower lip, a distraction that was amplified due to Lansing's nervousness. The voodoo priest ran his tongue over his mouth and lapped up the morsel.

"A shepherd and two pastures, two flocks of sheep and two dogs, one dog for each pasture," he said with an alluring tone to his voice, a confidence that both roused and troubled Lansing.

"One pasture is a vision of green, rolling hills, a river of clean water, sun and trees providing just the right amount of shade. And in this pasture is a dog, a quiet dog, with a beautiful coat, seeing eyes, and the power to allow his sheep to enjoy the gifts of the pasture while he protects them from harm. The shepherd stands on the border that divides these two pastures.

"In the other pasture are hills as well, although these hills are rolling, with rocks and jagged cliffs, patches of burned grass, thinning rivers and dying trees. There is either too much shade or not enough. And in this dying pasture we have another dog, loudly barking, steering his hungry, hoping sheep over the dying hills. They cannot see what is promised, but they continue on, having faith in this barking dog. 'Suffer these hills, and behind them is an abundance of green, rivers of crystal water. Follow me over these hills, suffer in your trust in me, and you shall be rewarded.' "

Valerian narrowed his eyes, and dear God, Lansing saw regret in those cold, black eyes. The voodoo priest shook his head in pity.

"And so the shepherd guides his flock into the hungry hills. And all the while, this dog keeps barking, loud and proud, and the sheep follow. They walk over the narrow roads and hills. They starve, drink the thin rivers filled with poison, and they suffer, holding on to the hope of one day frolicking in green pastures, listening to the dog that barks the loudest, led by the shepherd who guides them."

There was a thick silence, Lansing stunned to his marrow.

"My question, shepherd, is, which is the guilty dog, the one that stays quiet or the one that barks the loudest?"

The guilty dog barks the loudest, Lansing thought.

The voodoo priest reached toward his cup, took a long drink, set it down carefully, and then continued with his consumption of sugar cookies.

The guilty dark barked the loudest, the guilty dog being the liar. God being the liar was the implication. Lansing stood with a wobble, wanting nothing more than to leave the forsaken room with its milk-drinking demon. When his hand reached for the doorknob, Valerian spoke up.

"She has two days, shepherd. She drank the poisoned water that you lead her to drink. You had it backwards, shepherd. Backwards . . . "

That night, Lansing sat alone at the empty dinner table. Five place settings and only one remained in use. He felt incredibly lost. The table that once overflowed with laughter, discussions, good food and card games on Sunday nights was nothing more than a barren wasteland. Along the kitchen walls that had been painted, repainted and papered with yellow buttercups was a chalkboard with a smiley face that Summer had doodled. Pictures of the Lansing family, held with magnets, covered the entire fridge. Memorabilia of what had been spread into the dark halls and into the empty bedrooms, where everything remained as it was, as if one day he'd awaken form this nightmare.

The phone rang . . .

With the receiver still clutched in his trembling hands, long after the hospital had advised him to make preparations and long after Summer's nurse had hung up, he couldn't bring himself to move. He felt as if he stood on the edge of two valleys, a man divided by grief. Summer had only days to live.

God, the guilty dog barks the loudest.

Two pastures, two dogs. Divided and torn between two choices. In the dreamlike moment, he hung up the phone and stared down into a plate of untouched shepherd's pie which the Widow Duffield had dropped off. Grease oozed around the potatoes. He picked out a single corn kernel and ate it. Shepherd's pie, God. He pushed the plate away and felt a strange sensation, an awareness that raised the tiny hairs on the back of his neck, a sign that both terrified and numbed him.

A shepherd leading God's flock into an abyss of lies; the guilty dog barks the loudest. He was unable to pull himself to his feet. Instead he was drawn to minuscule, insignificant details at the table—the hundreds of carved, ivy-twined leaves that etched the edge of the cherry wood, he and Jonah had polished the wood until it looked almost black. He fingered a few of the leaves, holding back, hanging on the moment. Lansing feared every event that would follow once he rose from where he sat. He needed a sign, any sign from God, that would eradicate the seed that Valerian had planted in his head. He rose from the table and stepped outside to face the warm night.

The moon hung over the cottonwoods, its beams washing the white fluff in a soft blue hue. He stood on the long wooden porch that wrapped around his white brick home. He began to walk with slow, measured steps, eyes and ears alert.

Dear God, give me a sign; tell me what to do.

Along the wall were casseroles and other dishes left by his parishioners, Southern Baptists leaving signs of kindness at his door. Loyal servants of God that he'd led into the starving hills to drink the poisoned water.

He came to the back of his house, where a small creek trickled along, and continued through the grounds and past his church. He stood waiting, searching, but nothing came, just the constant hum of the nocturnal creatures. Tree frogs trilled in the hills, and a loon called in the distance The horned owl's deep call filled the sultry and fragrant air, air swept by the recent rain. Rain had washed over the floorboards of his porch, leaving drops of water hanging off the petals and leaves of the climbing jasmine. How beautiful . . .

But as wonder filled his heart, so did rage. He had no right to enjoy the world without them, yet he refused to yield to a life of loneliness. He called out into the darkness, screaming, "Dear God in heaven, a sign, I beg you. Give me a sign! Give me a sign, something, anything!"

But nothing. Until . . .

In the distance, an unnatural yet human sound dominated, a painful cry, a low moan coming from the shadows. Lansing walked through the spacious garden, stepping over the flowers that had sprung through the cracks of the walkway, and stopped before their oak tree. A single swing, made of board and rope, swayed in the night breeze, and sitting on the low arched branch above the seat was a large white bird with red reflective eyes. Lansing edged closer. A white raven? If so, it was the only white raven he'd ever seen, It opened its beak and let out a hurting cry, a low shriek that built up to a frightening moan. He was stunned. Was this the cry of angels? He was staring at the base of the old oak covered in a blanket of Spanish moss when utter fear swept over him, causing him to buckle at the knees.

A sign.

A dog-strangling vine, the dangerous weed that was known to kill and destroy trees and plants, had made its way into the Lansing garden. Like a serpentine predator, the lethal vines had crept in, killing their rose bushes and his wife's prized magnolias. The strangling vines had wrapped around their oak tree, trying to choke the very life from it. Lansing's rage became his driving force. He tore at the vines with his bare hands, weeping through his act of wrath, the vines cutting into his hands. He yanked and pulled, ripped and forced the killer vine until he exhausted himself, lying in the dirt, heaving in uncontrolled sobs. He had led his family to drink the poison, and all that remained was his baby girl.

Two days, shepherd.

The next morning Lansing pulled out the many tubes that ran into his dying daughter's arms and legs, and carried her away to a last-minute, two-way trip into Sao Paulo, Brazil, escorted by the milk-drinking demon.

And now Summer was dead. And he faced a crossroads.

Lansing opened eyes that had been closed to their approach; they'd arrived.

Valerian cut the engine and moved without saying a word, dropping the anchor into the ocean. Lansing squinted against the brightness of the sun and stared ahead at the intimidating island he knew to be overrun by dangerous golden lancehead snakes. Cool drips of sweat trickling down his back.

"How long?" he asked. Summer's bowels had loosened, and he felt the wetness through her pajamas. The hot sun was unbearable, and the smell of salt rose around them as the sweltering sun licked the ocean`s surface. He spied a few silvery fish swimming inches beneath the water.

"We wait," Valerian said, unfazed by Summer's death.

But why would he be bothered? Lansing asked himself. He was a reader of souls; he had known this would happen.

Valerian reached down, and pulled out two bottle of waters, passing Lansing one before slaking his own thirst. "Here they come," Valerian said, jerking his chin in the direction of a canoe.

Two men, both dark skinned, rowed toward them. Lansing felt faint, holding his dead child, not knowing what would follow once they reached land. The oarsmen pulled alongside the motorboat and waited. Valerian rose from his sitting position. The boat jerked sideways as he boarded the smaller craft.

"Pass her to me," Valerian demanded with his arms outstretched.

"You'll drop her," Lansing spoke his fear.

"You can hardly manage yourself…quick, give her to me."

The oarsmen steadied the boats, while Lansing cautiously transferred his daughter into the arms of the voodoo priest, before boarding himself with his small knapsack hung across his back.

There was complete silence, as the oarsmen faced the bow of the small vessel; they rowed in unison, reaching forward, the steady swish of the hull cutting through the waters, and then leaning back, toward the vessel's stern. They were lean and disciplined, wearing nothing save for loincloths. From behind, Lansing could see every muscle being worked and the thin sheen of perspiration glistening over their very black, hairless bodies. They paddled toward a narrow inlet and stopped along a sharp and jagged rock formation.

They all exited the boat and hiked up along a thin strip of land leading up the to the rock face.

"Stay close," Valerian called. "This is the worst of it, the most slippery." He carefully placed Summer into the reaching and capable hands of an oarsman before tackling the climb up without a hitch.

Slicker than snot on a doorknob, Lansing thought, his legs sliding over the stone's surface before making contact with Valerian's outstretched hand. He pulled him up in one swift gesture.

The sun was low, casting a glow that dappled over the panoramic scene. At first glance, the island looked no more forbidding than any other piece of land, with its high and low vegetation, rocky protrusion, and scattered puddles that filled the deeper recesses. Lansing spotted a single gray bird, which took a quick drink before disappearing into the foliage. This putrid land was a far cry from what he'd pictured an island to be, and the acrid smells reminded him of the swamps in Louisiana. He couldn't imagine how the soils would rebirth his baby girl. He immediately searched for her and saw that the oarsman had placed her into Valerian's arms. A few feet away he spied the only hint of civilization shooting up amid the shrubbery: a weathered wooden sign with faded words that Valerian translated: the Brazilian navy prohibited anyone from landing on the island.

That they were defying the government didn't sit well with Lansing, but watching Summer being carried by a seven-foot giant was even more disturbing. The rational man in him felt the urge to turn around and go back home and give Summer a proper burial. But the desperate man in him had nothing left to lose.

The oarsmen disappeared through the shrubbery, leaving Lansing and Valerian on their own. They journeyed along the rocky formation that led up to a thin pathway. From behind, Lansing noted that Valerian's thin white undershirt was sweat soaked and drips of sweat ran down his thick legs. Lansing tore off his sweat shirt and tied it around his waist before they penetrated deeper, through a thicket of strangely twisted trees. Birds burst through the branches overhead, twittering and fluttering against the golden sky. The scene felt like a dream. Like an unsettling illusion.

Hungry, exhausted, and almost delirious, he turned his gaze to Summer. How pitiful this was, her limp body being dragged around. She looked as if she were sleeping, peacefully sleeping, in Valerian's arms. But that too was illusion.

When he spotted her newly painted pink toes, tears swam in his eyes, and he reacted by wiping at them with the back of his hand. *Her socks—when did her socks fall off?*

When Summer was a baby, she'd had a habit of kicking off her socks, a habit that continued on into her adulthood. He walked alongside Valerian and glanced down at her. His breath caught and he tripped when he saw her wan skin against the depth of color in Valerian's. Summer looked dead, lifeless, as if she'd been dipped in wax. Lansing was weeping shamelessly now, loud sobs that made his nose run. He stopped hiking, and on bended knees he wept into his hands, exhausted by the insanity. He sobbed for his wife, he sobbed for Jonah and for Naomi who died in a car crash, alone, without his comfort, because of a loose wheel he'd forgotten to check. He sobbed for the faith he'd lost, for a God who'd forsaken him, who now took the only thing he had left, his baby girl with her little pink toes and no socks, her lifeless body carried by Lucifer's Chosen.

Taking several deep exhausting breaths, Lansing pulled himself up to come face to face with Valerian.

Whether the voodoo priest had read his mind or not, it brought Lansing a kind of unexpected comfort when Valerian gave him a look of understanding, his deep, black eyes soft. Valerian waited as Lansing covered Summer's toes and pulled the blanket over her emaciated chest where her pajamas had slipped and readjusted the wooden cross, which Brother Favreau had given her. It was an awkward moment, because Valerian exuded a compassion Lansing hadn't expected from Satan's own. Valerian shared a sad smile through his catlike lashes and kept his head down when Lansing kissed Summer's hard cheek. She'd been a private person, and humility was always her strength. Somehow the voodoo priest understood.

"It's not too late, shepherd," Valerian stated. "She's ready to fight her last battle."

Lansing's shoulders rose and fell in vague accord. "I'm still fighting for her, I won't give up."

A muscle in Valerian's jaw twitched, and he nudged his chin to the darkening foliage up ahead.

And so they were moving again. With a new resolve, they journeyed through a dense pathway where the rotting stench became stronger since the shade preserved the rot. A thin trickle of moving water marked a muddy trail as they trudged in silence. The odors, along with the heat that rose off of the stream-bed, caused Lansing's head to spin; when the trees became sparse and the air less humid, he went to lean against a tree.

"I wouldn't suggest leaning against any trees," Valerian said. "The snakes might think you a bird and attack."

"I haven't seen any serpents," Lansing said, so consumed over Summer's death that nothing else had mattered. But now armed with vigilance after Valerian's warning, he looked around. He saw something move in the trees, a flash of yellow. But just a quick hint. "There's something . . ." And then he did see. Quite clearly. "Sweet Jesus! They're everywhere!" Golden, scaly snakes hovering from almost every tree, shrub and root. Some looked two yards long. They hung from branches and emerged through the leaves, heads alert, parting the way, like Moses did the Red Sea.

"They're welcoming you," Valerian said, stepping without fear while in the undergrowth the serpents slithered alongside.

How could Lansing not have seen them? Long swards of grass shifted with each step they took, and before them at least a hundred golden snakes lead the way, guiding them along, while behind them other serpents slithered over their footprints, covering them as if they'd never been there.

"It's their island," Valerian explained. "They protect Lucifer's sacred grounds, that and the original tribe members from Benin who led Lucifer's Chosen into safety in the late sixteen hundreds."

"Benin?" Lansing repeated. "Benin, West Africa?" When Valerian didn't deny it, Lansing felt terror gripping him into submission. As a pastor and a missionary, he had traveled deep into the dangerous areas of Africa. Benin was in West Africa, bounded on the east by Nigeria and Burkina Faso, and on the west by Togo. It was no secret that voodoo and devil worship were rampant there. And now, here on Snake Island, Lansing was alone with those who practiced both.

"These were the original ancestors, those who aided my father in the late sixteen hundreds," Valerian explained. "You do remember the story I told you, about our history, how Lucifer's Chosen came to be?"

"Stories tend to change after a few hundred years," Lansing murmured. "I was hoping it was a myth."

As they moved deeper into the thickets, the oppressing heat became unbearable. A familiar sound assaulted Lansing—the sound of tribal cries, distant, but growing louder with each step. Lansing remembered Valerian's story, told on the long plane ride to Brazil.

Two brothers had set sail from Portugal to build a sugar plantation. One, Christopher, was ultimately chosen by God to save the Africans who'd been forced into slavery by arming them with Christianity. The other brother, Manuel, was chosen by Satan to crush Christianity when he brought a child into the world, Kamau, which the Africans said, meant Silent Warrior, who was Lucifer's Chosen.

Following the slaughter of Christopher's trained Christian foot soldiers, the golden lancehead snakes lead Kamau and twenty-two slaves to freedom on tiny Snake Island. Valerian explained that the small tribe's population always remained at twenty-two and that the tribe would sacrifice members following the birth of a new member, as a gift to the serpent God in exchange for the freedom of the island.

"My father, Lucifer's Chosen, remained on this island for less than two years. He then relocated to Mato Grosso, where he built his family. Seventeen children, chosen by Lucifer. I was his sixth-born son," Valerian had explained.

"And just how many lives have you lived?" Lansing had asked, tripping over a mess of corkscrew branches, but caught his fall just in time.

"Twelve." Valerian looked at Lansing from the corner of his eye. "I'm a warrior shepherd, just like you. I'll fight to the death for what I believe. And your little girl here, she'll have to fight her way back, just as me and my chosen brothers and sisters had to fight our way back into flesh."

"Have you seen it?" Lansing begged for assurance. "Summer's outcome? Will she win the battle for her body?"

Valerian stopped walking and spoke without turning around. "Her soul is strong, shepherd, stronger than most because she's been battling since long before her death. She's trained and ready."

"You haven't answered my question," Lansing said. "At home, you said her body would be restored, healthy, and that she stood a good chance." He circled Valerian and met his eyes.

"I told you she would have to battle another soul for her body," Valerian reminded him, "that there has to be a balance, a life for a life. I also said that I saw her alive and dancing again. But that could mean many things. There are twenty two tribesmen here on this island waiting for us. In a snake pit is a boy of seventeen, who just died under the venom of seven snakes. His soul will battle your daughter's for her body as a way to return; that is the only condition which allows them to leave the island. A warrior in camouflage. If he wins the battle, he'll keep Summer's body and return to the Valley of Souls, in Mato Grosso, where he'll learn our ways. This is a battle, shepherd, and the stronger soul will win. I done told you that, I explained it all the night you returned to me."

Lansing understood that Summer's soul could stray, in the after world, but realizing that another soul could wear his child's body made him sick.

"I don't want my daughter's body worn as some prize, like a string of Mardi Gras beads. I can't have some savage wearing her like a pelt." He laid a hand over her cheek. "Please, tell me something, anything, because I got nothing left."

The brief silence was infiltrated by the loud screams that carried through the bush. Above them, the sun was falling into the ocean. Night was approaching and Lansing was never more terrified.

Valerian gave Lansing a searching look, then said in a kind tone, "I won't lie to you. Most souls give up the battle, some become lost, wander off in a different sphere. But your child is still here. I done told you that."

The urgency in Valerian's eyes, made Lansing believe him, but there was still the chance that Summer could lose the battle for her own body, and worse yet, her soul would be lost. Yet the thought of witnessing Summer's body rising from the dead without Summer's soul left Lansing no choice. "If she doesn't win, I want you to promise me that you'll kill me. I cannot leave her alone, lost like that, wandering. Promise me." Lansing grasped Valerian's shoulder. "I need you to kill me, so she's not alone."

Valerian looked straight ahead without answering, "The battle awaits us."

In a natural clearing, surrounded with bird bones and slithering snakes, danced the original members of the tribe from Benin. They formed a circle, black-skinned men, women, a few children, and even a newborn babe that suckled on its mother's teat. They were dressed in snake skins, pieced together with stripped wood and worn as coverings, that barely concealed their breasts and groins, and around each neck a serpent's jaw. Some wore only one while the older tribesman had many.

Their dance didn't disturb Lansing because he'd seen it before. Gyrating hips and bodies slithering in the dirt followed by the release of cries and repetitive invocations. It was a dance that called on the gods, a gesture to be seen. He was certain that this ceremony, however, was for the battle between souls.

Valerian moved between them, Lansing following close behind, and came to the center of their circle, where a fire burned between two graves. One was unmarked, freshly padded down, with moist dirt and bits of white dust that Lansing knew to be crushed bone, sprinkled over it. The other was a hollowed grave, about three feet deep, prepared for Summer.

It was when Lansing approached the grave that he felt the power of the soil, a strange magnetic sensation that made his legs feel as if they were tugging toward the earth, as if metal had been poured into them.

"The boy's been dead for less than an hour," Valerian explained. "The tribe's keeping his soul close, so that it won't stray."

"And Summer?"

Valerian's eyes darted around at nothing in particular. "Just as stubborn as her daddy, ready to fight her last battle."

His hopeful words pulled Lansing from the ledge of his own dark abyss. He turned around for another look at the tribe. Completely hairless, high foreheads, large black eyes shaded by arched eyebrows. Their noses were flat, their lips broad and fleshy like Valerian's. They moved in dance without even a drum, issuing a sequence of hisses followed by quick flicks of the tongue. Now Lansing was disturbed because he knew that unlike the other ritualistic ceremonies he'd seen as a missionary, this was the real thing. There was no drinking of goat's blood, no cutting off of chickens' heads, no drinking blood out of a hollowed horn. These simple, people, that required no props and drums were that of demons that ruled the earth, no different from the single wooden table and lit candle in Valerian's room in New Orleans. All eyes were on Summer, their gazes on his child's body.

Two women stopped mid-dance, collected a contraption of some sort, and approached Valerian with their hands stretched out. Lansing planted himself between his daughter and them.

"What in hell do you think you're doing?"

The dance continued, and the women said nothing, seemingly understanding, as Valerian turned to him and explained in the gentle way that Lansing had come to depend on.

"They're going to clean her, wrap her in leaves, have her body prepared for the healing." Valerian glanced down at Summer. "Do you want her choking on the dirt? Or being reborn in her own filth?"

Socks, she has no socks.

"Well?" Valerian asked. "If she should win, would it not be wise to have her cleaned and ready, like a babe seeing the world for the first time, not covered in her own urine?"

Lansing was silenced.

Valerian inclined his head toward one of the women. "She's the boy's mother, shepherd. She has reason to care for this body; it may serve as her son's vessel."

For awhile, Lansing just stood there, thinking his options over and then realized that there were none. He gave a small nod, allowing the strong woman to place Summer onto a make-shift gurney made of lined wood held together with liana. Staring into the large eyes of the women, he saw that they had beautiful lashes, thick and curled. Lansing read the woman's sorrow in her eyes. He swallowed the dryness in his throat and whispered, "Please, she's my baby. She doesn't want anyone to see her without the scarf on." He reached out his hand and touched the thin fabric between his two fingers. "Her scarf, please . . . " He carefully removed the wooden cross from around Summer's neck and held onto it.

The mother gave him a knowing look through eyes that said she understood, then she eased him with a nod. Lansing turned away. It was all he could do.

Valerian approached him and gestured to the fire with his hands. "Stay by the flames, shepherd...souls see fire as life. We'll keep her close."

Nightfall crept through the trees like a prowling demon. The fire, along with a sliver of moon, was the only light on the island. Lansing felt anxious and remembered the bottle of Dreher Gold, a Brazilian brandy he'd purchased at the airport. He tore through his bag, pulled it out, and turned to Valerian.

"I don't drink too often, but I thought it best if I had something if and when the time came." He drank a mouthful and offered Valerian a taste. Valerian took a swig and passed it back. The taste was harsh—it burned the lining in his throat—but the ordinary gesture reminded Lansing of civilization. The alcohol calmed him. After a few mouthfuls, watching the tribe through the veil of alcohol and roaring flames, he felt as if he were in hell, an inferno filled with demons. And slithering in the undergrowth, Lansing spotted the snakes, which were circling the graves.

Across from him, Valerian was quiet, the flames reflecting in the blackness of his eyes. Lansing realized how safe he felt with him. With a voodoo priest who openly belonged to Satan. He laughed at the absurdity. Dear God, is this what it comes to?

Several mouthfuls later, Lansing felt the courage to ask, "How long?"

"Sometimes a day, other times a few hours. Depends," Valerian replied.

After a long silence between the two, Lansing leaned forward.

"Summer was my favorite child."

Valerian's fleshy lips curved into a genuine smile that chased away the darkness around his eyes.

"I might as well tell the truth and shame the devil, but she was always my favorite. No offence." He took another swig of brandy, wiped his mouth with the back of his hand, and passed the bottle to Valerian. "Spitting image of me. Same blue eyes, yellow hair—the little that's left, anyway." He ran a hand through his thinning crown. "So much like me." It was easy to talk to Valerian, especially without filters. Here he was simply a man desperate to heal his child, not a pastor standing before his flock.

"When she was three I was preaching about homosexuality and how God's plan was for man and woman to be as one, to multiply. I spoke about Noah's ark and how there were two of each animal, male and female." He lifted a brow at Valerian. "You know the story?"

Valerian swallowed a mouthful of brandy and nodded.

"I'd already told Summer the story the night before," Lansing continued. "She took a real interest in my sermons, but with her, I made all the sound effects. I growled like the lions, mooed like the cows, made the funny eyelid flutters like the big giraffes. And she loved it, she outright loved it. The following morning I stood before my congregation and spoke the sermon, and Summer stood up right in the middle of it, her hands set on her hips, and yelled out, "Daddy, you ain't tellin' it right; you forgot the sounds. Tell it right, Daddy." Lansing laughed and looked up to find Valerian chuckling as well.

"Tell it right, Daddy..." Lansing shook his head in regret, his emotions pulling at him. He wanted to laugh, needed to cry. Fought the compulsion to shout.

"That night, that dark night when I had to tell my baby that it was over, that the marrow hadn't worked, the look in her eyes was . . . " He dropped his head onto his hand, covering his eyes. Not wanting to see. Not wanting to remember. He reached into his pocket and pulled up the wooden cross, dangling by a suede string. 'It's only wood daddy,' Summer said. I brought this for her, it's made of olive wood from a tree which was chopped down in Bethlehem. Or so I was told."

A grave frown puckered the voodoo priest's forehead. He reached his hand out, and Lansing placed it into his palm. He looked the cross over, his frown replaced with a smile.

"It was, the West Bank region of Palestine and Israel actually. The older the tree, the darker the wood. Very nice," he said, still looking the cross over.

Lansing checked a stunned laugh.

"It's just wood, when you no longer believe," Valerian stated in a soft voice, handing the cross back to Lansing. "But I don't gotta tell you that."

Lansing strung the keepsake around his own neck and tucked it behind his shirt. "She no longer believed, and there was nothing I could do to change her mind. What could I say? That God had his reasons? That it was all in his plan? What could I tell myself? That I would one day be reunited with my loved ones?" Tears rolled down his cheeks.

"How in God's name was I supposed to save my child's soul and instill faith into her when I had none left myself? And even worse, how was I supposed to lead God's flock, those people who trusted every word I spoke with the faith that had brought them under the roof of my great-granddaddy's church? How could I teach them what I no longer believed?"

He turned to Valerian, but the other man was silent.

"A man without faith is nothing!" Lansing said, his voice rising. "A man must have something to fight for, or there is no point!"

As he spoke, he felt the vein in his temple pulsing as it did when he preached with vigor at his podium on a Sunday morning. "A man must have a reason, Valerian. Or he is nothing. He must believe in what he can't see, suffer the hills, in hopes that one day his loyalty and love and sacrifice shall be rewarded. To..." His words trailed off when he saw the tears in Valerian's big black eyes.

Valerian gazed at him. "What you asked me earlier, about killing you, if Summer should lose the battle? I promise to do that for you. But I also promise that I'll kill the boy...I won't let your child's body be worn by another soul."

It took Lansing a moment, before he reached over and shook hands with the priest. "Thank you, Valerian." It was a strange and unexpected thing, to have Satan's Chosen bring him the kind of comfort that no one else could. Coming from a man like Valerian, meant something. But what?

"Won't that be problem, you doing that for us?"

Valerian gave a soft laugh. "I rule this island, shepherd; I speak for Lucifer, and what I say goes. Besides, they have enough living bodies." He narrowed his eyes and said, "My question is what to do with your bodies in the event that she doesn't return. We can't send you back to New Orleans."

"What are my options?" For a moment, Lansing felt as if he was buying car insurance.

"Normally, we burn the bodies, crush the bones. We could spill them into the ocean, or I could take them into the valley with me, have your ashes set in stone. For those loyal to God, we have a ritual. A wall of souls."

Undecided, Lansing didn't give Valerian an answer. Instead, he let Valerian inside his heart, telling him everything significant about himself, starting from his childhood and going right up to the deaths of his wife and Jonah and Naomi, only stopping when he'd told him about Summer's unexpected leukemia.

Valerian was receptive, sharing a laugh when appropriate or a gentle pat on the shoulder when needed. And he spoke too, explaining Lucifer in a light that was surprisingly different from anything Lansing had ever heard, showing him as good. There were two sides of the story, Valerian explained. Lucifer was God's alter ego, and eventually God would surrender to his other half. Lucifer was a loving God, a misunderstood God.

"I'll say a prayer for you, to Lucifer, Son of Dawn," Valerian said. "To guide Summer's soul back to her body. That you and her—"

Sounds of static filled the air and a crackling blue haze danced over the flames of the fire. Lansing flinched and his ears popped.

Valerian stood and moved closer to the grave. The tribe also gathered and soon resumed their chanting and strange dance. Lansing was drunk and incredibly off kilter, but his eyes weren't fooling him: his baby girl was battling for her body. Both souls were distinct. One was a quick blue curl that whipped around the other soul; the second was a thicker, smokier haze, rather like a trailing smoke left behind by an extinguished candle. The souls fell into the earth and then shot back up, over and over battling for Summer's body.

The sounds of the tribe coupled with the screams and wailing, and the pressure in his head, made Lansing feel as if he was going mad. His knees gave out, and he dropped low to the ground, waiting and praying, but to whom? It wasn't clear. He wasn't clear. His petitions went to God, then to Lucifer. Back and forth he prayed, offering his pleas to either, to both, begging one of them to hear, to listen. To save. After almost an hour, as dawn reached the island, Lansing ripped the cross from around his neck, and tossed it into the fire-pit.

It's just wood, Lansing thought.

He bowed his head, clapped his palms together and paused. As a boy, Lansing learned early on that prayers were to be whispered into empty hands, and the words would follow to where the fingers pointed – heavenward.

Lansing summoned a breath, pointed his fingers earthward, and whispered his first words into empty hands. "Lucifer, Son of Dawn, God of earth. I beg you. Bring me my child back..."

And as the first bird took flight and spread its white wings against the golden sky, silence fell and all was still. The entire group waited. When the soil over Summer's grave began moving, earth turned and yellow fingers, not human but rather the heads of the golden snakes, pushed their way out and slithered away, disappearing into the undergrowth. Once the seventh snake had surfaced, the men and women began to excavate the grave, their hands tearing through the dirt, reaching, pulling, until they produced Summer's body, still wrapped in wet leaves.

Lansing stood away, his heart thrumming behind his chest bone. But he watched. And his hands shook.

And he was terrified.

Vomit, tasting like Dreher Gold rose in his throat when he saw movement inside the green cocoon. A few of the men placed Summer's body by the warm fire, and they all began peeling away the sticky covering. And then, there she was, naked as a babe, her hands and feet moving, feeling around with her eyes closed. The first and only miracle, apart from the birth of his children, that Lansing had ever witnessed.

Dear God, he thought, hovering a few feet away. She was alive. Her scarf had fallen, and her head was bald and smooth, just as it had been when his wife had birthed her twenty-one years before. He wanted nothing more than to hold her. But who was she? Several of the tribe's women scraped the sticky substance with leveled rocks, revealing skin fresh and pink. Lansing watched in absolute awe as her painted toes wiggled, and then she let out her first cry, a soft whimper, then a wail, just like the first day she came into this world, bringing in the gift of rain. He edged closer, moving between the others, close enough to touch her, when her eyelids fluttered open, blinking hard and fast. Her chaste blue eyes searched around until she saw him.

"Daddy," she said, reaching out to him.

He fell before his daughter and on bended knees, he let out a thunderous scream, rejoicing like a madman. Lansing laughed until his elation turned into jubilant sobs of relief as he cradled Summer to his chest. In disbelief, he looked down into her face, wanting to verify what his eyes were seeing.

And in that instant, as the rays of the morning sun made their way through the trees on Snake Island, darkness became light. And as he rejoiced with Lucifer's Chosen, celebrating the rebirth of his child, the earth became Lansing's heaven. And when Summer smiled and that smile reached those chaste blue eyes of hers, Lucifer became God.

Author's Notes:

Although my main characters are wholly fictitious, certain historic facts remain true. I have always had a deep appreciation for historical events, and when writing Angels in Stone, as well as the books that followed; my knowledge became useful, when spinning fiction from non-fiction.

Originally, Angels in Stone was written as a screenplay. The story was then very much the same, although key elements were left out. This is one of the downsides where scriptwriting is concerned. A writer must convey the story in a certain amount of pages, keeping in mind that the story is told through dialogue and scene setting, (what the camera sees). In a script, the writer has to transmit the emotions through action, leaving out the vital and most intricate details that one would otherwise read between the lines, such as the character's thoughts, back-story and so on. This is where turning my script into a book became the most liberating and rewarding experience as a writer. The manuscript was my stage. I was both actor and director. I was able to get inside of my characters, get under their skin, and feel their every emotion pertaining to each situation. I will admit that there were times that I recoiled at some of the scenes. What would my readers think of me? What would people— like my friends and family—think when reading some of the more sinister chapters? Is she like Claire? The calculating woman, steadfast in getting what she wants? Or is she like Esperança, the damaged soul in the midst of an evolution, trying to find her inner peace? The truth is, that along with my own twisted sense of humor, there are minuscule pieces of me inside of all my characters: portions that I have surrendered in order to be an honest writer.

Acknowledging those, who acknowledged me:

I need to lavish praise on three very gifted individuals. I praise these people, not because they thought that I had something special, or because they claimed to have enjoy my saga, along with my imagination. I commend them for being my 'stones,' my solid team, who supported my vision. I decided to omit the idea of traditional publishing, never even writing as much as a query letter. I wanted to remain unscathed. Writers lose a part of their souls. They bleed their essence onto paper, pour over keys, and write notes on the backs of utility bills, reminders for scenes they're working on. Writers are artists, lost inside of their mind's eye, they create, they spin; and most of all, writers are wrapped up in the written word. It's who they are.
I wanted writing to remain my first love and not my heartache. I also realized that if I wanted to get my series out there, I needed to do it myself. But nothing is done entirely alone. This is where I must give credit, where credit is due.

Donald Pratt: my enthusiastic and intellectual assistant: I truly appreciate your support, priceless effort, and fortitude. I cannot count the amount of times I said, "Thank goodness for Don!" You are a true artist, and your ability to comprehend the complexity of this series humbled me.

To Michael E. Dobson: a rebel, a businessman, and someone who goes off the beaten path. I am so grateful to you and trust in your ability to continue on, in being my mentor.

To Gregory Pratt: an incredible artist, who brought my story to life on paper. I thank you for your patience, and for creating the covers for my Stones Series. Your professionalism and acute attention to the details, was fundamental in creating the covers, which I had envisioned in my mind. Not only are you a remarkable graphic artist, but a fine musician, that made my covers sing.

Thank you for reading Angels in Stone. I only hope that I have made it worth your while. I invite you to read the next book, Ashes in Stone, where Claire's personal struggle continues, set against the majestic backdrop of the dripping jungles of Brazil.

About the Author

Tanja Kobasic was born and raised in Toronto, Ontario, Canada, where she currently resides.
She is the creator and author of Sugar Mountain – The Golden Key: a transitional children's book, linked with one of Canada's largest candy confectionery companies.
When Tanja isn't writing, she runs her paralegal firm, and is a proud and licensed member of The Law Society of Upper Canada.